MATING OF THE GODS

"Major Lange, do you mean to tell me that you're running a . . . a human *breeding* farm?" Lisl Rodl's lovely gold-flecked blue eyes widened.

"Why not? For centuries now man has put his best effort into the science of breeding cattle, pigs and horses. Can we do less for humankind?" The handsome S.S. Major smiled confidently at the beautiful young girl riding at his side.

"But . . . It seems so inhuman."

"It *is* inhuman," Lange said. "For it is above the human level, and on the level of the gods. We are at the dawn of the gods, Fraulein Rodl. And you and I can be part of it."

"You and I?" she gasped.

"Yes," he said, reaching over and squeezing her thigh. "I want you for breeding purposes, Fraulein Rodl. I want you to conceive my child."

"I . . . I can't do that," Lisl said quietly.

"Oh yes, you can do it, Fraulein," he said. "And you will do it, because it is the only way you can save your fiance, the Jew Maass!"

The War-Torn

THE BRAVE AND THE LONELY

MASTERS AND MARTYRS

MASTERS
AND
MARTYRS

Robert Vaughan

A DELL / JAMES A. BRYANS BOOK

Published by
Dell Publishing Co., Inc.
1 Dag Hammarskjold Plaza
New York, New York 10027

Dell ® TM 681510, Dell Publishing Co., Inc.

ISBN: 0-440-06370-1

Printed in the United States of America

First printing—February 1983

This book is for
JOHN BRYANS
who brought friendship
in a green bus

MASTERS
AND
MARTYRS

Headlines in the Schweinfurt Tageblat, September 19, 1939:

THE FÜHRER TO VISIT SCHWEINFURT TO-DAY! Will discuss vital war production with Herr Direktor-General Heinrich Rodl of I.G.N. Kugel-werks.

The citizens of Schweinfurt were waiting eagerly for the visit from Adolf Hitler. Thousands of people lined the streets waiting for the motorcade, crowding down to the curbs and shoving their children in front of them so they too could see Hitler. Flags were everywhere, hanging from lamp poles and specially designed arches, and suspended from upper floor windows. These were long swaths of blood-red cloth, bearing a black swastika centered in a white circle. From a distance the flags looked substantial, but up close one could see that they were made of the sheerest muslin through which light could pass and which filled and floated with the slightest breeze. Interspersed with the flags were stylized eagles, golden birds of prey, perched atop wreath-encircled swastikas, mounted on poles like the standards carried before the Roman Legions of Caesar's time. Below the wreathed swastika were the letters N.S.D.A.P.

At the airfield at Conn Kaserne, Lisl Rodl waited with half a dozen other dignitaries for the arrival of Hitler's airplane. It was said that Hitler had an eye for pretty girls, and if there was truth to that, then Lisl would certainly arrest his attention. She was tall and blonde, full-bosomed and thin-waisted, with long, slender legs which somehow seemed to express their sensuality even through the tailored skirt she wore. She had a delicate nose, fine lips and eyes which were green and flecked with gold. She was a strikingly beautiful young woman of twenty-one, the daughter of Heinrich Rodl, who was Director-General for the giant ball-bearing factory, I.G.N. Kugelwerks. She was also the sister of one of the heroes of the Reich; her brother Rudi was serving in Poland with the German Army.

Lisl was in love, engaged to Paul Maass, the Director of the Schweinfurt Philharmonic Orchestra. Tonight Hitler would attend a special concert of Wagner music, directed by Paul. Lisl and her mother and father would share Hitler's box at the theater. Lisl could barely contain her enthusiasm. It was wonderful to be young and German and in love during such exciting times.

"Oh, Paul, do you think he'll like the flowers?" Lisl asked, holding up the bouquet of yellow roses she intended to present to Hitler as soon as he landed.

"I don't think he will even look at them," Paul answered.

"What? Oh, Paul, you mean he *won't* like them?"

Paul laughed. "I mean he will be so dazzled by

your beauty that the flowers will appear as little more than weeds to him."

"Oh," Lisl said in relief. "Oh, you frightened me for a moment."

"Look!" someone shouted, pointing toward the northeastern sky. "Look, there is the Führer's airplane!"

"The Führer!" someone else called and the thousand or more people who were standing behind the police barricades began to push and shout in excitement as the black dot grew larger and larger in shape. Finally the dot became the three-engined Junkers which was carrying Hitler from Berlin to Schweinfurt. This same airplane, which Hitler called his *Luftchancellory*, or airborne capitol, had recently taken him to the Eastern front to observe the action of the German Army in Poland.

There were three Mercedes near the flight line, one of them an open car with Nazi flags flying from the front fenders. That would be the car which would transport Hitler from the airfield to I.G.N. Kugelwerks, where a special reception was planned for him. The other two cars were for the welcoming party which included, in addition to Lisl and Paul, the Gauleiter of the Schweinfurt District, and the Gauleiter of the Wursburg District, as well as other, lesser officials.

"Now," Gauleiter Dietering said, addressing the others just before the plane landed. "Let us be certain that each of us knows what we are to do." Dietering was the head of the Schweinfurt District. Schweinfurt was much smaller than Wurzburg, and under normal conditions, protocol would have demanded that the Wurzburg Gauleiter, an ex-locksmith named Schmidt, be in charge. But these were not normal circumstances. Hitler was coming to Schweinfurt specifically, and Dietering had informed Schmidt that he could come as a guest, but would have no official capacity. Dietering was now speaking, just to make certain that Schmidt knew his place.

"Anton, we all know what we are to do," Schmidt said. "You've gone over it enough times."

"Yes, yes, I know," Dietering said. "But one cannot be too careful when one is dealing with the Führer. Everything must be just right. Remember, I will greet him first, say a few words of welcome, and then I shall escort him over here where you, Fraulein Rodl, will present him with the flowers. After that, the rest of you may meet him."

The airplane was touching down at the far end of the field by now, and at the moment it touched down, a nearby military band began playing, though of course it was impossible for anyone in the plane to hear the music. The plane taxied across the field, then, increasing the power in the engine on the right wing, and decreasing the power of the other two engines, it pivoted around so that the door was facing the crowd. The engines were cut, and the propellers spun for a few seconds before coming to rest, gleaming silver in the afternoon sun.

Two men ran to the airplane and placed a low wooden step in place, then one of the men opened the door. The crowd strained to look through the door, but all they could see was the back of one of the seats. A figure appeared in the door for a brief second, and excitement rose until everyone realized that it wasn't Hitler.

"Where is he?" Lisl asked quietly. "Why doesn't he appear?"

"I think he was waiting for that," Paul answered, and he pointed to a formation of black-clad S.S. men,

Schutzstaffel, goosestepping smartly as they marched to the side of the airplane. They took their positions beside the door, forming a corridor through which Hitler would walk after he left.

"Oh, there he is!" Lisl said, and though she tried to whisper it, she was so excited that it came out louder than she intended, and Gauleiter Dietering looked at her sharply and disapprovingly.

Hitler paused for just a moment, framed by the doorway of the airplane. He looked out over the welcoming crowd, brushed the shock of hair back with his hand, then stepped down. The S.S. Honor Guard extended their right hands in the Nazi salute, and, as one, they shouted *"Heil Hitler."* Hitler, almost self-consciously it seemed, returned their salute not with a straight armed thrust like theirs, but with a rather jerky, bent elbow which brought his hand up almost as if he were waving.

"Heil Hitler, Heil Hitler, Heil Hitler!" the crowd behind the fence started shouting, and Lisl had never felt such tingling excitement. He was coming toward her now, and in just a moment, she would be handing him the bouquet!

"Mein Führer!" Dietering started. "As party Gauleiter of the Schweinfurt District, let me welcome you on behalf of the peoples of Schweinfurt. We are resolved to stand together for the glory of the Third Reich, and for the manifest destiny of you, our—"

"Thank you," Hitler said, cutting Dietering off in mid-sentence. Dietering, who had prepared a speech of some five minutes in duration, looked up in surprise, made one weak gesture with the paper, then saw that Hitler had already walked by him toward the line of people who made up the welcoming committee. Dietering had no recourse but to shove the unused speech into his pocket and follow quickly, or he would be left behind.

Though the first person in the reception line was Schmidt, Hitler walked by him with only a perfunctory handshake. He stopped in front of Lisl, where he again self-consciously brushed the shock of hair back from his forehead. He reached for Lisl's hand. Lisl was so awed by him that for a moment she forgot that she was supposed to give him the flowers, and when he reached his hand out toward her, she suddenly thought of the flowers, and she thrust the bouquet into his hands.

"Doesn't this seem a bit backward?" Hitler asked Dietering, who had fallen into position behind him. "I had always believed that a man should give flowers to a beautiful girl, not the other way around."

Everyone within earshot laughed, and their laughter was joined even by those who hadn't heard, because they thought it was expected of them. Hitler took the flowers from Lisl, then handed them to Dietering, who held them awkwardly. "Keep these for me, would you, Herr Dietering?"

When Hitler called Dietering by name, the hurt feeling Dietering had suffered over not being able to finish his speech were immediately soothed. He smiled broadly, and, with a click of his heels answered, "*Jawohl, Mein Führer!*"

Hitler took Lisl's hand then and raised it to his lips. Lisl felt the touch of his lips and the brush of his moustache as he kissed the back of her hand, then, as she looked into his eyes, she shivered involuntarily with the thrill of it. Beads of perspiration popped out between her breasts.

"I was told that Herr Rodl's daughter would be here to greet me. Would you be Fraulein Rodl?"

"Yes, Excellency," Lisl replied.

"Then I must congratulate my protocol officer for arranging such a welcome, though I think he should have told me of your breathtaking beauty."

"Thank you, Excellency," Lisl managed to mumble.

Hitler dropped her hand and proceeded directly to Paul, who stood beside her. Paul clicked his heels and took Hitler's hand in his.

"And you," Hitler said, "are *Orchester-Direktor* Maass."

"Yes, Excellency."

"I have spoken with those who have heard you conduct, and I am told that my evening at the concert will be most enjoyable. I, too, am an artist, you know. Of course, I express my art through painting and sketching, but I feel that all artists, be they poor painters like myself, or accomplished musicians such as you, share a common bond, a kinship of spirit, as it were." Hitler chuckled. "It is ironic, is it not, that I, an artist, should come to Schweinfurt to discuss such unartistic matters as ball bearing production? But soon, now, Germany shall occupy the position of power and influence necessary to preserve our Germanic way of life against all impure influences, and I will take great delight in stepping away from this difficult task I have set for myself, so that I may spend the rest of my days in support of the arts. Remember, my friend, as an artist, you shall always have entrée to my offices."

"Thank you, my Führer," Paul said.

Hitler went on to the next, and then to the next, until each had been greeted, then the welcoming party proceeded to their cars to follow Hitler's open Mercedes down the flag-lined Niederwern Strasse, toward the large ball bearing factory which employed more than half the city and comprised the major source of Schweinfurt's income. In a way the ball bearing factory and Hitler were synonymous in the eyes of the cheering, waving crowd, for before Hitler there was unemployment and runaway inflation. Hitler had stabilized the currency, and put the factories back to work. Now every family had a breadwinner, there was food on the table, clothes on the back, and even money left over for holidays and sportsfests. It was good to be a German, and even those who had not been early converts to the Nazi Party had to concede that Hitler had saved Germany from total collapse.

"*Herr Direktor-General*, I have just received a telephone call from the airfield. The Führer's plane has landed," Kurt Papf told Heinrich Rodl. Papf was Rodl's production foreman, and the second in charge of operations at the I.G.N. Kugelwerks, which was the largest ball bearing manufacturing plant in the world.

"Thank you, Kurt," Heinrich said.

Heinrich was standing at the window of his second floor office, and he glanced down toward Niederwern Strasse to see a gently flowing sea of red, white and black floating above the large crowd of people. Heinrich was fifty years old, with blue eyes and steel gray hair. He was barrel-chested and thick-waisted, though the overall illusion was one of great strength rather than paunchiness. In many ways he still looked like the Oberst, or Colonel, he had been in the Imperial Army of the World War. The command which sat easily with him in battle, remained with him in industry, and he was not intimidated by the responsibility of running such a large factory.

Colonel Rodl had returned from a lost war to find that the orderly world which had governed his life was gone. With the army limited by the treaty of Versailles to one hundred thousand men, there was no room on active duty for the reservists and home guards, so he was without rank.

The redefining of Germany's borders had taken away his lands, so he was without income and home. But Heinrich was a man of tremendous pride and self-discipline, and he wasted no time lamenting over his losses. Instead, he found work in the ball bearing factory which the Swiss built in Schweinfurt, starting as a laborer. He stayed with them, even during the terrible years of insane inflation when the value of German money reached one trillion marks to the dollar, and millions of Germans were quitting their jobs because there seemed to be little sense in working for worthless currency. When the Swiss owners of the factory asked Heinrich why he hadn't quit as so many others had, he replied that he worked for pride as much as for money, and as long as he had pride and self-respect, he was amply compensated.

Heinrich was rewarded by being made a shift foreman. In the beginning it was more of a gesture than a reality, for there were times when Heinrich had no one but himself to supervise. Still, he stayed with it, moving from shift foreman to production foreman, then to production supervisor and finally to plant supervisor. It was then that Heinrich met Emil Kirdorf, one of Germany's biggest coal barons, and Fritz Thyssen, the head of a giant steel trust. Heinrich was convinced by them that Hitler held the key to Germany's economic salvation.

It was not difficult to convince Heinrich of the evil of the Versailles Treaty. Heinrich had personally suffered as a result of that odious instrument. Therefore when Heinrich learned that Hitler intended to openly defy the treaty, he was impressed with the courage of

a leader who would free Germany from its brutal re-
strictions. The treaty had not only limited Germany's
military and reduced its borders, but it had also
stripped Germany's industry, and levied such repatri-
ation payments on the country that the best estimate
for a total economic recovery indicated that it would
be 1988 before the country could gain parity with
the other nations of the world.

If the Versailles Treaty rendered Germany's industry impotent and stripped its citizens of all self-respect, then the world financial interests, dominated by
international bankers, had manipulated Germany's
runaway inflation to profit from its collapsing economy.
Property bought on credit at pre-inflation prices could
be paid off at inflation rates. Companies and corpora-
tions worth millions of marks, when a mark meant
something, changed hands when ten million marks
wouldn't even buy a loaf of bread.

Heinrich was convinced that only production—the
generation of goods and products—would save Germany. The maggots who lived off the decay of a dying
society would have to be swept away, and Hitler
promised to do that, and to lead Germany to a new
industrial revolution.

Heinrich was instrumental in convincing other in-
dustrialists of the soundness of Hitler's production policy, and he visited and wrote letters to such people as
Georg von Schnitzler, of I.G. Farben, Aughust Rosterg
and Aughust Diehn of the potash industry, Cuno of
the Hamburg-Amerika line, and half a dozen others.

Heinrich came to power at the same time as Hitler.
The *Direktor-General* of I.G.N. Kugelwerks retired,
and Heinrich was appointed by the absentee owners
of the company as the new *Direktor-General.* The
Swiss owners were rewarding Heinrich for his long

years of loyal and efficient work, to be sure, but they also were not ignorant of the fact that as an early supporter of Hitler, Heinrich would be a good man to have in their camp.

But now the Swiss owners were afraid that they may have miscalculated, for the real reason for Hitler's visit to Schweinfurt was not to discuss production, as the papers stated, but to nationalize the ball bearing industry under the war materiels clause of the emergency powers enabling act. Heinrich's position of *Direktor-General* of I.G.N. Kugelwerks would now be on par with the German owners of German industries.

Peter Staub, agent for the Swiss Owners of I.G.N., was in Heinrich's office, waiting with Heinrich for the arrival of Hitler. Peter had come to protest Hitler's move, though he had known from the moment he left Geneva that his mission was a hopeless one.

Heinrich turned from the window and looked at Peter, sitting on the sofa. Peter had just informed him of the text of the official protest he would be filing with Hitler's government.

"Peter, my friend," Heinrich said softly. "And I call you my friend for we have been close for many years—since I was but a shift foreman. As a friend, you must listen to me—"

"As a friend, Heinrich, how can you be a party to this?" Peter interrupted. "You, who have always espoused pride and integrity. How can you stand by and watch your government steal this company from its rightful owners? Is this the reward we receive for placing our trust and confidence in you?"

"Listen to me, Peter," Heinrich went on. "Germany is now at war." Peter started to say something, but Heinrich held his hand up, stopping him so he could go on with his point. "I know, you are going to say that it is not Switzerland's war, and that is right. Switzerland is neutral and they will stay neutral in this war, as they always have. But suppose your government tells you that they fear the manufacture of ball bearings for use by a belligerent country is in violation of their neutrality? This factory would be closed, Germany would be denied the critical ball bearings that her own people are producing, and your employers would be denied the fair profit which is legitimately theirs. Don't you see, Peter? By nationalizing I.G.N. we are both protected. Germany will have her ball bearings and you will have your profit, for it is not the intention of the German government to steal the profit, only to ensure the production."

Peter looked at Heinrich for a long moment, then he smiled. "Heinrich, are you saying that the profits will continue to come to I.G.N.?"

"Precisely," Heinrich said. "Only the profits will be much larger, for I have been told that Hitler plans to increase production threefold. Your employers will realize three times the profit, Peter, and when the crisis has ended, this factory shall be returned. You will have your cake and eat it, too, so to speak, for who can fault you for making a profit from an operation over which you have no control?"

Peter stood up and walked over to the liquor cabinet to pour himself a drink. He turned and looked toward Heinrich.

"You do understand, of course, that I still have to follow through with my protest, and we shall also register an international protest?"

"Of course," Heinrich said. "You must, after all, maintain your neutrality."

Peter smiled. "I do have one question, however."

"What is that?"

"Do you suppose there is any way you could prolong the crisis for a period of two or three years?"

Heinrich laughed. "I see that you now comprehend fully what I was trying to say."

"Comprehend and appreciate, my friend," Peter said, holding his drink out as in a toast before he tossed it down. He wiped the back of his hand across his mouth. "In fact, in view of the circumstances, I'm certain that my principals may even see fit to return a fair portion of their profit back to you in the form of a bonus . . . a rather substantial bonus."

"I could not accept that," Heinrich said easily.

"Scruples, Herr Rodl?"

"I know it is hard for you to understand, Peter, but I am serious when I say that I am totally dedicated to the best interests of my country. I thought everything was lost after the last war. I feared that ten centuries of Germanic culture and influence had been destroyed and that destruction had been presided over by my generation. Now I discover that I may be an instrument in saving the old and building the new. I will extend every effort to produce ball bearings for the enrichment of these ideals, but not for my personal enrichment. For my part, I ask no increase in salary, nor production bonuses, beyond that for which we have already contracted."

"You are serious, aren't you?" Peter asked.

"Yes," Heinrich said.

"And you really think that National Socialism is the wave of the future?"

"I do."

"You have always been honest with me in the past, Heinrich, be honest with me now," Peter said. "Do you accept *every* aspect of the Nazi party, including the racial superiority and Jew-hating?"

Heinrich sighed. "That is a difficult thing for people outside of Germany to understand," he said. "I've given it a great deal of thought. There are Jews who have made a contribution to mankind in general, and to our society in particular. I would be a fool not to recognize that, though it is not something I would admit to everyone right now. I think the problem boils down to this. During the time of our greatest peril, when our country was teetering on the edge of total collapse, a very strong and highly *visible* Jewish banking element, profited from it. It was necessary to find a focal point, a theme if you will, which would unite all Germans. We had to have a concrete enemy, someone we could see and fight. We needed not just an abstract economic principle, but a flesh-and-blood enemy, and there were many Jews who were contributing to our plight. Now, mind you, I don't say they instigated it, as the official party line does, but I am convinced that they contributed to it and profited from its prolongation. And because they were there and visible, they were a natural rallying point. Germany underwent a revolution as surely as the revolution which overthrew the French Monarchy one hundred and fifty years ago. We are still undergoing that revolution, and as long as the revolution is in progress, then we must use the Jewish 'problem' to sustain it. Thus, as a matter of national necessity, all Jews, not just those who contributed to our troubles, but all Jews, must bear the brunt. It is unfortunate, for there are some who have done us no harm, yet they find themselves unwilling participants in the great crusade. You must remember also that Jews form only about one percent of our total population, so that numerically it makes sense to sacrifice them to the greater good for the greatest number. I am certain, however, that as the gains made by our revolution become secure, the need of an outside influence to sustain the revolution will be eliminated. At that time all who choose to enjoy the fruits of the new German Government will find this a good place to work and live; Germans and non-Germans, Christians and Jews."

"Do you actually believe that, Heinrich?"

"I believe it with all my heart," Heinrich said. "I could not support National Socialism if I didn't."

Peter smiled. "That is good to hear, Heinrich. That is very good to hear." He held his glass up again. "To your new Reich."

"To *Germany's* new Reich," Heinrich corrected.

2

Dr. Hans Werfel was studying the results of neutron bombardment on uranium atoms during tests he had conducted with Drs. Otto Hahn and Fritz Strassmann. He had already advanced the theory of energy conversion by isotope enhancement, and that theory was currently the leading candidate for releasing the energy contained in matter in accordance with Dr. Einstein's formula, $E = MC^2$.

Over the last few weeks, however, Hans had come to believe that his isotope enhancement theory, though possible, was simply not practical, and he was following all the leads in order to avoid stumbling over the same path again. It was a process of elimination, but on an enormous scale.

Hans was Professor of Physics at the University of Schweinfurt and, though the Nürnberg Laws had withdrawn teaching rights from Jews, it hadn't really affected Hans because he had devoted most of the past years to research anyway. Therefore, the University, which was pleased to have a man of Werfel's scientific credits on their staff, retained him even while dismissing the other "tainted" professors.

"Herr Doktor Werfel," a voice called from the door of the laboratory.

Hans didn't look up from his work, so the person who had called him—a laboratory assistant who was actually a student—cleared his throat and tried again. "Herr Doktor Werfel."

"Yes," Hans said, finishing the calculation. He looked up at the student and ran his hand across his forehead as if brushing back a shock of hair, but he had such a high forehead and such a receding hairline that there was nothing to brush back. Hans' eyes were large and brown and the lids drooped slightly, giving the suggestion of an Oriental appearance. His cheeks were red, as if he had just come in from a cold, brisk wind—though in truth they looked that way all the time.

"Albert, so you are still here, are you? I thought you would be out on the streets welcoming Hitler. Doesn't he come to Schweinfurt today?"

"Yes," Albert said. "But he has already made his parade, and now he is in meetings."

"Oh, and did you see the great man?" Hans asked, with just a touch of sarcasm to his voice.

"Herr Professor," Albert said, looking around to make certain that no one overheard. "Herr Professor, it isn't wise for you to speak so carelessly. One never knows who may be listening."

"Come now, Albert," Hans said with a little chuckle. "As the last remaining Jew in the University do you suppose my feelings for Hitler are secret?"

"Nevertheless, it isn't safe," Albert said.

"Yes, as you say, it isn't safe. Now, what is it? Why have you come to my laboratory? Surely not to discuss politics."

"Oh, I have come to tell you that there is a meeting

of the staff and faculty. Herr Doktor Funk is to speak on the new curriculum."

"Very well," Hans said, closing his notebook. "As I am still a member of the staff, if not of the faculty, then I shall attend Dr. Funk's address."

Albert, having delivered his message, hurried on, not wishing to be seen arriving at the library with Dr. Werfel. Under ordinary circumstances, Albert would have appreciated being seen in the company of a scientist so distinguished as to have been nominated for the Nobel Prize in physics. But these were not ordinary times and, if Dr. Werfel was a scientist of international acclaim, he was also a Jew and it was not good to be perceived as a friend of a Jew no matter how impressive his academic credits.

There were nearly two dozen in the library when Hans arrived. More than half were new to the University, having arrived in the last few years to implement the bizarre policies of Bernhard Rust, the Reich Minister of Science, Education and Popular Culture.

Under Rust, all German education was Nazified. Textbooks were rewritten, curriculums were changed, and teachers were hired to promote the ideology of National Socialism. Such courses as "Racial Science" were added while philosophy, history and sociology courses were either withdrawn or so radically changed to conform to Nazi ideology that they lost their identity.

Dr. Funk, the newly appointed president of Schweinfurt University, was one of Bernhard Rust's most dedicated lieutenants. He enthusiastically embraced all of Rust's directives, and held frequent meetings to ensure that his faculty understood what was expected of them.

As Hans took his seat in the rear of the room, he looked over to the other faculty members. Those who had been there the longest, many of whom had at one time called themselves his friend, avoided his gaze or returned it only briefly, a flicker of guilt passing over their faces. Only the new members looked squarely at him, and they did so with ill-conceived contempt. They made no effort to keep Hans from hearing their frequent references to the fact that they did not appreciate working on the same staff as a Jew.

Something new had been added. Dr. Funk was not wearing the simple brown suit he normally wore. Instead he was dressed in the splashy black and silver uniform of an S.S. Obersturmbannfuhrer, which in the strange and inexplicable S.S. ranking system was equal to a Lieutenant Colonel.

"Well, Herr Doktor Werfel," Dr. Funk said as Hans took his seat. Funk turned the corners of his mouth up as if smiling, but the effect did little to soften the features of a face which had cold, flat eyes and rather sallow cheeks. "I trust you have an adequate excuse for keeping the rest of us waiting?"

"Dr. Funk, I'm certain you did not find it necessary to delay the meeting on my account," Hans said.

"You are quite correct," Funk said. "We did not delay the meeting. However, when such meetings are called in the future, you will do well to attend them on time. Perhaps you don't understand how fortunate you are to still have a position here."

"I have a position here because I make a contribution here," Hans said. "That is the natural order of things."

"What contribution can a Jew make?" one of the new staff members spoke from the front of the room.

Hans wasn't able to see who the speaker was, and he knew that the atmosphere was so hostile that it would not be advantageous to try to find out. He sat back quietly, ignoring the remark.

Funk resumed his meeting, discussing the new classes he intended to put in—such classes as German physics and German science, as well as German literature and German culture. He had discussed these things with the Führer only this morning, he said, letting everyone know that he had enjoyed a special audience with Hitler.

"And tonight," Funk went on, "I shall be attending a special concert given in the Führer's honor. *Concert-Direktor* Maass is conducting the orchestra in a Wagnerian salute to the Führer."

At that, Hans looked up. So, Hitler would be honored by Paul Maass tonight? Everyone, it seemed, had been drawn into Hitler's camp. Even Paul Maass.

As the meeting broke up, the faculty members began filing out of the library. Hans had arrived for the meeting in an almost challenging mood, but now he found himself strangely depressed. He had tried to tell himself that eventually the citizens of Germany would wake up to what was being done in their country, and they would throw Hitler and his gang of hoodlums out. But that didn't seem to be the case. In fact, the situation seemed to grow worse with each passing day.

Hans avoided looking at any of the other faculty members; then, when the last one had passed him, he stood up to leave.

Hans was wrong. All had not left. There was one teacher, Dr. Mueller, still in the library. Dr. Mueller was one of the original professors who had been retained because an examination of his political philosophy justified his retention. Dr. Mueller had joined the Nazi Party in the 1920s, when it was still considered by the majority of the Germans as a minor radical party.

As Hans stood Dr. Mueller drew even with him and pushed him roughly, shoving Hans back into the chair.

"Jew, wait until the last!" Mueller said loudly and angrily, and Dr. Funk, who heard the commotion, looked around just in time to see Hans sit quickly in the chair to avoid falling.

"What's the matter, Werfel? Did you lose your balance?" Dr. Funk taunted.

"I'm sorry," Hans said, and quickly he looked toward the floor in what he hoped was a non-threatening way.

"Just learn your place, Jew," Mueller said as he left the room. Mueller's voice was dripping with venom, and Hans noticed that all those new members of the faculty were laughing smugly over the fact that one of the old members had been the one to turn on Hans.

The ones who were smiling smugly, though, did not know what Hans knew. They did not know that Dr. Mueller had merely shoved Hans aside as a means of putting a note in his pocket. At first, Hans had been surprised by Mueller's action. He and Mueller had never been friends, but they had never been enemies, either, so he was surprised and hurt. But, even before he had time to react, he realized that Mueller had put a note in his pocket, and took on the cowed expression which he knew would elicit the least attention.

Later, when Hans was alone, he took out the note and read it.

Hans:
You must leave Germany as quickly as you can!
You have been spared the fate of the other Jews
because you are working on a method of devel-
oping atomic energy. Hitler wants to use your
work to develop an atomic weapon. As soon as
he feels you have advanced far enough to enable
others to carry on with your work, he will have
you killed, and a weapon of massive power will
be put in the hands of a madman! Destroy your
notes and papers and leave at once. Do not ac-
knowledge this note! Do not speak to me; it is
far too dangerous!

Hans held the note over a bunsen burner until it flamed, then he put it in an ashtray to watch it burn. Next he took the notes he had been working on and began tearing them out of the book and burning them, one at a time. Finally, when all were burned and there was no trail left through which another scientist would be able to follow his progression from what had been a blind-alley theory to where he stood now, he was ready to leave.

Hans looked over his laboratory. There were a few things he would like to take with him, but he felt his best bet would be to leave things just as they were, so that it would appear that he had every intention of returning. All of the notes which had led him first into a blind alley were still here. Let them remain, he thought. Let Hitler follow them into the blind alley. Perhaps it would slow any scientist who hoped to develop an atomic weapon for the Nazis.

Hans turned out the lights and pulled the door closed behind him. He glanced at his watch. He would have to hurry if he wanted to make it to the concert hall in time.

The last notes of *The Ride of the Valkyrie* hung in the air in all their majestic grandeur, and the audience erupted into applause. In a box draped with bunting, Hitler stood with the cheering crowd and applauded the musicians. From Lisl's vantage point near him in the private box, she could see that his eyes were sheened with tears. Surely, she thought, no other leader in the world, not Daladier of France, or Chamberlain of England, and certainly not Roosevelt of America, had such depth of feeling. Would either of those men stand before their people unashamedly weeping over the beauty of music? Lisl thought not.

Hitler turned to Lisl and reached out to take her hand in his. "Your young man is a conductor of exceptional talent."

"Thank you, my Führer," Lisl said. "Paul will be most gratified to hear that."

Hitler dabbed at a tear, then looked toward Lisl's father and mother. "Herr Rodl, please do me the honor of coming to the Rathaus, where rooms have been prepared for me to spend the night, and be my guest at a small after-concert dinner. Bring your lovely wife and daughter and the talented young man who gave us such pleasure tonight."

"I would be honored, Excellency," Heinrich replied.

"And now," Hitler said, "I must leave the auditorium before the conclusion. It is the price one must pay for *verrut*," he added, laughing at his choice of the word "notoriety" over fame.

Two S.S. guards slipped in and Hitler left with them even as the opening bars of the encore swelled from the orchestra pit. It was planned that way to allow him to leave without being caught up in the press of the crowd. By the time the crowd realized he was gone, it would be too late.

Lisl watched him leave, then she turned back to the stage. This night was just too perfect. She felt her heart swelling in pride for her fiancé, and in the fact that she and her family had shared a private box with Hitler. If only Rudi could have been here with them. And yet, even Rudi's absence was a source of pride, for Rudi was a Panzer Lieutenant in Poland, bringing more glory to Germany upon the field of battle.

The music of the encore selection ended, and Paul turned around to acknowledge the applause of the crowd. He glanced toward Hitler's box and saw Lisl and her parents standing and cheering for him, and saw too that Hitler was gone. He knew that it had been planned this way, and he was able to realize a rather selfish sort of satisfaction over the fact that his music had held the attention of the audience well enough to allow Hitler to sneak away undetected. Perhaps it was not very patriotic to take satisfaction in upstaging Hitler, but it was ego-massaging.

The curtain drew shut, opened again briefly for a curtain call, during which Paul recognized his concert master and the other members of the orchestra, then it closed for the final time.

Paul tapped his baton on the stand and his musicians, as well trained as the members of an elite military force and as respectful of Paul's position as if he had been an army general, looked up at him.

"My thanks to each of you," he said. "This night belonged to us. The Führer was here but our music was the star of the evening." Paul applauded lightly. "I applaud you," he said.

The musicians beamed under Paul's praise, and they talked happily and excitedly among themselves as they began to pack up, laying their instruments lovingly in the felt cases, and carefully folding up the music sheets. The Schweinfurt Symphony orchestra was one of the finest orchestras in Germany, and those who were selected to be members were among the best musicians in the world. Every member of the orchestra, from the concert master down to the fourth chair, newest member, commanded the respect of all they encountered. It was a measure of the esteem in which they were held that Hitler's government, in this time of military conscription, had declared all members of the better orchestras exempt from military service in order that they might celebrate and sustain the Germanic culture for which the German soldiers were fighting.

Paul took his baton and his director's score to the small room in the theater which was set aside for his personal use. He used the room as his office when the orchestra was not on tour, and here he had a desk, a sofa, a piano for working out arrangements, and a rather generous library. It was a further indication of Paul's secure position within the Reich that many of the books which had been banned from distribution, and had been ceremoniously burned in a public, patriotic display, could still be found on Paul's bookshelves.

There had been much made over the public burning of books, the reaction had been exactly counter to Goebbel's intention, the entire world had been shocked, and many held the Germans up to ridicule. Paul had been secretly pleased by that. He was sure that the book burning was not Hitler's idea, but the idea of some of the people around him. Paul thought

Hitler was probably a reasonable man, but that Goebbels, Himmler and others were a disgrace. He hoped that Hitler would soon be able to see through such men.

Paul stepped into his office, then reached for the light switch.

"No," a quiet voice said from the shadows. "Just use the small desk lamp."

"What?" Paul asked, surprised by the voice. "Who is it? Who is there?"

The desk lamp clicked on and Paul saw Hans Werfel sitting behind his desk.

"Hans!"

"Hello, Paul. Are you surprised to see me?"

"Yes, I'm very surprised," Paul said. "What are you doing here?"

"I came to hear the concert," Hans said. "After all, even Jews have an appreciation for music, though I must confess that Wagner, who was never one of my favorites, is now even less of a favorite."

"It was a special concert," Paul explained.

"Yes, I know," Hans said. "For the Führer. *Heil Hitler,*" he added, raising his arm slightly in a lackluster imitation of the Nazi salute.

Paul looked around nervously.

"Don't worry," Hans said. "No one saw me come in here. You are perfectly safe."

"What do you really want, Hans?"

Hans sighed. "Paul, I have to get out of Germany."

Paul ran his hand through his hair and sat down on the sofa with a weary sigh. "I told you that three years ago," he said. "I told you then that you should leave before things got worse."

"I had tenure," Hans explained. "And my work was going well. I didn't want to interrupt it. Besides, I was like you; I was aware of things going on, but they were happening to others, not to me. Bankers, businessmen, property owners, they were the ones who were feeling the brunt of it all. I own no property, I'm engaged in no business. I thought I was safe."

"What happened to change your mind?" Paul asked. "Hans, have you been . . . have any of the S.S. thugs injured you?" Paul's voice, which had previously expressed almost the tone of one who was being put-upon, now displayed a genuine sense of concern.

"No," Hans said, and the expression in his voice was one of thankfulness that Paul could still care. "No, I haven't been injured. But I received a warning tonight."

Paul dismissed that with a wave of his hand. "Ah, the Nazis have been warning the Jews ever since they came into power."

"No," Hans explained. "This wasn't an official warning, this was a personal warning given directly to me."

"Who warned you?"

"I'd rather not say," Hans said. "It came from someone I always considered a Nazi zealot, but now I'm not so sure. Anyway, he told me that I had been left unharmed only because of the work I was doing. When I complete my work I will be killed, and Hitler will use my work for his own evil purposes."

"What work? What are you doing at the University?"

"I'd rather not say that, either," Hans said. "Paul, you've got to help me get out of the country. I have no one else to turn to."

"I can't help you," Paul said, shaking his head. "What makes you think—"

"You can help me," Hans insisted. "You and your musicians have the ability to travel almost anywhere without challenge. Issue me a pass to Geneva. Send me there for some reason which would not be challenged."

"Hans, if anyone stopped you and traced your pass back to me . . ."

"I'm not saying that it would be without some risk," Hans said. "But it's a risk I've got to take."

"All right, it's a risk *you* have to take, but why must you involve me?"

"I told you," Hans said again. "You are the only one I can turn to."

"Hans, this isn't fair," Paul complained. "You had your chance to leave and you didn't take it. Now, what right do you have to ask this of me?"

"You are my brother," Hans said, simply.

3

LIEUTENANT Rudolf Rodl stood in his tank with his upper torso protruding through the hatch of the turret as it rolled quickly alongside a road near Warsaw. The retreating Polish army had felled all the trees across the road, hoping thereby to form a roadblock, but the German Army had merely swept around the road, proceeding through the fields without a break in their progress. It had been like that since the first day the German Army had moved into Poland. Poland's army, thought to be one of the strongest in Europe, had crumbled before the German onslaught.

Rudi was wearing a headset with earphones and a mike, so he could speak to the driver and the gunner in his tank. He knew that he made an imposing figure protruding from the top of the tank like a knight in shining armor mounted on a spirited steed. Even the microphone added to the illusion, for it denoted him as one in charge. He liked to imagine what must be going through the minds of the Polish citizens who watched in fear as he swept by them, the very symbol of Germany's might.

Rudi turned to look behind him, and was startled to see that the other two tanks of his platoon were gone. Where were they? He had given them explicit orders to follow him.

"Sergeant Heibler, halt!" he shouted. "Stop the tank!"

Heibler, who was the driver, braked both tracks and the tank came to such a sudden stop that Rudi had to hold onto the turret ring to keep from being thrown out.

"What is it, Herr Lieutenant?" Heibler called up to him. "What is wrong?"

"I don't see Sergeant Kress or Sergeant Lutz. They were supposed to be behind us." Rudi removed the earphones and tried to listen for them but he could only hear the sound of his own tank engine. "Turn off the engine," he ordered.

"Herr Lieutenant, if we stop the engine we may have trouble getting it started again," Heibler warned. "I have been experiencing some difficulty."

"Turn off the engine," Rudi ordered again, angered that Heibler should question him. What good was it to be the commander if one had every command questioned?

"*Jawohl*, Herr Lieutenant," Heibler said, and the engine went silent.

"Now," Rudi said. "Perhaps now I can hear the other tanks."

Rudi crawled out of the turret and walked to the back of the tank, then strained to hear the sound of engines and clanking track which would signify the approach of the other two tanks.

Rudi could hear a far-off distant rumble of artillery, and an occasional rattle of small arms fire, muffled by distance and made hollow by the echoing sound through the trees. Closer he could hear wind in the gold and yellow leaves of the trees, but he heard nothing which sounded like tank engines.

The driver's hatch opened and Sergeant Heibler stuck his head up. "Ah," he said. "It is good to get a breath of fresh air."

"Heibler, have you the map?" Rudi asked.

"Are we lost, Lieutenant?"

Rudi glared at Heibler. "Did I say we were lost? It is Kress and Lutz who are lost. Why did not someone keep an eye open and let me know when they stopped following us?"

Rudi knew it was an unfair question. As the column leader he was the one who should have kept an eye open. He had only to look behind him ever so often to ensure that they were staying with him. But he didn't look around often enough, and the sound of his own tank plus the fact that his ears were plugged with the earphones prevented him from hearing when they dropped off. Now he was God-knows-where, and they were God-knows-where else.

"Here is the map, sir," Heibler said, handing it up to him.

"Thank you," Rudi said. He spread the map on the top of the tank, then he took his compass out and lay it on the map.

"*Reading a map without first properly orienting it is like using a set of scales to tell you how long something is. A map which isn't properly oriented is worthless,*" Rudi's map instructor had said in the classroom, and now those words came back to him. But something was wrong, the compass was going crazy, he couldn't . . . suddenly Rudi laughed, and he was glad that Heibler hadn't seen him. Of course the compass was going crazy, he was trying to read it from the top of the tank. All the metal in the tank was affecting it. He would have to jump down and walk from the tank, perhaps as far as fifty meters, before the compass would behave properly.

Rudi jumped down then walked across the open part of the field to a little glen of trees. There, he decided, he would be far enough away from the tank to read his map, and perhaps be able to make some sense of where he was.

When Rudi reached the line of trees, he realized that he wanted to urinate so he stood there for a moment relieving himself, thinking with a silent chuckle that even conquering warriors had found no way to defeat the call of nature. The concussion from the blast pitched him onto his stomach.

"Heibler, what is it?" Rudi shouted, raising himself up to his hands and knees, spitting out dry leaves and dirt.

Rudi could hear the sound of fire and he looked back toward the tank, then gasped, for it was burning, and three figures were climbing out. Heibler had jumped from his driver's hatch onto the ground in front of the tank, and even now he was running toward Rudi. The other two crewmen, the gunner and the loader, were trying to come through the top turret hatch, and Rudi saw with horror that both of them were on fire.

"Heibler!" Rudi shouted, pointing to the gunner and the loader. "Gunz and Brandt are on fire. Put them out! Push them in the dirt!"

Heibler looked toward the two burning crewmen, but before he could take one step toward them, shots rang out from behind one of the trees which had been felled across the road, and both Gunz and Brandt went down. They lay very still as the flames continued to consume them, and Rudi stood with his hand against a tree watching in fascinated horror. For the moment it didn't sink in. It did not seem real that two of the men who had been in the tank with him were now burning pieces of meat lying face down in a Polish field, and he just stood there as if this were some bizarre drama being played for his benefit alone.

Heibler ran toward the two burning corpses, and Rudi watched him disinterestedly, wondering what he was doing there. Then he saw Heibler scoop up the two machine pistols and dart across the field toward him.

"Get down, Lieutenant!" Heibler called. "Get down, you'll be hit!"

As if to underscore Heibler's warning, Rudi suddenly heard a buzz, angry and wicked sounding like a swarm of large hornets, followed closely by the crack of small arms fire. One bullet hit the tree against which Rudi was leaning, and Rudi was suddenly and effectively jerked from his semi-trance. They were shooting at him! It seemed incredible! Why would anyone want to shoot at him? "This is Rudi!" he wanted to shout. "Who would want to kill Rudi!"

Rudi dropped to the ground, then, on his stomach, he scooted back, feeling a small depression behind him. He managed to get out of the line of fire.

Heibler reached him at about that time and dived to the ground beside him, then turned around and wriggled back up to look toward the roadblock. He pointed and Rudi could see a little puff of white smoke drifting away through the limbs of the felled tree. "There," Heibler said. "They are behind that tree."

"What did they hit the tank with?" Rudi asked.

"It was a satchel charge," Heibler answered. "They crawled up from the other side. We didn't see them."

Another puff of smoke and the sound of a shot, but the bullet was so high over their heads that Rudi didn't even hear it.

"What should we do now?" Rudi asked. Heibler was a sergeant of the old Army, and Rudi didn't hesitate to ask him for an idea. After all, it had been easy being the platoon leader during the advance when Rudi had orders to follow. But now with no tank and no orders it was a different story. "I wonder how many there are?" he added.

"I have seen four guns," Heibler replied. Heibler rubbed his chin and looked into the woods behind him. Rudi saw him looking around, then perceived at once what was on his mind. Yes, Rudi thought. Yes, that might be it. If he could reach the woods, he might be able to follow the woodline around until he was even with the roadblock, then, perhaps he could come upon the Poles who were shooting at them without the Poles even seeing him. It might work and, best of all, it was his own idea. He could not abrogate his responsibility to Heibler now, no matter how urgently he wished to do so. He would try it! Rudi smiled to himself, and nodded his head in determination, not realizing that he was giving visible indications of his thought process.

Heibler saw Rudi smile and nod.

"What are you thinking, Lieutenant?" the Sergeant asked.

"Heibler, you fire at them from here," Rudi said. "I am going to try and get into the woods and fire from over there." He pointed to the edge of the woodline which was even with the road block.

"What if there are more in the woods?"

"If there are more in the woods we have no chance

anyway," Rudi said, "for surely they will come on us. Now, fire."

Heibler smiled at his Lieutenant, as an approving instructor would his student, then he raised his machine pistol and squeezed off a short burst. Rudi could see the leaves fly from the limbs just above the ambushers, and he was impressed with the accuracy of Heibler's fire.

With Heibler keeping the Poles' heads down, Rudi was able to dart into the tree line. He wanted to run quietly through the woods, but that was impossible, for the ground was covered with fallen dry leaves and they crunched with every step. Rudi ran in long steps, thinking that the longer he made his steps the fewer steps there would be and the less noise he would make. Finally, Rudi reached a small stream bed, so small that the water was all but choked out by the leaves; here, the leaves were soggy and dank-smelling and he found that he could move through them without making quite as much noise.

Twice Rudi moved up to the bank of the stream bed to check his bearings until, finally, he was just where he wanted to be. He dropped to the ground behind a tree whose roots were exposed. Rudi pulled himself up to peer through the roots, and he could see, a short fifty meters away, the four Poles who had destroyed the tank. Two of them were up against the tree trunk firing methodically toward Heibler. One of the other two appeared to be working on his rifle, while the fourth was just sitting on the ground with his back against the tree trunk drinking from a bottle with as little concern as if they were on a picnic.

Rudi heard one of them say something and the other three laughed, and he felt an intense anger at that precise moment. They had murdered two of his men, left them out there to burn like so much trash, and now they joked and laughed and drank as if they were on a picnic.

Rudi felt the anger rush to his head and his ears buzzed loudly, and he thought of nothing at that very moment except how much he wanted to smash these people, these four men who had no reason to fire at his men except for their own evil desire to commit murder. The war was lost for the Poles, and everyone knew it. Why were they not with the rest of the Polish Army? What did they hope to gain by all this?

"Ahhhh!!!" Rudi screamed from deep in his throat, suddenly standing up and rushing toward the tree firing his pistol in short bursts from the hip. The two men who were at the barricade were hit by his first burst, and that was fortunate for Rudi for they were the only ones who had weapons in their hands. The Pole who had been working on his weapon tried to bring it around into position to fire at Rudi, but Rudi caught him with a burst in the chest before he could do so. The fourth Pole, the one who had been drinking, saw his three companions killed and he began shouting, and he stood and raised his hands.

"*Nein, nein, nicht shiessen!*" the Pole shouted in German.

Rudi stopped shooting, and the echoes of his firing came back to him. He could smell the cordite, and out of the corner of his eye he saw the blue smoke from the powder drifting away. He felt a muscle jumping in his leg, and his throat was hurting, and his mouth was dry. His tongue felt as if it had swollen to twice its normal size. He pointed his gun toward the Pole.

"*Nein, nein!*" the Pole begged, holding one hand out

in front of him as if in so doing he could hold off the bullets if Rudi decided to fire. The Pole looked to be about fifty, his face now white with fear, and his eyes wild-looking like those of a trapped animal.

"I'm not going to shoot you," Rudi said quietly. He looked at the other three men. Now they were crumpled, bleeding, lifeless forms where, but a moment earlier, they had been living human beings.

Rudi had killed them. He had never even shot at anyone before other than direct the fire of the tank's gun toward distant and impersonal targets. Now he had not only shot at men, he had killed them.

Rudi felt dizzy, then a sudden wave of nausea overtook him, and he clutched his stomach and spun away from the Pole and began to retch.

"Lieutenant, look out!" Heibler called and Rudi, in the middle of retching, turned just in time to see the Polish prisoner raising one of the rifles and taking aim at him. Just as the Pole raised the rifle there was a burst of machine gun fire from Heibler's machine pistol, and the man with the rifle went down.

"Are you all right?" Heibler asked. He was standing on the tree trunk with one hand on his hip and the other holding the smoking machine gun by his side.

"Yes," Rudi said. "Yes, I'm all right. Thank you, Sergeant."

"You can't trust any of these sons-of-bitches," Heibler said, jumping down from the tree. "Like now, for instance. We should make certain they are all really dead." He walked over to the four bodies and kicked each one of them as hard as he could, and held his gun at the ready should any of them show signs of life. All appeared to be dead.

"You did some good shooting, Lieutenant," Heibler said, smiling broadly.

Rudi was just beginning to recover from his bout of nausea, and slowly reason began to return. He had done only what he had to do. He was a soldier, and he had been fired upon by the enemy. He had returned fire, and he had been victorious.

"Yes," he said, taking a deep breath as he fought his senses and emotions back to normal. "Yes, thank you, Sergeant. And thank you for your timely intervention."

"I guess that'll teach them not to lay an ambush for us, eh, Lieutenant?" Heibler said, still smiling. He was enjoying it, Rudi thought. He was actually enjoying it.

"Yes," Rudi said, showing more bravado than he actually felt. "And at four Poles to two Germans, I would say the odds were about even, wouldn't you?"

"I'd say so, yes sir," Heibler agreed, smiling even more broadly.

Of course, Rudi thought, that did not take into consideration the fact that when the engagement began, the odds were four to four and the Germans had a tank.

"What do we do now?" Heibler asked.

"We must go back to recover the map," Rudi said. "With the map we can find one of our own positions."

"Lieutenant, excuse me, sir, but before we get to our own position, wouldn't you like to button your trousers?"

Rudi looked down at his trousers and saw that they were still open from when he was urinating at the opening shots. He had fought the entire battle, including his wild charge from the woodline, with his trousers unbuttoned and his privates exposed!

Suddenly the ludicrousness of it all struck him as humorous, and he began to laugh. But his laughter was for far more than just the humor of the situation; it was also a release of the tension, and consequently his laughter was wild and uncontrolled and Heibler, too, began to laugh so that both men sat down and spent the next several moments wiping tears away and laughing, and trying to regain control of themselves.

"Perhaps they were mesmerized by the snake," Heibler suggested, and thought such a personal statement from an enlisted man to an officer would border on impertinence under other conditions, Rudi and Heibler had just shared an experience which transcended military rank. Rudi found his observation hilarious, and both men began laughing anew.

The building rose before them, a great, dark shadow thrusting into the night. Rudi and Heibler were crouching behind a wall looking down a small, dirt road toward the building. The road glowed a soft silver in the moonlight.

"It's a church," Rudi said. "It's the church of Postowycz."

"I thought our army would be here," Heibler said.

"It was our objective for the night," Rudi said. "I don't know why they aren't here."

"Perhaps they've already been here and gone on," Heibler suggested.

"No, if they had done that, there would be someone left behind. Come on."

"What are we going to do?"

"We're going to go there and wait for them," Rudi said.

Rudi looked around back toward the village of

Postowycz. There was not one light shining in the entire village, but that was normal for a town in the middle of a war zone. Somewhere in the village a dog barked.

"Wait until I am across," Rudi said to Heibler. "If I make it safely, you follow. If I am shot, go back to the woods and stay there until our army comes through."

"Right," Heibler answered.

Rudi took a deep breath then darted out into the road. He ran in a low crouch along the edge of the road holding his hand on his canteen and gas mask to prevent them from clanking too loudly. Finally he made it to the church yard, then, with a sigh of relief, he darted inside.

The church had been hit with artillery fire, but whether by the Germans or by the Poles he didn't know. But there were large holes in the roof and charred timbers lying across the pews, many of which were overturned. Shafts of moonlight streamed in through the holes in the roof, and in the moonlight he could tell that the reredo had been removed. In fact, all of the religious articles had been removed; there were no icons, statues, or crosses to show that this building even was a church. Only its general shape remained to speak of its purpose.

Rudi heard a sound and he whirled around quickly, only to see that it was Heibler arriving after his own dash down the road. Heibler stood leaning over one of the rear pews gasping loudly as he tried to regain his breath. "Any . . . one . . . in . . . here?" he finally managed to gasp.

"No," Rudi said.

Heibler pushed some of the trash aside and cleared

away a place on one pew. "Lieutenant, if you don't mind, sir, I'm going to take a little rest."

"Yes," Rudi said. "I think that would be a good idea. You sleep for two hours, then I shall sleep for two hours. One of us should stay awake at all times."

Heibler lay down on the pew using his gas mask container as a helmet. He laid his machine pistol on the floor beside him and folded his arm across his eyes. After a moment of silence, he spoke.

"What if they don't come tomorrow?" he asked.

"They'll come."

"But what if they don't? What if their orders were changed and they've gone another way? We'll be behind the enemy lines."

"We've been behind the enemy lines all day today and we've done all right," Rudi said. "We shall do all right tomorrow as well."

"I hope we can find something to eat tomorrow," Heibler said.

Rudi walked over and sat down with his back to the wall looking toward the door. The front door wasn't the only entrance into the church, but it was the most logical. Besides, from this position, he would be able to see anyone else before they saw him no matter how they entered the building.

Heibler was asleep within seconds and Rudi could hear his deep, rhythmic breathing. Heibler was older than Rudi—by almost ten years, in fact. He had been a member of the army during the peacetime limit of one hundred thousand men, and was a professional in the truest sense of the word. And yet, today, he had followed Rudi's orders without question, and even depended upon him. It made Rudi feel a sense of pride that he had been able to function so under such adversity.

Damn Heibler though—he wished the Sergeant hadn't mentioned finding something to eat tomorrow. Rudi had not eaten since breakfast, and the day had been busy enough so that he hadn't missed it, until Heibler mentioned it. Now Rudi was hungry. He wished he had some of the field rations which had been in the tank.

4

Hans read the letter he had been given by Paul.

I have the honor of introducing Herr Professor Hans Werfel: Please extend to Dr. Werfel all due courtesy as my representative in the negotiations for the right to present a public concert of the special Geneva Philharmonic arrangement of Tannhauser.

In a recent concert presented by the Schweinfurt Symphony Orchestra for the Führer, the Führer expressed a desire to hear this music, and it is the wish of the Schweinfurt Symphony to grant the Führer this wish at some future date.

Dr. Werfel is authorized to arrange for payment at a mutually agreed upon figure.

Heil Hitler,
PAUL MAASS
Orchestra Direktor

Hans actually did have the authority to negotiate with the music publisher who held the copyright to the *Tannhauser* arrangement, and that publisher had been contacted and told to expect Hans' arrival. It was also true that Hitler had mentioned the music to Paul, thus giving credibility to the letter.

Hans and Paul had decided that this would be the best method of providing a cover for Hans' escape from Germany. The passport was Hans' actual passport. Hans wasn't worried about using his own name. His name was well known in scientific circles; he had written many articles over the last ten years, and had been the subject of many more. But Hans Werfel was not a name generally known by the public, and the place on the passport which listed his occupation stated only that he was a "professor," a title which was supported by the letter he carried. It did not specifically state that he was a professor of physics. And, though the law required it, Hans' passport did not carry the fact that he was a Jew.

Hans folded the letter carefully and put it back in the envelope, then returned the envelope to his inside breast pocket. He had enjoyed a moment of solitude to look at the letter, for the others who had been sharing the compartment with him left the train at this stop. Now he was only ten miles from the Swiss border.

For a while Hans thought he would be alone in the train compartment for the last ten miles, but just before the train pulled out of the station, a rather portly, jolly-looking blond man came in and sat on the seat across from Hans. He was wearing *lederhosen*, the traditional leather shorts in the Black Forest, and he sat down and hooked his thumbs in his suspenders and looked out the window, letting out the sigh of one who is relieved to sit after a long stand.

"So, my friend," the fat man said to Hans. "You

are coming to the Black Forest, eh? Is it a holiday for you, then?"

"No," Hans said, "I'm going across the border into Switzerland."

"Switzerland, is it? You would rather take your holiday in Switzerland than in Germany's *Schwarzwald*?"

"It isn't a holiday," Hans said. Hans had no wish to get involved in any conversations, even though his compartment companion seemed affable enough.

"My name is Werner May," Hans' companion said, and he extended his hand to take Hans' in a hearty handshake. "Who are you?"

"I am Professor Hans Werfel," Werfel answered.

"A professor is it? Do you teach in the University?"

"No," Hans said. "I represent the Schweinfurt orchestra."

"A musician then," Werner said. "Good, good, the world needs much music."

The train whistle blew, a high-pitched sound which carried across an open field to the Granite Mountains nearby, then returned in a haunting echo. There was a puff of steam, then a creak of wheels as the car began to jerk forward.

The train pulled away from the station and the small village, then followed alongside the Rhine, which flowed in picturesque grandeur along the western edge of the forest. The forest consisted of a thick growth of dark fir and spruce trees from which the region derived the name "Black Forest". It all combined to make the region like a picture in a storybook. Indeed, many of Germany's legends and fairy tales were associated with the Black Forest for just such a reason, and Hans knew that when outsiders conjured up a mental image of Germany, the Black Forest was what they saw.

"Look," Werner said as the train rounded a curve and they were treated to a majestic view. There had been something added to the trees, rivers and mountains, however, as hundreds of flagpoles were erected alongside the tract, while large red swastika flags fluttered from them, adding a splash of garish red to the more natural shades of nature's fall palette. "Even here that fool Hitler must fly his flags."

Hans was surprised to hear anyone make such a negative comment about Hitler with no regard for who overheard him, and if Werner wasn't frightened to say such a thing aloud, then Hans was frightened for the both of them. He looked around to make certain they weren't overheard.

"Ach, don't worry, Herr Professor," Werner said expansively. "There is no one here. Besides, we are both men, *ja?* Has it come to the point that a man cannot express what is on his mind?"

"You should not say such things before strangers," Hans said.

"I see," Werner laughed. "It is all right to speak so in front of friends, but not in front of strangers, is that correct?"

"It is at least more prudent," Hans said.

Werner laughed again. "How cautious you are," he said. "You will not even agree that my statement is correct for fear of making it appear that you yourself are speaking against Hitler."

"I will not speak against the Führer," Hans said cautiously.

Werner studied Hans for a moment, and though Hans tried to read Werner's eyes, he was unable to do so.

"Well," Werner finally said. "Perhaps you are right.

Perhaps it is unwise to say such things. So we will talk of other things. Do you know the Black Forest? Have you been here before?"

"Yes," Hans said. "My father brought me here on holiday when I was a child."

Hans saw a small boat on the Rhine, and he remembered another boat many years ago, the last summer he had come to the Black Forest. He had gone boating with his father, a famous cuckoo clock maker, and it was the first time he had ever known that there were some who did not approve of his father, just because his father was a Jew, named Jastrile Werfel.

"Why doesn't the Kaiser want the clock, father?" he had asked. They had been very proud when Hans' father got the commission to do a special commemorative clock for the Kaiser, and Hans had watched it take shape under his father's skillful hands. Then, suddenly, the commission was cancelled and the clock was put onto the shelf in the shop, just one of the many others, no longer magic by its association with royalty. Jastrile had been told that the clock was rejected when the Kaiser discovered that Jastrile was Jewish and was afraid of offending non-Jewish artisans.

"Because of a nasty thing known as anti-Semitism," Jastrile answered. Jastrile was rowing the boat, and Hans was sitting at the stern, holding the tiller.

"Anti-Semitism? What is that?"

"It's a disease which affects some people," Jastrile tried to explain. "For over two thousand years the Jews have experienced this. It is a way of life which we cannot change. It means that there are people who don't like us, you and I, because we are Jews."

"And mama?"

"No, not mama," Jastrile said. "Your mama is not a Jew."

"But she's married to you, papa."

Jastrile smiled. "I know. Your mama is not a Jew, and she does not have the disease of anti-Semitism. There are many who are like your mother. In fact, there are more who are like your mother than there are people like the foolish person in the Kaiser's entourage who feared that buying a clock made by a Jew would be a bad thing to do. It is only because there are more people who are like your mama than there are those who are anti-Semitic that life is worth living."

"Can't we just stop being a Jew and be something else?" Hans had asked.

"Can you stop being a boy and become a girl?" Jastrile replied with a smile.

"No," Hans laughed.

"Why not?"

"Because I was *born* a boy," Hans said, as if unable to understand why his father couldn't comprehend such a simple fact.

"Then that also answers your question," Jastrile explained. "We are born Jewish, and that we cannot change. I wouldn't want to change it, even if I could."

"But why not?" Hans asked. "If there are many people who dislike us because we are Jews, then I would think it would be nice to change if we could."

"We are a blessed people," Jastrile said. "It was to us, the Jews, to whom God chose to manifest Himself as the one true God of all mankind. It was we, the Jews, who rejected Rome when Rome was at the peak of power, and stopped the spread of Roman paganism around the world. And it is we who have the richest and the longest history of any civilized body of people. Is it too much to have to pay for this rich heritage and this God-given honor by suffering a little jealousy from others?"

"But the Kaiser, papa. He is Germany!"

"No, he is not Germany," Jastrile said. "He is only one man in Germany. And no man, not even the Kaiser, could ever impose his anti-Semitism upon the entire German People."

The train whistled shrilly, and then began to slow, and in doing so, it interrupted Hans' thoughts, and brought him back to the present. How glad he was now that his father had died before he could see what had become of his beloved Germany and his equally loved Jewish heritage.

"We have come to the border," Werner said. He stood up and looked down at Hans. "Have you anything you wish to tell me?"

"Tell you, Herr May? What would I wish to tell you?" Hans asked.

"Perhaps I can help you," Werner suggested.

"Help me with what?"

"Herr Professor, let me tell you something. I have an eye for some things and my eye tells me that there may be something you do not wish the authorities to know. If this is true you are indeed lucky, for I am an understanding and compassionate man who has no love for the authorities. I am also a—how shall I say it?—an opportunistic man. Yes, that is an accurate statement. I am an opportunistic man, and I sense a possible opportunity here."

"What type of opportunity, Herr May?" Hans asked.

"If I were to cooperate with you in whatever scheme you have to defy the authorities, you might see fit to reward me, *ja*?"

"I'm sorry, Herr May," Hans said. "But I have no scheme to defy the authorities. I have only one mis-

sion and that is to secure the permission of a certain
music publisher to perform *Tannhaüser* for the
Führer. This I shall do."

"It's a pity we can do no business," Herr May said.
He looked out the window. "Look at them, so many
authorities for one small train. It would be foolish to
be on this train now and try and trick them in some
way." He looked toward Hans. "Unless, of course, one
had a plan?"

"It would still be foolish," Hans said. "And treason-
ous as well. Our country is at war. We should all be
behind the Fatherland during these trying times."

Werner chuckled. "To be sure, Herr Professor, to
be sure. If you will excuse me, I will visit the toilet
during the border inspection."

Hans watched as May left the compartment, then,
left alone he sat quietly and stared through the window at the Rhine River. On this side of the bridge
he could see the guard house of the German officials
with the swastika flying above it. Just across the river,
at the other end of the bridge, he could see the Swiss
border guard house with the red flag and white cross
which was Switzerland's National ensign flying above
it. It seemed so close, a man on foot could walk across
the bridge in less than a minute. And yet he knew
that the last few hundred feet were the most difficult
of all.

Ironically it had once been easy for Jews to leave
Germany. Early in Hitler's term of power, they had
actually been encouraged to leave. Of course, there
was a heavy penalty for leaving. The Jews who left
had to forfeit all they possessed. Many Jews left anyway, feeling that it would be better to start fresh in
a new country than to remain in Germany and face the
increasing hardships Hitler was causing for them.

Many more tried to beat the system by leaving and attempting to smuggle diamonds or other valuables out with them. Some made it, but those who were caught paid the penalty of being put into a concentration camp.

Hans had not left when he had the opportunity because he was too involved with his work. Now the opportunity had passed, for Jews were no longer allowed to leave. Those who were caught were sent immediately to concentration camps, and though no one knew exactly what went on in the camps, it certainly was not to be considered as a desirable condition.

Hans heard a woman scream, then begin to shout and cry, and though he couldn't hear her clearly enough to make out what she was saying, he realized from the tone of her voice that she was terrified of something. He pressed his face against the window and saw her being pulled, fighting and crying, away from the train by two burly guards. Behind her, walking at a slow, defeated pace, with his head down, came a man whom Hans took to be the woman's husband. A car was brought up and they were both shoved into the back seat, then the car drove off.

Hans felt a sick, sinking sensation in the pit of his stomach. Who were they, and what had they done to warrant such treatment? Were they Jews trying to cross the border? Would he join them shortly?

There was a knock on the door of Hans' compartment, but it was a knock which mocked courtesy. It wasn't requesting permission to enter, it was harsh and challenging, *demanding* entrance. Three men followed the knock into the compartment, one dressed in a policeman's uniform, another dressed in the uniform of a border guard, and the third dressed in the uniform of the S.S.

"Let me see your passport and papers, please," the police officer said. His "please," like his knock, was a mockery.

Hans took a deep breath, then reached for his passport. He called upon every ounce of reserve strength to force himself to be calm. Though his stomach was churning and his heart pounding, he knew that the slightest display of nervousness, a bead of perspiration, or the shake of a hand could betray him.

"You are a professor?"

"Yes," Hans said easily.

"Where do you teach?"

"I do not teach," Hans answered easily. "I am the business agent for a symphony orchestra."

"A symphony orchestra," the border guard said. "I don't like that kind of music. That is the music of highbrows. Give me the music of a good oompah band in a beerhall." He held his arms out as if playing a tuba, and began imitating the sound, "oompah, oompah," while bending his knees in rhythm.

"Yes," the police officer replied, laughing. "That is where the real music comes from." He handed the passport back to Hans. "Are you on holiday, Herr Professor?"

"No," Hans said. "I am going to Geneva to arrange for some music. I must return to the orchestra as quickly as possible."

"Very well," the police officer said. He turned to leave. "We have only one more car to examine and then we can—"

"Wait," the third man interrupted. He was the one in the S.S. uniform and he had not spoken until this moment.

"Is something wrong?" the policeman asked the S.S. man.

"I am not yet satisfied with the Professor," the S.S. man said. "Have you some paper or authorization to cross the border?"

"The passport is the only authorization I need," Hans said, quoting the law. "I do have a letter of introduction to the music publisher authorizing me to do business on behalf of the orchestra."

"Let me see the letter, please," the S.S. man said, holding out his hand.

"You must be very careful with it," Hans said, handing the letter over. "It is the only way I have of introducing myself so that I can conduct my business properly."

The S.S. man took the letter without responding to Hans and removed it from the envelope. He read it, then looked at Hans coldly.

"I am always suspicious of someone who uses the Führer's name," he said. He thumped his finger against the letter. "It is as if the most common criminal, or the stinkingest Jew, can hide behind the name. Is that what you have done here?"

"No," Hans said. "No, of course not."

"Still, there is something here which is causing my nose to itch," the S.S. man said, and he scratched his nose to emphasize his statement. "I have been at this business too long to be fooled."

"Waste no more time with this one," a new voice suddenly said. "He is of no consequence to us. I have checked him myself, and I do not make mistakes."

"*Jawohl, Hauptsturmführer*," the three inspectors said, suddenly coming to attention with a click of their heels.

Hans turned toward the sound of the voice, then noticed that it was the beer salesman, Werner May. Or at least, Hans had thought he was a beer salesman.

Now he saw May in the uniform of an S.S. captain.

Werner May's smile was no longer jolly. Now it was almost sinister.

"You must excuse the little game I played with you," S.S. Captain May said to Hans. "But you would be surprised at how many people, who have made it this far, give themselves away to someone they think can help them go the final step."

"You are an S.S. officer?"

"Yes," May said. "I am in charge of this sector." He smiled broadly, and Hans was amazed to see how evil such a smile could make one look. "Since I have hit upon my little charade, I have increased the number of Jews caught by tenfold."

"Yes," Hans said. "Yes, I can see how such a ruse might work."

"I wish you good luck in your acquisition of the music, Herr Professor, and I hope the Führer is not disappointed."

"I'm sure I will be successful," Hans said. "Thank you for your concern."

"Now, gentlemen, shall we get on with it?" Werner said. He turned back toward Hans and clicked his heels and raised his hand. "*Heil Hitler*, Herr Professor."

"*Heil Hitler*," Hans answered as the four men left the compartment. It was odd, but Werner May had looked natural, even dignified, in the short lederhosen and the garish suspenders. Now, in the stern military cut of his S.S. uniform, he looked ludicrous.

Hans watched through the window as three more people were pulled from the train and he had to begrudgingly admire the grim efficiency which allowed a would-be escapee to be caught at this, the last possible moment.

The train gave another shrill whistle, then it began to move. Hans took in a deep breath and held it, not daring to breathe as the train started through the raised bars and out onto the bridge. He looked out and saw the cobblestone banks of the river, and then the river itself. He vowed to hold his breath until the middle of the river was crossed, for then and only then would he be in Switzerland and be safe.

The river was crossed and the train passed through the Swiss gates, then stopped for the Swiss border inspection. It was swift and simple, a mere declaration of possessions, then the train was waved on, then Hans lay his head back on the seat and wept in relief.

Hans Werfel was free.

5

ARTICLE in the Schweinfurt Tageblat, September 28, 1930:

VICTORY IN POLAND!
Lieutenant Rudolph Rodl mentioned in Colonel Guderian's dispatches!

The German Army has achieved a marvelous victory in Poland, finally righting the terrible wrongs which Poland has, for so long, heaped upon the peaceful and productive German citizens who lived near the Polish-German borders.

The Führer stated in an announcement released from Berlin that, "Germany has shown the world that reckless behavior with our legitimate rights will be dealt with in an unrelenting manner. The Polish problem, so long the festering cause of war, has been eliminated. Today Germany is satisfied, content at last that all wrongs have been righted. I appeal to France and England to join with me now in assuring peace in Europe."

It is not known whether the Führer's sensible and heartfelt appeal for peace will be listened to, or whether the bloodthirsty governments of England and France will insist upon carrying out their bellicose threat of war. While extending the offer of peace, Chancellor Hitler also cautioned England and France against the folly of war, by pointing out the ease with which the German Army defeated Poland.

With the victory of the German Army in Poland, comes news of the courage of our brave fighting man. One such man is Lieutenant Rudolph Rodl, son of Herr Director-General Heinrich Rodl, of I.G.N. Kugelwerks.

Colonel Heinz Guderian, commander of the 19th Panzer corps, said of Lieutenant Rodl: "With great disregard for his own personal safety, Lieutenant Rodl continued to press his attack, even when an unexpected pocket of stiff Polish resistance held up the rest of his Panzer company. Lieutenant Rodl pressed on, thrusting deep into the Polish lines where, outnumbered by the defenders, he lost his tank to enemy artillery. Lieutenant Rodl then rescued his crew and led them through the Polish lines, destroying one fortified position and capturing in hand to hand combat the objective which had been set for his company. When the rest of the company arrived in force the next morning, they found Lieutenant Rodl and his one surviving crew member in command of the military objective."

Rudi stood just off the edge of the road in the grass, hoping to avoid getting mud on his shoes and trouser legs. The driver of the little open scout car which had brought Rudi to this point sat behind the steering wheel and drummed his fingers nervously as Rudi examined the little town which was at the bottom of the hill one kilometer away.

Rudi looked through binoculars at the little town which was typical of the dozens of other Polish villages he had seen over the last month. The town was composed of dirty, mud-mortared, and thatch roofed houses dominated by a stone church with a steeple which rose majestically above the cluster of weathered buildings around it. The town differed somewhat from the others, because the war had not touched this town. Not one artillery shell had landed within the town limits, and not one German soldier had set foot upon its cobblestone streets. Now, however, with the surrender of Poland, the town was to be occupied, and Rudi's Panzer platoon had been selected to be the first German military unit to enter.

"What do you think, Lieutenant? Is it safe?" the driver asked.

"Yes," Rudi said, lowering the binoculars. "In fact, I think it is empty."

"Empty?"

"I didn't see any sign of life."

"Well, where could they have gone?" the driver asked.

Rudi chuckled. "Perhaps they have all gone to a party. Come, let's go."

The driver hesitated. "I don't know . . . if the town is empty, it may be some sort of trap."

"Kaspar, you worry like an old woman," Rudi said. "Come on, let's go down there."

Rudi's assurances did nothing to ease the driver's fear, but he obeyed his lieutenant's order and drove on down the hill and into the little town.

A dog ran out from behind one of the houses, barking and nipping at the tires. The dog followed for about one hundred meters, then he gave up the chase. Ahead, in the center of the town, was the center square. There was a fountain here, not a pretty, ornate fountain, but a serviceable fountain from which many of the townspeople drew their water. Water was pouring out of a metal pipe into a cement dish which was green with algae. The water splashed over the lip of the cement dish into a larger collecting pool at the base of the fountain.

"Turn off the engine," Rudi said.

Kaspar turned off the engine, then he reached into the backseat for the machine pistol and he brought it up and moved the safety off. He looked around the square with his eyes searching every building for a possible sniper.

It was silent. Rudi could hear the engine popping as it cooled and he could hear the cool splashing sound of the water. The bubbling fountain made him thirsty. He got out of the car and walked over to the fountain, then leaned across and cupped his hand under the pipe to form a pool from which he could drink. He took long, deep swallows; the water was cool and more delicious than anything he had tasted in quite a while.

"Lieutenant!" Kaspar said quietly, but with a sense of urgency. "Lieutenant, someone is coming!"

Rudi straightened up and wiped the back of his hand across his chin. He looked in the direction Kaspar had pointed, then he laughed a low, relieved laugh. Two girls were walking toward them. One was dark and full-bodied and she held a bouquet of fall flowers in her hand. The other girl was somewhat plainer in appearance, and she hung back just a little from the first.

"Welcome to our village, Lieutenant," the pretty, dark girl said, extending the bouquet toward Rudi. "We are pleased to see the German army."

"You speak German very well," Rudi said.

"Better than I speak Polish," the girl replied with a little laugh. "That has caused me a little trouble over the past couple of years."

"I can see that it might," Rudi replied. He took the bouquet. "I thank you for the flowers, they are lovely, though, in truth, your own beauty makes them rather bland."

The girl laughed and her laughter sounded throaty, earthy, like the splash of water from the community fountain.

"Lieutenant, I do believe you have a way with women."

"Where are the others of the village?" Rudi asked.

"Gone," the girl said. "All gone except for a few of the very old or very sick. They believed the rumors that all German soldiers would murder and rape."

"And you?" Rudi said. "Did you not believe the rumors?"

The girl smiled. "You don't seem like the murdering kind," she said. She thrust her hip out slightly, then tossed her head to move the hair back. She licked her lips and looked at Rudi with dark, smoldering eyes. "And if I'm willing, it wouldn't be rape, would it?"

Rudi was surprised by the frankness of her statement, and he caught his breath as he felt a sudden heat leap to the pit of his stomach. "Are you willing?" he asked.

"Come with me," the girl invited.

Rudi looked toward Kaspar, who was now being entertained by the other girl.

"Kaspar."

"Yes, Lieutenant."

"I am going with this girl to reconnoiter the town. I shall be gone about an hour. I want you to stay with the scout car."

"Yes, Lieutenant," Kaspar said. "Uh, Lieutenant, if Captain Kant should come, what should I tell him?"

"Tell him that I am making a thorough examination of the town to be certain that there are no snipers or dangerous agents."

"Yes, Lieutenant," Kaspar said. Kaspar wasn't fooled for a moment by Rudi's charade, and Rudi knew that Kaspar wasn't fooled. But the propriety of relationship between the ranks dictated that both pretend to believe.

Rudi followed the girl across the square and up a small, twisting street, so narrow that no vehicle, not even a horse cart, could move through it. Rudi thought he could feel eyes staring at him, looking out from the shadowed rooms behind closed shutters, but when he turned to try and catch someone he saw nothing.

Finally they reached a garden wall and the girl stepped through a door and Rudi followed her. The door was so small that Rudi had to bend down to step through it, and on the other side he saw a small courtyard with the browned plants of what had been a summer garden.

"Up here," the girl said, and Rudi saw another door in the side of a two story building. The stairway which led to the upper floor was so narrow that Rudi had to twist his body sideways to ascend. The stairway was dank and dark and smelled foul from the scattering of chamber pots and the emptying of bladders. Rudi held his breath and wondered how anyone —even Poles—could live in such filth.

"This is my room," the girl said, opening a door

at the top of the stairs and stepping inside. "I'll open the window and give us a little light and air. I think we could use the air . . . my landlords are as filthy as all the others."

"Your landlords?"

"Yes. I work in the fields for the farmers of the village and I rent this room. You do not think I would keep my own house so filthy, do you?"

"No," Rudi said. "No, of course not."

The girl's room was noticeably cleaner than the rest of the house. The floor was of bare wood, but it was scrubbed clean. The walls were just as clean as the floor, and the bed smelled of fresh linen. A clean muslin curtain filled with the breeze and stood out toward the middle of the room.

"You may put your clothes there," the girl said, pointing to a table which stood at the foot of the bed. Even as she spoke, she began removing her clothes, using a shadow here, a soft light there, a movement to hold her body just so, so that by the time she was undressed she had managed to portray a sensuality which had enflamed Rudi's desire to a fever pitch.

The girl smiled at Rudi, then got onto the bed and stretched out, pointing her toes down toward the foot of the bed and raising her arms above her head. The breasts flattened a bit as she raised her arms, but they were still well rounded and sensual.

"Come to me now," she said. "Come to me, my beautiful god of war."

Rudi climbed onto the bed with her then and took her in his arms, kissing her and pulling her body against him. He could feel the soft yielding of her body, and a rapidly spreading need which her touch generated within him. He was the conqueror and she the conquered, and nothing seemed more right in Rudi's mind at this moment than this.

For whatever reason drove her, the girl was as eager as Rudi, and he could feel her kisses becoming more demanding as the tip of her tongue darted across his lips, tentatively seeking entrance. He opened his mouth and the girl's tongue stabbed inside, changing the warmth to fire.

He felt himself growing larger, and he was aware of a tremendous sense of sexual power as he moved his hard and demanding body over her soft receptive thighs. The girl let out a soft moan of passion as he thrust into her. She raised her legs and wrapped her arms around him, stroking his shoulders and raking her fingers down his back.

The power Rudi felt grew and grew as he thrust himself into the girl again and again, driving, plunging with wild abandon, now oblivious of everything except for the sensory connection between them. The girl began to whimper and flail about as her body was struck by pleasure's lightning, and with that Rudi also climaxed, feeling as if his entire being were sliding through that which connected them, there to burst in a fountain of fire and spent energy.

After several moments, Rudi got up. The girl stayed in bed, now ready for a nap, having done all she could do to welcome the brave liberators, and just before Rudi pulled the door shut, he looked back at her and saw the way the sun, shining through the slats of the shutter, painted alternate bars of light and shadow across her nude body. It was a scene which was as visually stimulating as the physical stimulation had been but a few moments earlier, and he would have returned to her had it not been for the fact that he had left Kaspar alone in the square.

The walk down the smelly stairs and through the dirty courtyard and alley quelled the lingering vestiges of desire so that by the time Rudi returned to the square in the center of the town, he was glad to be away from the girl and back to doing his duty.

Kaspar had gotten out of the jeep and was sitting on the edge of the fountain. The girl who had stayed behind with him was now working her flirtatious ways with him, and as Rudi approached them he could see the girl rubbing her pelvis against his leg and looking up at him with invitation in her eyes.

"Has anything happened?" Rudi asked.

Kaspar had not seen Rudi returning, and he was so startled that he stood up quickly and turned toward him to salute. "All is quiet, Lieutenant," he said in a crisp, military way.

Rudi smiled. "That is good," he said. "I see the young lady is still with you."

"Yes, sir," Kaspar said. The girl said something, speaking so quietly Rudi couldn't hear her, and then Kaspar cleared his throat. "Uh, Lieutenant, do you suppose it would be all right if *I* reconnoitered the place?"

"Private, are you trying to suggest that I didn't do a thorough job?"

"No, sir, it's not that, sir, it's just . . ." Kaspar's apologetic rejoinder hung in the air, pregnant with disappointment.

Rudi smiled. "Now, if you would like to take about an hour to find the best place to park all our vehicles, I could see where that would be helpful."

"Find a place to park the vehicles, sir?" Kaspar replied, not yet grasping Rudi's meaning.

"Yes," Rudi said. "You might want to take the

young lady with you. I'm certain she would be a big help."

"Take the young lady to help me find a place?" Kaspar said. He still didn't understand, but now the girl did, and she started tugging eagerly on Kaspar's arm.

"Oh!" Kaspar said, suddenly realizing the implication of Rudi's offer. "Oh, yes, take the girl with me! I understand, Lieutenant. Yes, I'll go look for a place to park the vehicles now."

"See that you are back in less than an hour," Rudi said, once again the stern military commander.

"I will be back, Lieutenant," Kaspar said, and he and the girl left, disappearing down one of the many narrow alleyways which ran, like spokes in a wheel, away from the town square.

Rudi watched until they were gone, then he leaned over the fountain and cupped his hand under the pipe to take another drink of water.

"So, the German pig has come to the Polish trough for water, eh?" a man's cold, angry voice said.

Rudi whirled around quickly, frightened that perhaps a Polish soldier who had decided not to surrender with the rest of the country was now about to kill him. He wished that he had not been so stupid as to get this far away from his weapon.

Rudi breathed a sigh of relief. It wasn't a soldier, it was an old man, and the man held nothing in his hand any more frightening than the cane he used to help him walk. That wasn't quite right, though, he noticed. The old man was a soldier, or at least had been a soldier, for he was wearing a World War I uniform, complete with ribbons and medals.

"Hello," Rudi said. He didn't really know what else to say.

"Why have you come here?" the old man asked. "Why have you sacked and pillaged my country?"

"You've got that all wrong, old man," Rudi answered. "Poland attacked Germany. This was merely a counterattack."

"Lies," the old man said. "All Germans are full of lies."

Rudi felt a degree of sympathy for the old man. Certainly he must feel as if the world as he knew it was gone. But his sympathy did not extend far enough to allow him to put up with the man's vicious slander. Didn't the man read the newspapers at all? Could it be true that he had no idea of the events which led to this war? Didn't he know about the repeated Polish provocations?

"Listen," Rudi said. "The war is over now. Let us start the peace by being truthful with each other."

"The German doesn't know the meaning of the word truth."

Rudi sighed. "I know you are upset," he said. "I will do nothing to make you any more uncomfortable. You will find, to your surprise I think, that we are decent, civilized people."

"What if I told you I was a Jew?" the old man said. "Would your decency and civilization extend that far?"

"Yes, of course," Rudi said. He laughed. "I see that you have fallen for the old propaganda which has been put out about us. Jews who have caused no problems for Germany will have no trouble with Germany. The whole thing has been blown out of proportion. A few troublesome Jews have caused difficulty for their entire race. But with peace and stability will come justice and fairness. You will soon see that no one has reason to fear us."

"How good of you to reassure me, Lieutenant," the old man said sarcastically. The sound of engines reached Rudi's ears then, and he looked back toward the top of the hill from which he had first surveyed the town to see the remainder of his company. The column was being led by a tank from which flew the red, white and black Nazi flag. "And now, the locust plague is upon us," the old man said quietly. He turned and left, walking laboriously across the cobblestone floor of the square. Rudi could hear his cane tap, tap, tapping as he walked away, even above the sound of engines and jangle of track of the coming vehicles.

Rudi walked over to the scout car and took out a flare pistol. He checked the color of the flare, then fired a green rocket into the air. That was the agreed upon signal that the town was safe for all to enter.

Before the column reached the town, a scout car pulled out from deep in the line and raced quickly ahead of the tanks leaving behind a pair of roostertails of dust trailing out behind the wheels. The little car left the dirt road then bounced across the cobblestones until it reached Rudi where, finally, it stopped.

Captain Ernst Kant, the commanding officer of Rudi's company, stepped out of the car and returned Rudi's salute.

"Well, Rudi," Kant said, fitting a monocle into his eye. "What do you think? Is the village secure and ready for our occupation?"

"It seems to be, sir," Rudi said. "I have, myself, conducted a most thorough reconnaissance, and at this moment I have Private Kaspar out seeking the best parking place for the vehicles."

"Good, good," Kant said. "Excellent work." Kant stuck his baton under his left arm, then with his hands folded behind his back, and his cheek and eye socket squeezed into position to clamp the monocle securely, he slowly looked around the town. The remainder of the convoy arrived then, and there were shouts and laughs, and the occasional gunning of engines. The track of the tanks clanked and squealed, and there was the groaning whine of electric motors as the turrets traversed into position to set the guns at the desired angle and elevation. It was an exciting moment, and Rudi felt himself quivering inside. Surely no man could ask for more than to be a German officer in this magnificent army. He wished the old man had hung around to see this. It would teach him the proper respect for the German Army.

6

Spring, 1940

SLIGHTLY south and west of Schweinfurt, close enough to the city to see the smokestacks and higher buildings of the factories but far enough away to be surrounded by open land and farmers' fields, stood the house of Heinrich Rodl. The house was a very old house, built by an early land baron during the mid nineteenth century. It was two stories of stone and brick, and only recently had been updated with inside plumbing and electrical wiring. The grounds of the house were enclosed by a high stone wall, and though there was a gatekeeper's shack, Heinrich did not actually employ anyone for that purpose.

Heinrich bought the house shortly after he had been promoted to the position of Director-General of I.G.N. Kugelwerks, because he felt that such a home was befitting one of his position. He also bought it to try and recapture some of his lost heritage, for had it not been for the deprivation of his lands by the Versailles Treaty, he and his family would have inherited such a home.

The place was a fine example of a Bavarian manor

house, almost, but not quite on the order of a castle. It made a quaint picture, and would have been suitable as one of the decorative pictures one often sees on the walls of a travel office. It was even more lovely now than usual, because it was dressed in the bright color of fresh spring growth.

Inside the house on the upper floor Heinrich was pacing back and forth nervously, and he reached into his watch pocket to remove his watch. He looked at it, then tapped it and raised it to his ear to see if it was running, then he looked at it again. He snapped the lid closed and cleared his throat.

"Frauka, will you please hurry?" he called impatiently. "Rudi's train arrives at ten o'clock. Would you have us late on the first day he is home?"

"You do want us to look nice, don't you, papa?" Lisl asked.

"Of course I do," Heinrich said. "Everything must be perfect for Rudi."

"Then you'll have to give us a moment," Lisl said.

"All right, but only a moment," Heinrich said. "And then, do hurry down. I shall wait by the car."

Heinrich hurried down the stairs, passing the large old paintings which had graced the walls when he bought the place, and which seemed so much a part of the house that they remained, though he had no idea who any of the subjects of the paintings were. On the front wall there was a shield with a sword and mace crossed over it, and to the right of that, a new sculpture, a bas-relief eagle with its talons clutching a wreath-encircled swastika. Great oaken doors led from the entrance hall into a library, the shelves of which, like the library belonging to Paul Maass, still contained books which had been officially banned by the Nazi state.

"Herr-Dircktor-General, Gauleiter Dietering is here," Wili Arndst told Heinrich, as Heinrich reached the bottom of the steps. Wili Arndst was Heinrich's personal secretary, a man that Heinrich often spoke of in English as "his man Friday."

"What does Dietering want?"

"It is about air defense, I believe," Wili said.

"Herr Direktor, if I might have just one moment, please?" Dietering said then, stepping into the entrance hall from the parlor where he had been waiting.

Heinrich looked at his watch again. "All right," he said impatiently. "But only a moment, please, for my son is arriving from Poland today and we are going to have a picnic."

"How nice," Dietering said. "I am pleased for all of you on such a joyful occasion. Please offer my congratulations to your son. I recall reading of his heroic action in Poland."

"I shall," Heinrich said. "Now, Herr Gauleiter, what is it? What do you need?"

"I need your authorization to implement an air defense plan for the factory," he said. "If you will allow me, I have a plan here I would like to show you."

Heinrich walked over to a hall table where Dietering had a briefcase, and he watched over Dietering's shoulder as Dietering opened it and removed the contents. He spread a map open to show to Heinrich.

"Here," he said, "we have a map showing the location of the ball bearing factory. As you can see, any bombing airplanes would have several excellent landmarks by which to orient themselves, the sports stadium here, the railroad yard here, and this complex of apartment buildings here."

"Yes," Heinrich agreed.

"Now, here is my proposal," Dietering said. He put the map to one side and opened a folder to show another paper, this one featuring an artist's drawing of I.G.N. Kugelwerks. "What do you think?" he asked.

"What do I think?" Heinrich replied, puzzled by the question. "What do you mean, what do I think? It's simply a drawing of the factory. What should I think?"

Dietering smiled broadly. "Look again, Herr Direktor."

Heinrich looked at Dietering in confusion, then looked back at the drawing. "What do you mean, look again?" he asked. "Look, here is the main building here, and here are the rolling . . . wait, your drawing is incorrect, these windows should be . . . ," Heinrich paused again and studied the drawing intently for several seconds. "Herr Gauleiter, this isn't the factory at all. What is it?"

"Now look," Dietering said, and he showed another drawing, this time a bird's eye view of that section of the city where the factory was located. Heinrich looked at it, and saw that the factory was in the wrong place, moved by as much as two miles.

"I don't understand," he said. "Why would you want to move the factory to here? Look, the sports stadium is still here in the same relative position, the railroad yard still there—it would be just as easy to pinpoint."

"Precisely," Dietering said smiling broadly. "And that is just what we would want to happen. Don't you recognize the buildings, Herr Rodl?"

Heinrich looked more closely. "Why, these are . . ." he paused and looked again to make certain. "These are the Adolf Hitler People's Apartments."

"Yes," Dietering said. "You see, we've moved the

smokestacks from the factory over to the apartment
buildings, and the smoke will be routed over to them
by a series of pipes. We've moved all the signs, here,
we've built what will appear to be a cooling tower,
and there you have a factory. Only it isn't a factory.
The real factory is where it has always been, but now
without the smoke stacks, signs, cooling tower, and
so forth."

"But that is preposterous!" Heinrich said.

"Why do you believe it is preposterous?" Dietering
replied. "Herr Rodl, you were yourself fooled for a
moment and you should know the factory better than
anyone. If you were fooled, think of the pilot of an
enemy bomber flying at night with only the moon to
guide him. I assure you, Herr Rodl, when this plan is
adopted the only bombs to fall on I.G.N. Kugelwerks
will be the result of an accident."

"But what about the apartment buildings?" Heinrich asked. "What about the people living there? You
are the Gauleiter of Schweinfurt. These are your
people!"

"They will be evacuated to bomb shelters in the
event of an air raid," Dietering explained easily. "It
is much easier to evacuate people than to move heavy
machinery."

"But they'll lose their homes," Heinrich protested.

"It is easier to rebuild homes than to rebuild factories," Dietering said. "Herr Rodl, don't you see the
beautiful simplicity of my plan?"

"No," Heinrich said. "No, I don't see it at all."

"It is too bad that you don't see it," Dietering said,
now some of the enthusiasm in his voice gone by the
unexpected reaction from Heinrich. "Because I have
already discussed it with the minister of home defense
and he has given me his approval."

"Then you have wasted your time," Heinrich said. "For you do not have *my* approval."

Dietering picked up the papers and put them in his briefcase, then clicked his heels together and gave Heinrich a small, perfunctory bow. "As you yourself have already noted, Herr Rodl, *I* am Gauleiter of Schweinfurt. I wasn't here for your approval, I was here for your cooperation. I don't need your approval and, as you shall soon see, I don't even need your cooperation. *Heil Hitler*, Herr Rodl."

Dietering turned sharply on his heel and walked away carrying the briefcase under his arm as gingerly as if it contained secret war plans. Heinrich watched him, at first, with a sense of bewilderment, and then with a sense of anger. By the time he heard Dietering's car drive away, he was seething with anger, and he wished that he had thrown Dietering out.

"Well, there, you see," Lisl's voice said as she and her mother came down the stairs at that moment. "It didn't take so terribly long after all, did it?"

Heinrich looked at his beautiful daughter, and at his equally lovely wife and, for the moment at least, he was able to forget about Dietering. After all, there was plenty of time before Dietering would be able to put his insane plan into operation, and Heinrich was reasonably certain that he would be able to find some way to stop it.

Wili was waiting outside with the door of the car open when Heinrich, Frauka and Lisl left the house. The car actually belonged to I.G.N. Kugelwerks, though, as its director, Heinrich had access to it at all times. Private ownership of automobiles in Germany was still possible though exceedingly difficult, not only because of the price, but because of the cost and availability of fuel. Therefore, though one of the highest paid men in Schweinfurt, Heinrich did not own a personal car.

Wili slammed the door, then moved quickly around to get behind the steering wheel. He started the car and they pulled out onto the road heading for the railroad station and a meeting with Rudi.

On the train which Heinrich and his family hurried to meet, Rudi sat watching the fields roll by outside the train window. They were now less than fifteen minutes from Schweinfurt and he was getting anxious to see his mother and father again and, of course, his sister. She had written him about meeting Adolf Hitler, and Rudi took a measure of pride in realizing that Hitler had apparently appreciated her beauty as much as Rudi and his family did.

A farmhouse slid by outside, neat and clean, with a beautiful flower garden adding a touch of color. How different the German farmhouses from the Polish farm houses, Rudi thought. In Germany all the houses were clean and orderly, with an obvious attempt by the owner to make a contribution to the eyes as well as the stomach of all Germans. In Poland, the farmhouses were little more than functional shelters, devoid of styles and in many extreme cases, devoid even of cleanliness. It was very good to be back.

Rudi not only appreciated the sights and smells of Germany (Poland not only looked dirty, it *smelled* dirty, he thought), but he also appreciated the people of Germany. Everywhere he went in his uniform, he was surrounded by well-wishers; men who bought him beer, women who gave him flowers, and children who practically worshiped him. Flush with victory now, the German citizen could not do too much for the German soldier.

Rudi looked around the compartment at his travelling companions. There was an old man and old woman in the compartment who had shared the compartment all the way from Frankfurt. She had offered Rudi a piece of cheese when they first came in and, when he had refused, she begged him to take it. Her grandson was in Poland, a private with Army Group North, and giving some cheese to him made her feel as if she were doing something for her grandson.

Rudi was embarrassed by it, but he accepted the cheese, then asked the private's name, making a mental note to look him up and see if there was something he could do for him when he returned from leave. It was a well intended idea, but in less than half an hour he had already forgotten the private's name, so he knew it would all come to nothing.

Two nuns boarded the train and sat in contemplative silence for most of the journey, then two men in civilian clothes and, finally, three rather loud S.S.

Rudi looked at the three S.S. They were wearing their uniforms like heroes, and yet he knew that even if they had been to Poland, which he doubted, they had gone there for the free ride. This branch of the S.S. did not participate in combat with the other soldiers. They were policemen, and honor guards and, Rudi often suspected, cowards. Why was it, he wondered, that while other men did the fighting, it was the S.S. members who found it necessary to swagger about so?

A few years ago the S.A. was eliminated. Some said it was because Himmler did not wish so powerful a group competing with the Führer for attention. Others said it was because Hitler himself feared Roehm. Whatever the reason, they were gone, and though Rudi had never publicly so stated, he wished the S.S. would suffer the same fate.

The door to the train compartment slid open and an old woman stood there. She looked around, saw that there was no seat, and sighed.

"There are no other places," she said. "Would it be all right if I sat on my suitcase here."

"Go somewhere else, old woman," one of the S.S. men said, and the other two men laughed.

"Madam, allow me," Rudi said quickly, standing and offering his seat to the older lady. "I know that someone of your age might tire easily."

"Bless you," the old woman said, accepting his seat eagerly.

Rudi looked over at the three S.S. men, wanting them to look him in the eye so he could shame them. In fact, he was hoping against hope that one of them might go so far as to challenge him. In the past, it would not have been healthy to get into an altercation with a member of the S.S., but since the victory in Poland, the army was enjoying privileged status.

None of the S.S. men returned Rudi's icy stare, so he stepped out of the compartment into the narrow aisle which ran the length of the car and leaned against the raised window, enjoying the fresh, clean smell of Germany in the spring and looking at the neat villages and fields roll by. Behind him he could hear the loud, raucous laugh of the three S.S. men, and then he heard one of them make an off-color comment. He thought of the women and the nuns in the compartment and of how rude the comment was, but he didn't go back into the compartment or say anything.

The S.S. men were a mystery to Rudi. How could

Hitler, whose brilliance had saved Germany, allow such a group to attain so much power? He hoped that Hitler would soon realize that whatever purpose the S.S. was created for had been served, and it was time to eliminate such people from the new order.

The conductor came through the car then and his passage interrupted Rudi's thoughts.

"Schweinfurt," the conductor called out. "The next stop is Schweinfurt."

"That's my stop," Rudi said, pulling away from the window and moving down to the end of the car near the entrance.

"Are you coming home on furlough?" the conductor asked pleasantly.

"Yes," Rudi said. "This is my first since I went in, so I am very much looking forward to it."

"I'm certain you would be," the conductor said. "Are you coming from Poland?"

"Yes."

The conductor pointed to the black armband around his arm. "This is for my son," he said. "He was killed in Poland fighting for the Führer."

"I'm so sorry," Rudi offered.

"There is nothing to be sorry for," the conductor replied. "One can die no more noble a death than to die for the Führer."

"I agree," Rudi said. "I just meant that I was sorry that you are now without your son."

"I still have him," the conductor said, and he put his hand across his heart. "I have him here, and all Germany has him here." The conductor clicked his heels and raised his arm in the Nazi salute. "*Heil Hitler!*" he said.

Saluting, when it was done on the front, was generally done by the more conventional method, and the Hitler salute nearly caught Rudi off-guard, but he recovered in time to return it. *"Heil Hitler,"* Rudi said.

The engineer gave several loud whistles, then Rudi looked forward to see that they were going into a train shed. The bright sunlight of a beautiful spring day was shut out by the cool shadows of the interior of the shed. The train stopped, let off steam for a moment, then started backing and Rudi saw that they were backing along a track which ran by a long boarding platform. On the other side of the platform sat another train, either having just arrived, or just preparing to leave, Rudi had no idea which. He stood up straight, brushed his hand against his uniform and prepared to get off.

"Oh, papa, there he is, see!" Lisl squealed in delight, as she saw Rudi coming through the large gate from the train shed. She pointed to her brother, who was standing there is his gray-green uniform, looking around as if slightly confused by everything. "Rudi!" she called. "Rudi, over here!"

"For heaven's sake, Lisl, don't scream so," Heinrich growled, but Frauka, who was even more anxious than Lisl, yelled as well and Heinrich knew that it was a losing battle.

Rudi might have missed Lisl's call but there was no way he could miss the shouts of both his sister and his mother, and he looked toward them, then broke into a big smile and hurried over to them. They met in the middle and embraced fondly.

In another part of the city Paul Maass was reading the morning mail to see if there was anything he would have to attend to before he joined the Rodls at the picnic honoring Rudi's return from Poland. Most of the mail was routine, then he saw a letter addressed to him from a Dr. Phillip Jones, U.S.A. Paul reached quickly for it and examined it closely before he opened it, to see if he could determine whether or not a censor had already opened it. It didn't appear to have been opened, but Paul knew that it would be in code anyway, just in case. The letter was not really from Phillip Jones, it was from Hans Werfel. Phillip Jones was the name they had agreed upon before Hans left, and with the receipt of this letter Paul knew that Hans had made it safely to America.

> *Dear Direktor Maass:*
>
> *I have been informed that you are interested in a certain piece of Wagnerian music, the copyright of which is held now by Liveright and Adams Co. of Boston, U.S.A. I am pleased to inform you that the copyright contains a codicil which allows this music to be performed in Germany without violation. Therefore, Mr. Maass, you are not to concern yourself with any details about the arrangement. You are free to use it as you wish.*
>
> *Sincerely,*
> *Phillip Jones*

The letter meant that everything had gone off perfectly, there were no hitches, and no possibility of recriminations coming back to Paul. For that, Paul was thankful.

Hans was Paul's half brother. Before Paul's mother married his father, she had borne Hans by an earlier marriage. Hans was nearly twelve years older than Paul, and had spent much of his time with an uncle (the brother of Hans' father) and, thus, Paul had seen very little of him as they grew up. Paul's mother had died ten years ago, and with her death the last, tenuous connection between Paul and Hans had been broken, so that, until Hans arrived on the night of Paul's concert for Hitler, Paul had not seen him for years.

Paul had not helped Hans to escape out of a sense of brotherly love, for in truth he felt as if he barely knew him. There had been a much more practical reason for Paul to help Hans escape. Hans was Jew, and he was Paul's brother. Even though Paul had none of the blood in his veins which made Hans a Jew, the fact that they were half-brothers could, possibly, have an adverse effect on Paul's career. Therefore, it was decidedly to his advantage to be rid of Hans, even if it meant undertaking a small risk to do so. Paul undertook that risk, if not enthusiastically, then at least willingly, in order that the possible blot on his own record be kept clear.

Paul burned the letter after he had read it. He was glad that it was all over, and that Hans was now safe in America. His mother would have approved of that, and it made Paul feel almost self-righteous. For the moment, he could even forget the selfish motives which had prompted him to help Hans in the first place.

7

"Oʜ, please," Rudi said, rubbing his stomach gingerly and smiling at his mother who was offering him another sausage. "I can't eat another bite, honestly."

"But you look so pale and thin," she said. "Doesn't the army feed you in Poland?"

"I'll admit that during battle there were times when we were on the move and we had no time for anything except field rations," Rudi said. "But the occupation hasn't been bad. Of course, I've had nothing like all this." Rudi waved his hand over the display of food which was on the tablecloth spread out on the lawn in the park near the river. There were sausages, cheeses, breads, potato salad, wine and beer.

Frauka smiled proudly that she had pleased her son with the special picnic spread. "I'll bet I can tempt you with one more thing," she offered.

"No," Rudi said. "Really, I couldn't eat another bite of anything."

"Not even this?" Frauka said, opening a basket with a flourish.

"Oh, *puffer torte*!" Rudi said, seeing the cake which

was his favorite and which his mother had prepared especially for this occasion.

"Of course, if you can't eat it," Frauka teased, closing the lid again.

"No," Rudi said, reaching for the basket. "I've suddenly decided that I am starving to death. I could eat this entire cake and another like it."

"You'll not eat all of *this* cake," Paul said. "Not unless you want to fight me."

"Oh and such a fight it would be too," Lisl said, laughing. "A Panzer officer against a symphony direktor."

"Yes, but don't forget, I can also play the timpani and I will play the timpani on Rudi's head if he attempts to eat my share."

"Ow," Rudi said, laughing and putting his hands over his head. "That I do *not* want. Don't worry, Paul, you shall have your share."

Frauka began cutting the cake and two children from a family which was having a picnic close by ran by them to the river laughing and shouting as they ran. On the Main River a young man and young woman were drifting by in a boat and in the far corner of the park a band was playing. There were dozens of uniforms in evidence—Hitler Youth, S.S. and Wermacht, though the Wermacht was the least represented.

"So many uniforms, and so few army," Rudi mused.

"What?" Heinrich asked, surprised by his son's statement.

"I was just commenting upon the large number of S.S.," he said. "It is good that the war was so quickly won in Poland. With so many in the S.S., there are few left to fight."

"But how can you say that?" Lisl wanted to know. "Aren't the S.S. men fighters?"

Rudi laughed a small, scoffing laugh. "Yes, if you count rounding up Jews as fighting."

"But, didn't they fight bravely against the Poles? In the newspapers and in the newsreels we see so many S.S. in Poland."

"Now that the fighting has ended there are more S.S. than army," Rudi said. "The S.S. arrive after the battle to take over the job of running things. They confiscate the food, the wine and the most comfortable buildings, while the soldier eats field rations and sleeps on the ground. The S.S. round up the Jews and close down his shops and businesses, while the army goes after the straggler who does not yet know the fighting is over. The S.S. men get their pictures taken by the newspapers and the newsreel cameramen while the soldier cleans his tanks and his guns. It is no wonder that you see so many S.S. In fact, you see too many, for I feel the S.S. should be eliminated."

"Rudi," Heinrich warned. "You shouldn't talk like that."

"Why?" Rudi answered easily. "Because it is unpatriotic, or because you feel it is dangerous?"

"Both," Heinrich said.

"Ah, don't worry about it, father," Rudi said, dismissing the entire incident with the wave of his hand. He smiled. "I am one of the brave defenders of the Fatherland, no one would do anything to me. Besides, I think if Hitler realized what a bunch of thugs Himmler's boys have become, he would eliminate them. Perhaps some day he will discover it."

"Perhaps so," Heinrich said. He looked around still a little apprehensive over the direction the conversation was going. "Still, I don't feel comfortable talking about such a thing."

"Tell me, Rudi," Paul asked. "Do you think we will have war with France and England, or will they make peace?"

"We will have war," Rudi said.

"But surely not," Frauka said. "It has been six months now and nothing has happened. Maybe the French and English will be reasonable."

"Neither the French nor the English are known for their reason," Rudi said. "If reason prevailed, then they would have not declared war on us in the first place."

"But what else could they do?" Paul asked. "After all, they did make a public declaration of support for the Poles. They threatened to declare war if we moved into Poland. We moved into Poland and they declared war."

"Yes, but even that was an example of the irrational aspects of their policy," Rudi said, parroting what he had heard over and over in the policy briefings to which all officers were frequently subjected. "Their threat of war was intended to preserve Poland's repressionist government. But that government is no longer there to preserve, and, in fact, neither England nor France made a move to help Poland. So my question is, why would they insist upon fighting a war when the purpose of the war no longer exists? And the answer is, because they are irrational peoples, led by irrational and irresponsible leaders. Thus, the sad but inescapable conclusion is that we will have war."

"But surely you won't have to go again?" Frauka said. "You have done your duty for the Fatherland."

Rudi laughed at his mother's wishful naiveté. "Mother, if not those of us who were in Poland, then who?" he asked. "Of course I will go."

"I fear we shall all go," Heinrich said solemnly.

"All go, papa? What do you mean?" Lisl asked, puzzled by his strange comment.

Heinrich sighed. "The airplane has brought war to everyone," he said. "What happened in Warsaw can happen in every city. Berlin, Frankfurt, Hamburg, Nürnberg, even Schweinfurt, could be bombed."

"Why would anyone bomb Schweinfurt?" Lisl asked. "We are such a small city compared to all the others."

"Schweinfurt will be a target because your papa is a target," Paul said simply.

"Papa is a target?"

"In a manner of speaking," Heinrich agreed. "The factory will be very important."

Lisl laughed. "Papa, you are teasing, aren't you? Why would they want to bomb your factory? You don't make guns or ammunition. All you manufacture there are little ball bearings."

"Lisl, do you know how many bearings are in just one of my tanks?" Rudi asked. "Multiply that by the number of tanks in the army, then add all the trucks, cars, planes, and artillery pieces, and you can see how important father's little ball bearings become."

"Heinrich, is this really true?" Frauka asked. "Could Schweinfurt be bombed?"

"Not if we believe Goering," Paul laughed. "He has sworn that if so much as one enemy bomb ever falls on Germany, his name isn't Hermann Goering."

"Does that mean he would admit to being a bastard?" Rudi teased.

"Rudi, you shouldn't say such a thing!" Frauka said, but though she acted scandalized, even she couldn't help but laugh, for Goering was famous for his claim to aristocracy, and his insistence upon fastidious propriety among all his entourage.

"By the way," Heinrich put in, "according to my sources, Goering has bought up another *eigentum*, this time in textiles."

"*Eigentum*," Paul asked. "What do you mean, property?"

"It's the euphemism the business world has adopted to refer to Jewish businesses which have been forced into bankruptcy. There have been many juicy pieces of property taken over in that way in the past couple of years."

"Heinrich has had his opportunity at more than one of them," Frauka said, "but he won't buy any of them."

"No," Heinrich said. "No, I won't buy any of them. I am as much in favor of the laws which prevent the Jews from ruining our economy as anyone else. I well remember seeing businesses stolen during the bad days by the unscrupulous Jews whose money manipulating created the economic chaos in the first place. I say any law which prevents those Jews from ever again attaining such power over the rest of us is good. But I do not feel right in profiting by some of the harsher aspects of the laws."

"What are some of the harsher aspects, Herr Rodl?" Paul asked.

"Well, such things as we are speaking of now," Heinrich answered. "The laws were designed to break the backs of those Jews who held the economy of Germany, indeed of all Europe, in a vise-like grip. They would have brought the entire world to their knees had they been allowed to continue business unchecked. I supported Hitler, even before he came to power, because he understood that and was willing to take the unpopular stand to correct the situation."

"Do you really think it was an unpopular stand?" Paul asked. "Or do you think Hitler simply called forth the anti-semitism which was just beneath the surface in everyone?"

"No, I think it was basically an unpopular stand," Heinrich said. "Unpopular but necessary."

"Why do you think it was unpopular? There has always been bias against the Jews."

"Bias, yes, but not open mis-treatment. Now, one has to agree that under the current laws, things are being made very difficult for the Jews," Heinrich explained. "We Germans are a decent people with a long history of moral obligation to civilization. It is asking the German to go counter to one thousand years of heritage to ask him to treat with such harshness a group of people who are what they are by an accident of birth." He paused and took a sip of water.

"But the laws have to be tough laws with a net drawn so tightly as to prevent the guilty from finding some loophole through which to escape. Unfortunately, like a fishing net drawn from the water, some fish are caught which we don't intend to catch in order to make certain that we catch those fish we do want to catch. Thus, the innocent Jews are pulled down with the guilty, and their holdings, like the businesses of the guilty, become *eigentum.* I have no wish to make an unfair profit from such a situation."

"There are many who hold no such scruples," Paul said.

"I know," Heinrich said. "And many of those people are in high government positions. But it is my belief that they will have to answer for their actions one day, when everything has stabilized, we are once again at peace, and the German people can hope for and expect the best men available to fill the most important positions. Those who exhibit character flaws now will be dealt with later. And that includes that grand peacock, the Reichsmarschall."

"Herr Rodl, are you saying you don't think Hitler knows, or approves, of what Goering and the others are doing?"

"No, not exactly," Heinrich said. "But I do think that Hitler has established certain priorities, and Goering, Himmler and the others who are making an unjust profit from the current emergency, are way down on the list."

"Tell me," Paul said, pulling a grass stem from the ground and leaning his back against a tree, as if this were just part of a casual conversation. "Suppose a Jew came to you, someone that you know and have known for a long time, and ask you to help him leave the country. Would you help him?"

"I have asked myself that question many times," Heinrich said. "In fact, I'm certain that many Germans have asked themselves that question."

"And did you answer yourself?"

"I answered myself," Heinrich said. "I would not help."

"Papa," Lisl said. "You mean even if someone like Dr. Rosenthal came to ask you for help, you wouldn't help him? He was our doctor for many years."

"Dr. Rosenthal is dead," Heinrich said.

"I know, but suppose he were still alive. If he came to ask for help, wouldn't you help him?"

"No," Heinrich said again. He sighed. "I know this sounds harsh, but look at it this way. The Jews had ample warning to leave Germany. In fact they were encouraged to do so. Most of the innocent ones did leave. The only ones who stayed were those who had selfish reasons to stay. Besides, if the net is drawn tight to capture all the destructive Jews, is it not possible that in opening it to allow the escape of one Jew we consider innocent, could weaken the net to the degree that some of the guilty may escape? I'm afraid that my answer would have to be no, regardless of who asked my help." Heinrich looked at Lisl and smiled. "And as far as our dear Dr. Rosenthal, I think it would do us no good to dwell upon such a hypothesis. He was our friend when he died, and I prefer to keep his memory that way. I am glad that he did not live to see this problem arise."

"Why did you ask such a question, Paul?" Lisl asked. "Has a Jew come to you for help?"

"What, a Jew come to me?" Paul replied, laughing. "Of course not. Why would a Jew think *I* would help?"

"Because you are an artist," Lisl said. "And many Jews gravitate toward the arts."

"Enough talk of Jews," Rudi interrupted. "For the last three months we've scarcely had a chance to do anything in Poland except count Jews. Do you know that only about one-third of the new crop was put in? Poland may starve this year for lack of food, and it's all because the army has spent its time in locating and identifying Jews, when we should have been seeing to the orderly transition of Polish life from Polish rule to German rule—and that includes making certain the farmers put in their crop."

"I agree with Rudi," Frauka said. "All this talk of Jews is depressing, anyway. They all look so long-faced and sullen nowadays. No matter where you go you see this wretched bunch of people, all huddled together, wearing awful-looking clothes, and with such down-trodden looks about them. I don't like to even think of them."

"Rudi, tell us some stories about your adventures," Lisl asked.

"I didn't have too many exciting things happen to me," Rudi replied.

"You could tell us how you captured your unit's objective in hand to hand combat," Heinrich said. "That was in all the papers."

Rudi grinned sheepishly. "Did the papers say it was a church, and that Sergeant Heibler and I stumbled across it in the middle of the night, and just went inside to get some sleep?"

"No," Lisl said, laughing. "Is that all there was to it?"

"That was it."

"You mean there was no fighting, or discomfort? You weren't even in danger?"

"Oh, I wouldn't say it was all that easy," Rudi said. He laughed. "We had to go nearly thirty hours without anything to eat. I was starving by the time the rest of the group arrived."

"Tell us about it," Lisl said. "Tell us all about it."

"Well, it all started when I left the tank so I could use the map and compass," Rudi said, and he began to tell the story of the adventure which got him a mention in the dispatches.

Paul had invited Lisl to the theatre office in order to hear some new records recently made by the Berlin Symphony Orchestra. Had the invitation been to his apartment, Lisl would have been unable to accept, for Heinrich would never have approved of her going to a man's apartment alone, even though she was engaged to Paul and they planned to marry soon. If Heinrich had known what went on in Paul's office, he wouldn't have allowed her to go there either, for

Paul and Lisl, like so many other young couples of the day, had merely found a way to circumvent the old-fashioned ways of their parents.

"Did you lock the door?" Lisl asked, as she stood beside the sofa and began removing her dress. The sofa folded out into a bed and Lisl, quite expert by now in manipulating it, had turned it down as soon as they went into Paul's office. Paul, following their routine, pulled down the shades and locked the door.

"Don't I always lock the door?" Paul replied. "Why are you so worried?"

"I would not like to see Herr Baumann come in on us," Lisl said, laughing. Baumann was the *Koncert-meister*, an old-maidish man, much older than Paul, but so respectful of any position of authority that he could scarcely speak to Paul without stuttering.

"Why not?" Paul replied, laughing with her. "It might put a little excitement into his life." Paul was at the record player, stacking records on the spindle. When he was through, he turned the machine on, then started toward the sofa-bed, where Lisl, now totally nude, lay waiting for him. The records clicked, then there was the rushing sound of the needle searching the track, and after that, the rich sound of Beethoven's *Pathétique*.

Lisl looked up at Paul, feeling the quivering anticipation deep inside her as she watched him remove his clothes. Paul was the picture of grace in everything he did, whether it was directing the orchestra or removing his clothes, and though he was unaware of the sensuality of his action, as Lisl watched him strip it was in itself a form of foreplay.

Finally when jacket, shirt, trousers, and underwear were removed, and the shoes and socks taken off and everything neatly and precisely stacked on a chair beside the bed, Paul's lean, graceful body came to the sofa-bed with Lisl, and he reached for her and pulled her to him for a kiss.

Lisl had been a virgin until she met Paul. She had studied piano and thought at one time she would like to be a concert pianist, so when she heard that the orchestra needed a music clerk, she took the job, hoping that by being close to the orchestra, she would be inspired to greater work on the piano. Quite the opposite was the case. She realized almost at once how poor her talent for playing the piano really was, in comparison to the other musicians.

But if she lost interest in the piano, she gained interest in Paul Maass, the youngest musical director in Germany, and before that first summer was over, she had not only fallen in love with him, but had been loved by him, losing her virginity one rainy night after the last concert of the season.

Now as they kissed, there was no sparring nor tentativeness. From the very first kiss they were lovers, and as Lisl felt Paul's lips on hers, she felt her insides growing white with the heat of passion she felt for him.

Paul's lips traveled knowingly and excitingly from her lips, and down her throat, then out onto each breast, leaving a trail of silken sensation as his tongue touched the flesh of her breast, and then his lips pursed over each nipple.

Lisl lay back under his lovemaking, listening to the strains of Beethoven in music which seemed orchestrated just for them. She could feel the rough texture of the bed linen against her bare legs and back, then the muscular texture of Paul's legs against hers as he moved over her. As Paul's weight came down on her, she thrust up against him, giving him willingly, eagerly, that which he sought. They moved against each other, in time with the music it seemed, in fact, almost a *part* of the music, with the sensations of pleasure rising and falling, quickening and slowing, waxing and waning. Finally it began, a tiny, tingling deep inside, moving independently of the music, growing quickly to match and then overtake the tempo so that it, and not the music was the master, exploding over Lisl's body in rapidly widening circles until her entire being was caught up in the maelstrom of sensation. There were a million tiny pins pricking her skin and involuntary sounds of pleasure came from her throat.

She lost consciousness for just an instant, and lights passed before her eyes as her body gave its final, convulsive shudders. And through it all the music of Beethoven surrounded them, wrapped them in the erotic blanket of its theme, then matched its movement to their own, finally reaching a thundering crescendo with the two lovers.

They lay together for a few moments while Lisl experienced secondary orgasms, less explosive but greatly satisfying. Finally Paul withdrew, then walked over to the record player and turned it off.

"Oh," Lisl said from the sofa. "I was enjoying it."

"Lisl, there is something I must tell you," Paul said.

Lisl sat up quickly. There was something in Paul's voice, something frightening, which caused a constriction in her heart. There wasn't another woman? Surely, not another woman? She heard herself put the question into words, frightening and explosive.

"No," Paul said. "No, nothing like that."

"Then what?" she asked.

Paul walked over to sit on the bed beside her, then he put his hand gently onto her shoulder. "I, I helped a Jew to escape," he said.

"Oh," Lisl said, breathing a sigh of relief. "Is that

all? Darling, you scared me to death. Do you think I care if you helped a Jew escape? You could help an entire trainload escape as far as I'm concerned. I think this whole business is awful anyway if you want to know my opinion. I know Papa can justify it, but I can't. I'm glad you helped a Jew escape."

"He was my brother," Paul said.

"Your brother?" Lisl asked, and now there was a renewed sound of fright in her voice.

"Don't worry," Paul said. "We have the same mother, but a different father, and it is from his father that he is Jewish."

Lisl breathed a sigh of relief. "Oh, I'm so glad," she said. "Not that it would change anything if you were Jewish—anything between us, I mean. I love you Paul, and nothing can change that. But if you were Jewish, I would be frightened to death for you all the time." She put her arms around and kissed him again. "Nothing must ever come between us, darling. Nothing," she said.

"I'll never let that happen," Paul promised.

8

As the panzers rumbled through the streets of Louvain, the historic University city near Brussels, Rudi looked around at the destruction of the city. Block after block of buildings were now little more than piles of rubble. Telephone poles were down, and bundles of wire crisscrossed the roads and hung like wet spaghetti from the broken walls and twisted wreckage. In a few places the fires still smoldered, though there were no large blazes remaining.

Rudi knew Louvain—"Leuven" the road signs read —because he had visited the city. He particularly remembered the library, and he found himself searching for it, confused by the fact that many of the landmarks were either gone, or so badly damaged as to be unrecognizable. Then he saw it.

"Sergeant Heibler," he said, speaking into his headset. "Halt."

The tank stopped.

"Why have you stopped?" Captain Kant's voice asked.

"I have seen something I wish to examine, Captain," Rudi answered.

"Is it a danger to the column?"

"I think not," Rudi said, not wanting to admit that he just wished to satisfy his curiosity about the library. "But I would like to examine it anyway."

"Very well. Rejoin the column west of the city."

"*Jawohl*," Rudi answered. Rudi ordered the tank to pull over and stop, so that those following him would have room to pass.

"Lieutenant Rodl, do you wish one of us to accompany you?" Sergeant Heibler asked.

"No," Rudi said. "I shan't be long."

Rudi climbed down from the tank, then walked through the rubble strewn streets toward what had been the library. Two lines of gray-green clad soldiers were streaming by, their eyes on the necks of the men before them; proud, strong men who looked like the conquerors they were. A captain was moving with them, and Rudi saluted him as he out through the ranks.

"Is there a problem, Lieutenant?" the captain asked, pointing toward Rudi's tank. "Have you broken down, or run out of gasoline?"

"No, Captain," Rudi said. He pointed toward the gutted library. Some of the girders which held the roof still remained, though, even as he watched, a large section of the Tudor facade fell in. "I want to look at what is left of the library."

The infantry captain stopped as Rudi stepped up to the ruins. "Did you know the library?"

"Yes," Rudi said. "It was a beautiful place."

The solemn line of marching soldiers continued on by, oblivious of the ruin through which they passed. Rudi kicked at some of the rubble with his foot.

"It is a shame about the buildings in the town," the infantry captain said, sensing the degree of sadness in the tone of Rudi's voice. "But there was bitter fighting here."

Rudi scraped away some of the black dust from one of the stones and read the inscription: AIDED BY FUNDS FROM STANHOPE COLLEGE, MOUNT EAGLE, ILLINOIS, U.S.A. AMERICAN GENEROSITY, REBUILDING WHAT GERMAN BOMBARDMENT DESTROYED DURING THE GREAT WAR.

"The Americans will again have something to be self-righteous about," Rudi said.

"Did you know about this?" the Infantry Captain asked, surprised by the inscription.

"Yes," Rudi said.

"I didn't know about it. I guess the British and American newspapers will be full of it now, won't they?"

"I'm sure they will."

Rudi walked into the building, despite a caution from the Infantry Captain, and he looked around the blackened interior. With most of the roof collapsed, and one entire wall down, there was easily enough light from the sun to allow him to see. He saw the tumbled bookshelves and the piles of books, now charred and darkened, and then, quite by coincidence, he saw a burnt copy of *Mein Kampf*. He couldn't help but chuckle at the irony of it.

"You!" someone shouted from outside. "What are you doing in there?"

Rudi looked toward the sound of the voice and saw a colonel in the Pioneers, the engineer unit which was already beginning to organize for the cleanup of the town.

"I thought I saw something suspicious in here," Rudi lied. "I was investigating."

"This building is unstable," the engineer colonel

said gruffly. "Come out of there at once and return to your unit."

"*Jawohl*," Rudi said easily.

Rudi left the library and walked back across the road to his tank. The three other crewmen of the tank had climbed out, because it had become unbearably hot while they were sitting, and as they saw him coming back, they returned to their positions. Heibler hung back.

"Is everything all right, Lieutenant?" Heibler asked.

"Yes," Rudi said.

"Lieutenant," Heibler said softly, so quietly that the others couldn't hear, "you should not let others see that such things bother you. It would look bad for you."

"What are you talking about?" Rudi asked, surprised by Sergeant Heibler's observation.

"We have been together for nearly a year now, Lieutenant, and I am proud to serve with you. I would not want someone to believe that you do not have the will of iron all Panzer officers must have."

"Tell me, Sergeant Heibler," Rudi said. "Do you think I am lacking in iron will?"

"No, Lieutenant," Sergeant Heibler said. "I think you do have an iron will. But you are also a man of intelligence and sensitivity, and there are those who would misinterpret that intelligence and sensitivity. And it is not worth the risk, because intelligence and sensitivity are not always rewarded in the army."

"Did you take philosophy courses along with your gunnery training, Sergeant?" Rudi asked, but he was smiling as he asked the question. He liked his sergeant, and was at first surprised by his observation of traits which were not always consistent with the average soldier of his rank.

Once he had suggested to one of his superior officers that Sergeant Heibler should be commissioned, only to find out that Sergeant Heibler was considered to be a good soldier, but adjudged as politically unfit. That was when he discovered Sergeant Heibler's history. Sergeant Heibler had been in the 19th Infantry, the Army unit which broke up the famous Beer Hall *Putsch* in November of 1923. That was Hitler's early ill-fated attempt at a political coup, the failure of which put him in Landsberg Prison. Heibler had graduated with distinction from the officer candidate school of Kadetenstalt, but at a time when the German Army was limited by the terms of surrender to the number of officers it could commission. Heibler would have eventually been commissioned, but an accident of duty caused him the misfortune to be a part of the unit which broke up Hitler's Beer Hall *Putsch,* and that put him in bad with the Nazis. Once they came to power, Heibler was to be denied his commission forever.

Other men might have left the army under such circumstances, but the army was the only thing Heibler knew, and he gave no thought of doing anything else. Because of that, Rudi had as his tank driver, a man who, by education and length of service, would have, under any other government, likely been a Division Commander.

"*Herr Lieutenant,* the Commandant is calling," the gunner said, and Rudi jumped onto the tank to hold the earphone to his ear. He spoke into the mike.

"*Ja, Herr Commandant, Lieutenant Rodl.*"

"Have you completed your investigation, Rudi?"

"Yes," Rudi said. "It was nothing."

"Good, then come quickly. We have taken over a

fine restaurant which has not been damaged, and the officers will be taking their evening meal here."

"That is good," Rudi said. "We are coming now."

A thick layer of blue tobacco smoke hung just beneath the ceiling of the Café Metropole. The rattling overhead fans caused the smoke to drift and curl through the room and collect in a small cloud. It was a rich, aromatic smoke, from fine American tobaccos, eagerly bought up by all the German officers who smoked, including Rudi. Rudi had bought two cartons of American cigarettes, choosing that particular brand, because he liked the name Lucky Strike.

"It means *glucklich stossen*," Rudi, who spoke English very well, explained to the others, and they, intrigued by the name also bought Lucky Strike until the supply was exhausted.

Dinner was exceptionally good, with a dozen waiters behaving as correctly and politely to the German officers as if they were tourists, and not conquering warriors. After the sausages and cheeses and the pastries and ices, came the brandy. It was excellent, and as Rudi tasted the controlled fire of its fruit, he felt his head growing light, and a warmth in his chest. He leaned back in his chair and looked around at the others, and he felt a tremendous sense of pride in the fact that he was German and victorious.

"We'll be in London in two months," Hauptsturmführer Lange was saying. Lange was the S.S. political officer assigned to Rudi's Panzer company. Though he was not the tactical or combat commander, Lange had an inordinate amount of power over everyone, because he was the final authority on the intangible "attitude" of the soldiers.

Lange was an exceptionally handsome man, very dashing in his black and silver S.S. uniform, and because he was the epitome of the Aryan ideal, his photograph had appeared in many German magazines and newspapers. Such publicity greatly increased Lange's already high degree of cockiness.

"*Hauptsturmführer*, I have as much confidence in our army as anyone," Captain Kant said. Kant was Rudi's commanding officer, and had been, even in Poland. Lange had not been with them in Poland. "But I would remind you that we have two obstacles between us and London. The Maginot Line and the English Channel. The Maginot Line we will handle easily, the English Channel, not quite so easily."

"You dismiss the Maginot line so easily?" someone else asked, surprised by Kant's comment.

"Yes," Kant said. "It is little more than a glorified trench, bigger and grander than in the last war, but a trench none the less, built with all the comforts. They even have a room with a sunlamp."

"Yes," Lange said, laughing. "I recall seeing a photograph of six French soldiers sunbathing nude, on their stomachs with their naked butts up, ready for buggering, should one of the French High Command happen by."

Though Lange's comment was a bit crude for Rudi's tastes, the brandy had been good, and he was feeling good, and he joined the others in their laughter at the ribald joke.

"What the French forgot," Kant went on, explaining about the Maginot Line, "is that the trenches were used in the last war. They could have just as well have spent their money on bows and arrows, for the art of war changes, and while the German General Staff understood that, the French High Command did not. The Maginot Line will be defeated by the simple process of outflanking it, as we have already done here, in Belgium. But it is England which will cause us a problem."

"England?" Lange scoffed. "The English soldiers we have encountered in Belgium and France have shown us nothing but their backsides as they ran. England will be nothing."

"England will retreat to her little island," Kant said. "And then we must go there, but the channel cannot be flanked, and it cannot be driven across with Panzers. The channel is a formidable obstacle."

"Captain Kant, are you saying we cannot defeat England?" Lange asked.

"No, of course I'm not saying that," Kant replied. "I'm merely saying we will not be in London in two months."

"I do not agree with you, and neither does anyone else," Lange said.

"I agree with him," Rudi heard himself saying. He was enjoying this opportunity to discuss geopolitics with the others. Though political indoctrination had been a standard fare of Army training for some time now, this was not of the same ilk. Here there was give and take, room for thought and question. "Blitzkrieg will not work across the channel. Blitzkrieg only works in terrain which is suitable for Panzer warfare. I am also concerned about the Americans."

"The Americans?" Lange scoffed, with a mocking laugh. "Did you say you are concerned about the Americans?"

"Yes."

"Why would you be concerned about the Americans?" Kant asked. "We aren't at war with America."

"The Americans came into the last war," Rudi explained. "I believe they will come into this war as well. They are too closely bound to England to let England lose a war to us without trying to help."

"Ach, America is a mongrel country," Lange scoffed. "Have you not heard my racial theory about the Americans?"

"I suppose there is no way to avoid hearing it now, is there?" Kant mocked.

"The American," Lange went on, paying no attention to Kant's sarcasm, "is already in the third generation of mixing the races. There, one finds the mingling of the blood of the black race, the oriental race, and the Jewish race."

"There are many Germans who migrated to America," Rudi reminded Lange.

"That merely proves my point," Lange replied. "Even pure Aryan blood, such as that which we supplied to America, can be polluted when fouled with other racial specimens. If America does not awaken to what it is doing to itself, it will spawn increasingly more mongrelized creatures until, one hundred years from now, there will be an entire continent of sub-human species. Their cities will fall into ruin, their social structure will break down, and civilization as we know it will die. One can already see the beginnings of this in the gangster elements of Chicago."

"I don't agree at all," Rudi said, leaning forward eagerly to continue this conversation which had so stimulated his imagination. "I see that as America's secret strength. As alloys strengthen steel, so do the mixing of races and cultures strengthen America. Why, America has an industrial strength which we cannot even imagine. Do you realize that nearly every family in America has a car? There are enough cars in America for every man, woman and child to ride at the same time."

"You do understand, don't you, Lieutenant, that you are spouting the same kind of lies our enemies put forth? By denying the truth of racial purity, you are denying National Socialism."

"I think National Socialism is strong enough to stand up to the winds of legitimate questions," Rudi said. He laughed. "Do you remember Gustav Nagel? He traveled naked around Germany with a beard which reached to the ground. It was his claim that Utopia could be achieved if only mankind would shed its clothing, give up shaving, and abolish all capital letters. What if he had succeeded in establishing a government?"

Those around the table laughed.

"Are you comparing our Führer with that fool?" Lange asked angrily.

"Of course not," Rudi said. "I'm merely using that as an illustration. Had Nagel been successful, surely his strange theories would have been questioned by thinking people, would they not? I'm merely saying that any theory should be subject to question, even the theory of racial purity."

"And so you suggest that because America can produce so many cars, that it brings up questions about our sacred theories of racial purity?" Lange challenged.

"Yes," Rudi said, pleased for scoring a point. He was glad that Lange understood. "What does America's amazing production of cars mean to you?"

"It means they are a nation of soft, fat weaklings," Lange scoffed. "It is a sign, if such a sign were needed, of their decadence and weakness. They are making cars, while Germany, under National Socialism, is making tanks and planes."

"No," Rudi said. "It is a sign of their strength. Don't you see? If the Americans wished, they could just as easily produce tanks and planes as cars. My father is the Director-General of I.G.N. Kugelwerks, and he receives all the world's industrial publications. He has in fact modeled his production procedures after the Americans."

"I see," the S.S. officer said. "And tell me, Lieutenant, would your father use Jews?" Lange's tone of voice was now cold and menacing, and the good, almost effervescent feeling Rudi had felt during the conversation was suddenly over. Now he realized that it was no longer a discussion of fellow officers, but the almost dangerous challenge of one of the more radical members of Germany's new society.

Rudi put his glass on the table and slid his chair back. He looked at the others around the table and saw that they, too, had grown uneasy by the sudden turn in the conversation.

"I, uh, must get back to my platoon, *Herr Commandant*," he said to Captain Kant. "I hope you will excuse me."

"Of course, Rudi," Kant said.

"Captain," Lange said. "It would be to your advantage to ensure that all of your officers are more thoroughly indoctrinated with the purposes and goals of the Führer, and are imbued with the spirit of racial purity for which we are all fighting."

"Lange," Kant replied, purposely omitting the S.S. officer's title. "Lieutenant Rodl is in *my* command, and *I* am satisfied by his performance of duty. He has served the fatherland bravely and well, and I would gladly take others just like him."

Rudi looked at his commanding officer then with more respect than at any time since he had served with him. It took a high degree of courage to stand up to an S.S. officer, even one who did not outrank you, and Rudi greatly appreciated Kant's defense of him under such circumstances.

Captain Kant stood then, and fixed his monocle pointedly. "And now, gentlemen, I too must be going." Kant reached for one nearly full bottle of brandy, then saluted and started away with Rudi. It was only then that Rudi noticed that Kant was even more intoxicated than he was. In fact, Rudi believed that Kant was nearly drunk.

"I appreciate what you did for me in there," Rudi said, after they left the hotel and began walking down the street. There were no civilians visible outside, even though Louvain was a city of more than forty thousand people. There were, however, German soldiers standing guard about every twenty-five yards along the curb.

It was dark, because the blackout was being strictly enforced, even though it seemed very improbable that France or England would launch an air attack against the small Belgium town. Despite the lack of artificial light, there was an exceptionally bright moon, a moon that was now being popularly called a "bombers' moon" and it hung low over the hulking shadows of gutted buildings, dividing the city into patterns of silver and black. Silver and black, like the uniforms of the S.S. police, Rudi thought, and somehow the analogy to a bombed-out city seemed appropriate.

"You are quite right about America's potential, you know," Captain Kant said. "Our only hope is to end this war so quickly that America will have no reason to fight. At least, the broad, popular sentiment in

America now is against the war. After all, they didn't enter into any ironclad alliances, as did England and France."

"Do you think we will win, quickly?"

"Yes," Kant said. "We will win the war, of that I have no doubt. But will we win the peace?"

"I don't understand," Rudi said.

"You left Poland and returned to Germany before I did," Kant said. "Do you know what is happening to Poland's Jews? Do you know what is going on there?"

"I know that there has been a great deal of resettlement there," Rudi said. "But that is to be expected, isn't it? After all, isn't it important that we establish security?"

"I think much of it is going beyond security," Kant said. "The S.S. have been little more than murderers."

"I am sure that there must have been a few occasions which warranted harsh treatment of some prisoners," Rudi said, remembering now that his sergeant had advised him to always show a will of iron. In fact, Rudi had often been distressed by the treatment he had observed. He would have preferred that those people who represented Germany behave in a manner to bring credit to Germany. Realistically, though, he knew that wasn't the case.

"It is more than mere harsh treatment," Kant said. "There were occasions when—well, let me just say that there will be an accounting someday for what went on in Poland, and I hope it is we who are making the accounting. Otherwise . . ." he hinted darkly.

"Otherwise what?"

Kant pulled the top off the brandy bottle, and it came out with a hollow thump. He turned it up and took several swallows, then he wiped the back of his hand across his mouth and handed the bottle to Rudi. As he did, he saw two women emerging from the shadows of one of the buildings which had not been too badly damaged. The women started toward the officers, walking with a swinging, seductive gait which, even in the dark, was unmistakable.

"Otherwise," Kant said, looking toward the two women, "we had better enjoy ourselves while we can. Come, Lieutenant. As your commanding officer, I order you to partake of a little rest and relaxation. I want the one on the right."

9

5 *July, 1941*

Dear Father,

At last I have the chance to write you a letter. This letter comes to you from near Dvinsk, Russia. Yes, father, I was part of Operation Barbarossa, and I am certain now you can understand why I could say nothing of it before this moment.

It is good to hear that the factory is in good order and that at home all are well. Tell mother I miss her puffer-cake more than anything, and tell Lisl that she has spoiled me, for I shall probably remain a bachelor until I can find a girl as pretty as my sister.

I am glad to be away from France. I do not know what kind of Frenchmen I dislike the most, those who make no pretense about hating the Germans, or those who smile silkenly as they betray their own countrymen, selling information to the authorities, Judas-like, for their thirty pieces of silver.

In Poland and in France, I was with the 19th Panzer Group. Now I have been assigned to the

41st (so greatly has our army grown), and I am
pleased to report that now I am an Oberleutnant,
and the commanding officer of my own company.
Hauptmann Kant, my old commander, is now
Major Kant, and a staff officer at Battalion. He is
pleased with his promotion, but he is not pleased
to be taken from the field.

Allow me to speak of an action in which I recently participated, and for which I have been
recommended for the Iron Cross First Class. As
we approached the river Dvina, which separated
our advance from the town of Dvinsk, there was
fear that a bridge would be blown which would
strand our tanks on the west bank. I suggested a
ruse which Major Kant immediately accepted,
and I undertook.

I recruited 40 men from my company, and we,
dressed in Russian uniforms, and driving commandeered Russian trucks, drove immediately to
the bridge. On our way, we passed three companies of retreating Russian soldiers, and so well
were we disguised that they even waved at us,
and shouted to us to give them cigarettes. One of
our number who speaks Russian without an ac-
cent, called back to them and tossed several
cartons of Russian cigarettes to them. They were
very strong and foul-smelling anyway, so we
didn't consider that too great a sacrifice for the
success of our mission.

As we neared the bridge a Russian sentry
stepped out to challenge us. The driver slowed
to a near stop, then grew frightened and stepped
on the accelerator. I had planned to use the Russian speaking soldier to convince the Russian engineers that we should blow the bridge, but now

our plan was compromised and we had no choice.

We raced to the far end of the bridge, where my men jumped out of the trucks. Some were deployed as infantrymen, attacking the Russian engineers, while others began at once to dismantle the explosives the Russians had put in place. The battle lasted for half an hour, and seven of my men were killed, but we managed to secure the bridge and less than one hour later I had the privilege of taking the first tank across.

The battle goes well and the Russians we have encountered seem no more formidable than were the Polish, Belgian, or French. I have stopped being amazed by the success of our army. Truly, no army in history has ever known such triumph.

　　　　　　　　Respectfully, your son, Rudi

Heinrich folded the letter from Rudi and placed it to the side of his desk. He had not known that Rudi was in Russia until receipt of this letter. Now he felt a tremendous sense of pride in that fact, for it meant that Rudi had served his country in all three engagements of the war. Frauka may not be as happy about it as Heinrich, but that was because she did not understand. Rudi was a soldier, and it was a soldier's duty to go to the sound of the guns.

Heinrich looked at the framed pictures on his desk, the one of Lisl, a girl as beautiful as the most beautiful movie star, and the one of Rudi, a handsome blond soldier with features so close to the mythical Germanic ideal that it would have warmed Goebbels' heart to see him. And there was also a picture of Frauka, a woman who was as beautiful to Heinrich now as she was when they first married.

There was a discreet knock at the door to Heinrich's office.

"*Hereinkommen*," Heinrich called.

Kurt Papf, the production foreman, stuck his head into the office. "*Herr Direktor*, about the shipment we expected today?"

"Yes, what about it? Was it correct?"

Papf cleared his throat. "I regret to say, *Herr Direktor*, that the shipment did not arrive at all."

"What?" Heinrich replied, looking up in surprise at the statement. He looked at the calendar. . . . It was July 25, and there, on the calendar, the shipment was marked due. "But I don't understand, it is due today, isn't it? Get me the invoices."

"Here are the invoices," Papf said, the ever efficient foreman holding out a sheaf of papers.

Heinrich walked over to take the invoices and looked through them quickly. "Yes," he said, tapping them with his fingers. "Yes, it is right here. The shipment is due today. Call the consignor."

"Begging your pardon, *Herr Direktor*, but I have already done so."

"What did they say?"

"They shipped the order as agreed, on the date agreed. Here are the shipment numbers and the train numbers."

Heinrich took the numbers from Papf. "Get Dr. Dorpmuller of the Reichsbahn on the phone for me," Heinrich said.

Papf smiled. He had gone as far as he could go with the situation. Now something had to be done at the top level, and Heinrich showed no hesitation about going directly to the ministry of railroads.

"*Jawohl, Herr Direktor*."

Heinrich returned to his desk and sat behind it as he waited for the call to be put through. It seemed impossible, but somehow an entire shipment had become lost. Without the shipment, Heinrich would not be able to meet the quota of bearings expected of him.

Papf was talking into the phone, and he covered the mouthpiece with his hand. "*Herr Direktor*, it is Dr. Dorpmuller."

"Dr. Dorpmuller, Heinrich Rodl here, Director-General of I.G.N. Kugelwerks. I'm inquiring about train number 15-5-27. It was supposed to—"

"Train 15-5-27 was preempted by government order," Dr. Dorpmuller interrupted.

"Preempted? What do you mean, preempted? Where is it?"

"It has been selected to go to Russia," Dorpmuller said.

"Oh," Heinrich said, now somewhat pacified. "Oh, well, of course, if it is being used for strategic purposes, then I suppose I can't really complain. But I am concerned about the location of a shipment which was to be aboard that train. Do you have any idea where it might be?"

"I can trace it down if I have the shipment number," Dr. Dorpmuller explained.

"Good," Heinrich said. "I will have my production foreman give you the shipment number. But this is a very critical shipment for a war-critical industry. Do you suppose it might be possible to secure some sort of priority for the next train?"

Dr. Dorpmuller laughed. "Herr Rodl, not even the army has been able to get a priority number for a train, and we have fifteen divisions still awaiting shipment to Russia."

"What?" Heinrich asked, puzzled by the strange

statement. "What do you mean? I thought you said the army already had priority. You said that's where my train went."

"No, Herr Rodl. I said your train went to Russia, and it did. But it didn't go for the army, it went for the S.S., and it went empty."

"What?" Heinrich asked, the question literally exploding from his lips. "Dr. Dorpmuller, what in the hell are you talking about? How could the S.S. enjoy a higher priority than a combat unit, and why would anyone send a train to Russia empty when there are goods and materials to be shipped?"

"The S.S. enjoys a higher priority because their mission takes precedence over the mission of the army."

"The army is fighting a war!" Heinrich said. "What could take precedence over that?"

"Jews," Dr. Dorpmuller answered simply.

"Jews?"

"The Führer has ordered the resettlement of all Jews in all conquered lands. They are to be taken to special camps in Poland."

"Yes, I've heard this," Heinrich said. "But surely such a program could be delayed until the more pressing business is attended to."

"*Herr Direktor-General*, there is no more pressing business than the settlement of the Jewish problem once and for all."

Heinrich sighed. "Very well," he said. "I consider it a waste of fuel, but I shall send company trucks to pick up the shipment. Kindly tell Herr Papf where everything is." Heinrich signaled for Papf to get the information, then, as Papf started talking into the receiver and jotting down notes, Heinrich walked over to the window and pinched the bridge of his nose, then looked out over the town.

Heinrich had a disquieting feeling about what he had just been told. Oh, he was aware of the official view of Jews, The Nürnberg Laws on Citizenship and Race, passed in September of 1935, made clear to every German, if such clarification was needed, that the Jews were going to have a hard time of it in Germany.

Heinrich had not protested the passage of The Nürnberg Laws, which revoked the Jews' citizenship. Jews could not vote, or marry Aryans, or employ female domestics of German or kindred blood. They could not attend schools, libraries, theaters, or use public transportation facilities. Passports were stamped with the word "Jew" and all Jewish men had to add the middle name "Israel," while Jewish women had to add the name "Sarah."

But those laws were merely the extension of centuries of anti-semitic feeling in Germany. Heinrich had accepted the laws when they were passed, because he felt them an expression of general public sentiment with regard to Jews. As long ago as the sixteenth century, such respected men as Martin Luther had preached against the Jews, calling them a plague, pestilence, and pure misfortune. There had been anti-semitic uprisings in 1805, and again in 1813. In 1840 when the German constitution proposed to grant rights to Jews, anti-Semites collected eighty thousand signatures on petitions opposing Jewish rights, and the constitution was rejected. So Hitler was merely carrying out the historical will of the people.

Heinrich had not only respected Hitler's honesty in voicing publicly what many hypocrites would say only in private, but he also approved of the political use of Jews as a rallying point. When Germany was in the throes of defeat and on the verge of starvation, Hitler had brilliantly contrived a scapegoat, a means for Germany to raise itself from the ashes. But Germany was anything but in the throes of defeat now. Germany stood at the head of all the nations of the world, victorious in war, and master of Europe. The political purpose of the Jews had been accomplished, it was no longer necessary to use them as a convenient vehicle.

Why, then, if they had already served their purpose, would the government go to all the trouble and expense of relocating them? And what made this relocation so important that it took priority even over the movement of combat units and critical production material? If anti-Semitism as a governmental policy went so far as to interfere with the conduct of other operations, then wasn't the medicine worse than the sickness? Besides, it could not be looked upon favorably by the rest of the world if Germany systematically uprooted the Jews and forcibly settled them elsewhere.

"Papa!" Lisl said, suddenly bursting into the room smiling happily over some excitement or other. "Papa, look at what I have!" She waved an envelope under her father's nose, so close that he couldn't see, and when he moved away to attempt to focus upon the envelope, she laughed and teased him, and shoved it so close that once again it slipped out of focus.

"How can I look when you wave it so?" he asked.

Lisl laughed. "If you weren't so old and your eyes so poor, you could see at once what this is," she said, and then she held it perfectly still, allowing Heinrich to focus on it.

It was a small, white envelope, bordered with a silver band, and embossed with a silver eagle, its wings outstretched, and a wreathed swastika in its talons. In the upper left hand corner of the envelope were the initials A.H.

"What?" Heinrich asked, surprised by the envelope and looking up at his daughter with a questioning stare. "Lisl, what is it?"

Lisl laughed happily, then pulled out a card. The card, like the envelope, was white, bordered with a silver band, also with an embossed eagle, but this eagle was gold in color, while the wreath in its talons was red and the swastika black.

Liebe Frauline Rodl

I have the pleasure of inviting you to visit with me at my mountain residence in Berchtesgarten on Saturday next. It is my hope that you will come and spend the weekend with me and my guests.

Ihr ergebener

AH

"I don't understand," Heinrich said. "Why would the Führer invite you?"

"Oh, papa, you know they say he likes pretty girls," Lisl said, and she swirled around the room once, letting her skirt fly out.

"That's what I mean," Heinrich said, and now there was a twinkle in his eye so that Lisl knew that he was only teasing. "So why would he invite you?"

"Oh, you are only teasing," Lisl said. "Papa, I can go can't I? You will let me go?"

"Of course, I could scarcely refuse to allow you to accept such an invitation. But what about Paul? How will Paul accept this?"

"I've thought of that," Lisl said.

"And?"

"I simply won't tell him."

"He'll find out," Heinrich said. "You can't keep such a thing secret."

"I know he'll find out," Lisl said. "But he won't find out until after the fact, and then, no matter how mad he gets, I can make him forgive me. In the meantime, I will have enjoyed my visit to the Berghof. Oh, papa, isn't it the most wonderful thing? Just think, I will spend an entire weekend in the company of the greatest men in the world. I shall look at everything, and pay the closest attention so that I will remember every detail for the rest of my life."

"I am happy for you, Lisl," Heinrich said. "It isn't every girl who receives such an opportunity. I am blessed to have such a daughter. Oh!" he literally shouted. "And such a son! Did I tell you? We received a letter from Rudi today."

"From Rudi? How is he? Is he enjoying France? Has he gone to the opera? Oh, papa, do you think I could go to Paris to visit Rudi?"

"Rudi isn't in Paris," Heinrich said. He picked up the letter and handed it to Lisl. "He's in Russia, and he has been nominated for the Iron Cross First Class! There have been many soldiers in the family Rodl, but no one has ever received the Iron Cross First Class."

"Rudi is in Russia?" Lisl asked, taking the letter. "But why was he sent from Paris? Was he being punished?"

"Punished? Heavens no, didn't you hear what I said? He is going to receive the Iron Cross. Read the letter. See for yourself what he did!"

Lisl read the letter quickly, and when she got to the part where he described the battle, she gasped and raised her hand to her mouth.

"Oh," she said. "Oh, papa, what a dangerous thing that was. Rudi could have been hurt or worse—he could have even been killed! And look, there were seven men who *were* killed," she said, pointing to the line. "How dreadful!"

"Dreadful? Oh, yes, about the poor soldiers who were killed. But their families will be compensated by the fact that their sons died bravely. I am sure that Rudi will write a letter to each of their families in which he conveys to them, just such a sentiment. I myself had to write many such letters in the last war. It is a sad thing to write them to be sure, but one feels such a stirring of pride in the deeds of such fine men that it fills the heart to the point of bursting."

"Pride?" Lisl said. "Papa, what if such a letter came to us, telling us of Rudi's heroic death on the battle-field? Would pride compensate us for the loss?"

"Nothing can ever compensate fully for the loss of a loved one," Heinrich admitted. "But when losses occur as they inevitably will, then it is good to have pride to help ease the pain. For without pride, we would have nothing."

"I don't like to think of such things," Lisl said.

"During time of war, such thoughts cannot be avoided," Heinrich said. Then he smiled. "But there are better things to think of now, yes? Such as your exciting news. Have you told mama yet?"

"No," Lisl said. "Papa, you don't suppose mama would object, do you?"

"Why should she object?"

"I don't know," Lisl said. "It's just that I have never done anything like this before. I mean, I've never spent a weekend with a man, not even with Paul."

Heinrich laughed, and he laughed so hard that tears began to pool in his eyes. He slapped his knees, then pulled out his handkerchief and wiped the tears away, then he laughed again.

"What is it?" Lisl asked, confused by his strange reaction. Then her confusion began to change to hurt and anger. "Why are you laughing at me?"

"I'm sorry, *liebling*," Heinrich said, putting his handkerchief away. "It's just that I wouldn't really think a social visit to the Chancellor at the Berghof, amidst two dozen state guests could be classified as spending a weekend with a man."

Lisl saw the humor of it then, and she too laughed. "I see what you mean," she said. "I suppose the whole thing is just so exciting to me that I couldn't think clearly. Then you don't think mama will mind?"

"I'm certain she will not mind," Heinrich said. "In fact, I'm certain that she will be very pleased by the whole idea."

Frauka was more than pleased. She was proud, so proud that she personally supervised the purchase of a new wardrobe for her daughter. "All new," she insisted. "Everything must be new and beautiful. My daughter is paying a social call on the Führer," she explained to the others in one of the dress shops, enjoying the looks of awe on the faces of those she told.

During the shopping expedition for dresses, hats and shoes, Frauka and Lisl noticed, perhaps for the first time, a dramatic effect of the war. There had been no new "season" this year. The Paris designs which had brought color and style to all of Europe were not present now.

"Oh, it's awful," Frauka said, picking through the paucity of styles, colors, and materials which were available. "These are so *ugly*, and there are so few to choose from."

"I'm sorry, madam," the store clerk said, stung by Frauka's remark. "But the cloth which is normally used for the new dresses is now being used to make clothes for our soldiers."

"Oh, mama, what if some of the cloth is used to make an overcoat for Rudi this winter?" Lisl asked. "Wouldn't that be more important than a cape or a wrap for me?"

"Yes," Frauka said, patting her daughter's hand affectionately. "Yes, of course you are right, dear. We have no business complaining about such a thing." She smiled sweetly at the store clerk. The store clerk, amazed at the miraculous change in her customer from belligerency to understanding, went out of her way to be nice to her important customer.

"Perhaps madam would care to see some of last year's Parisian fashions which were not shown?" she suggested.

"You have such clothes here?" Frauka asked.

"Yes," the store clerk said. She looked around cautiously, as if taking Frauka and Lisl into her confidence. "It is not something we tell everyone," she said quietly. "But in a few cases, when we encounter someone of rare taste and appreciation, we allow them the opportunity to look and buy."

"Oh, mama, may we look at them, please?" Lisl asked excited by the prospect.

"Yes," Frauka replied. "No daughter of mine is going to meet the Führer in clothes which are unsuitable. Bring on last year's designs, madam. We shall make a selection."

"Oh, mama, I do hope we find something nice," Lisl said. "I so want to make a good impression."

"You will make a good impression, dear, that I promise you," Frauka said.

10

WHEN Lisl stepped off the train in Berchtesgarten, a middle-aged, rather stiff-looking S.S. officer approached her, bearing a bouquet of long-stemmed roses. He looked at her questioningly.

"*Fraulein Rodl?*"

"Yes," Lisl answered.

"Ah, good," the S.S. officer said. He clicked his heels together sharply, then bowed graciously, while extending the bouquet of flowers. "Allow me please, to present you these flowers on behalf of the *Führer*. I am *Oberführer* Max Brandt, of the Berghof Guards. You will come with me, please."

"Thank you, *Oberführer*," Lisl said, taking the flowers. She sniffed them. "How lovely they are."

"There is a card, Fraulein," Brandt said.

"Oh, so there is," Lisl said, removing the small card, which, like the invitation which had summoned her was embossed with the eagle and swastika.

> *Once a lovely girl presented me with flowers.
> Now I return the gesture.*
>
> AH

"Where is the Führer?" Lisl asked.

"He is in his chalet, up there," Brandt said, pointing to the mountain which rose just behind the railroad station.

"Am I to go up there?" she asked.

"Yes."

"But it is so formidable! How does one get there?"

"There is a road to the house," Brandt said. "Of course the road is well guarded, as you can imagine, but we will have no difficulty. Come, someone is waiting in the coffee house to meet you."

"Oh, my bag," Lisl said, and she started toward the luggage cart which was rolling away from the baggage car of the train.

"Do you have the claim ticket?"

"Yes," Lisl said, taking the ticket from her handbag.

Brandt snapped his fingers, and, seemingly from nowhere, a soldier appeared, clicking his heels together sharply. Brandt handed the man the claim ticket and he took it to claim Lisl's bag.

Lisl followed Brandt to the coffee house where he said someone waited to meet her. There were half a dozen tables on the sidewalk in front of the coffeehouse, each table occupied by one or more patrons. A very handsome young man in the uniform of a *Luftwaffe Generalmajor* sat drinking a beer and reading a newspaper. ENGLAND TRIES TO BRING AMERICA INTO WAR, the headlines read.

The Lüftwaffe officer looked up just as Lisl passed his table and he smiled broadly and started to stand, but was stopped by a stare from S.S. *Oberführer* Brandt.

Inside a very pretty blonde woman was sitting at the corner table, the table normally reserved only for the most important of guests. Brandt led Lisl to the table, and the woman smiled pleasantly at Lisl.

"Fraulein Braun, may I present Fraulein Rodl," Brandt said formally. "Frauline Rodl is to be a weekend guest at the Berghof."

"Well," the girl said. "And won't we have a good time? My name is Eva, Lisl. I hope you had a pleasant journey."

"Yes, most pleasant, thank you," Lisl said, wondering how this girl knew her first name without being told.

"Fraulein Braun is a secretary on the Führer's staff," Brandt said, as if it were somehow necessary to explain the girl's presence to Lisl.

"Be a good fellow, Max, and run fetch the car for us, will you?" Eva said with a preemptive wave of her hand.

"Yes, of course, at once," Brandt said, and he clicked his heels—as obedient to the young woman as the low-ranking soldier had been obedient to him a few moments earlier.

Eva saw Lisl's expression of surprise and she laughed. "You are wondering how I can command someone of such high rank and make him jump?"

"Yes," Lisl admitted. "I must confess that I do find it a little confusing."

"There's nothing confusing about it," Eva said. "I am the Führer's mistress."

"What?" Lisl gasped, surprised not only that such a person could exist, but equally surprised to hear the person admit it. "I didn't know the Führer had anyone, I mean . . ."

Eva laughed, a rich, throaty laugh. "Come now, Lisl, don't tell me that you came up here harboring some hidden desire that *you* might be—"

"No!" Lisl said sharply. "Absolutely not!" And she

was so firm in her denial that Eva was absolutely convinced.

Again, laughter bubbled forth from Eva's throat. "No, I can see this is not the case. I hope you don't think I was rude, but I thought it would be better to get it out in the open, once and for all. The Führer and I are not married, because he feels it would be wrong to marry before the end of the war. But our commitment is as strong as if we were married.

"Now," she said, and the moment of seriousness which had passed across her face disappeared, to be replaced by a broad smile. "I see that the flunky has brought the car around. Shall we go up to the Berghof then?"

"Oh, yes," Lisl said.

"You'll like it. It's a little like a museum sometimes, filled with paintings and flags and the like, but we have a marvelous time during our weekend get-togethers. Goering is going to be here this weekend, you know."

"I've never met the *Reichsmarschall*," Lisl said. "What is he like?"

"Well, he is like any other man who weighs 150 kilos, wears a hair net, rouge and eye-shadow, and dresses in lavender uniforms with medals from his neck to his knees," Eva said, and though Lisl would have been hesitant to laugh about the number two man in all of Germany before anyone else, she couldn't help but laugh at Eva's description of him.

Brandt held the door open for the two women and they climbed into the back of the large, open Mercedes, and the driver started up the narrow, winding road which led up to the Berghof.

The road kept curving back on itself as they

climbed, and often Lisl would look over the side of the car and be totally unable to see the roadbed upon which they were driving, because it was so narrow that the car hung over the shoulder. She could look several meters below them though, and see the road snaking its way up the side of the mountain, while several meters below that she could see it again, and then again, all the way to the bottom where it began as a narrow ribbon winding out of the little village, now no more than a cluster of toy houses far below.

All the way up the side of the mountain Eva kept Lisl laughing, regaling her with funny stories, describing in unflattering terms all the men whose names were synonymous with power: Himmler, Goebbels, von Ribbentrop and many others.

The car finally reached the top of the road, where they were stopped by a closed gate. The driver honked the horn, but no one was there to open the gate for them.

"Where is the guard?" Brandt asked impatiently.

"Guard, yoo-hoo, come and open the gate quickly, or you will be sent to Russia to fight in the real war!" Eva shouted, standing in the back and cupping her hands around her mouth as she called.

About twenty meters off the side of the road was a small outhouse, and the door of the outhouse suddenly banged open as a man, still adjusting his pants, hurried to the gate. Eva laughed, and the others in the car, including Lisl, joined in. The guard stood at attention as the car passed through the gate and drove the rest of the way up to the house.

The house was beautiful. It was far grander than the typical mountain chalet. It was a large, and luxurious villa, making use of the ground on which it stood to provide the occupants with a most marvelous view."

"These are the rules of the stay here . . ." Brandt said, turning in his seat to talk to Lisl.

"Rules?"

"Oh, absolutely," Eva said. "Even I have to abide by them. Oh, damn—I could have smoked two more cigarettes while I was down there," she said.

"That is the first rule," Brandt said. "The Führer does not smoke, and does not wish to be around anyone who does smoke. You will not smoke while you are here."

"I don't smoke," Lisl explained.

"Then you will have no trouble," Eva said. "I do smoke, though if you tell the Führer I will deny it, and I am the one he will believe."

"I wouldn't tell," Lisl said.

"You know what he wants to do? He wants to force the cigarette companies to put a slogan on all their packages of cigarettes saying, *Danger, smoking causes cancer and can kill!* Could you imagine putting something like that on cigarette packages? Max, talk about something else or we are going to have to go back down the road so I can have another smoke."

"No whistling."

"He hates whistling," Eva explained. "He says it hurts his ears. I think he is still shell-shocked from the last war."

"No dancing."

"He says it is a waste of time," Eva said. "I love dancing. Come to think of it, I'm not sure what I see in him." She laughed.

"No heavy make-up or nail polish."

Lisl touched her cheeks. She had applied rouge and eye make-up before leaving the train.

"Don't worry," Eva said. "The only one who wears more make-up than he can stand is Goering, and somehow he finds the strength to accept even that."

"No letter-writing or diary-keeping," Brandt went on.

"We'll have too much to do for that anyway," Eva said.

"And, this is most important," Brandt said. "Absolutely no political discussions."

"That's as much for me as for him," Eva said. "I hate politics and I don't understand what National Socialism is supposed to be about. So we only talk about fun things while we are here."

"Oh, that will be no problem," Lisl said. "I'm afraid I'm not very political."

"Good, you will be to the Führer's liking," Eva said. "And mine too. Now, Max, if you are through, I shall take her inside and show her to her room."

"When do I—" Lisl started, then she stopped. "I mean, shouldn't I see the Führer to let him know that I am here, and to pay my respects?"

Eva laughed. "Lisl, nobody but *nobody* sees the Führer before noon. I imagine he will rise at about twelve, and we will take our lunch at one. That is when he will greet you."

"Of course," Lisl said. "I didn't mean to be presumptuous."

"You aren't presumptuous in the least," Eva said. "Now, come, let me show you around the place."

Eva escorted Lisl through the spacious rooms of the luxurious villa, taking as much pride in it as if it were her own house, and she the proud *hausfrau*. The house was constructed of beautiful woods and liberally embellished with Carrara marble. Expensive oriental rugs were on the floor of every room, and heavy, richly-upholstered furniture displayed both elegance and comfort.

"Here is the terrace," Eva said, opening the French doors and sweeping out onto the stone and cement porch.

Lisl gasped, then walked over to the low wall surrounding the terrace. She looked out over the magnificent vista which was displayed before her. Far below, the Königssee Lake sparkled in the sunshine, and in the distance she could see the Alpine mountains purpling in their grandeur.

"Do you like it here?" Eva asked. She stepped up onto the wall then struck a ballet pose. "I could do *Swan Lake* here," she added. "Only Wagner didn't write it, so the Führer probably wouldn't like it."

Lisl laughed at Eva's antics, then Eva jumped back down to continue the tour, leading Lisl across the large flagstones, to a well-tended garden. "Often we have tea here," Eva explained. "And I like to read here." Two small black Scotties bounded across the garden toward Eva, and she stooped down to pet them. "Ah, here you are my lovelies," she cooed, as the dogs happily jumped and rolled under her administrations.

"These are my babies," Eva explained. "The Führer has a big German shepherd named Blondi, and he thinks Blondi is the only dog that ever lived, but for my money, you can't beat my babies."

"Fraulein Braun, the Führer is coming," Brandt said, appearing from the house.

"Ah, his royal highness has awakened," Eva teased. "Come, as mere peasants, we must stand in line to receive our morning greetings." She looked at her watch. "Well, surprise of surprises. It actually *is* a morning greeting—he has five minutes until noon. Such a thing could make me jealous, you know. He must be very anxious to see you, to get up this early."

Eva made the comment with such jocularity in her voice that Lisl sensed no threat in it. She laughed and followed this young woman whom she had met only this morning, but to whom she had taken an instant liking, back to the terrace to wait for Hitler's arrival.

As they waited on the patio, Eva cupped her hands to her mouth and blew into them, smelling her breath. "Oh, I hope I don't smell like cigarettes," she said.

Adolf Hitler stepped through the French doors onto the patio and looked around. He was wearing a uniform of dark brown trousers and a double-breasted jacket of a lighter shade of brown. A military visored hat was perched on his head, so that the famous forelock of hair was not immediately discernible. Over his breast pocket he wore the Iron Cross First Class. He looked toward Lisl and Eva and smiled, then walked toward them.

"Ah, Fraulein Rodl. I am so delighted you could accept my invitation."

Hitler took Lisl's hand and raised it to his lips. His eyes were a brilliant, cobalt blue, strikingly intense and penetrating. Lisl looked at the hand which held hers. It was pale and soft, as sensitive as the hands of an artist. "Have you been shown your room?" he asked.

"Not yet, my Führer," Lisl replied.

"I've been showing her around," Eva said.

Hitler smiled. "Well, there is plenty of time yet. In the meantime, you must consider this as your home."

Hitler dropped Lisl's hand then took Eva's and repeated the gesture, kissing her hand as formally as if she, too, were just a temporary house guest. At first, Lisl was surprised and she wondered if Eva had been misrepresenting the truth. After all, there had never been the slightest hint of the existence of a mistress in Hitler's life. Then she saw something which verified all Eva had told her, for the intense sparkle in Hitler's eyes took on an intimate glow which could be seen by even the least observant.

"Well, then," Hitler said, his greetings concluded. "Shall we have lunch?"

"Lunch, so early?" Eva teased. "Whatever makes you think someone might be hungry? Just because we've been up for several hours with nothing to eat?"

"We can wait until later, if you prefer," Hitler said.

"No, no, lunch will be fine," Eva said quickly, and Hitler laughed at Eva's easy surrender.

Lisl followed Eva and Hitler back into the house, down the hall, and into the dining room. There were half a dozen people in the dining room, and it surprised Lisl, for she had not seen anyone since she arrived, and she wondered where they had all been. She recognized one of them right away. It was *Reichsmarschall* Hermann Goering. Goering looked just as Lisl had described him, and she had to consciously fight against breaking into a smile. Goering was wearing a light blue uniform with a broad gold stripe down each pant leg. He had an array of medals which covered his broad chest, and diamond rings glistened and sparkled from his fat fingers.

Hitler spoke to the others and they returned his greeting, then waited patiently as Hitler helped first Lisl and then Eva into their chairs. Lisl noticed that Eva was seated next to Hitler.

"Now," Hitler said, sitting to the table and joined by the others. "What have we for lunch?"

"My Führer, I've taken the liberty," Goering said, snapping his fingers at one of the white-jacketed S.S.

waiters who stood by, "to bring some *wildschwine wurst.*"

A plate of sausages was put on the table. They were smoking hot and aromatic, filling the room with a rich, spicy aroma.

"I see," Hitler said, looking at the sausages. "And did you murder the poor beast yourself?"

"I took him in a hunt, yes," Goering replied.

Hitler sighed and looked at his table guests. "I am a tolerant man and therefore do not apply my dietary habits to others," he said. "But if any of you wish to become corpse-eaters, eating the flesh of this dead animal that the *Reichsmarschall* murdered, you have my permission to do so."

"Thank you, my Führer," Goering said, and he signaled to a waiter who transferred a generous portion of the sausages to Goering's plate. Goering leaned back in his chair with his hands laced across his large belly and watched appreciatively.

"Are you an avid hunter, *Reichsmarschall*?" Lisl asked, wanting to participate in the conversation, but feeling out of place here among such luminaries.

"Yes," Goering replied. "I've hunted all sorts of game."

"There is nothing to excite one about hunting," Hitler put in, accepting a bowl of cabbage soup. "How can one get excited about hunting, when anyone with a fat belly can shoot any animal from a safe distance?"

"Hunting is as old as mankind, my *Führer*," Goering tried to protest.

"That's just my point," Hitler said. "It is exactly such things as this, that directs my efforts to bring about a world revolution. Just think about it. Eons ago, when man lived in caves, his only way of survival was to eat the animals who didn't eat him. Then he discovered agriculture, and with that discovery, mankind was freed for all time. Man can grow his own food, it is more healthful, and it supplies his every need. Freed from the necessity of hunting animals just to stay alive, man was able to develop in other ways, ideas were born and culture was begun. And yet, there are still some who cling to the prehistoric barbarism of murdering animals and eating dead flesh."

Hitler's monologue was persuasive enough to cause many of the others to stop eating the sausage, but Goering continued to relish the meat, totally unaffected by Hitler's disapproval.

Throughout lunch Hitler continued to dominate the conversation. It turned from diet to religion. "The church is necessary. It is a powerfully unifying element. I will, at some time in the future, unite all the German churches into one church, as was done in England. Then the church will adapt itself to the goals of National Socialism."

Lisl noticed that Hitler didn't carry on a conversation in the normal sense. There was no exchange of ideas from the others, no differing points of view. Hitler expressed a thesis, and then he expounded upon it. His audience was little more than a sounding board.

After lunch, Hitler invited everyone to take a stroll through the grounds to a place he called the teahouse. Here they were served apple-peel tea and cake. Lisl noticed that Hitler had as large an appetite for cake as Goering had for the sausages. Here, too, the monologue continued; Hitler spoke about such things as art, travel, astrology, and the importance and sanctity of motherhood.

By six o'clock that evening, Lisl was beginning to wonder why she had been invited. Other than the initial greeting, Hitler had not even spoken to her. In fact, except for the brief visit with Eva before she met Hitler, no one had spoken to her. What she had thought would be a weekend of excitement and gala activity had turned boring. But how could this be? she wondered. How could she be in the company of the most powerful man in the world and be bored?

They returned to the main house shortly after six, watched a movie, ate dinner, then retired to the parlor, where Hitler continued his monologue, now repeating some points he had already made earlier in the day. At about midnight, Lisl felt that she could hold her eyes open no longer, and she yawned, then quietly asked Eva where her room was, for she had not had the opportunity to visit it all day.

"There is one more rule you must observe," Eva noted. "No one goes to bed until after the Führer."

"Of course," Lisl said. "I had no wish to leave yet, I was just concerned as to where it was."

"I'll show you when we start to bed," Eva promised, patting Lisl's hand as a mother would pat the hand of a fidgety child.

It was two in the morning before Hitler finally stood abruptly, bowed stiffly, then wished everyone a good night. Lisl noticed that the other guests seemed to be as tired as she was and as eager to go to bed, for there was absolutely no lingering after Hitler's departure. Everyone left immediately.

"What did you think?" Eva asked, as she led Lisl through the hallway to her room.

"It was a fascinating day," Lisl replied, thinking it would not be wise to suggest that she had been bored and exhausted by it all.

"Yes, wasn't it?" Eva said. "I think it is wonderful that he has ideas on so many subjects. If only all of his enemies could see him at these moments as I see him. No, they speak only of his harshness toward the Jews, or of the invasions of Poland and Russia. They see him as a one-dimensional man. I see him as the most marvelous human being who ever lived. And you will too, by tomorrow night. Here is your room."

"Thank you," Lisl said. "You've been a wonderful friend today, Eva."

"It is I who should thank you," Eva replied. "I'm not really in a position to make many friends, and when I do make one, it is a treat indeed. Goodnight."

Lisl pulled the door shut and walked over to the bed where wearily she undressed and slipped under the covers. If tomorrow was as long and hard as today, she would welcome the end of the weekend.

11

"BRING hot tea, *brochen* and marmalade to the terrace," Eva was saying right outside Lisl's door.

"At once, *gnädige fraulein*," a man's servile voice answered.

There was a rap on Lisl's door.

"Lisl? Lisl, are you awake?" Eva called.

Lisl ran her hand sleepily through her hair, and for just an instant wondered where she was, and why someone was calling her. Then, almost at once, she remembered, and she called out.

"Yes, Eva, I'm awake," she answered.

Lisl heard the door opening and she was shocked, because when she went to bed the night before—or was it really the night before, it had been so far into the morning that it was just a few short hours ago—she had locked the door. Eva came into her room, smiling as brightly as the early morning sun which streamed in.

"I see you locked your door," Eva said, holding up the key which gave her access to the room. "That is probably a good idea."

"You have a key?" Lisl asked.

Eva laughed. "I have a key to every room in the house, including the Führer's room." She dropped the keys into her apron pocket, and Lisl saw that, this morning, Eva was dressed as a Bavarian peasant, with a dark print skirt, a puffy sleeved blouse, and a white apron. "The Führer doesn't like anyone to eat until he rises. Then we all must take lunch together as we did yesterday," Eva said. "But sometimes I sneak in a small snack. Otherwise I couldn't make it. Would you join me this morning?"

"Of course," Lisl said, now swinging her legs out of bed and reaching for her dressing gown. "Why do you call him Führer?"

"Because he is my leader, just as he is the leader of everyone else in Germany," Eva replied easily.

"Yes, but, you are also his *maitresse*. Surely you call him by a more personal name?"

"He wishes me to call him that," Eva said. "That way, there is never any problem of my slipping and saying something I shouldn't before someone who shouldn't hear."

"I would ask that you, also, respect the Führer's desire for privacy," Eva went on. "Don't speak of me to others when you return."

"No, I shan't," Lisl promised.

Eva smiled. "I was sure you wouldn't, and so was the Führer. Otherwise, you wouldn't have been invited."

"Why was I invited?" Lisl asked. Now she was looking through the clothes she would wear that day, and though she didn't realize she was doing it, she was trying to make a selection which would compliment Eva's dress. Lisl had brought only the smartest clothes with her, and it was difficult to find a wardrobe which would be compatible with Eva's simple dress.

"Because the Führer enjoys having pretty women around," Eva said. "I didn't think *that* was a secret," she went on, laughing.

"Well, no, I've heard that," Lisl said. "But he has hardly spoken to me. I've felt as if he didn't know I was here."

"That is the way it is supposed to be," Eva said. "If you were anything more to him than a pretty vase, or a lovely painting, then I should be terribly jealous and we couldn't be friends. Now you wouldn't want that, would you?"

"No," Lisl replied. "Of course not."

"Wear that one. I think it would be lovely," Eva said, pointing to a gray dress. Lisl had been about to choose a red one, but she took the gray at Eva's suggestion.

"Very well," Lisl said, taking off her dressing gown and slipping into the dress Eva had chosen for her.

After the light breakfast, which Lisl and Eva took on a terrace, overlooking the magnificent scenery of the mountains and lake, Eva asked Lisl if she would like to complete the tour which was interrupted by Hitler's arrival on the day before.

"Yes, I would like that," Lisl said. From the moment the Führer had arrived yesterday, he had been the center of all activity. All the guests ate when he ate, walked when he walked, and listened when he talked. Because of that, Lisl had seen very little of the house, other than the outside views she had enjoyed with Eva before Hitler came on the scene.

"Let's start downstairs," Eva offered. "Then we'll come back up here and I'll show you everything except the Führer's room. I can describe that room to you if you wish," she added, with a possessive smile.

Eva led Lisl down a spiral staircase to the antechamber, one wall of which was glass opening onto a courtyard. The other side of the antechamber led into a very large drawing room which featured an enormous fireplace of green faience. The drawing room had a tremendously large picture-window looking out toward Untersberg peak.

"I've seen pictures of this," Lisl said, suddenly recognizing it.

"You should have," Eva explained matter-of-factly. "It's on about twenty million postcards. Come, here is the dining room. I know you ate two meals here yesterday, but did you get a chance to really look?"

"No," Lisl admitted. "I did notice that everyone sat in armchairs, rather than straight-back chairs, though."

"That's the Führer's idea. He likes to make his meals last two hours or more, and he feels that arm-chairs are better suited for that pace."

Silently, Lisl agreed. She remembered the long, drawn-out meals and Hitler's rambling monologues and realized how much more uncomfortable she would have been had she been subjected to all that while seated in a straight chair.

The dining room was paneled with pine and the furniture was of the same wood, so that there was an exact matching. There were several medieval-type lamps of heavy wrought iron, while along one wall there was a cupboard filled with exceptionally beautiful china and vases.

After the dining room came the main hall, where the movie had been shown the night before. Lisl had not noticed then, because they had been pulled up to lower the screen, but one wall was covered with beautiful hanging tapestries.

"Oh, how beautiful!" Lisl said, walking over to the tapestries and running her hand over one of them.

"They are authentic Aubusson-Gobelins," Eva said, as proudly as if they were her own. "Oh, and these mosaic tables and the fireplace are a gift from Mussolini."

"What is Mussolini like?" Lisl asked.

"Mussolini is a comical character," Eva said. "He follows the Führer around like an obedient puppy. But his son-in-law, Count Ciano, ahh," Eva folded her arms across her chest and made a move as if she were dancing. "How handsome he is, and how beautifully he dresses! I have some photographs of him which I sometimes look at and dream about. I do believe it makes Woulfe jealous."

"Woulfe?"

"The Führer," Eva explained. "You wanted to know my pet name earlier? When I first met him, he was introduced to me as Herr Woulfe. It is the name he used to use when he wished to be incognito. But I really never use it anymore, for he doesn't like me to. Now, come upstairs."

Lisl started toward the spiral staircase, but Eva called out to her. "No," she said. "Come this way."

There was another staircase, one Lisl had not seen. It was covered with red velvet, and Eva explained that it went up to the main apartment. "My rooms are up there," Eva said. "And so are the Führer's," she added.

Lisl had not seen this part of the house, and she was struck with the size of the upstairs corridor, which was every bit as imposing as the main hall on the first floor. The walls were covered with huge paintings and lined with tables of marble and expensive woods. Vases, busts, small statues and expensive bric-a-brac occupied places on the tables.

"Take off your shoes and walk quietly," Eva whispered. "The Führer is still sleeping."

Lisl and Eva slipped out of their shoes, then laid them beside the stairs, and walked down the long, thickly carpeted hallway. Two S.S. guards stood, totally immobile, outside one door, and Lisl did not have to be told that it was the door which led to Hitler's apartment.

"This is my room," Eva whispered, and she opened the door and ushered Lisl inside. The walls were lined with silk, and the room was heavily furnished. Above the sofa hung a painting of a nude woman. Lisl gasped when she saw it.

"Yes, it's me," Eva said, smiling proudly. "The Führer claims that it is scandalous to have a nude painting of oneself on display, but I think he likes it secretly. Besides, it is certainly better than the photograph he wishes me to keep of him." Eva pointed to the photograph of Hitler. The photo was completely black, except for a face, staring out in an almost spectral image. The eyes, always intense, were absolutely hypnotic in this picture. "Frightening, isn't it?" she said.

Eva opened a door and Lisl looked into the bathroom. The tub was of marble, and it was huge. The fixtures were gold. The bathroom was a large room, and there was another door opening from the other end.

"That door leads into the Führer's apartment," Eva whispered. She let Lisl look around, then she pulled the door to. "Now you've seen everything," Eva said. "What do you think of it?"

"I think it is beautiful," Lisl said. "What a grand place to live."

"Or be imprisoned," Eva said, and Lisl was surprised by her strange statement. "For that's what I am," Eva went on.

"I don't understand. You mean you can't leave here?"

Eva smiled sadly. "Of course I can leave here," she said. "But once I leave here I become Miss No Private Life, unable to let the world know what I feel in my heart. Tell me, Lisl, are you in love?"

"Yes," Lisl said. "I am in love with Paul Maass, the *Orchestra Direktor* of the Schweinfurt Symphony."

"And have you told anyone, or do you keep the secret locked up in your heart?"

"Of course I have told others," Lisl said. "My parents, my friends, everyone knows. We will be married some day."

"Ah," Eva said. "And so now you know. Isn't part of the beauty of being in love being able to share it with others? Who would want to be in love and keep it always a secret? Here at the Berghof, it is not necessary for me to keep it a secret, for all who visit this place are people who can be trusted. When I leave this place, however, I must keep secret the very thing I would prefer to shout from the rooftops. I am a prisoner here, but the only restraint upon me is the restraint on my heart."

At that moment, Lisl felt an almost overwhelming pity for the young woman who, on the surface at least, would seem to have everything she could ever want.

The rest of the day passed much the same as the previous day. Hitler came down at a few minutes after twelve, greeted all his guests with almost shy formality, then treated them to another long afternoon of rambling monologues. There was one moment during the seemingly endless afternoon which stayed with Lisl, however. At one point during the discussion Hitler had fallen silent and the others, sensing that Hitler wanted the silence, were also quiet. They were sitting in the great drawing room, looking through the window at Untersberg peak. After several moments, Hitler spoke.

"If I am successful with all I have set out to do, I will be considered one of the greatest men in the world. But if I fail. . . ."

"Fail, *Mein Führer?*" Goering interrupted, protesting the very idea that Hitler might fail.

Hitler waved Goering's interruption aside with an impatient move of his hand, as if it were imperative that he finish his thought.

"If I fail," Hitler went on, "I shall be condemned as the most dreadful criminal in the history of mankind, and I will be damned for eternity."

There was such an ominous tone to Hitler's voice as he made the statement that it caused Lisl to shake with a chill. It was the type of chill which used to prompt children to say: "Someone just stepped on your grave."

The late summer had brought beautiful sunshine and pleasant weather to the guests at the Berghof, but it merely brought more rain to the beleaguered troops who were advancing toward Moscow. That rain, compounded by the rain which had already fallen over the last several days, made quagmire pits of the roads and fields, and the Blitzkrieg had been halted, not by the Russian troops, but by something the German soldiers called, *"Herr General Schlamm,"* or, "General Mud."

Tanks which had been advancing at a speed of one hundred miles per day during the dry summer, were now slowed to ten miles per day when they could move at all. Even horse-drawn wagons had a difficult time of it, though the German press assured the German public that the army would be on the move again as soon as the weather cooled and the mud congealed.

Rudi was concerned about the cooling weather for a different reason. He knew of the brutal Russian winters, and his entire Panzer company was totally without winterized equipment. There were none of the canvas shrouds, and pre-heaters which were a part of the table of equipment supposed to be available for a Panzer company. Without those shrouds and pre-heaters, the tank engines would get so cold that it would be difficult to get them started.

There was an even more pressing lack, however, which Rudi discovered when he went to Division Supply to inventory the support equipment. There was no winter clothing. All the uniforms in stock were summer cotton. There were no winter uniforms, no winter parkas, hats, boots, or mufflers. There weren't even any overcoats, field jackets or extra blankets. The division was totally without support for men who would be in the field during cold weather. As soon as Rudi made the startling discovery, he went at once to his old commander, Ernst Kant, now a Major on the Division Staff.

"But surely there are," Kant replied, surprised by Rudi's statement. "Why, I myself signed the requisition forms six weeks ago. I was assured the supplies would be sent along with the next shipment."

"There are no winter supplies," Rudi said. "Not for the vehicles, not for the men."

Kant was sitting behind a desk in what had been a school building in a small village, and he reached for the field phone and cranked the handle, demanding to be put through to the Division Supply Officer.

"*Hauptmann* Janicke, Major Kant here. What about

my requisition for winter supplies? One of my field commanders had just come to me with the unbelievable story that we have none."

"*Ja*, Major Kant, your field commander is correct. We have no winter supplies in the Russian Theater," Captain Janicke replied.

"But that is impossible!" Kant said. "The requisition did go through, did it not?"

"*Jawohl, Herr Major*," Captain Janicke answered. "The requisition did go through. But it has not been filled."

"Are you telling me that the German Army does not have winter equipment? Not even back in Germany?"

"We have the equipment, Major," Captain Janicke explained. "But the shipment priority has been downgraded severely. The trains are being used for other purposes."

"Other purposes? What other purposes?" Kant asked.

"Jews, Major. The trains are being used to round up all the Jews within the occupied territories, and the Jews are being shipped back to Poland."

"Thank you," Kant said. He hung the phone up and then polished the eyepiece of his monocle as he looked at Rudi. "Jews," he said.

"Jews?" Rudi replied. He laughed, a scoffing, disbelieving laugh. "I know the government blames everything on the Jews, but how do they manage to blame this on the Jews?"

"Because it is true," Kant said. He sighed. "The trains which should be used to transport supplies and material are being used to transport Jews back to Poland."

Rudi blinked his eyes in disbelief. "Ernst, you can't

be serious," he said, using his superior officer's first name in what would normally be a serious breach of military etiquette.

"I'm afraid I am," Kant said quietly. Kant stood up and walked over to the door then looked out into the hall. He closed the door, then returned to the desk. "Rudi, you mark my words, no good is going to come of all this. That bunch of fanatical S.S. bastards is going to bring this entire war crashing down on our heads. Here we are, totally immobilized by this damned mud, facing the prospect of spending the winter right where we stand, and we can't even get the most basic supplies because of this insane business with the Jews."

"What is going on, Major?" Rudi asked. "I mean, what are they doing with all the Jews? What is happening to them when they reach Poland?"

Kant shrugged his shoulders. "Who knows?" he said. "Sent to farms and factories as involuntary labor battalions, I suppose. I don't know. I guess there are greater minds than mine at work here. But I fail to see what good it does to use slave labor to produce food and supplies if you can't get that food and supplies to the army for which it is being produced in the first place."

"What are we going to do?" Rudi asked.

"What do you mean?"

"I mean, if the winter supplies don't get here soon, what are we going to do? How are we going to handle it?"

"Rudi, my boy, your guess is as good as mine," Kant said. He sighed. "Now, if you have nothing else to say, I have work to do." He pointed to a pile of papers. "Believe it or not, that is a census report on the number of Jews living in our area of responsibility. I'm counting Jews when I should be counting winter coats."

"It could be a hard winter, Major Kant," Rudi cautioned.

"Tell it to the people in Berlin," Kant said.

Rudi watched Kant return to his work, then he left the little schoolhouse to wade through the mud back to his unit's field position. It wasn't a field position picked because of the terrain and tactical control, it was a field position picked because four of the tanks had become so bogged down that they could go no further that day.

For the first time, Rudi began to wonder about the invincibility of the *Wehrmacht*.

12

Early Spring, 1942.

"WILL this miserable winter never end?" Frauka asked, pulling the curtains to one side to look out at the snow which was falling. "It is March. Surely the worst is over by now."

"Mama, if we are miserable, think of poor Rudi in Russia," Lisl said. Lisl was sitting on the sofa with Paul, who held his hands out to accept a skein of yarn. Lisl was knitting a woolen scarf to send to her brother.

"I don't like to think of Rudi, or of any of the other poor boys out there in this miserable weather," Frauka said. She let the curtain close then walked over to stand by the stove and held her hands out to warm them. The stove roared merrily, supplied with coal which Heinrich managed to bring home from the factory. Officially, they were supposed to have a fire only four hours per day, but Frauka openly and without apology violated that law, and kept the fire going twenty-four hours a day, though she did bank it at night.

"I wish they would just go ahead and capture Moscow," Lisl said. "Surely there are places where one can stay warm in Moscow? I mean, after all, the Russians have lived there for a great number of years."

Paul chuckled. "Don't you think they would have captured Moscow by now if they could?" he asked. "I'm sure they aren't staying outside by choice."

"Paul, what are you saying?" Lisl asked. "Are you suggesting that the Russian Army is beating our Army?"

"Well, we don't really know, do we?" Paul said. "The only news reports we get are that the German Army has 'dug into winter positions'. That doesn't sound very encouraging to me. It sounds to me like we are just hanging on."

"I don't know, Rudi has never suggested anything like that in any of his letters," Lisl said.

"He wouldn't," Paul reminded her. "First of all, he wouldn't want to worry you. And secondly, I doubt that the censors would let the letter through if he did try."

"You are a pessimist," Lisl said. "The papers say we shouldn't listen to pessimists."

"The newspapers aren't always right, are they?" Paul said. "The newspapers said that America would not come into this war. Their people have no will to fight, I think was the way it was put."

"The Americans are too busy with the Japanese," Lisl said. "They will never come to Europe to fight."

"Listen to who is the military expert now," Paul teased. "One visit to Hitler, and she knows everything."

There was the sound of car tires rolling on snow, and Frauka got up and walked over to look through the window.

"It's your father," she said. "I wonder what he is doing home at this hour?" Frauka went to the front door and opened it while Heinrich stamped his feet on the porch to rid himself of the snow.

"You have it too hot in here," he said.

"No, I don't," Frauka replied. "It's nice and comfortable in here. You've just been out in the cold. What is it, Heinrich? Why are you home? Is something wrong?"

Heinrich took his coat off and hung it on the hall-tree and nodded at Paul before he answered. "Have we any hot tea?"

"I'll get some," Lisl offered.

"Thanks," Heinrich said.

"Well?" Frauka said. "Are you going to answer?"

"Lubeck was bombed by the British last night," Heinrich said. He let out a long, slow sigh. "The city was almost totally destroyed. Burned to the ground. Over fifteen thousand people were made homeless by the raid."

"Oh," Frauka said, putting her hand to her mouth. "Oh, how brutal! And in such weather! The British really have no spark of decency in them, do they?"

"Frauka, it can happen in Schweinfurt, too," Heinrich said quietly.

"But surely not," Frauka said. "I mean surely the authorities realize that something will have to be done, won't they?"

"They have realized," Heinrich said. "They are completely re-doing the Air Defense system. We are putting in radar, like the radar used by the English. That way we will be able to detect the bombers long before they approach their targets, and we'll be able to guide our fighter aircraft to them."

"Well, I'm glad to see that something is being done," Frauka said.

"I have volunteered you," Heinrich went on.

"Volunteered me? Volunteered me to do what?" Frauka asked.

"To work with the aircraft plotters," Heinrich said. "I hope you don't mind."

"Mind? Of course I don't mind," Frauka said. "I would be glad to do something, anything, to make a contribution."

"You aren't the only one," Heinrich said. "I've had my reserve rank activated. I am now a Colonel in charge of the Schweinfurt air-defense artillery."

"And what about me, father?" Lisl asked, returning to the room then with a cup of hot tea. "Have you found no duties for me to perform?"

"You will be married to Paul this summer," Heinrich said. "It is not my place to volunteer you to work."

"But I want to do something to help," Lisl insisted.

"You can help me," Paul said.

"Help you do what, fiddle while Schweinfurt burns?" Lisl snapped.

"Lisl!" Frauka said, surprised by her daughter's unkind remark.

"Well, it's true," Lisl said. "I'm sorry, Paul, but I can't help but think about it. Poor Rudi and the others are facing such horrible conditions and all you can do is stay back here where you are safe and warm and criticize."

"I see," Paul said quietly. He sighed, and slipped the skein of yarn from his hands and lay it on a nearby table. "Perhaps I had better be going."

"Oh, I'm sorry," Lisl said. "I guess I'm just a little edgy because I'm concerned about Rudi. Please, Paul, don't be angry with me!"

Paul looked at her and smiled, but there was a deep sadness behind his smile. "I can't be angry with you,

Lisl. And I especially can't be angry with you when you are right. I am at home, warm and safe."

"You are exempt by the special artists' decree," Frauka reminded him. "And I agree with the government. If we are to have no culture, then all we are fighting for is useless. Don't put yourself down so. Lisl was out of line."

"I was," Lisl said. "And I admit it."

Paul put his hand at the junction of Lisl's neck and shoulder, and squeezed lightly. "I know you didn't mean anything by it, Lisl. But, as I say, you merely expressed aloud thoughts I have often entertained. Now, if you will excuse me, I really must be going."

"Won't you stay for dinner, Paul?" Heinrich offered.

"No, thank you. I'll be giving a concert for some wounded soldiers tomorrow afternoon, and I need some time to prepare."

"Do you need some help?" Lisl asked.

"Not tonight," Paul said softly. "Tomorrow morning."

Lisl went to Paul and kissed him, full and unashamedly on the mouth. "Until tomorrow morning, then," she said.

Paul smiled at her. "For a kiss like that, I would gladly go through another little spat," he teased, and his tease evoked laughter from Lisl and her parents, just as he hoped it would. He walked over to the hall-tree and slipped on his coat.

"Would you like me to have Willi drive you to the concert hall?" Heinrich asked.

"No, thank you," Paul said. "It is but a one kilometer walk until I reach the trolley stop. I will be all right."

"I'll see you tomorrow, Paul," Lisl called again, and

Paul could tell by the tone in her voice that she was still sorry she had lashed out at him.

"Tell me what an aircraft plotter must do," Frauka was saying to Heinrich as Paul closed the door, and he knew that the subject had already gone on beyond him as he walked out across the snow toward the road which would take him to the trolley stop.

Paul had thought about his situation—the fact that he was exempt from service while so many were fighting and dying for the fatherland. No, not the fatherland—the Führer. There had been an entire page of death notices in the *Schweinfurt Tageblate* this morning. *"In a hero's death for the Führer, there died on February 22, 1942, in the fighting in Russia, my beloved husband and the father of our children,"* etcetera, etcetera, etcetera.

Paul did not want to die for the Führer. Already, Paul had begun to ask himself questions about the Führer . . . questions that he could never ask aloud. Paul answered the questions he asked, and the answers were disturbing to him. Hitler bode evil for Germany, Paul was now convinced of that. The bombing raid at Lubeck on the night before, that Heinrich spoke of, seemed prophetic to Paul. Paul had only to close his eyes, and he could see all of Germany going up in flames.

Paul reached the trolley stop, then stood there with his back to the blowing snow until the next streetcar came by. He stepped onto the car, dropped his coin in the box, then took a seat. This far out on the line the car was nearly empty, and there were plenty of seats available.

Across the aisle from Paul sat a soldier with one leg. His uniform trousers were tucked into a tight roll where one leg should be. A well-worn set of crutches leaned against the seat. There were only about six others on the car, but they all seemed to be consciously avoiding the soldier, as if embarrassed by his condition, or as if unwilling to be reminded about it. That was quite a change from a year earlier, when a wounded soldier was treated as a hero everywhere he went.

"Russia?" Paul asked, nodding toward the leg.

The soldier nodded in the affirmative.

"Is it pretty bad there?"

Paul saw something in the soldier's eyes then. What was it? Contempt for a civilian who had to ask? Disdain for someone who was not one of them, and therefore undeserving of an answer? Or was it fear that he would say the wrong thing at the wrong time to the wrong person? The soldier licked his lips nervously, and looked around at the others.

"We've dug in for the winter," the soldier said, parroting the reports carried by all the newspapers. "We'll move into Moscow in the spring."

"I have no doubt," Paul said, now wanting to end the conversation. He was making the soldier uneasy, and he had no desire to do that.

The trolley stopped, letting off a few passengers and picking up more, gradually taking on more than it let off, until by the time it reached the concert hall it was quite full, and Paul got up to give his seat to an old woman whose eyes looked accusingly at him for not being in uniform.

Paul walked across the sidewalk from the trolley stop, to the door which led into the concert hall, and as he was unlocking the door a man approached him.

"Herr Maass? Herr Paul Maass?"

"Yes," Paul said, looking toward the man. "I am Paul Maass."

"I would like to speak with you, Herr Maass," the man said.

"What about?" Paul replied. The man's strange behavior made him nervous.

"Please," the man went on. "May we step inside?"

"I don't know," Paul said. "Are you with the police? What is this all about?"

The man looked around to make certain that no one was close enough to hear him, then he said, very quietly: "It is about your brother, Herr Maass. It is about Hans Werfel."

Had the man suddenly poked Paul in the stomach, he wouldn't have been more stunned nor suffered a greater loss of breath. He felt the blood rushing from his head and a sinking sensation in the pit of his stomach, and for a moment he feared that he might pass out.

"What . . . what are you talking about?" he finally managed to ask.

"Please, Herr Maass, inside," the man insisted, and Paul, without further resistance, opened the door and stepped in from the street. The stranger came behind him. Paul closed the door and led the man through the dim shadows of the hall, behind the concert stage, and to the room which served him.

"In here," Paul said, opening the door. "We can talk in here."

"Without danger of being overheard?"

"Why should we mind being overheard?" Paul asked.

"What I have to tell you shouldn't be heard by anyone else," the man said.

"Then I'm not at all certain I want to hear it," Paul protested. "Look, Herr—"

"Doctor," the man answered. "I'm Dr. Benno Mueller."

Paul stuck his hand out as an automatic reflex, and shook hands with Dr. Mueller. "Yes, well, as I said, Dr. Mueller, I really don't wish to be a party to any secrets which might be—"

"You should know this secret, Herr Maass," Dr. Mueller said, "as it concerns you."

"It concerns me?"

"Yes."

"In what way?"

"Oh, in a very important, one might almost say, desperate, way," Dr. Mueller said.

"I don't know what you are getting at," Paul said, then he suddenly remembered that Dr. Mueller had mentioned his brother's name. "Is it Hans? Has something happened to Hans?"

"Hans is safe in America," Dr. Mueller said. "You should know this, because you helped him get there."

"How do you know?" Paul asked, still suspicious of the man.

"Because I am the one who gave him the warning that his life was in danger," Dr. Mueller said. "You see, I am on the staff at the University, and I worked with your brother for a long time. Your brother is a brilliant man, Herr Maass. He has nearly unlocked the secret of the sun's power."

"The secret of the sun's power? I don't know what you mean."

"No, nor do most people," Dr. Mueller said. "And we can be thankful for that, for if Hitler really knew how close your brother was, how . . ." Dr. Mueller let the words trail off. "Well, never mind. He is in America now, and his secret is safe with him. It is your secret we are worried about now."

"I have no secret," Paul said.

"Oh, but you do," Dr. Mueller said. "It is, as I say, a most desperate secret. But it is safe with me, as long as I can count on your cooperation."

Paul said, "My cooperation in what?"

"Herr Maass, as you have no doubt figured out by now, I am not a supporter of the Hitler regime."

"You must be," Paul said. "You would not be on the University staff otherwise."

"Unless my true feelings were not generally known," Mueller said. "I am going to be frank with you, Herr Maass, because I can afford to be frank with you. I am on the University staff because I joined the Nazi Party in 1923. That makes me one of the oldest and most trusted members of the party. But even before this war, I became disenchanted with the Nazis. Now, I am working to rid our country of Hitler and his band of criminals."

"Why are you telling me all this?" Paul asked. "I told you, I don't want to hear it."

"Ah, but you must hear it," Dr. Mueller said. "I am a dedicated anti-Nazi, Herr Maass, dedicated to overthrowing the Nazi government. I am what Franco called a 'Fifth columnist.' "

"You are taking a terrible chance by telling me all this," Paul warned him. "I could report you and have you shot."

"You could," Dr. Mueller said, "but you won't. I told you, I know a secret about you as well."

"What, that I helped my brother to escape? That was a long time ago, I could—"

"No," Dr. Mueller said. "I don't mean that. I mean the fact that you are a Jew."

At first Paul was shocked, then, suddenly, he laughed. "Dr. Mueller, I thought Fifth Columnists were more careful than that. Do you realize what you have done? You have exposed yourself to me in the hopes of being able to blackmail me into helping you, and you have no ammunition for your blackmail scheme. I'm not a Jew."

"Why do you say that?" Dr. Mueller asked. "Because your mother was no Jew, and Herr Maass, her second husband was no Jew?"

"Of course that is why I say that," Paul said. "Hans is a Jew because his father was a Jew."

"Hans' father and your father are one and the same," Dr. Mueller said.

"No, Hans' father died and my mother remarried," Paul said easily. "My father is Aaron Maass."

"Your father is Jastrile Werfel," Dr. Mueller said again. "Your mother was already pregnant with you when she married Aaron Maass. She was made pregnant by her first husband, Jastrile Werfel, and Aaron Maass agreed to adopt you and give you his name."

"I don't believe that," Paul said.

"I have the proof," Dr. Mueller said. "I have all the documentation that I need."

"But why wouldn't I know this, if it were true?"

"It was Herr Maass' wish that you be raised as his own son, and never know the difference. He arranged for a private proceeding to make it legal, then he arranged to erase all record of it. I managed to find one record he couldn't erase, however. An entry was made into the national census."

"How did you come by such information?"

"Oh, I have ways," Dr. Mueller said. "I am not the only anti-Nazi in Germany, you know. And I'm certainly not the only one who is working to overthrow

Hitler's regime. There are many working with us. And soon, you will join us."

"No, I won't," Paul said.

"Come, Paul," Dr. Mueller said, using Paul's first name for the first time in this conversation. "Do you expect me to believe that you are in one hundred percent support of everything Hitler has ever done since he came to power?"

"Well, maybe not one hundred percent, but—"

"But what?" Dr. Mueller asked. "Are you going to say that he created jobs and saved Germany?"

"He did, didn't he?"

"Germany was saved by a world-wide economic recovery," Dr. Mueller said, "that would have occurred with or without Hitler. We would have enjoyed an economic recovery, but without plunging the world into war or the wholesale murder of Jews."

"The wholesale murder of Jews? Isn't that a bit of an overstatement?"

Dr. Mueller looked at Paul with an almost patronizing look. "Is it possible that you don't know?" he asked. "Is it really possible that you don't know at all?"

"I know that this government is repressionist as far as Jews go," Paul said, dismissing Dr. Mueller's comment with a little scoff. "But I wouldn't go so far as to say that they were committing the wholesale murder of Jews."

"What do you call it when thirty-five thousand Jews are marched to the edge of a ditch—men and women, and mothers carrying their children—and shot down in cold blood, then covered with dirt and quicklime?"

"I've never heard of such a thing happening," Paul said.

"It happened."

"Where?"

"In Russia," Dr. Mueller said. "At a place called Babi Yar."

"I don't believe it. That is merely propaganda put out by the Russians."

"It is true."

"How do I know you aren't Communist? If you are, you would believe anything your Communist masters in Russia tell you," Paul challenged.

Dr. Mueller smiled. "I have no Communist masters in Russia. I am a German and I am working for Germany. I didn't hear this from Russians, Herr Maass. I heard this from Germans, and the Germans I heard it from are not Communists either. Many of them started out to be good National Socialists, just as I did."

"But, how can this be true?" Paul asked. "The whole world would know if thirty-five thousand people were murdered in cold blood."

"It isn't thirty-five thousand," Dr. Mueller said. "That figure represents only those who were killed in one day at Babi Yar. To date, as nearly as we can determine, there have been more than a quarter of a million Jews systematically murdered."

"I can't believe it," Paul said. "This is staggering to the senses. Why don't you go to the authorities? Why don't you—"

Dr. Mueller laughed, a cold laugh, without humor. "Paul, my good man, have you not yet caught on to what I am saying? It is the *authorities* who are committing the murders!"

Paul sat down in his chair, stunned by the words he had just heard. Dr. Mueller opened his coat and took out two envelopes, one brown and one white.

"Here," he said. "In the white envelope, you will find the only paper in existence which identifies you as a Jew. It is a census report for the year 1914, in which it states that Paul Maass, the adopted son of Aaron Maass, was born of the Jew father, Jastrile Werfel. Destroy that, and you destroy any hold I have over you."

"Why are you giving it to me?" Paul asked.

"Because," Dr. Mueller said, "after you examine the contents in the brown envelope, I feel certain that you will help us of your own volition," Dr. Mueller touched his forehead in a salute. "I will be hearing from you," he said, as he left Paul's office.

Paul looked at the two envelopes. Inside the white envelope, as Dr. Mueller had said, was a document from the Imperial Government of the Kaiser's Germany, attesting to the fact that the man he had thought was his father all along was not his father at all. There, also, was the word which suddenly changed his entire life. *Jew.*

Paul slid the paper back into the envelope and lay it to one side, then opened the flap of the brown envelope. Inside was a packet of photographs.

The first photograph showed a stark field somewhere. The featureless prairie suggested that the picture was taken in the vast, open spaces of Russia. To the left of the picture was an S.S. trooper, taking careful aim with a rifle at a woman who was clutching a baby, no more than five meters away from the trooper.

Paul put it aside and looked at the next picture. In it, a man of about forty knelt at the edge of a large hole. In the hole below him were dozens of bodies with legs, feet and arms akimbo. The man who was kneeling had a look of resigned stoicism on his face, while behind him an S.S. trooper held a pistol inches away from the kneeling man's head. Behind the S.S. trooper were ten more S.S. men, looking on as if they were witnessing something as mundane as a card game rather than the execution of a human being.

That was followed by several more pictures of the same type—men linked together arm in arm at the edge of a common grave while their executioners stood behind them. Men, women and children stood totally naked, and in fear, as S.S. troopers nearby laughed and jeered.

And then there was a picture which affected him more than any other. A group of four women and three girls stood in front of a large pile of clothing, staring fearfully at the camera. The women were dressed in their underwear—three of them young and very pretty, and the fourth old, with hollow eyes and sunken cheeks, a grandmotherly type who would receive the offer of a seat from any gentleman in the world, if he encountered her on a trolley or bus, in fact, no different from the woman Paul had given his seat to and that very day. The two little girls had their faces hidden in the slips of the older women.

There were dozens of other photographs, piles of bodies, grotesquely thrown together so that it became one indistinguishable mass, bones, skulls, and one inexplicable picture of a severed hand.

A strange thing happened to Paul while he studied the photographs. One hour earlier, he had not even realized he was a Jew. When he found out, it was with a sense of disbelief, even resentment. Now, from some genetic imprint deep in his subconsciousness, he felt a keen sense of awareness of his Jewishness, and an outrage at the horror being visited upon people whose only crime was to be born as he was born, as a Jew. He also felt a sadness, a sadness more profound than all the sadnesses he had ever experienced in his entire life.

Paul took the brown envelope with him and left his office to go to the darkest recess of the great, empty hall. There, sitting in a dark corner all alone, Paul wept.

"Herr Direktor? Herr Direktor, are you in here?" Baumann called from just outside Paul's door. He knocked lightly and the door, which had not been completely shut, opened under his knock. *"Herr Direktor?"* he called again.

Baumann stepped into Paul's office. He wasn't here. It was just like him not to be here. He was the boy genius, the musical wonder who had won accolades all over Germany, and yet no one knew as well as Baumann that it wasn't Maass's direction which elicited the best from the orchestra—it was the leadership he, the concert-master provided. Everything was left to Baumann: the practice schedule, the distribution of the arrangements, the overseeing of the problems and petty squabbles the musicians had among themselves.

Maass couldn't handle those kinds of things . . . they were beneath him. Ha! Beneath him? Beyond him was more the case. Maass did not have the experience to handle them, so Baumann handled things for him. Baumann would like to see how well the orchestra would perform without the leadership of the concert-master. Perhaps one day he would call in sick, just before a critical concert, and let the boy genius see how it was to try and handle it alone.

But even as Baumann thought that, he knew he wouldn't actually do it. He had too much loyalty to the orchestra to do that. He should have been chosen as the orchestra conductor, everyone said so. He believed that it was a mark of his professionalism and dedication that he had not been petty about it when he was passed over for Paul Maass. He had stayed, doing what needed to be done, to insure that the orchestra perform well, despite the youth and inexperience of its leader.

Now, there was the concert of the wounded soldiers tomorrow afternoon. Herr Maass knew about the concert, but as yet had made no mention of what music was to be played. How could Baumann oversee the distribution of the arrangements, if he didn't even know what music was to be played?

"Herr Maass?" Baumann called again, though by now he was well inside the conductor's office, and knew that he wasn't here. Still, it made him feel somewhat uneasy to be in an office without being invited. There, he thought, on the corner of the desk. There is a small, white envelope. Perhaps the program for tomorrow's concert is in that envelope.

Baumann opened the envelope and pulled out the paper. At first he was confused by it, then, when he realized what it was he was shocked! The shock was followed by fear, then, after a moment, the fear was replaced by something else. There was an opportunity here, Baumann sensed. An excellent opportunity.

13

THE tank engine rumbled in the background. Rudi was afraid to shut it down, because it was so cold that he feared they wouldn't get it started again. The Pioneers had fixed a blade to the front of the tank, and used it to rip a hole in the cold Russian soil, big enough and deep enough to hold twelve of Rudi's men who had died during the night. They had died, not from enemy action, but from the bitter, freezing cold and the lack of warm clothing.

Rudi stood on the edge of the pit, looking at the pitiful pile of men. They were lying as they had died, frozen into the twisted, grotesque positions they had assumed to try and keep warm. Some were wrapped in curtains they had taken from Russian houses, and one bearded soldier, was wearing a beaded and sequined woman's coat. Rudi would have removed the garments for his other soldiers had it not been for the fact that they were frozen onto the bodies.

Kaspar was one of the men down there—young, eager Kaspar, who had driven the car for Rudi when they occupied the little Polish village, and who had taken the Polish woman with him as he reconnoitered the village, "looking for a vehicle park area". Kaspar had been through the victories in Poland, Belgium and France, and the early victories in Russia. Now he, like hundreds of thousands of his comrades, lay dead on the harsh Russian soil.

The German Army had been stopped short of Moscow when hundreds of thousands of fresh, well-armed, and well-clothed Russian troops swept down on them from Siberia. The massive Russian counter-attack caught the German High Command completely by surprise. They had believed the Russian army defeated and Moscow defenseless, and they reeled back under the attack, suffering tremendous losses, not only to the enemy, but to the weather.

Rudi had been present at many staff briefings when he heard the proposals and counter proposals put forth by the High Command.

"We must withdraw," some said. "We can withdraw to a safer position, then counter-attack in the spring."

"Withdraw to where?" another would ask. "We have no fixed withdrawal positions. Remember if you will, the *Grande Armée* of Napoleon. The withdrawal of the French became a full scale flight of panic. Would you have the *Wehrmacht* undergo that humiliation and suffer that loss?"

In the end the decision was made, not by the field commanders, but by the Supreme Commander himself, Adolf Hitler. Hitler's order was printed and distributed not only to the senior officers, but to every officer and man of the German Army, in order that the Führer's words may "inspire and lift the spirits" of the fighting men.

> *To Field Marshall von Rundstedt, and the German Officers and Men: I, along with the grateful German people, have watched your heroic battle in Russia with utmost trust in your bravery and dedication to duty. In your current situation there can be no consideration except holding fast, of not retreating one step, of hurling into battle every gun, every man, every round of ammunition. You must resolve yourself, for the national weal, to seek victory or death.*
>
> *ADOLF HITLER*

And so the German troops had dug in and struggled to hold. They were holding, Rudi thought, against impossible odds. Oddly enough, as he stood here watching the dirt and snow pushed back over Kaspar and the others who lay frozen in the bottom of the common grave, he felt a sense of pride in the German Army which transcended even the pride he had felt during the victorious days in Poland and France. The German Army was proving to the world that they could fight not only when conditions were perfect, but when conditions were unbelievably bad, as well.

Rudi pulled the Russian private soldier's coat about him, and ran through the litany of troubles in his mind. They were outnumbered, and fighting on the enemy's home soil. German soldiers were freezing to death, and those who weren't dying were suffering from frostbite and other exposure problems. But it wasn't only the men who suffered. The bitter cold affected guns and machines as well. Ice jammed up the tank tracks, and the fuel and oil congealed, not only in the vehicles, but in the guns. The telescopic gunsights were useless, and even had they worked, many of the guns were frozen so solid that they couldn't be fired. And still the army held.

"Lieutenant," Sergeant Heibler called down to Rudi. Heibler was standing on a small elevation, looking out across a frozen plain toward a woodline, far in the distance. He was standing lookout during the burial.

"Yes," Rudi called back. "What is it?"

"Russkis, Lieutenant. They're moving out across the field." Sergeant Heibler pointed with an arm which protruded from beneath a woolen blanket, and Rudi scrambled up to the ridge to see for himself. At first he saw nothing except a field of snow. Then, after a second, he realized that some of the snow was moving. Troops, dressed in snow-camouflage white, were coming across the field toward them. There were hundreds of them!

"My God!" Rudi said, lowering the binoculars. "Where did they come from?"

"That's not the problem," Sergeant Heibler answered quietly. "The problem is, where are we going? They are between us and our headquarters."

Rudi sighed. "Sergeant Heibler, I'm not even certain we *have* a headquarters anymore," he said. He looked back toward the burial detail. There were seven of them, including the four men who made up the tank crew.

"We could all crowd onto the tank," one of the men suggested.

"No," Rudi said. "We'd be sitting ducks. They'd pounce on the tank in a—wait a minute." Rudi rubbed his chin with his hand, and looked back toward the common grave. "Sergeant, we have to dig up some of our men."

"I beg your pardon, sir?"

"Dig 'em up, Sergeant," Rudi said. "I need four men."

"What are you going to do?" one of the others started, but Sergeant Heibler cut him off with an impatient command. "Do as your officer commands you," he said, and he led the detail in pulling away the dirt and snow which had not had time to freeze again. Within a moment, four German bodies, still frozen in their crouched position, were lying beside the grave.

"Now," Rudi said. "You," he pointed to the tank driver. "Get the tank up onto the ridge and depress the gun as far as you can. Open fire on the advancing troops."

"Lieutenant, if we fire from the ridge, we'll be silhouetted against the skyline. We'll be an easy target," the driver protested.

"That's what I want," Rudi said. "Fire no more than two rounds, then put them in there." Rudi pointed to the frozen bodies. "If we are lucky, the Russians will hit the tank and by the time they get here, they'll just see four burning corpses. They may think that was all of us, and it'll give us a chance to get away."

"I hate to do this to our dead comrades," one of the soldiers said.

Rudi noticed that one of the four bodies was Kaspar. "Put Kaspar behind the gun," he said. "He always wanted to be a tank gunner instead of a scout-car driver. Now he shall get his wish."

The tank moved into position on the ridge, and the gunner fired two quick rounds. The sound of the gun was amazingly loud in the stillness of the afternoon, and after the second round was fired, its sound rolled

back in a distinct echo from the distant trees. Rudi
watched the shells explode in the midst of the approaching soldiers, and was gratified to see that one of
them, at least, had some effect.

"Load the bodies quickly and let's get out of here,"
Rudi commanded, and the gunner and loader scrambled out of the tank, while the others dropped the
frozen bodies down through the hatch. The first Russian artillery round burst on them just seconds after
the bodies were loaded, and the fourth round scored
a direct hit on the tank. It went up with a whoosh, and
Rudi turned to look back at it as the brilliant red-
orange fire and black smoke rolled up against the white
background.

Suddenly Rudi felt a scaring, burning pain in his
thigh, and then he was lying on the crisp, white snow,
watching, almost disinterestedly, as the snow began
to turn a bright crimson from his blood. Why was he
lying down? What was he doing in the snow?

Sound and vision dimmed and the initial shock of
pain gave way as a warming numbness spread through
his body. Sergeant Heibler came running back toward
him.

"What happened?" Rudi asked Heibler. "Why am
I down here?"

"You were hit with a piece of shrapnel, sir," Heibler
said. He bent down and scooped Rudi up in his arms.

"What are you doing?" Rudi asked.

"I've got to get you out of here."

Rudi was a good-sized man, but Sergeant Heibler
picked him up as if he had been a child.

"Thank you, Sergeant," Rudi said in a silly sort
of formality, as if the sergeant had just given him a
cigarette.

Another Russian shell burst nearby, and Rudi

could hear the angry buzz of shrapnel as jagged pieces of metal spread out in a lethal fountain. He watched the little smoking pieces, as if watching a fireworks display. Sergeant Heibler continued to run, but finally the snow and Rudi's weight became more than he could handle. After several steps Heibler tripped and fell, sending both of them sprawling.

"I'm sorry, Lieutenant, I'm sorry," Heibler apologized in horror.

"Think nothing of it," Rudi said easily, calmly. He couldn't understand why Sergeant Heibler was so concerned. He wished Sergeant Heibler would just stop running. Why couldn't both of them just stop running for a while and sit down here to rest? He outranked Sergeant Heibler. He would just order him to stop running.

Rudi could hear voices now, strange sounding voices. They were Russian voices.

"They are close," Heibler said, breathing heavily. Heibler looked around and saw a wrecked truck. "Here," he said, pulling and dragging Rudi. "Get under the truck."

"Get under the truck?" Rudi replied. "No, we must make a stand."

"Damnit, Lieutenant, I've no time to argue. Get under the truck," Heibler said, and he shoved Rudi under the truck, shoving him so roughly that Rudi felt a sharp pain return to his thigh. With the return of pain, came also the return of awareness, and now Rudi was acutely aware of the situation, and what the sergeant was doing for him.

"Get out of here," Rudi said, and the tone of his voice was such that Heibler knew Rudi was under control again.

"In a moment," Heibler said. "First, I've got to

hide you." Rudi wondered what Heibler was doing, as he struggled with the snow, then he realized that the Sergeant was building up the snow pile so that Rudi would be concealed. Rudi helped from inside, and in just a few seconds the snow wall was finished.

"I'll be back," Heibler whispered harshly. "I promise you, I'll be back."

Rudi heard Sergeant Heibler leave, then he lay there, feeling a warmth begin to diffuse over his body. He didn't know if the warmth came from the numbness of the wound, from the snugness of the igloo built for him, or if it was the first sign of dying by freezing. Whatever the cause of the warmth, Rudi welcomed it. Even if he were dying, it would be good to have a momentary respite from the bitter cold.

Rudi lay for over an hour, clutching the pistol with a round in the chamber, ready to fire if need be. The Russian soldiers were all around, he could hear them, talking and laughing among themselves. One of the soldiers leaned his rifle against the overturned truck, then Rudi heard the sound of water spattering on the snow, and he realized that the Russian soldier was relieving himself at the truck. A second later another soldier joined the first, and then another, so that by unspoken agreement, the truck was turned into a urinal point.

"*Toten Deutsch*," One of the soldiers laughed, saying the words "Kill German" in German. The effect of hearing his own language spoken so close by almost shocked Rudi into giving himself away.

After a while, the strong smell of the urine drifted in beneath the truck and joined with the smell of Rudi's own blood, and it made him sick. He couldn't keep from puking, and he was afraid that the sound of his retching would attract them to him, but it didn't.

Finally the Russian soldiers left, and Rudi lay still for what seemed an eternity. He drifted in and out of consciousness, and fought the cold and the pain. Several times he contemplated shooting himself, and once he even went so far as to put the barrel of the pistol in his mouth. He hesitated, only because he was afraid that the wound would not be fatal, then he would be in worse shape than he was now, and unable to do anything about it.

It was dark, and Rudi dozed off. He heard the sound of digging, and his eyes came open and he stared at the wall of snow in fear. Slowly and quietly he raised the pistol and pointed it at the wall. He was frightened, and with every nerve in his body he wanted to pull the trigger now, to shoot through the snow, but he managed to hold that impulse in check. Finally the digger broke through the snow, and Rudi saw the dark outline of a man's head peering through.

"Lieutenant Rodl, are you all right?" a voice called, and Rudi saw Heibler's big silly grin, looking in at him.

"You've come back," was all Rudi could say.

Heibler had constructed a travois, and he placed Rudi on it as gently as a mother would a baby. The night passed in a blur of images, sounds, and pains. Rudi had moments of consciousness, when he would feel the pain and the cold, then there would be long periods of unconsciousness when he would feel nothing and be aware of nothing. There were periods of hiding; once Rudi came to only to feel Heibler's hand clamped securely over his mouth to prevent him from crying out, and he was vaguely aware of the passage of several Russian soldiers nearby. Then there would be the traveling—long, tiring periods of motion with Heibler plodding along, never complaining, rarely speaking, stopping only periodically to look at Rudi's wound or to adjust the coat around him. And then after one particularly long period of unconsciousness, Rudi opened his eyes to see Major Kant staring down at him, smiling at him, and he knew that he was back with his own headquarters.

"You are a lucky man," Major Kant said.

"To have survived?"

"No, that wasn't luck, my friend, that was Sergeant Heibler. The luck comes from the fact that you are going home tomorrow."

"What? I'm going home? Why? Is my wound that serious?" Rudi asked, surprised by Major Kant's announcement.

"Not really," Kant said. "But there's a Ju-52 flying back to Germany in the morning, and the orders are to take back a load of wounded. You got wounded at the right place and at the right time."

"Sergeant Heibler? Where is he?"

"Back on the line," Kant said.

"I wanted to thank him," Rudi said.

"You already did."

"I want to thank him again," Rudi insisted. "And Ernst, I'd like to put him in for the Iron Cross, First Class."

"Impossible."

"Impossible? What do you mean, impossible? Damn-it, man, he saved my life!"

"His records are stamped 19th Infantry. You know what that means. No member of the 19th Infantry will ever be given a medal or a promotion above the rank they now hold."

"Heibler was only doing his duty when he raided the beer hall that day," Rudi protested.

"It's not my rule," Kant said. "It's Hitler's rule."

"Hitler's rule?" Rudi said.

"Yes."

"The same Hitler who says we are not to withdraw one foot from the Russian advance?" Rudi asked. "The same Hitler who used the trains which could have brought us winter equipment and clothes to haul Jews out of Russia? Is that the Hitler you are talking about?"

"Rudi, be careful," Kant cautioned him.

Rudi looked around the field hospital, at the other wounded soldiers who lay swathed in various degrees of bandaging.

"Don't worry, Ernst," Rudi said. "This is a hospital for men who were wounded in battle. There are only soldiers in here, there are no S.S. The Jews don't shoot back."

Kant looked over the other men as well, then he turned back to face Rudi and Rudi could see an expression in Kant's eyes, as if Kant had already resigned himself to an acceptance of his fate.

"We are soldiers, Rudi," Kant said quietly. "We do not have the right to question the orders our superiors send down."

"Not even when those orders cost us the lives of our men?" Rudi challenged.

"Men are killed in battle," Kant said. "That is the nature of war."

"Killed in battle, all right," Rudi said. "That we can expect as soldiers. But there is no justification for letting us freeze to death because of incompetence bordering on insanity."

"But what can we do about it, Rudi, you and I?" Kant asked.

And that was the crux of it, Rudi thought. There was nothing he, a junior officer, could do to alter the situation by one whit. He did not have it in his power to clothe one soldier, or provide one hot meal. And now he was about to be out of it entirely, for tomorrow he would be flying back to Germany.

Rudi thought of the last time he had gone back to Germany. He had returned as a conquering hero, fresh from victory in Poland. There had been a picnic in his honor, and his family was excited because they had been visited by Hitler. It was warm then. That was in the summer of 1940, less than two years ago. Was it that short a time? It seemed decades ago.

There were 22 people on the three-engined Junkers transport as it winged its way back to Germany. Up front there were the two pilots, and in the cabin, there were two doctors, walking up and down the aisle between the stretchers which were placed in a double deck along each side. There were eighteen stretchers, and in one of those stretchers Rudi lay. Rudi was on the lower stretcher, which was good, because it allowed him to look through the window.

"How are we feeling?" one of the doctors asked, stopping by Rudi's stretcher and putting his hand on Rudi's forehead.

"We are feeling fine," Rudi said quietly and without expression.

"Good, good," the doctor said. "That is good." The doctor moved to the next stretcher and asked the same question, to receive the same noncommittal answer, and he responded in the same way. "Good, good, that is good."

Rudi listened to the doctor's, "good, good," float up the aisle, until the worthy doctor moved far enough away so that the constant drone of the three engines drowned him out. Rudi turned and looked out across the gray-black, corrugated wing, over the black cross on the wing tip, and down to the gently rolling, snow-covered terrain below. Were they still over Russia? Would Russian fighters come swooping down on them from out of the sky?

Below, Rudi could see a small house. It was all alone, miles away from the next nearest structure. Who lived there? Were they ever lonely? Why would anyone want to live in such isolation? Had they been touched by the war, or had the war passed them by?

"How are we doing?" the good doctor asked again, again putting his hand to Rudi's forehead.

"We are doing fine," Rudi answered.

"Ah good, good," the doctor replied. "That is good."

14

ON the night of April 20, 1937, at exactly
the hour of midnight, Manfried Lange, a poet who
had never sold a line of verse, cloaked all his frus-
trations in a black and silver uniform and stood, along
with 213 other black-clad young men, to become an
officer of the *Schutzstaffel*. The *Schutzstaffel* was Hitler's elite protection corps, better known as the S.S.

The ceremony in which Lange was inducted was
like many other ceremonies which had taken place
during the '30s and early '40s. It took place in flicker-
ing torchlight amidst symbols and artifacts of Teu-
tonic mythology, and Lange and the others took a solemn oath, not to their country, but to Adolf Hitler.

> *I swear to you Adolf Hitler,*
> *As Führer and Chancellor of the German Reich,*
> *Fidelity and Valor.*
> *I swear to you and to the superiors*
> *whom you may appoint*
> *Obedience unto death,*
> *So help me God.*

Though it was conceived as a guard unit, the S.S., under the direction of Heinrich Himmler, became an empire within a state, and busied itself with dozens of roles. It had a police force in the dreaded Gestapo, and an intelligence division in the S.D. The S.S. ran the labor and concentration camps, and did genealogical research to ensure the purity of German racial quality. It published newspapers and conducted human breeding farms, and collected data on such things as astrology, phrenology, Teutonic-knight rituals, classification and ranking of human skulls, alchemy, and the production of racially acceptable food. S.S. members did not escape the organization, even in death, for the S.S. had selected and validated Valhalla sites for their dead.

Lange had taken eagerly to the ideology and the rites of the S.S., and his blond and handsome features had served him well. He was a favorite of photographers, and his picture had appeared in many newspapers and magazines within the Reich.

Lange served the S.S. well in Poland, receiving a letter of commendation from the *Obersturmbannführer* who was immediately over him in the *Einsatzgruppen* to which he was assigned.

To: Obersturmführer *Manfried Lange*
Einsatzgruppen D (4)
April 20, 1940
  It is with a great deal of pride that I personally commend you for your dedication to duty in carrying out your difficult assignment with this command. You personally commanded a special task squad which settled accounts with 1,893 Jews, bandits and sub-humans by method of extermination.

An examination of the bodies after the operation showed that the extermination was carried out in a humane and civilized manner. This is particularly evidenced by the decreased amount of feces, urine, and the lack of convulsive reaction in the facial features of the deceased.

> *Heil Hitler*
> Martin Reichart
> S.S. Obersturmbannführer
> *Einsatzgruppen D (4) Commanding*

After Lange's successful foray into Poland, he followed the *Wehrmacht* into Belgium and France, where his main duty was the location and identification of Jews who were trying to conceal their identity and race.

In Paris, Lange made a startling discovery. He could identify those people who were tainted with Jewish blood, no matter how clever their disguise and how non-Jewish their looks, by their reaction to art. Lange had only to expose a subject to a painting, piece of sculpture, music or poetry, observe his reaction, then determine his racial makeup.

He applied this new-found technique to many suspects while he was in Paris, and was sufficiently convinced of its success that he wrote a letter detailing his discovery to S.S. *Reichsführer* Himmler himself.

"Though it may seem startling," he wrote, "the principle differs not from the Rohrshach test, which as you know, *Reichsführer*, is a test of personality in which a subject's interpretations of abstract designs are analyzed as a measure of emotional and intellectual functioning. The Rohrshach is now widely accepted by educated men all over the world. It is not difficult then, to believe one could apply a measurement to the reaction, not to abstract, but to concrete forms, such as art. I have realized a 93.2% success ratio in the application of this system, the figures substantiated by further interrogation in the usual controlled-pain application method.

"I now request that this method of Jew determination be instituted throughout the S.S. sphere of influence, as it will determine quickly and accurately whether or not a person is a Jew, and it will do so without the unpleasant side effects of inducing pain to extract a confession."

Lange's idea was not adopted throughout the S.S., but Himmler, who was always looking for something new and different, thought it was a good enough idea to warrant further investigation. Himmler promoted Lange to *Sturmbannführer*, and moved him back to Germany to carry out his experiments. Himmler conceived of a most unique way for Lange to conduct his trials. Lange was placed in command of a Lebensborn home in the village of Gildersheim, very near Schweinfurt.

A Lebensborn home was a maternity home, where young women who were endorsed as biologically flawless and racially pure, were sent to mate with S.S. officers. This was done in an effort to bring about a great increase in the number of Aryan children born to the Reich. Lange, as commander of one of the homes, had the task of subjecting the young women to a screening for possible Jewish pollution, and then certifying them as pure and worthy of cohabitation with members of the S.S.

An added benefit of which Lange frequently availed himself was the unlimited visitation rights to any member of the home who was not more than three months pregnant. Those whose pregnancy had already gone into the fourth month were given special treatment to ensure the safe, healthy birth of their child. They were provided with a special diet, they had no duties to perform, and they had private, clean rooms.

When the German Army invaded Russia, Lange made application to go, but the application was turned down by the *Reichsführer*, who insisted that Lange continue with his work. Lange, who may have impregnated as many as fifteen of the "Little Blonde Sisters," as the residents of the home were known, answered that he would, of course, continue to serve the Führer in whatever capacity was most fitting for him, and would remain at his post. His heart, he insisted, was in the field with Germany's fighting men.

Lange had been at the Lebensborn Home for over a year, but not since the previous summer had he made an effort to leave and return to the field. He told all who would listen that he had been stuck here by the personal orders of Himmler, and during the long, cold winter when reports managed to filter back about the terrible conditions under which the Germans in Russia were serving, he added several more lumps of coal to the roaring fire in the stove in his office, and declared that he should be in the field with his comrades, sharing their hardships and dangers as he had shared them in Poland, Belgium and France. He made the declaration often, but only verbally. He never submitted another application.

Lange opened the door to the stove and poked around at the burning coals with the long, iron poker, until the flames blazed up again, then he closed the door and walked back over to his desk and sat down. He felt a satiation in his groin, because less than thirty minutes ago he had done his duty by one of the newest "Little Blonde Sisters" of the home. She had papers which stated that she was eighteen, but Lange knew she was only sixteen. She had been sent there by her widowed mother, whose husband had died in Russia, and who was unable to adequately care for a sixteen-year-old daughter on a widow's pension.

The girl had been a virgin, and she bled a little and whimpered a little, and gave absolutely no indication that she had enjoyed his visit at all. Lange was a handsome man who knew of his appeal to women, and the fact that the young girl had not been able to recognize that and show gratitude for his visit, had angered him, so he took it out on her by using her roughly, despite her tender years and virgin flesh. Her whimpers of pain merely excited him on to greater fury. Virgins, he thought derisively as he left. Who needs them? He'd take a woman with experience over a virgin anytime. Still, the moment was not without a certain animalistic appeal.

There was a light knock on Lange's door, and he sighed and turned his mind back to business. Though this job did have its compensations, Lange was certain that no one knew of its demands. He had to render innumerable reports, not only on the actual administration of the home, but on the progress of his special project as well. Now there was no doubt another job which only he could satisfy.

"Yes," Lange called.

Lange's first sergeant opened the door and stepped into the room, clicked his heels and saluted sharply.

"Yes, Ebert, what is it?"

"Excuse me, *Sturmbannführer*," the first sergeant said. "But there is a Concert Master Baumann here to speak with you."

"Concert Master Baumann? I know no such person."

"The guard who escorted him brought this letter, sir," Ebert said, handing an envelope across the desk to Lange, who opened it and looked at it closely. The letter was on the stationery of *Brigadeführer* Proust, Chief of Sensitive Matters.

To: Sturmbannführer *Manfried Lange*
  Project Officer, Jewish Identification via art reaction.

The man I have sent you is one Otto Baumann, Concert Master for the Schweinfurt Symphony Orchestra. Herr Baumann is making a claim that the Director of the Orchestra, Paul Maass, is a Jew, and he has a census form which may substantiate his claim. This is a most sensitive matter for the following reasons:

(1) Director Maass has performed special concerts for the Führer on past occasions, and the Führer has gone on record as saying that Maass is the most brilliant young conductor in the entire Reich. One can see the embarrassing condition this would place the Führer in, should Baumann's claim be substantiated. Chancellor Hitler has frequently spoken in a most critical fashion of all Jewish musicians and conductors.

(2) Director Maass is known to be engaged to Fraulein Lisl Rodl. Fraulein Rodl is the daughter of Herr Heinrich Rodl, Director-General of the I.G.N. Kugelwerks Ballbearing Factory in Schweinfurt. Herr Rodl was one of Hitler's earliest financial supporters, and as an industrialist, is of tremendous importance to the war aims of the Third Reich. Fraulein Rodl's brother, Rudi, is the holder of the Iron Cross First Class, and

was wounded, while fighting in Russia. And lastly, Fraulein Rodl herself, an exceptionally pretty woman, is a favorite of the Chancellor's, having recently been an honored guest at the Berghof.
(3) For obvious reasons, it would be to the advantage of the Third Reich to validate the biological purity of Director Maass. The document held by Herr Baumann seems to substantiate Baumann's claim, but this document may be falsified, motivated by Baumann's desire to succeed to the Directorship of the Orchestra, should Director Maass be discredited and removed. Your artistic screening method would be of sufficient proof to validate Herr Maass's racial purity, and thus justify the Führer's statements as to the talent of Herr Maass.

I gave the guard this letter in a sealed state. Neither he nor Baumann are aware of the contents, believing only that the matter has been referred to you for further disposition. Please assign this your top priority, and get back to me at once with your findings.

> *Heil Hitler*
> *Stefan Proust*
> *S.S. Brigadeführer*
> *Chief, Sensitive Matters*

Lange felt a thrilling leap of his heart as he read the letter. So, now he was going to be able to put his theory to work in a matter of the greatest national importance! Surely there would be the greatest recognition for his ability, and an immediate promotion as a result of his special talent.

There was something about one of the names in the letter which stirred his memory. Rodl! Lieutenant

Rudi Rodl, the Panzer Officer he had known in Belgium. Yes, he remembered him now. He had seen pictures of Rodl's sister. She was a beautiful woman.

"Send in Baumann," Lange said.

"*Jawohl*," the first sergeant said.

Baumann came in a moment later, a meek little man, holding his hat in his hand and keeping his head down, looking up at Lange from a position of subservience.

"Do you realize the significance of your implication?" Lange asked.

"Yes, I understand," Baumann said meekly.

"Director Maass has been acclaimed by the Führer as one of the most talented musicians in all of Germany. By the *Führer*!" Lange shouted.

"Yes," Baumann said.

"And yet you have the audacity to make the accusation that this man is a Jew."

"The document, *Sturmbannführer*," Baumann said. "I discovered the document—"

"Ah, yes, you discovered the document," Lange taunted. "And in so discovering it, thought you had found a method of advancing yourself, is that it?"

"No, *Sturmbannführer*," Baumann mumbled. "I was merely doing what I thought was my duty. I thought it was my responsibility to bring this information to the proper authorities."

"Yes, yes," Lange said. "Well, this is as it should be. You did the proper thing."

"You will investigate this?" Baumann asked.

"Yes, of course I will investigate this," Lange said.

"And I," Baumann said, now licking his lips and gaining a bit more courage as it became obvious that Lange was going to look into it, "will I be rewarded?"

"Rewarded, Herr Baumann?" Lange asked, smiling

now at a private thought. "Yes, you will be rewarded. Wait in the outerchamber. I shall speak with Sergeant Ebert about your reward."

"I . . . I seek no money," Baumann explained. "I seek only justice for the Reich, and, of course, the opportunity to serve the Reich in whatever capacity in which I may be capable."

"Such as Director of the Orchestra?" Lange asked.

Baumann now found enough courage to smile. "Yes," he said, glad that he and Lange were finally on the same wave length. "Yes, of course. I should be only too happy to serve in that capacity."

Baumann left Lange's office to wait in the anteroom, just as the First Sergeant came in to answer Lange's call.

"*Ja, Herr Sturmbannführer?*"

"This man, Baumann," Lange said. "Take him out and have him shot at once."

"*Jawohl, Sturmbannführer,*" First Sergeant Ebert answered without blinking an eye.

15

"I am told that I shall always have a limp, but when one considers the alternative, a limp isn't all that bad," Rudi said. "Besides, it might help with the girls. You know, a romantic symbol, like a scar from a dueling fraternity." Rudi patted his right leg, which was in a heavy cast. The cast was suspended by weights and pulleys from a contraption on the ceiling above Rudi's bed.

Lisl was sitting in a chair beside his bed, dressed in a dark green skirt and a deep red sweater. She had come to the military hospital in Wertheim to visit her brother, and she brought not only a splash of color to the interior of the hospital, but a vision of loveliness, for she was clearly the most beautiful visitor the hospital had received in some time. Rudi couldn't help but notice the steady procession of all the ambulatory patients by the door of his room. Each found an excuse to stop and look inside.

"They won't believe you are my sister," Rudi said with a small laugh. "They will think I am just being possessive of you, to keep you to myself."

"Well, just let them believe what they wish." Lisl said. She reached over and brushed a lock of Rudi's hair away from his forehead. "Anyway, what difference does it make to us? You are back from Russia now, and that's all that is important."

Rudi got a far-away look in his eyes. "There are thousands who aren't back, and many thousands more who will never make it back."

"But we are winning, aren't we?" Lisl asked anxiously. "I mean, all the newspapers say we are winning."

Rudi looked at Lisl, and in that moment she wasn't his sister at all, but merely one of "them." "Them" was anyone who wasn't a part of that fraternity of close-knit men who had served on the Russian front. Lisl and the others like her did not understand, and could not understand, even if someone explained to them what it was really like. A screen dropped across Rudi's eyes, and though Lisl didn't see it and didn't realize it, she was, at that moment, effectively shut out of that part of Rudi's soul which only had room for those who knew and understood.

"Yes," Rudi said flatly. "We are winning."

"Oh," Lisl said, breathing a sigh of relief. "You had me worried there for just a moment. You know, there has been some defeatist talk going around, rumors about such things as our army retreating in Russia, rumors that we will withdraw from the country this summer. I've had letters from Eva, such talk disturbs the Führer. I wonder where such rumors get started?"

"I have no idea," Rudi said easily.

"Was it bad there? I mean, the cold and all? They say Russia gets awfully cold in the winter."

"It was cold," Rudi said.

There was a knock on the door, and Rudi and Lisl

looked toward the door to see a tall, handsome S.S.
Officer standing there, looking in at them.

"So, Lieutenant Rodl, here you are," the S.S. officer
said stepping into the room with a pleasant smile on
his face. "When I heard that an old friend of mine, an
old comrade from past battles, had been wounded, I
hurried at once to call. How are you doing?"

"*Hauptsturmführer* Lange," Rudi said in surprise.
"What are you doing here?"

"It isn't captain anymore," Lange said, pointing to
his insignia of rank. "As you can see, I have been promoted to *Sturmbannführer*. That's equal to a major
in the Army."

"Yes," Rudi said. "Excuse me."

Lange looked at Lisl, clicked his heels together gal-
lantly, and reached for her hand. He brought it to his
lips. "And this must be your beautiful sister, Fraulein
Lisl Rodl. Surely, Fraulein, the words of praise of
your beauty do not do you justice. And now I see
why. You are more beautiful than mere words can
describe."

Lisl smiled, and despite herself blushed at the
excessive flattery. "I—I thank you," she said. "You are
too kind."

"It is certainly easy to understand why the Führer
would have wanted you as a special weekend guest,"
Lange went on.

"You . . . you *know* that I was a guest of the Führer's?" Lisl asked, surprised by Lange's comment.

"My dear, I am an S.S. Officer in a position of no
little importance," Lange said. "I am aware of everything that goes on in this district." He smiled once
again at Rudi. "That is why when I heard that my
old friend and comrade-in-arms, Rudi Rodl, had been
wounded on the Russian front, I came here."

"You know, it's funny, Major, but I never really remembered us as being such good friends," Rudi said sarcastically, remembering the argument they once had in a Belgium café.

"Rudi!" Lisl scolded. "Rudi, now is that any way to be? Major Lange came all the way down here to see you, and you say such a thing?"

Lange laughed easily. "Ahh, don't worry about it, Fraulein Rodl. Lieutenant Rodl has the combat soldier's right of caustic comment. How well I remember my own days of combat when I, too, was set apart from the rest of the world. Now," Lange sighed, "now I have been promoted to a duty which is more demanding to be sure, but certainly less satisfying than an assignment in the battlefield."

"Well, I apologize for my brother if he won't apologize for himself," Lisl said.

"You are most gracious," Lange replied. "By the way, did you come from Schweinfurt on the train?"

"Yes, of course."

"Then, perhaps you shall accept an invitation to ride back with me?" Lange suggested. He looked down modestly toward his tunic and removed an imaginary piece of lint. "One of the nice things about my present assignment is that I do have a car at my disposal, and as I shall be going back through Schweinfurt anyway, I would be more than happy to take you home."

"I'm sure my sister would not wish to put you out," Rudi said.

"Rudi, I can answer for myself," Lisl said quickly, showing a small degree of pique at Rudi's usurpation of her prerogative.

"Then you will ride with me?" Lange asked hopefully.

"I appreciate your offer, Major," Lisl said. She

looked at the pained expression on her brother's face. "But perhaps I had best decline."

Lange smiled easily, and bowed slightly toward Lisl. "Very well, I shall return alone, the more lonely because of the thought of the beautiful lady who might have been my travelling companion." He turned toward Rudi's bed, clicked his heels together, and thrust his hand out in the Nazi salute. "*Heil Hitler!*"

Rudi raised his hand from the elbow, returning the salute, but he said nothing.

"Rudi, you were absolutely rude to the Major," Lisl said, after Lange left.

"He isn't a Major, he is a *Sturmbannführer*," Rudi said with a derisive twist of his mouth. "That is an S.S. rank, not an Army rank."

"But isn't that the same as a Major in the German Army?" Lisl asked.

"It depends on how you look at it," Rudi said. "By my ranking, it's three notches lower than the lowest-ranking private in the German Army."

"How can you say that about someone as handsome as the *Sturmbannführer?*" Lisl said, and she smiled to try to tease Rudi into a better mood.

"Do you think he is handsome?" Rudi asked, surprised by his sister's comment.

"Of course," Lisl said. "Who wouldn't think he is handsome?"

"Paul might not think he is handsome," Rudi said, and Lisl laughed. Rudi laughed with her, and the temporary tension which had developed between the two of them broke.

"You are correct," Lisl said. "Paul would find it difficult."

"How is Paul doing now?"

"He is troubled," Lisl said. "He has a concert scheduled for this weekend and his concert master, Herr Baumann, hasn't been seen in five days."

"Where is he?"

"That's just it," Lisl said. "No one seems to know. It is all very mysterious. Paul has gone to the police but they have done nothing. No one in the orchestra has heard from Herr Baumann. Even Baumann's family knows nothing of his whereabouts. Paul is going to appoint a new concert master this week."

"And mother and father?" Rudi asked. "Are they still doing well?"

"Yes," Lisl said. "They are both doing very well. Mama is enjoying her position as plotter for the air defense. She says it is exciting to be able to talk to our pilots while they are actually in the sky flying attacks against the bombers." Lisl laughed. "You know, it's positively a wicked thing to say, but I believe Mama is actually *enjoying* the war. Well, that part of it, anyway. Before the war she was relegated to the position of 'Frau Rodl'. Now, she is *Valkyrie*."

"Valkyrie?"

"It's her radio call sign," Lisl said. "Isn't that ironic? In Norse mythology, Valkyrie is the goddess who selects the warriors to die, and escorts them into Valhalla. Mama is aware of the symbolic nature of her code name, and she confesses that sometimes it gives her a chill just to think about it—especially as the pilots she talks to could be killed that same day."

"What about the plant?" Rudi asked. "Has production been going smoothly?"

"You know how little Papa speaks of his problems," Lisl said. "I do know he has experienced occasional transportation problems. The trains have been diverted by the needs of the war, so that sometimes he is late getting material. But he understands the priority of the front, so he doesn't complain too much."

"If he only knew about the trains," Rudi mumbled.

"What do you mean?" Lisl asked innocently.

"Nothing," Rudi said. "I was just thinking out loud."

"Oh, and last week one of the rolling machines had to be taken apart and cleaned, then put together again. That slowed things down by three days. There was sugar in the oil bath," Lisl laughed. "Can you imagine that? How on earth would sugar get into an oil bath?"

"Someone put it there, of course," Rudi said.

"But why?"

"To sabotage the plant."

Lisl gasped and put her hand to her mouth. "Rudi, you don't mean someone purposely tried to damage papa's plant?"

"But I do mean that," Rudi said. "Lisl in case you haven't noticed it with your visit to Hitler's mountain resort and your concerts and parties, there *is* a war on, and there are people who would like to see Germany destroyed."

"Well, our enemies, yes, but—"

"Some of those enemies are among us," Rudi said.

"I don't understand," Lisl said. "I just don't understand how a loyal German could do such a thing. It's disgraceful."

"Nowadays, there are many Germans disgracing themselves," Rudi said, ominously.

Out in the hall of the hospital a bell rang, and Lisl looked toward the door. "Oh dear," she said. "That's the signal for all the visitors to leave, isn't it?"

"I'm afraid it is," Rudi said. He reached for Lisl's hand. "Thank you, Lisl, for coming by to see me today."

"I will try to come again," Lisl promised, and she leaned over to plant a light kiss on Rudi's lips.

Outside it was bright and warm, and birds warbled in cheery contrast to the gloominess of the inside of the hospital. Here, also, several soldiers were sitting in wheelchairs taking in the air, attended to by uniformed nurses, and they looked at Lisl with expressions of frank approval as she passed by. Lisl smiled prettily at them, and walked on through the flower garden, bright with color, to the trolley stop where she would catch the trolley to the train station.

"Fraulein Rodl?"

Lisl was startled by the fact that someone called her name and she stopped and looked around to see Major Lange standing beside his car.

"Major Lange?"

"I wanted to extend you my offer for a ride one more time," Lange said easily.

"Major, I'm embarrassed," Lisl said. "You've been so nice, and you've gone to such trouble, and yet again, I feel I must refuse."

"Why, because of your brother?"

"Yes," Lisl said. She gave a small laugh. "I must apologize for him again, I don't know why he was so rude. I don't remember Rudi as a rude person."

"Battle often does that to men," Lange said. "I quite understand your desire to honor your brother's wishes, particularly because he is a wounded hero. However, what your brother doesn't know won't hurt him, and I feel now that I must tell you, there is another ulterior reason, for my asking you to ride with me."

"Really, Major? And what would that be?"

"It concerns Herr Maass," Lange said. Now the smile, and the friendly manner left, and he looked at

Lisl through narrowed eyes. "It is not good, Fraulein Rodl. It is not good at all."

"What?" Lisl asked, gasping in quick fear. "Major, what are you saying? Has there been an accident? Has Paul been hurt?"

"Not yet," Lange said, "but he may be."

Lisl got a puzzled expression on her face. "I don't understand, Major Lange."

"Please, get in the car," Lange said. "It is something better discussed in privacy."

Now Lisl made no protests, but got into the car quickly, and sat quietly as Lange started, then drove away. She said nothing until they were on the autobahn. Finally she spoke.

"All right, Major, I have come with you. Now tell me what danger Paul faces."

"Paul Maass is a Jew," Lange said.

"What? Don't be ridiculous," Lisl scoffed. "Paul's father was a well known—"

"Clockmaker," Lange interrupted. "His name was Jastrile Werfel."

"That was the father of Paul's brother," Lisl said. She sighed. "I knew that couldn't be kept secret, but that really has nothing to do with Paul. You see, Hans Werfel, the famous scientist—"

"The famous Jew," Lange spat out.

"Yes, well, Hans Werfel and Paul share the same mother, who is not Jew. But Hans' father and Paul's—"

"Are one and the same," Lange interrupted.

"No, they aren't. I'm trying to explain that."

"Fraulein Rodl, I have no time for any of this," Lange said, and the gentlemanly, solicitous behavior was gone now. Lange's tone of voice was cold and superior. "I have proof that Paul Maass is a Jew. He was adopted by Herr Maass at the time he was born, but he was fathered by the Jew, Werfel, before Werfel died."

"Oh, my God," Lisl said, feeling the bile of fear building up inside her. "Oh, my God, what is going to happen?"

"What is going to happen, Fraulein Rodl? What is going to happen? I will tell you what is going to happen. Paul Maass is going to be arrested by the Gestapo, then taken to a concentration camp where he will be thrown in with the other Jewish scum."

"But no, please," Lisl sobbed.

"Unless . . ." Lange said, letting the word hang.

"Unless?" Lisl asked with a desperate note of hope. "Major Lange, you mean there is a chance that it might not happen?"

"There is a chance," Lange said. "It all depends on me."

"It depends on you? How?"

"Allow me to tell you a little about a method of racial genetic classification I have developed," Lange said. He then launched into an extensive explanation of his method of determining Jewish blood by watching the reactions of suspects to various works of art. It was being considered by Heinrich Himmler as the one definitive method of determination, he bragged, and for the moment Lange was so pleased with the chance to expound on his personal theory that he almost forgot the business at hand. But Lisl interrupted him.

"Please, Major Lange, what does all this have to do with Paul? And why does it depend on you?"

"I was merely trying to explain," Lange said, showing his agitation over being interrupted. "Despite the existence of the documents which state that Maass is a Jew, the final decision as to whether or not he is a Jew rests with my interpretation of his reaction to the racial genetic classification tests. If I say he is a Jew, then Maass is a Jew. If I say he is not a Jew then he is not a Jew, no matter what the documents may say."

"What?" Lisl asked, now realizing what Lange was telling her. At first she had been terrified by his revelation to her, and now she was beginning to see a glimmer of hope. "Major, *you* can make the decision?"

"That is what I have been trying to tell you," Lange said. "If you would just listen to me, you would realize that I am trying to help you."

"You're trying to help me? You mean help Paul? Oh, Major, would you do that? Would you help Paul?"

Lange looked over at her and smiled, but for some reason the smile didn't look as pleasant as it had before. That was strange—he had just offered her a small ray of hope in what would have otherwise been a hopeless situation, and yet his smile looked almost sinister.

"Yes, I will help," Lange said.

"Oh, Major," Lisl said, with a sob of relief. "Oh, Major, thank you! Oh, I can't thank you enough, you are—"

"Yes, you can," Lange said.

"I can what?"

"You *can* thank me enough," Lange said.

"How?"

"There is something I want you to do for me," Lange said. He looked over at her again, and again he smiled, the small, sinister smile.

"What do you want?" Lisl asked, and she felt a chill of foreboding pass over her.

"Tell me, Fraulein Rodl, what do you know of the Führer's Lebensborn home program?"

"Isn't it a place for unwed mothers to go and have their children?" Lisl asked.

"Oh, it's much more than that," Lange said. "I am in charge of the Gildersheim Lebensborn home, Fraulein Rodl, and I can tell you that we are doing a tremendous service for the Führer, and for our country."

"But what are you doing?" Lisl asked. "I mean, if it isn't a place for unwed mothers to have their children, what is it?"

"It is a place for Germany's fairest and purest maidens, to conceive children by Germany's most racially pure Aryan men. It is the place where Germany's future is being bred."

"Bred?" Lisl gasped, then she chuckled. "Major Lange, do you mean to tell me that you are running a *breeding* farm?"

"Why not?" Lange answered easily. "For centuries now, man has put scientific effort into breeding pure-bred strains of cattle, pigs, and horses. Can we do less for humankind than we are doing for the animal world? What a glorious world this will be when the next generation is the product of selective breeding!"

"But, it seems so . . . so inhuman," Lisl said.

"It is inhuman," Lange said. "For it is above the human level, and on the level of the gods. We are at the dawn of the gods, Fraulein Rodl. And you and I can be a part of it."

"You and I?"

"Yes," Lange said. He reached over and put his hand on Lisl's thigh, then squeezed it gently. Lisl felt a revulsion at his touch, but she closed her eyes tightly and fought against the urge to jerk away from him.

"I want to use you for breeding purposes, Frauline Rodl. I want you to come to the Lebensborn home, and I want you to conceive my child."

"I . . . I can't do that," Lisl said quietly.

Lange moved his hand further up on her thigh, bunching her skirt up between her legs. "Oh, yes, you can do it," he said. "And you will do it, because it is the only way you are going to be able to save the Jew Maass."

"You mean, if I go to bed with you, you will certify Paul as a non-Jew?"

"Yes," Lange said.

Lisl felt the tears sting her eyes and she looked out the car window at the side of the road. They were passing a small religious icon which was set up in a farmer's field, and in the icon there was a statue of the Madonna. The Blessed Mother. My god, Lisl thought, could she possibly be the mother to a child conceived by this man? Maybe she wouldn't conceive. Oh, dear God, please, let me not conceive!

"All right," she finally said. "Let's go and get it over with."

"Oh, you misunderstand, my dear," Lange said easily. "There's no 'getting it over with' until you are pregnant. You will make frequent visits to the Lebensborn home, where you will make yourself available to me. Such visits to terminate only when you are pregnant. Do you understand?"

"But surely you could be satisfied if we just try?" Lisl pleaded.

"It is not for my personal satisfaction, but for the glory of the Reich," Lange said. "Now Fraulein Rodl, do we have a deal?"

"Yes," Lisl said in defeat.

"Good, good," Lange said easily. "We will start today, and then continue on every day until we have done our duty to the Führer. *Heil Hitler.*"

"*Heil Hitler,*" Lisl said dully.

16

INSIDE the Lebensborn Home, the lobby was cool and elaborate. It was appointed with marble fixtures, wall tapestries, oil paintings and exquisite furniture. Behind the desk there was a gigantic painting of Adolph Hitler, and the painting was draped with a banner which stated: *"The Reich future is nursed at the mother's breast."*

"You must register," Lange said, pointing to a desk at the rear of the room.

"Please," Lisl said. "I'd rather we just—"

"Fraulein Rodl, you are not some trollop I picked up in a bar," Lange explained patiently. "What we are doing is for the good of the Reich, and the glory of the Führer. There is no shame, there is only pride. You will register, please."

Lisl looked back toward the desk, and at the woman who was sitting behind it. She was a powerful-looking woman, with mannish shoulders, thick arms and big thighs. Her blonde hair was tied back in a neat bun, and her face was totally devoid of any make-up. She opened a book and picked up a pen, then motioned toward Lisl.

"Come," she said to Lisl. "I must get some information."

Lisl walked over to the desk and looked at the big woman apprehensively. "What information do you need?" Lisl asked hesitantly.

"Do you swear to be absolutely free of all Jewish blood?"

"Yes," Lisl said quietly.

"Are you now or have you ever been married?"

"No."

"Are you a virgin?"

"I . . . I prefer not to answer that question," Lisl said.

"You will answer the questions, Fraulein," the woman behind the desk said quietly, but with enough force to let Lisl know that she meant business. "Again: are you a virgin?"

"No," Lisl said quietly. She mouthed the word so low as to be almost inaudible.

"What?" the woman asked. "I didn't hear you, Fraulein. Are you a virgin?"

Lisl cleared her throat. "No," she said again.

"Have you engaged in sexual innercourse with more than one man?"

"No," Lisl answered quietly.

"Have you engaged in sex with another woman?"

"What? What kind of question is that?" Lisl asked.

The woman looked up at Lisl, and for one terrible moment Lisl felt a fear unlike any she had ever before experienced. She saw, or *believed* she saw, the same look of raw desire in this woman's eyes she had learned to recognize in men's eyes when they looked at her.

"Answer the question, Fraulein," the woman behind the desk said. "Have you ever engaged in sex with another woman?" There was a leering quality in the woman's voice which both shocked and frightened Lisl.

"No, of course not," Lisl said. Then, quickly, to ensure that the woman understood her thoroughly, "I would never do such a thing."

"You will not be asked to do such a thing here, Fraulein. The purpose of the Lebensborn Homes is to conceive children," the woman said. "Are you now in your period of the menstrual cycle?"

"No," Lisl said.

"How long has it been since your last period?"

"I . . . I don't know," Lisl said.

The woman looked up. "Fraulein, you must cooperate," she said.

Lange, who had left Lisl at the desk for a few moments, now returned. "I have a few things to attend to in my office," he said to Lisl. "As soon as she is finished with you here, she will tell you where to go."

"*Sturmbannführer*, the fraulein is not cooperating with the registration questions," the woman complained.

"You have no choice, Fraulein Rodl," Lange explained. "You *must* cooperate, if you want my cooperation. I think you see what I mean."

"Yes," Lisl said. She ran her hand through her hair. She had not purposely tried not to cooperate, she just wasn't sure when her period ended. She chose a date. "My last period ended three weeks ago."

"The date, Fraulein," the woman said. "What was the date?"

"June the fifth," Lisl said, as she watched Lange walk away, across the wide carpeted lobby.

"Have you had sexual intercourse since that time?"

"No," Lisl said.

"Age, at onset of menstruation?"

"Twelve," Lisl said.

"Are you a frequent masturbator?"

"No! Of course not!"

"Age when you began to masturbate?"

"Why are you doing all this?" Lisl asked. "This isn't necessary, is it?"

"Answer the question, please," the woman insisted.

"I . . . I don't know," Lisl replied. "About fourteen or fifteen, I guess." She put her hand to her forehead and began to sob silently. "I don't know why you are doing all this. Why are you asking all these questions?"

"Are you able to orgasm during intercourse?" the woman asked, paying no attention to Lisl's discomfort.

Lisl stood there, her shoulders shaking silently, as she sobbed. The woman tapped the pen impatiently on the desk. "You *must* answer all the questions," the woman said.

"I didn't hear the question."

"Are you able to reach orgasm during intercourse?" the woman asked again, asking the question as clinically as if she were asking her name.

Lisl thought back to the moments of rapture she had spent with Paul, the blazing fires they had started together, the lightning bolts of pleasure which had jolted her body, the ebb and flow of sensation, the tenderness of the afterglow, and then she heard again the cold, clinical word—*orgasmus.* How can such love and depth of feeling be incorporated into one cold, harsh word?

"No," Lisl answered defiantly.

The woman looked up at Lisl and smiled, then allowed herself an editorial comment. "Perhaps you have been with the wrong lover," she suggested.

Lisl shuddered.

The woman turned the book around and handed
the pen to Lisl. "Sign here, Fraulein, then," the woman
opened a drawer and took out a key, "go to this room.
You will find a robe on the hook there. Get undressed
and put on the robe."

Lisl nodded her understanding, too numbed by
everything to speak, then she signed her name to the
bottom of the page the woman had just completed.
Afterward she took the key and followed the directions
down one long hall until she reached her room.

Just across the hall from the room to which she was
sent, there was another room, and the door was standing open. There, a young woman sat in a rocking
chair, holding a nursing baby to her bare breast. She
looked up at Lisl and smiled. "Good luck," she called
sweetly.

Lisl just nodded at the young woman, then unlocked
the door to her room and stepped inside. She started
to lock the door behind her, but realized there would
be other keys and it would be just an empty gesture,
so she didn't bother. Slowly and deliberately she undressed, stacked her clothes neatly on a small white
table, then slipped the robe on over her nude body.

There were three small windows in the room, but
they were high on the wall, too high for Lisl to look
through, though they did allow the evening sun to
stream in, casting white spears of light through the
floating dustmotes. Besides the white table which now
held Lisl's clothes, there was a rocking chair, a baby
crib, a dresser, a small trunk, and a bed. The walls
were decorated with pictures of Hitler, as well as
posters and pictures extolling the joys of motherhood.
Quite incongruously, Lisl thought, there was also a
large crucifix.

Lisl sat on the trunk and waited.

About ten minutes later the door opened, and Lisl turned, expecting to see Lange. Instead, she saw a short, rather heavy man with a bald head and a monocle stabbed into the socket of his left eye. It magnified that eye greatly and gave him an unbalanced appearance. He was wearing a white doctor's smock, with a stylized eagle and swastika symbol over his right pocket. He clicked his heels together and bowed stiffly from the waist.

"My dear, I am Dr. Ruden. I have come to examine you."

"Why must I be examined?"

Ruden smiled. "Really, my dear, you don't expect the *Sturmbannführer* to engage in sex with someone unless he has the confidence that that person is free of disease, do you?"

"And what about me?" Lisl asked. "Am I not to get the same reassurance?"

"That is a reasonable request," Ruden said. "I have examined the *Sturmbannführer* often, and I find him free of any disease. Now, does that satisfy you?"

"I really have no choice, do I?" Lisl replied.

"Please remove your robe," Ruden said, and when Lisl hesitated, Ruden chuckled. "Please, my dear, remember that I am a doctor."

Lisl untied the belt and opened the robe, then let it slip down from her shoulders. She felt the air of the room against her nude body, and though she had been nude a moment earlier when she put on the robe, this time it seemed as if there were a greater chill in the air.

Ruden crossed his arms on his chest and raised one hand to his cheek as he examined Lisl's nude body. He took in an audible breath. "Oh, my," he said. "I examine so many naked women that I thought I had become immune to all, but you, my dear, are a vision of breathtaking beauty."

"Thank you," Lisl said almost automatically. Lisl was now trying to get through one moment at a time. She did not look forward to the next day or the next hour or even the next moment, but only the one here and now. She felt no sense of pride or shame or fear over his compliment. She felt only a sense of numbness.

"Would you get on the bed, please?" Ruden asked.

Dully, Lisl lay on the bed, then she watched almost disinterestedly as Dr. Ruden spread her legs to conduct a pelvic examination. She felt his short, blunt fingers probe and poke, and she winced as some of her pubic hair was pulled. Finally he raised up and looked at her.

"You have wonderful pelvic construction my dear," Ruden said. "Nature has been most generous with you. You have been given a beautiful body to inflame the sexual ardor of the male, and the equipment to conceive, carry, and deliver children. May you have many children for the glory of the Führer."

Ruden left then, and Lisl remained on the bed, not bothering to put the robe back on, or shield her nudity. The bars of sunlight bent and dimmed as the sun dropped lower throughout the long afternoon. When there were no discernible sun bars left, but only the diffused silver of twilight, the door opened and Lange came into the room.

"Dr. Ruden has given you high marks," Lange said as he began to remove his clothes. When he was totally naked, he stood beside her, looking down at her body. Had the scene been captured on an artist's canvas, it would have been one of exquisite erotica. The woman on the bed was long of limb, with smooth, supple skin and gently molded curves and valleys. The breasts were seductive suggestions of flesh, topped by tightly drawn nipples which added a sense of dynamic tension. The blonde nest of hair at the junction of her legs provided texture to the flaring pelvis, drawing the eyes to a focal point, although no focal point was needed in this vision of beauty. The man standing beside the bed was angular and handsome, with a broad chest, a flat stomach, slim hips, and a proud badge of manhood thrusting at an arrogant angle over the body of the woman it would soon enter.

As Lange moved onto the bed and spread Lisl's legs to make the connection, roughly and without fanfare, the pain in her womb was nothing compared to the agony in her soul.

Later, when Lisl finally returned home, she said nothing to her parents, who had been strangely anxious for her, but brushed by them and ran up the stairs to her bedroom.

"What is it, dear? What is wrong?" Frauka asked anxiously, calling up from the bottom of the stairs.

"Don't bother her," Heinrich said. "You know how sensitive she is. I'm sure she is just emotionally drained from seeing Rudi."

"I suppose so," Frauka said. "Do you think we should wait dinner?"

"No," Heinrich said. "I've work to do tonight. She can eat later."

Lisl had stood just inside her bedroom, leaning against the door, and she heard her mother and father's conversation. Let them think what they will, she thought. I cannot tell them, I cannot tell anyone, of the hell I have been through.

Lisl dropped her hands to feel that part of her body

which had always tingled with pleasure long after she
made love with Paul. Now it throbbed with a dull
ache, and she felt an irritating itch, as if she were
dirty there.

Dirty, Lisl thought. Yes, that's it. She would take
a bath. A very hot bath.

Lisl opened the door slightly, saw that no one was
there, then she moved down to the bathroom and
began drawing hot water into the large, porcelain tub
which sat on lions' feet, dominating the room which
had been converted into a bath years after the house
had actually been built. Maybe the bath would purify
her.

But even as she thought of it, she knew that the
bath could do nothing to negate the real impurity of
her body. She could still feel the heavy wetness of it,
the slimy sperm Lange had injected into her womb. If
there were only some way she could kill it. Lisl saw
a bottle of rubbing alcohol then, and in that instant
she knew what she was going to do.

As the tub filled with hot, soapy water, Lisl took
her feminine syringe down from the top shelf to the
closet where she stored her personal things. She filled
the bulb with alcohol, then turned off the water and
slipped down into the tub. She lay back and raised
both legs, and looked at herself for a long moment.
Then she plunged the syringe deep into her vagina
and squeezed the bulb.

The alcohol burned with a fire she had not been
able to imagine, and she had to bite her lips to keep
from crying out. And yet, it was only in that wash of
pain that she was able to bind the bleeding wounds
of her soul. She squeezed the bulb again, welcoming
the tongues of fire which raced up through her womb.

17

"I shall consider your qualifications, Herr Krebbs, but you must realize that there are others equally qualified who have also applied for this position," Paul was saying.

Paul was in his office behind his desk at the concert hall, interviewing prospective applicants for the position of Concert Master, a job vacated by the disappearance of Baumann.

"Excuse me please, *Herr Direktor*, but I would also ask that you consider my recommendations from certain influential people. If you will notice, Herr Dr. Goebbels has given me his personal endorsement."

"Yes, I am certain that Herr Goebbels' taste in music should deserve the utmost of consideration," Paul said, somewhat sarcastically, though the sarcasm was lost on Krebbs.

Krebbs was a small man with thin blond hair and watery blue eyes. He sat very stiffly in his chair and kept his hands folded across his lap. The hands, Paul noticed, were small and without calluses.

"I shall hear from you soon?" Krebbs asked, standing as he saw Paul close his portfolio.

"Yes," Paul said. "Soon."

"How soon?"

"Soon," Paul said, a little irritated by Krebbs persistence. "First, I want to make certain that Herr Baumann doesn't return."

"He will not return," Krebbs said.

"How do you know?"

"I believe he is dead," Krebbs said. "If he were not dead, you would have heard from him by now."

"I hope you are wrong," Paul said.

"I believe you will find that I am correct in my assumption," Krebbs went on. He turned to leave, then stopped just as he was about to exit. "I would like to say, *Herr Direktor*, that should you decide in my favor, I shall consider it a rare privilege to work with one as brilliant and as famous as you. I am told you are one of the Führer's personal favorites."

"I try only to do the best I can," Paul said. "When someone is pleased, I am honored."

Krebbs smiled and bowed at least two more times as he scraped his way backwards out of Paul's office. When the door was finally closed, Paul sat back down and drew a line through Krebbs' name. He did not wish to employ Herr Krebbs.

There was a light knock at his office door, and Paul checked his schedule. He had thought Krebbs was the last applicant he was scheduled to see, and, according to the appointment book, he was. Who, then, was knocking at the door?

"Yes," Paul called. "Who is it?"

"Herr Maass, it is I, Dr. Mueller," a voice replied. "Am I in the way of one of your appointments?"

"No," Paul said, opening the door and inviting Dr. Mueller in. "Come on in, I have just seen the last one for the day. Would you care for a cup of tea? I've some hot water."

"Yes, thank you," Dr. Mueller said. "That would be nice."

Paul walked over to the tea cart and poured tea into two cups, then handed one of the cups to Dr. Mueller. "And to what do I owe the pleasure of your visit?" he asked.

"I just wanted to see how the interviews were going," Dr. Mueller said. "I know that you are looking for a new concert master, and, of course, the city is anxiously awaiting the concert in the park." As Dr. Mueller was talking, he looked around the room, checking for anything which might compromise his conversation. Finally Paul realized what he was doing, and Paul spoke.

"We can talk if you wish, Dr. Mueller. There is no one here but us."

"Good, good," Dr. Mueller said. He sat in the chair recently occupied by Krebbs and leaned back and sighed. "It is good to get away from the summer's heat." He fanned himself with a concert program which was lying on the front of Paul's desk. "I've some bad news for you," he went on.

"Bad news? What sort of bad news?"

"It's about your concert master," Dr. Mueller said. "Herr Baumann is dead."

"How do you know?"

"One of our operatives told us," Dr. Mueller said. "He was executed by the S.S. What we do not know is why he was executed."

"My God, Baumann was *executed*? But, why wasn't I told? I mean wouldn't the authorities inform some- one if they did something like that?"

Dr. Mueller laughed a short, bitter laugh. "Paul,

have you not yet realized that the Gestapo owes no one an explanation?"

"Yes, of course I realize that," Paul said. "They are saying nothing about the extermination of the Jews, why should they say anything about the execution of one poor concert master? But Baumann? It seems so unbelievable. What sort of thing would Baumann ever do to get himself into such a fix? See here, Dr. Mueller, was Baumann involved in—"

"No," Dr. Mueller said, interrupting Paul's question. "At least, we know he was not associated with any known group. Our guess is that the Gestapo must have somehow made a mistake. They got the idea he was involved in espionage, and rather than take any chances with him, they just killed him."

"Poor Baumann," Paul said.

"Well, at least we can take some satisfaction in the fact that his death may have bought a little time for someone else," Dr. Mueller said. "Now, tell me, how did your attempt at sabotage go?"

"It was a total waste of time," Paul said. "Dr. Mueller, for the life of me, I don't know what I have gotten myself into. I agreed to help, and then I received orders telling me to pour sugar into the oil bath of one of the machines of the I.G.N. Kuglewerks plant. I did it, but the machine was only out of commission for four days. What possible benefit could my little effort have had? I risked my reputation, my freedom, probably even my life, and all for nothing."

"I'm sorry," Dr. Mueller said. "But all assignments cannot be the assassination of Hitler."

"I didn't say I wanted to assassinate Hitler," Paul protested. "All I said was that if I am going to be asked to risk my life I would like to have an assignment worthy of the risk."

"You will forgive us, please, Paul, but we thought it necessary to test you once."

"Test me? You mean you were afraid I would report you to the authorities? Is that what you were afraid of?"

"No, not at all," Mueller assured him. "You are an intelligent man, Paul. You have now seen the proof of what Hitler has in store for the Jews and for anyone else who doesn't agree with him. I know you are dedicated to eradicating that evil, and I know you would do nothing to jeopardize that goal. We weren't testing your loyalty at all, merely your ability to carry out an assignment under difficult conditions. After all, if you had failed in your assignment, it would not have mattered much."

"It would have mattered a great deal to me," Paul said.

Dr. Mueller smiled. "Yes, I'm sure it would have." He leaned forward in his chair. "But now, my friend, there is an assignment which does matter. It matters a great deal. Will you assume it?"

"Yes," Paul answered.

"You would assume it without questioning what it might be?"

"Dr. Mueller, I told you, I am ready to help rid our country of such men as control it now. You have said that the assignment is important, and that is all I need to know. Just tell me what you want me to do."

"We want you to help someone escape from the country," Dr. Mueller said.

"All right," Paul said. "How do I go about it?"

"Naturally, we will depend upon your position as director of the Schweinfurt Symphony Orchestra to help us carry out the plan we have devised. Would you like to know who you are helping?"

"Yes," Paul said.

"His name is Dr. Ludwig Bernhardt. He, like your brother, is a physicist, and, like your brother, he is working on the problem of converting matter to energy. At least, he was working on that for a while. Then when he realized the mass potential for destruction such a device would have, he stopped work. That was when the Nazis put him in prison."

"Dr. Bernhardt is in a concentration camp?" Paul asked.

"No," Dr. Mueller said. "He is in a prison, or rather a small dungeon. He is being kept in an old castle near here, which has been taken over by the S.S."

"I know the castle," Paul said. "It's on the Main River about ten kilometers from here."

"Yes, that is the one," Dr. Mueller said. "We are going to break him out of that prison, then send him to the United States."

"Dr. Mueller, what makes you think you and I can get Dr. Bernhardt out of prison? I don't know the first thing about such an operation."

"You don't have to know anything about that," Dr. Mueller said. "Someone else is working on that. They will take Dr. Bernhardt from the prison and deliver him to you. You must take him to a small landing field near Wurzburg, where a Moon Plane from England will land for him."

"A Moon Plane?"

"It's a special plane designed for such purposes," Dr. Bernhardt said. "It's small, made of plywood to help defeat the radar, and painted black so as to be nearly invisible against the night sky."

"I see," Paul said. "Dr. Mueller, this all sounds very dangerous."

"It is extremely dangerous," Dr. Mueller said. "But

it must be done if we are to get Dr. Bernhardt safely out of Germany."

"Does Dr. Bernhardt know of the danger?"

"Dr. Bernhardt doesn't even know we are planning this."

"What?" Paul asked anxiously. "Dr. Mueller, you can't seriously plan to do something like this without the cooperation of the man involved, can you?"

"We believe we will have his cooperation," Dr. Mueller said.

"And if we don't?"

"If we don't, we will take him anyway," Dr. Mueller said. "You know the ways the Gestapo have of making people talk. If they realized the value of the information Dr. Bernhardt has locked up in his mind, they will keep at him until they break him."

"What if we don't have his cooperation and we can't get him out?" Paul asked.

"We won't leave him for the Germans."

"I don't understand."

"You won't have to worry about it," Dr. Mueller said. "The extraction team will make that determination before they ever take him from the prison. If they can rescue Dr. Bernhardt, they will do so. If they cannot, they will kill him."

The words sounded cold and clinical, and Paul winced when he heard them.

"It's harsh, I know," Dr. Mueller said. "But it is a harsh world, Paul. We may have no choice."

"And so we may resort to murder," Paul said.

"It isn't murder," Dr. Mueller assured him. "It is a necessary action."

"By any euphemism, it is still murder," Paul said. "Dr. Mueller, I won't do murder for you."

"I told you," Dr. Mueller said. "You won't have to

worry about it. The extraction team will make that decision. All you have to do is get him from Schweinfurt to Wurzburg."

"But why me?" Paul asked. "If the extraction team takes him from the prison, couldn't they take him to the landing field near Wurzburg?"

"No," Dr. Mueller said. "The operational plans call for a different escort. That has to be you. You are an artist who has won Hitler's admiration, and Hitler has a blind spot for artists. If anyone can bluff their way through the roadblocks at night, it has to be you. I'm not saying it is without any risk. I'm just saying that is our only hope."

"When does all this occur?" Paul asked. "Will I have the opportunity to make any dry runs?"

"Oh, it happens tonight," Mueller said easily.

"Tonight?" Paul asked. "But no, it can't occur tonight. I didn't have any chance to make plans or anything."

"The plans have already been made," Mueller said. "You are known to be interviewing people for the position of concert master. When you encounter a checkpoint you will merely explain that you have concluded the interview and are taking Herr Cuno home."

"Cuno?"

"Dr. Bernhardt will have identification papers stating he is Viktor Cuno, musician of Wurzburg," Mueller explained. "After you have taken him through the final checkpoint you will go exactly fifteen kilometers, where you will see a fence on the right side of the road. There will be a handkerchief tied to a rail of the fence. You will stop the car and let Dr. Bernhardt off there. He will have instructions to cross the fence at that point, and someone will be there to meet him."

"I see," Paul said.

"Are there any questions?"

"Just one."

"What?"

"Tell me, Dr. Mueller, now that you have everything figured out: where shall I get a car?"

"You shall have to come up with one," Mueller said. He looked at his watch. "You are a very resourceful fellow, I'm sure you will have one here by twenty-one hundred hours."

"But that's only two more hours," Paul protested.

"Then you must hurry," Mueller said. He stood up. "Come, we should go to a *gasthaus* for a few moments so that this would appear to be a social call."

"Very well," Paul said. "There is one next door."

Paul and Dr. Mueller left the concert hall, then walked down the street together as if they were very old and very dear friends. They conversed about music and a few other things as they turned into the *gasthaus*. Dr. Mueller ordered the first round and Paul got the second round. After he completed his second beer, Paul started to leave the *gasthaus* when he was addressed by Herr Dietering, the *Gauleiter* of the Schweinfurt District. Paul remembered Dietering and the way Hitler had ignored him to make much over Lisl and Paul. Dietering had shown Paul a trace of animosity ever since that day, and Paul felt that it was because Dietering was jealous.

"*Herr Direktor*, will we be honored by a concert in the park this weekend as planned?" Dietering asked.

"Yes," Paul said, "if I am able to select a new concert master in time."

"Please make a concerted effort," Dietering replied. "I have invited several important officials. I would be embarrassed if there were no concert. You *must* have the concert."

Suddenly Paul got an idea, and he narrowed his eyes and looked at the *gauleiter* cunningly. "Herr Gauleiter, there is a way I could guarantee a concert, if I could count on your help," Paul said.

"Of course you can count on my help," Dietering said. "Just name what you want me to do and I shall provide any assistance necessary."

"I have a number I wanted to do, which was arranged especially for the Führer himself," Paul said. "I had hoped to be able to perform it for him, but, of course, he won't be here. However, I could still do it, if I could find a very important dignitary to help with the staging. That's where you could help me, *Herr Gauleiter*. You are an important enough personage to fill that vacancy for me, if you would do us the honor. I want you to take the throne of Odin in our production number. Would you do that?"

Dietering smiled broadly and his chest expanded noticably. "You want *me* to sit on the throne of Odin?"

"Yes. We will be playing the *Ride of the Valkyries*, and I've arranged for dancers to salute the throne. But we must have a dignitary of great importance on the throne. May we count on you?"

"Yes, yes, of course you can count on me," Dietering said. "After all, I am the *gauleiter* of this city and district, and I owe it to my people to let them view me, do I not?"

"That is exactly what I was thinking," Paul said. He smiled and rubbed his hands together. "Now, I see no reason why we can't do the concert, and . . . oh . . . no, wait a minute. Wait a minute, we can't do that number. I'm sorry, *Herr Gauleiter*, I thank you for being so gracious as to offer your help, but it will be impossible for us to do that number."

"Why not?" Dietering asked, clearly crestfallen over

the idea that he might not get to sit on the throne as Paul had suggested.

"I don't have the proper arrangement here," Paul said. "I took it to Wurzburg, where I planned to use *Gauleiter* Schmidt in the—"

"Schmidt?" Dietering exploded. "You were going to use Schmidt?"

"Well, yes," Paul said. "When I thought there was a possibility to perform for the Führer I was looking for a suitable dignitary and *Gauleiter* Schmidt came to mind. So I took the arrangement to Wurzburg, where I intended to ask him if he would participate."

"Why Schmidt?" Dietering asked angrily. "Why Schmidt instead of me?"

"Well, after all, Wurzburg is larger than Schweinfurt and—"

"But you are the director of the Schweinfurt Symphony, not the Wurzburg Symphony," Dietering insisted. "By rights you should have asked me first."

Paul smiled. "Well, I *did* ask you first, Excellency. I just took the music to Wurzburg. I haven't yet asked *Gauleiter* Schmidt."

Dietering's chest expanded again when he heard Paul use the word "Excellency" in addressing him.

"Then there is no problem," Dietering said. "You haven't asked that clown from Wurzburg, and I have said that I will do it."

"The problem, Excellency, is that the arrangement for the music is in Wurzburg. I would have to go there and get the music, then return to Schweinfurt to start the rehearsals. It is too late to go by train and I have no other way. Even if I could borrow Herr Rodl's car, there is a blackout on the roads, and a restriction against night travel unless one has the highest priority. I would be turned back at the first road-check."

"Yes, you would," Dietering said, then he smiled. "Unless you had my help."

"Your help, Excellency?"

Dietering held up his hand and wagged a finger back and forth triumphantly. "It isn't for nothing that I am the most important man in the district. I will let you use my car and I will issue a pass which will allow you to get through the roadblocks."

"*Gauleiter* Dietering, would you really do that?" Paul asked.

"Of course I will do that," Dietering replied. "I owe it to my people to make an appearance in this concert. We are at war, and my people have a right to see their leaders in inspirational settings and scenes, in order that we may lift their morale. You go and attend to your errands and be back here in one hour. At that time I will have the car and the papers ready for you."

"You are most kind, Excellency," Paul said, and waving happily at everyone else in the *gasthaus*, he left. Dr. Mueller smiled broadly at him, and Paul was showman enough to appreciate the fact that there was at least one person in his audience who had an unique understanding of the performance he had just given.

Schweinfurt was in a Condition II blackout. Some lights were authorized, but only the most essential. Those cars that did move drove through the city streets with "cats-eyes," narrow slits in the black headlamp covers which barely lit the way, but which would give little help to any night bombers trying to guide their way by ground lights. Not only the cars but also the buildings were restricted, so that only the barest number of lights could be used. Uniformed block wardens patrolled the streets at night, inflated with their importance, and armed with the power to

enter any building without warrant and without warning, to extinguish all unnecessary lights.

Because of the Condition II blackout, Paul had
only one small lamp burning in his office, and he sat
on the sofa with his head tilted back on the cushion,
waiting to be contacted. A big Mercedes touring car,
adorned with Nazi flags and bearing a high priority
license plate, sat at the curb in front of the Concert
Hall. The keys to the car were in Paul's pocket, along
with a signed pass authorizing him to drive at night.

Paul heard a sound from the auditorium, and he
got up and walked quietly to the door of his office and
looked out toward the sound.

"*Herr Direktor?*" a voice called from the darkness.

"Yes," Paul said. "I am Maass. Who are you? What
do you want?"

"I have come to inquire, *Herr Direktor*, if you've
an empty chair for another flutist?"

This was the question Paul was told would be asked
by his visitors, but there was a careful response, then
counter response required before a secure identification would be established. Paul responded in the correct way.

"I may be interested," he said. "Where were you
schooled?"

"At the Augsburg Conservatory," the voice answered.

"Ah, at Augsburg. Did you study with Dr. Meyers?"

"No, *Herr Direktor*, I studied with Dr. Drexler."

Paul signalled to the form in the darkness to come
into the light of his office. "Did you have any trouble?"
he asked, now that the identification was thoroughly
established.

"No, we had no trouble," the voice said. Paul noticed
that there were two more shadows behind the first,
and then the three shadows became men as they

moved into the light. "I am Helmut, this is Franz. I must confess, we nearly passed you by when I saw that big car at the curb. Whose car is it, and why is it parked here?"

"The car belongs to the Schweinfurt *gauleiter*," Paul said. "Before the Nazis came to power he was a gardener who couldn't even afford a bicycle. Now he is one of the few with a car. Such are the strange events of a world controlled by Nazis. But I should not speak ill of him, for he has loaned us the car for the night."

Helmut laughed. "I take it that the *gauleiter* has no idea of what use you will make with the car?"

"No," Paul said. "He believes I am going to go to Wurzburg for a musical score."

"Good," Helmut said.

Paul looked beyond Helmut and Franz to the third man. The third man had not yet spoken, and he was standing quietly, as if unsure of himself.

"You must be Dr. Bernhardt," Paul said quietly.

The man looked toward Helmut and Franz with questioning, frightened eyes.

"You must forgive him," Franz said. "He has been a prisoner of the Gestapo for eighteen months. He had no idea a rescue attempt was even being planned until we took him less than one hour ago. He is still quite confused."

"Is he cooperative with our plan?" Paul asked.

Helmut smiled. "You do want to get out of Germany, don't you, Dr. Bernhardt?"

"Yes," Dr. Bernhardt said eagerly. "Yes, I want to leave this place. I will do whatever I must."

"Good," Paul said. He breathed a sigh of relief. "I must say it makes our job a little easier to have him cooperating with us instead of fighting us." He looked at Dr. Bernhardt again. "I am the brother of Dr. Hans Werfel," he said. "I believe you know Hans."

"Yes," Dr. Bernhardt said. "Hans was my friend."

"He is still your friend," Paul said. "You are going to work with him just as soon as we can get you out of here."

"Yes, Hans is my friend," Dr. Bernhardt said again. "But I don't see much of him anymore, he doesn't come around to visit."

Paul looked at Helmut and Franz in confusion. "What is this?" he asked. "Isn't Dr. Bernhardt lucid? Now I'm concerned as to whether he will be able to play out his role."

"He is quite obviously confused," Helmut explained. "But, as I said, he has been subject to the Gestapo for some time, and their methods are quite harsh. But he is stronger than you think. A weak man could not have survived at all."

"I hope he can get on the plane all right," Paul said.

"He must get on the plane," Franz said.

"Does he understand all he is to do?" Paul asked.

"We have explained it to him," Helmut said. He sighed. "We can only hope . . ."

"I will put him on the plane," Paul volunteered.

"Paul, that is very dangerous," Helmut said. "Your orders call only for you to stop where you see the handkerchief tied to the fence. Someone will meet him there."

"I intend to see him on the plane," Paul said, resolutely. "What is the password for the contact at the fence?"

"He will ask if he can be of help. The response is 'I am looking for the house of Herr Berger.'"

"Good luck," Franz and Helmut called to him, as he led Dr. Bernhardt out to the car.

* * *

The *gauleiter*'s car was one of the more luxurious models of Mercedes. The seats were large, tooled leather, soft, and very comfortable. It was roomy and quiet, and there was even a radio. Paul turned on the radio and was surprised to hear one of his own recordings. He hummed along with the music and tapped his finger on the steering wheel as he drove through the dark, quiet streets of Schweinfurt.

The first group of police Paul encountered didn't even attempt to stop him. They recognized the car and came to attention, saluting as he passed them. Surprisingly, the roadblock just out of the city wasn't even manned, and within a short time Paul found himself out of the city, and driving through the country.

"So far so good," Paul said to his traveling companion, "Now, if we are stopped, you do know what to do, don't you?"

"I will say nothing," Dr. Bernhardt said. "They will get nothing from me."

"Dr. Bernhardt, you don't understand," Paul said. "We aren't trying to resist interrogation here, we are merely trying to bluff our way through the roadblocks. You should tell them you are Viktor Cuno, a musician."

"I will tell them nothing," Dr. Bernhardt said again.

Paul sighed. "Yes, well, we shall see how that works."

Approximately ten kilometers later, they encountered a roadblock which stopped him. The guard who approached the car was not a policeman but a member of the army, and he was not as awestruck by the license plates of a party *gauleiter* as the police in the city had been.

Paul rolled his window down as the soldier approached.

"This road is closed for travel at night," the soldier explained. "What are you doing out here?"

Paul handed the soldier the *gauleiter*'s letter of authorization, which allowed him to go to Wurzburg for the musical score. He explained it as he handed the letter to the soldier.

"You mean you would chance enemy bombing by driving to Wurzburg just to get music?" the soldier asked, as if unable to believe the letter.

"Of course," Paul said easily. "Without the music I cannot give the concert."

The soldier looked at the letter for a moment, and at the car, then he rubbed his chin. "I don't understand it," he said. "But someone in a pretty high place must really have an appreciation for music. And who is he?" he went on, pointing to Dr. Bernhardt.

"He is Viktor Cuno, an applicant for the position of concert master in my orchestra," Paul said.

"Can't you answer for yourself?" the soldier asked Bernhardt.

Dr. Bernhardt merely stared, close-mouthed, at the soldier.

"Lieutenant, you must forgive him," Paul said. The soldier was only a sergeant and Paul knew that. He hoped to flatter him by the use of the rank.

"I am only a sergeant," the soldier replied.

"I'm sorry," Paul said. "I must plead the ignorance of an artist. I thought anyone who had this important a position must surely be a Lieutenant."

"Yes, I really should be," the sergeant said. "In some cases the roadblocks are commanded by officers, but my captain says I am as trustworthy as an officer," he added proudly.

"Oh, I am certain that you must be," Paul said. "But, please let me explain why Herr Cuno does not answer.

He is disappointed because I have decided not to use him as the concert master for my orchestra. He has not spoken a word since I made that decision."

The sergeant laughed. "I get it. He's a temperamental artist, is he?"

"Yes," Paul said. "And, unfortunately, I must ride with him all the way to Wurzburg."

The sergeant stepped away from the car. "Better you than me," he said. "A temperamental woman is bad enough—a temperamental artist, I don't even want to be around." He waved the car on through and saluted. "Be careful on the road, *Herr Direktor.*"

"Yes, I will, thank you," Paul said, putting the car into gear and pulling away.

"Are you all right?" Paul asked Dr. Bernhardt as they drove away.

"Yes," Dr. Bernhardt said. "I want to thank you. I was too frightened to say anything."

"It worked out all right," Paul said. "Don't worry about it."

They drove in silence for another fifteen kilometers, then Paul saw the handkerchief tied to the fence. He pulled the car off the side of the road and stopped. "We get out here," he said.

It was exceptionally dark outside. There was no moon, which was one of the reasons this particular night was chosen for the rescue attempt. The sky was slightly overcast as well, so that even the stars were dimmed. There was not the slightest breeze to cool the warm night, and mosquitoes were biting. Frogs serenaded them.

"Hello," Paul called softly. "Hello, is there anyone here?"

Suddenly a dark form stood up from the ditch alongside the road. "May I help you?" the man said.

"I am looking for the house of Herr Berger," Paul said.

"Why did you stop? You were supposed to drive on."

"I wanted to see that Dr. Bernhardt got away safely," Paul explained. "He is frightened and confused."

"I don't know," the man in the ditch said. "It is not good to change plans."

"I will see him safely away," Paul insisted.

"Very well," the man said. "But we cannot leave the car there. I will drive it away, and you may deliver him. You take the doctor three kilometers that way," he pointed. "When you come to a haystack, stop. When you hear an airplane approaching, listen to see if he cuts his motor three times. When he does, start the generator which is covered by the hay, and that will light the landing strip."

"Where will you be?" Paul asked.

"Do not worry about me," the man said. "I will stay with the car. When I have heard the airplane leave, I will bring the car back for you."

"All right," Paul said. "Come, Dr. Bernhardt, you have a plane to catch."

Paul led Dr. Bernhardt through the fields and a small patch of trees until he saw the haystack. He stopped by the haystack and looked around. Paul was not a flyer, but he had ridden as a passenger on airliners, so he was familiar with airports. This looked nothing like an airport, and he had no idea how an airplane could possibly land here. He said nothing about it to Dr. Bernhardt though, because Bernhardt was already frightened enough, and he had no wish to frighten him more.

After a wait of several minutes, during which Paul

slapped at mosquitoes and other biting insects, he heard the sound of an approaching airplane. Paul walked over to the generator he had uncovered and put his hand on the starting rope. When he heard the pilot cut the engine three times, Paul jerked on the rope. It took him about five jerks before the generator roared into life, and then he saw a double string of lights stretched out through the small pasture, outlining a runway.

At first, Paul thought that the airplane must have overflown the field, or missed them, because he heard nothing and he saw nothing. Then, amazingly, he saw a black shape rolling up before him. The plane had already landed, but so well was it able to hide in the darkness that he didn't even know it was here until it was right upon him. The plane turned, stopped, and the door opened.

"Come, quickly," someone called from inside the plane.

Paul looked at Dr. Bernhardt, and Dr. Bernhardt hesitated for a moment.

"Go," Paul said. "Dr. Bernhardt, for God's sake, go now, or all will be lost!"

From somewhere deep inside, Dr. Bernhardt seemed to gather his last bit of courage, and, with a resolute set of his shoulders, he sprinted across the pasture to climb onto the plane.

Paul stood there watching, and he returned Dr. Bernhardt's wave just before the door to the plane was closed.

The plane took off into the darkness. As soon as it was off the ground, Paul turned off the generator and the string of lights went dark. He could hear the distant drone of the plane's engine as it flew away, but already he could not see it. Within moments he could no longer even hear it. Dr. Bernhardt had made good his escape.

Paul turned and started back to the road to get the car. The tension which had built up inside him fell away and he laughed. Only now did he realize what an exhilarating experience it had been.

18

"WILD Boar, this is Valkyrie," Frauka was saying into the mouthpiece she wore on a neckcollar.

"Ah, so it is Valkyrie again, is it?" the voice said into Frauka's earphones. The voice, Frauka knew, came from a pilot who was in the close quarters of a Messerschmitt 109, somewhere in the cold, upper reaches of sky high over Germany. He was up there, all alone, facing death, and yet there was a vitality, an air of buoyance to his voice. How could he do it? Frauka wondered. How could he go up, day after day, knowing full well that each day might be his last?

"I have a bomber stream report," Frauka said.

"Tell me, Valkyrie, what do you look like?" Wild Boar asked. "No, don't tell me, let me guess. Let me see, you have blue eyes, *ja*? And hair a light brown in color, which falls softly about your face."

"Wild Boar, you must not say such things over the radio," Frauka cautioned. "Don't you know we are being monitored?"

Wild Boar laughed. "And tell me, Valkyrie, what will the big, bad monitor do to me for such a violation of radio procedure? Will he fire me and send another up to take my place? Will he take my place?"

"Please," Frauka said. "Stick to business."

"Ah, yes, to the nasty business at hand," Wild Boar said. "Now, tell me, my sweet, lovely, Valkyrie—what are the coordinates of the bomber stream?"

"Sector G-5," Frauka said. "Altitude 9,000 meters, speed 350 kilometers. There is a very large dispersion pattern."

"Ahh, the Americans and their B-17s," Wild Boar said. "They are interesting planes to shoot down. They can take so much punishment."

"Head 245 degrees true," Frauka said.

"Two-forty-five true," Wild Boar replied, and now he was all business.

Frauka had two light-guns in front of her, and she projected the bomber position with one and Wild Boar's position with the other on a large map in front of the room. As she continued to plot the course of the converging flights, she continued to project the plot on the map, so that she and the others in the room were able to watch the drama as it unfolded.

"Wild Boar, you are five minutes from contact," she said.

"Five minutes," Wild Boar acknowledged. "I'm forming into attack teams now, and climbing to . . . say now bomber stream altitude."

"Nine thousand meters," Frauka said.

"Wild Boar flight climbing now to 10,000 meters." Frauka could hear the roar of the engine over the voice of the pilot, and her stomach tensed and she could almost imagine that she was there, in the plane with the brave young officer who was Wild Boar.

Gradually the dots grew closer together on the large map, then Frauka heard from Wild Boar.

"Valkyrie, we have contact. It is a large bombardment group, consisting of at least fifty B-17s. We are going in on our first attack now."

Wild Boar left the microphone keyed, probably because of the tension of the moment, Frauka thought, and she could hear the terrible scream of the engine as the airplane started on its long dive.

"Valkyrie, are you there?" Wild Boar asked.

"What? Yes, yes, I'm here," Frauka answered, surprised by the call.

"I thought I'd let you go on this one with me," he said. "Will you send me a kiss for good luck?"

"Yes, yes," Frauka said, now feeling a fear unlike anything she had ever before experienced. She wasn't actually in the cockpit with him, she was safe in the underground flight control headquarters, and yet, she could hear the roar of the engine, and even the breathing of the pilot as he started his run.

"I'm lined up on the lead plane now," Wild Boar said. "Ah, they've seen us, and they are opening fire. We are out of range right now, but the Americans don't care about that. They spray bullets out of their guns as one squirts water from a hose, in a never-ending stream. I must say, Valkyrie, seeing a solid stream of tracer bullets like that does give one a start."

Frauka heard a heavy hammering sound, and at first she didn't know what it was. It lasted for about two seconds, then it stopped. "Oh, sweet, I do believe I hit them in their inboard engine," Wild Boar said, and then Frauka knew that she had been hearing his guns.

"Ah, I did hit them there, I saw it as I dropped through the formation. Now I've got to twist around and make another pass. I'll be climbing on them now so they'll have a better chance at me. Are you enjoying this, my love?"

"No," Frauka said. "Oh, Wild Boar, please, be careful."

"I am called Max," Wild Boar said. There was a loud, popping noise, unlike the sound of the gun she had heard earlier.

"Max!" Frauka called. "Max, what was that?"

"I've a few holes in my fuselage I didn't have before," Max chuckled. Frauka heard the sound of Max's guns again, then she heard a dull thump. "He blew up!" Max said. "What a sight! He blew up, right in front of me."

Frauka heard more engine noise and more gunfire, then she heard Wild Boar's voice again. "Valkyrie, turn to 129.9 and you can hear the Americans talking."

"No, I want to stay with you," Frauka said.

"I'm not going anywhere," Max said. "I'll be here when you come back."

With shaking hands, Frauka tuned her receiver to 129.9, and then was greeted with a cacophony of voices. The Americans not only squirted their machine-gun bullets out like a water hose, they also flooded the airwaves with radio talk. Only the lead planes of the German fighter groups were equipped with radios. But evidently all the American planes were, and every one on every plane must have had access to a microphone.

"Jeez, look at that son-of-a-bitch with the yellow nose! He's crazy! He's flyin' right through everything we can throw at him!"

"We're hit, we're hit, we're goin' down, we're goin' down!"

"Bail out, bail out!"

"There they go, look, see the first one!"

"There's number two, three, four, five, six, I think they are all going to . . . my God, he blew up! Cap'n, did you see him, he just blew up!"

"Two more comin' in at two o'clock, heads up, guys, pay attention to what the hell you are doing."

"There's that son-of-a-bitch with the yellow nose again! He must be their leader . . . I got 'im! I've got a confirmed kill, he's on fire, he's . . . damn, he's trying to get out. Shoot the son-of-a-bitch, don't let him out of the plane!"

Frauka was frightened that Wild Boar had been hit, and she returned quickly to the command frequency. "Wild Boar, Wild Boar!" she called. "Max, Max, are you all right?"

Frauka heard Max chuckle. "Yes," he said. "I'm all right. Are you worried about me, love?"

"I was listening to the Americans," she said. "They said they hit a plane with a yellow nose, I thought it was you."

"No, it is one of the group leaders."

"Did he get out?"

"Yes," Max answered. "There goes another bomber, that's ten they've lost, but forty of them are going to get through. You'd better tell the people ahead to get ready."

"Yes, I will," Frauka said. "I'll be passing them off to the next control as soon as you break off your attack."

"That will be four minutes from now," Max said. "We have enough fuel for one more pass."

"Max, please, be careful," Frauka said.

"Ah, you are worried about me, aren't you? I'm

going to come see you when I get on the ground to let you know I am all right."

"No!" Frauka said. "No, you can't do that!"

"Oh I can't, can I? We are both based in Schweinfurt, so you just watch for me."

"Wild Boar, please," Frauka said, "you mustn't!"

"Valkyrie, this is Wild Boar, breaking contact with bomber stream. Ten bombers shot down, four damaged, pass it on to the next unit, please."

"This is Valkyrie, passing control on," Frauka replied.

The radio connection with Wild Boar was broken, and Frauka sat there listening to the rush of static for several seconds, until she realized that someone was tapping her on the shoulder.

"Yes? What is it?"

"Have you passed the bomber stream on? The controller-director wants to know."

Frauka reached down and changed frequencies so she could speak with the controller-director. "This is Valkyrie."

"Valkyrie, what is wrong? I have been trying to contact you."

"I'm sorry," Frauka said.

"How many bombers did your flight element get?"

"Ten," Frauka said. "And four damaged."

"That is good," the controller-director said. "We lost twelve fighters, but it was a worthwhile exchange."

"Twelve? We lost twelve?"

"Yes."

Frauka closed her eyes and pressed against her eyelids with her fingers. Twelve young men who, but moments ago were vibrant and alive now may be dead. Of course, she knew there was a chance some of them escaped. But the likelihood was that more of them were killed than escaped. Frauka suddenly realized that the controller-director was talking to her.

"I'm sorry," Frauka said. "Were you speaking to me?"

"Yes," the controller-director said. "I said you did well."

"Thank you," Frauka said. "This is Valkyrie, closing the station."

Frauka took the headset off and hung it on the hook in front of her station. She put a lens cap on the light gun which projected the light dots to the plotting board, then she put on her jacket and left the room. Already the new group was coming on duty, ready to follow the bomber stream back out of the country, and vector new fighter elements onto them. Without the earphones to filter out all but your own conversation, the dozens of voices came across as an unintelligible babble. Frauka was glad to finally leave the plotting room and step into the relative peace and quiet of the front office.

"I hear they are working a bomber stream," the woman at the front desk said, as Frauka started to leave. The woman's name was Hannah, and she was a friend of Frauka's.

"Yes," Frauka said. "I believe it is headed for Nürnberg."

"Nürnberg? That's not very far from here, is it?" Hannah said with a shudder.

"No," Frauka said.

"And to think that Hermann Goering said that if one enemy bomb ever landed on German soil we could call him Mayer," Hannah added.

"So tell me," Frauka joked. "How is Herr Mayer doing these days?"

"At least they haven't bombed Schweinfurt," Hannah said. "And I hope they never do. By the way, when is the wedding to be? Your daughter is getting married, isn't she?"

"No," Frauka said. "That is, yes, but there has been no specific date set as yet."

"What are they waiting for, the war to end?"

"I suppose so," Frauka said. "I know they don't want to get married until things become a little more stable. Well, you know how young people are."

"I thought I knew," Hannah said. "But the young people I know would be rushing to get married, not waiting."

"Well, perhaps the war has changed them," Frauka said. "For myself, I can't say that I am too anxious for Lisl to get married yet. She is still young. There is still time."

The phone on Hannah's desk rang, and as she answered it, Frauka waved good-bye and left the building.

It was cold outside, and Frauka pulled her coat about her as she walked, quickly, to the nearest trolley stop. A sign in a store window said, "Merry Christmas, '42." Below the sign was a gaily painted wreath of holly, and in the wreath, a bright red candle.

The window sign was the only indication that Christmas was but a few days away. None of the lampposts sported greenery, or lights, or any other type of decoration. How different Schweinfurt was this year from all the previous Christmases. Of course, there was a war on, and that explained it, but it didn't keep Frauka from feeling sadness over the situation. At that, she realized, Schweinfurt had much more to be thankful for than many other cities in Germany: not one bomb had fallen on Schweinfurt.

Frauka didn't think Schweinfurt would be bombed. She had plotted the bomber streams coming into Germany day after day and night after night now, and not once had any enemy bombers given the slightest indication that they might head for Schweinfurt. Heinrich, on the other hand, was convinced that it was only a matter of time until the city was bombed, because he believed the ballbearing plants made an ideal target for a raid. Because of that he had placed all the anti-aircraft guns in a ring around the city, to deliver deadly accurate fire against any bombers which might actually try to bomb Schweinfurt. In addition to the active defenses, Heinrich had also prepared underground tunnels to accept the machinery, so that if the factory were bombed, the machinery could be moved and production could continue.

The machinery wasn't the only thing Heinrich had moved into the underground tunnels. He had moved his office, and even his bed, and lately, with the production schedules at peak, Heinrich had been spending a lot of time at the plant. Frauka's busy hours as an aircraft plotter, and Heinrich's busy schedule at the plant, meant that the two only saw each other about two or three times per month.

Frauka was particularly frustrated now, because she wished to discuss Lisl with Heinrich, but he was never around for her to talk to. The truth was, Frauka was worried about Lisl.

Frauka told Hannah that Lisl and Paul postponed the wedding because they were waiting for the situation to stabilize. That was true, to a degree, but the stability that was needed was not in the war, but in Lisl and Paul's private lives. Lisl had changed drastically. Frauka wasn't sure what brought about the change, but she was fairly able to place when it happened. It happened during the summer, when Lisl went to visit Rudi.

At first, Frauka had thought that it was because Rudi was wounded, and Lisl couldn't adjust to that. But when Rudi left the hospital for two weeks of convalescent leave at home, Frauka saw that he had not been wounded badly enough to cause Lisl's odd behavior. Then, when Rudi received orders to go back to duty, his orders sent him not to Russia, but to Italy, the warmest and safest assignment in the entire German Army. So, it could not be worry about Rudi that was causing Lisl's strange behavior.

What was it then? Why did she spend long periods of morose silence? Where did she go so often? And what had happened between Lisl and Paul?

Lisl wasn't the only one to change, though. Paul had changed as well. He no longer seemed as sweet and as full of innocent, boyish charm as he once was. But then, Frauka asked herself, who was the same? The war had affected everyone, even her.

The trolley stopped and Frauka got on, then shuffled tiredly to a seat in the rear. She wondered if Heinrich would be home tonight. If so, she had nothing to fix for supper. It was very difficult to go shopping now, not only because of the difficult hours she kept, but also because there was so little of everything in the stores. "Sorry, war shortage" signs seemed to fill every sausage and meat counter, and were even beginning to take over the vegetable stalls as well. Frauka had some black bread, and she could make some cabbage soup if Heinrich or Lisl came home for supper. If not, she would just eat a piece of bread, drink a cup of hot tea and go right to bed.

Down inside, Frauka was ashamed to a degree for

feeling sorry for herself. At least she had a bed to go to. There would be many families in Nürnberg tonight who could not make the same claim. At least ten bombers wouldn't be adding to the misery of the Nürnberg citizens though, she thought. She was glad that ten were shot down, and she wished all of them had been destroyed. She wondered if the German people knew how much they actually owed to men like Wild Boar. Max, he said his name was. Frauka wondered about Max. How old was he? What did he look like? He was handsome, she decided. He was definitely handsome.

What was she doing? Frauka's face flushed red, and she looked up in embarrassment at the others in the trolley, as if they could read her mind. She was actually thinking about Max, not as a disembodied voice over the radio, but as a man. And not just a man, but a *handsome* man. What was worse, during that period of fantasy, Frauka had even realized a warm dampness in her loins, and a thought of forbidden thrill passed unbidden over her as she wondered what Max would be like in bed.

"More wine, my dear?" Lange asked. He held up a bottle of fine, vintage Bordeaux, and it gleamed richly in the soft candlelight.

Lange was speaking to Lisl, his dinner companion of the evening. Lange was dressed in his finest S.S. uniform, and Lisl was wearing a beautiful Paris creation. They were in the special suite, and the table was set with the finest silver, china and crystal, while a Christmas centerpiece provided the soft glow of candlelight to capture the wine's beautiful color.

"Yes, thank you," Lisl said. "It is very good wine."

"It should be," Lange said. "This wine, like the

dress you are wearing, came from Paris. I managed to"—Lange cleared his throat—"liberate, shall we say, several cases of the finest vintage, along with several gowns, dresses, and some jewelry. The spoils of victory, you know."

Lisl held her glass as the wine was poured, then smiling, she raised it to her lips and drank it down, enjoying its rich, full-bodied flavor, without the slightest feeling of guilt. After all, she had earned this evening, she thought. She had been coming to the Lebensborn Home for nearly six months, fulfilling her obligation to Lange at every trip. She had not become pregnant, but she had tried. She really had tried, because after the first crude attempt at an alcohol contraception, she hadn't done anything else to interrupt nature.

Lisl had not become pregnant, so Lange continued to have her visit him once or twice a week. But now the visits did not seem as odious to Lisl. After all, Lange often gave her gifts, presenting her with things she could not get otherwise. He had given her such things as silk, wool, jewelry, and sometimes sausages and meats Lisl had not seen in the market place in over a year. Besides, her relationship with Paul certainly wasn't progressing. Her marriage to Paul had been postponed indefinitely, by Paul's wish, not hers. She tried to talk to him, to tell him how desperately she needed him now more than ever, but to no avail. He was becoming a stranger to her, and she didn't like it. Sometimes, she felt like telling him that he had no right to treat her this way. After all, he was alive, only because she had sacrificed herself to save him. She was doing what she was doing, to protect the fact that Paul was a Jew, and the least Paul could do, she thought, was to show a little gratitude. Very well, if he wished to treat her that way, she could find other diversions.

"I've a gift for you," Lange said, handing a small, beautifully wrapped package across the table to Lisl.

"Oh, for me?" Lisl exclaimed, accepting it easily and without shame. "But what kind of gift?"

"A Christmas gift," Lange said. "Go ahead, open it."

"But shouldn't I wait for Christmas?"

"No," Lange said. "Open it now."

Lisl tore off the wrapping, then let out a gasp of pleased surprise. The gift was a black nightgown made of the sheerest lace. Lisl put her hand under it, and saw every finger as clearly as if her hand were before her face.

"Why," she said. "Manfried, this is absolutely scandalous."

"Put it on," Lange said.

"Put it on? I might as well wear nothing."

"Please," Lange said. "Put it on."

"Can't I wait until after dinner?"

"Put it on," Lange said. "You will be my dessert."

Lisl laughed a low, throaty laugh. "Very well," she said. "I'll just step behind the dressing screen while I change."

Lisl moved from the table to the dressing screen in the corner of the room and quickly changed into the nightgown. When she stepped out from behind the screen a moment later, every curve of her body, every smooth inch of her skin, was totally visible.

"Oh, yes," Lange said, letting out a long, slow, breath. "Beautiful. Absolutely beautiful."

"Show me," Lisl heard herself saying. "Show me how beautiful you think I am." She had closed her mind to everything now except the hedonistic desire for pleasure. In a world which was not of her making, pleasure was the only reward, and the only escape. And Lisl had decided to escape in whatever way she could.

19

Rudi walked along the Via Tiburtina Vetus in the section of the city known as Ancient Rome. On his left stood the Colosseum, while ahead of him the specially braced Arch of Constantine bridged the road. He had been in Rome for nearly nine months now, and the remnants of the mighty Roman Empire still impressed him, not so much with their individual magnificence, as with their collective reminder of man's transient status on this planet. Countless generations had been born, made their puny efforts, then turned to dust while these structures stood by in haughty grandeur.

A poster, faded by weather, and torn on one side, decorated a kiosk on the corner. It had a picture of the face of Mussolini, with his jaw thrust out and his lower lip rolled down, snarling into space like a man who could envision the future. Behind Mussolini's face there was a ghost-like image of a Caesar from the days of the Roman Empire, and beneath the picture, the words:

*Il Duce and the Caesars of old, a wondrous past,
a glorious future!*

Street vendors displayed their wares on the sidewalk. One black market vendor had eggs, and though they were going at the high price of four marks apiece, the vendor was doing a brisk business. As Rudi passed them by, they all turned their backs to him, hiding their faces from him, lest he decide to enforce the law against black marketeering. The law was very strict; those who engaged in the black market could be shot. Realistically, however, Rome was a city which now existed on about 900 calories per day per citizen, and without the augmentation of black market supplies, many would be starving to death. Therefore the law was enforced only sporadically, and prosecution was seldom, if ever, carried out.

"German swine," Rudi heard from a group of people, though he pretended he didn't hear it. The Italians were allies. Some allies, he thought. The Poles, Belgians, and French he had encountered in those conquered countries, were more trustworthy than the Italians, and they were supposed to be the enemy.

Rudi had very little respect for the Italian Army. They were slovenly, ill-trained, and apt to break and run at the first sign of trouble. There seemed to be no discipline in the Italian Army, and one might as well talk to a private as an officer when trying to get something done.

And yet, despite the constant undercurrent of antagonism which seemed to exist between the German and Italian Armies, Rudi rather liked the Italian people. They bore up under the hardships with a stoic determination which spoke well of their 2000-year history. It was as if the people, like their ancient monuments, were determined not to be changed by the temporary insanity which had come over the world. They would survive, with their personality and their nationality intact.

Rudi knew of one Italian in particular who seemed to embody that noble Roman spirit. She was a very beautiful girl, with dark, flashing eyes, and soft, chestnut brown hair. Her name was Maria Todaro, and Rudi had met her in an art gallery six months before. She was the daughter of one of Italy's best-known artists, though her father's contemporary art style was not in favor with the Fascists and Nazis, so he had fallen onto hard times. Maria had to work at the gallery to support them.

Though Rudi made an effort to befriend her, Maria had not been receptive to Rudi's earlier advances, and in fact discouraged them. Rudi kept returning to the gallery where she worked, and when he asked her to dinner for the third time, only to be turned down for the third time, he asked her why she would have nothing to do with him.

"You are a German officer, and as such, you represent everything I hate," Maria answered.

"You hate the military?"

"No, I do not hate the military. I think the military is a necessary evil for any country. Perhaps if Italy had a more efficient military, we would not now be under the yoke of the German occupation."

Rudi laughed. "Italy and Germany are allies," he said.

"We are allies? You have stolen our food, looted our art treasures, and gutted our industries. You have taken Italian citizens off the streets and shipped them to concentration camps in Poland—"

"Only the Jews," Rudi interrupted.

"Jews who were Italian citizens," Maria went on. "And, the most terrible crime of all, you have robbed every Italian of his dignity and self-respect. Now, Lieutenant, if that is what you do to your allies, what do you do to your enemies? No, I don't hate the military, I just hate the Germany military, and what it represents. Therefore, I cannot help but hate you."

Rudi had never before encountered such hostility on a personal basis, and he mounted a campaign to show Maria that she was wrong, that not all Germans were as she perceived them. It was for that reason and no more that he began pursuing her, or at least, that was what he told himself. But somewhere the reason for his persistence changed. Rudi discovered that the fire-and-ice personality of Maria, combined with her smoldering beauty, made her a creature of exceptional merit. He began pursuing her because he wanted her. Then, one spring day, Maria surprised Rudi by agreeing to go out with him.

"What?" Rudi asked, shocked that Maria had answered yes.

Maria was cataloging the art in the gallery, going from painting to painting with a notebook and taking notes on each one, as Rudi followed along beside her.

"I said yes," Maria said. "If I don't go out with you, I'm afraid you will come in here every day and bother me, and that would be bad for business."

"Yes," Rudi grinned. "Yes, it would be bad for business, wouldn't it? So, where do you want to go? I know a wonderful little sidewalk café that—"

"We will go to visit my cousin," Maria said.

"Your cousin?"

"Yes. He has a place in the country near here and there is to be a picnic on Saturday. There are no soldiers there, and no Germans. It is very nice."

"Yes, without Germans, I'm sure it is nice," Rudi said, trying for sarcasm but missing, and not even caring that it missed, because she was so beautiful and so full of spirit and life and he wanted her more than he had ever wanted anyone or anything.

There were dozens of people at the little country house, all cousins or aunts or uncles of Maria, and Rudi soon lost track of who was who, but he didn't care. Rudi was Maria's guest, and because of that he was welcome, so there was no talk of politics, or war, or hardship. There was only wine and food—more food than Rudi had seen in a long time. In addition to the wine and food, there was song and dance, and Rudi laughed and danced, and for one afternoon at least, the war did not exist.

It was one o'clock in the morning, and Rudi was lying in the bed in the small cloakroom he was using as a bedroom, thinking about the day. He lay with his hands folded behind his head, staring at the silver-dappled pattern on the wall. The silver came from the bright moon which hung in the soft, Italian night sky, and the dappling came from the orchard trees which moved under the gentle breeze just outside the farmhouse.

Somewhere in this house of cousins, aunts and uncles, Maria was in bed, and though Rudi wasn't with her, his thoughts certainly were. He laughed at his thoughts. He was a warrior, an officer of an army which had conquered most of Europe. There had been many women over the last three years, in Poland, Belgium, France, Russia, and even here, in Italy. He had taken them all as Germany had taken their countries, as a victorious warrior plundering the spoils. And yet, he had not taken Maria that way, or any other way, and, as badly as he wanted her, he knew that he did not want her unless she wanted him as well.

Rudi fluffed the pillow and tried to get comfortable. It seemed strange that he couldn't get comfortable on this bed. He had slept in mud, snow, rain, in hot-bouncing tanks and on hard rocks. Why couldn't he sleep in this bed?

Finally, with a sigh, Rudi got out of bed and walked over to the dutch door which led from the cloakroom to the courtyard. He opened the top half of the door, leaned on the bottom half and looked out. The hills were moon-painted in silver and shadow as they rolled away from the house, and in the distance he could see the dark mass that was Rome. Rome was blacked out against possible air radio now, but he knew that in normal times it must gleam like a cluster of diamonds among the hills.

Rudi pushed open the bottom of the door, then walked outside. He was wearing only his undershorts, but he knew that it was so late that everyone else must be asleep, so he didn't bother to pull on his trousers. Besides, the breeze felt good to his bare legs.

Outside, the grass felt soft and cool, and Rudi walked across the small lawn, then climbed the low stone fence, and sat on the side of the hill just beyond the fence, looking out over the peaceful countryside. The gentle breeze carried on its breath the aromatic perfume of sweet shrubs and high-blooming verbena. Just below where Rudi was sitting, a stream bubbled and splashed its way down the side of the hill, and from there Rudi could see the water breaking white around the rocks. He stood up and walked down to be closer to it.

"When I was a little girl, I thought that stream

made music only for me," a woman's voice said from behind Rudi; startled, he turned to see Maria. Maria laughed, her laughter bubbling out with as light and lilting a sound as that made by the brook. "I'm sorry," she said. "Did I startle you?"

"Yes," Rudi admitted. "I didn't really expect anyone to be awake now."

"I was looking out the window from my room and I saw you come down here," Maria said. She smiled, and her teeth gleamed white and lovely in the moonlight. "I couldn't resist the impulse to come down here with you."

"I'm glad you did," Rudi said.

"Did you enjoy the day?" Maria asked.

"Yes," Rudi said. "I enjoyed it very much."

"It wasn't exactly what you had in mind, though, was it?"

"What do you mean?"

"You wanted to go out with me. You didn't bargain for my entire family."

Rudi smiled. "No, I didn't," he said. "But they are nice people. I like them, and I enjoyed the day. I wish everyone could . . ." Rudi gave a little laugh then let his thought drop in midsentence.

"What?" Maria asked.

"It's silly."

"No, please, what were you going to say?"

"I wish everyone could see everyone else as I have seen your family," Rudi said. "I mean if Germans could see Poles, and the English could see the Germans, and the Americans could see the Italians as family, cousins, brothers, aunts, and not as alien cultures, there would be no war."

"And the Jews?" Maria asked.

"We Germans are going to have much to answer

for," Rudi said. "We are all guilty, if not by commission, then by omission, because none of us have done anything to stop it."

"Are you saying you don't approve of your country's policy toward the Jews?"

"No," Rudi said. "I don't approve. But I have done nothing to stop it."

"What can you do?" Maria asked with a frustrated sigh. "What can any of us do? The whole world is guilty of the crime of omission, Rudi. You Germans aren't alone."

"You called me Rudi," Rudi said, pleased at the sound her voice gave his name. "I like that."

"Does it please you?" Maria asked, and at that moment, Rudi knew that he was going to make love to her.

"Yes," Rudi said. "It pleases me very much."

"I'm glad it pleases you," Maria said.

Rudi looked into Maria's eyes, trying to gauge their depth. They were dark and flashing, and they seemed to go on forever. Somewhere down there he could see her very soul, and he liked what he saw. Rudi put his hand to her face, let his fingers linger for a moment to caress her cheek, and finally pulled her lips to his for a kiss.

Maria opened her lips to Rudi's kiss, then leaned into him and rested her soft, sensuous body against his. Rudi was engulfed with overwhelming and bewildering sensations. He recognized the unmistakable signs of sexual arousal, but he did not recognize the soft, tender feelings which swept over him.

Maria's graceful hands and supple fingers moved down Rudi's bare back, leaving a trail of fire in their wake. The tenderness he felt commingled with the heightening desire, and Rudi knew that he was losing

control of his own actions. He was subservient to the
will of the beautiful woman with him, and when he
opened her bodice to bare her hot breasts, it was as
if his hands were drawn there by some powerful
magnetism, and not by his conscious direction. His
hands cupped her breasts, warm and supple, and he
stroked the swollen nipples with his thumbs.

"Oh, yes, Rudi," Maria breathed.

Gently, but with a passion he was barely able to
keep within bounds, Rudi pulled Maria's gown over
her head, then lowered her to the grassy slope beside
the splashing brook. He moved over her, and Maria,
willingly, even eagerly, spread her legs to receive him,
pushing against him, stabbing her darting tongue into
his mouth as he thrust into her. She moaned and
whimpered with the joy of it. Beside where they made
love the dark water continued to spill over the rocks,
supplying a symphony to accompany the lovers, from
the bass roar of the rushing current to the soprano
trill of the rock-formed eddies.

They made love, not in the selfish quest of individual pleasure, but in the unselfish joy of giving to
each other all that could be given. They knew several
moments of shared ecstasy, during which time Rudi
approached the precipice many times, only to back
away so as to continue the sensations longer. Then,
when he could no longer hold himself back, he found
himself propelled over the edge in a burst of rapture
which came from every nerve-ending in his body.

Afterward they lay together arm in arm, and shared
the wonder that had come to them, and Rudi knew
that for the first time in his life, he was in love.

Rudi knew that Maria returned his love, even before
she would admit it, and he knew how difficult it was

for her, so he was patient and understanding and soon all her reserves were broken down and now they shared a life together which made Rudi's months in Rome the most wonderful period of his entire life.

Rudi was a liaison officer between the German Panzer Corps and the Italian Armor Command. Though the use of the term "advisor" was frowned upon, because officially it made it seem as if the Italian Army was inferior to the German Army and thus needed advice, in truth that was what Rudi was. He had been promoted to captain, and yet within the Italian Army he had the status and respect of one much higher in rank. Lieutenant colonels and colonels listened to Rudi when it came to developing tactics and employment techniques for the Italian armor.

Because of Rudi's position, he was able to rent an apartment in Rome where he spent the nights, and he commuted to work by day, just as a civilian would. Maria shared his apartment with him, and they often had other couples over, just as if they were a man and wife entertaining. It was a way of life Rudi would have welcomed for the next forty years.

The apartment was just beyond the Arch of Constantine, up a narrow flight of stairs between a tobacco store and a shop which sold straw baskets. Here, the Italians Rudi encountered were more friendly. They knew that he lived as they lived, and in fact shared his apartment with one of them. They even respected Maria and treated her not as a German whore but as a woman in love, and when Rudi started up the steps they smiled and greeted him with friendly words.

The smell of cooking drifted down the stairs as Rudi started up, and his stomach growled in eager anticipation. Despite the food shortages, Maria somehow managed to come up with meals which were deliciously satisfying. In fact, if there was any one thing Rudi had to complain about, it was that Maria fed him too well, and when easier days returned, he feared she would make him fat.

Rudi pushed the door open to his apartment, and called out to Maria. "I am home."

Maria came from the kitchen at his call, wearing an apron and smelling of tomato sauce and cheese, smiling happily to see him. She kissed him, then, with her hands locked just behind his neck, leaned away from him and looked into his face. Her eyes sparkled brightly, and she laughed, a playful little laugh.

"I have a secret," she said.

"What sort of secret?"

"There is someone here to see you."

Rudi looked at Maria with surprise. "Someone is *here* to see *me?*"

"Yes."

"Who?"

"Someone you thought you would never see again," Maria said.

"But who would it—"

"For God's sake, girl, we'd better tell him or he'll have a stroke trying to figure it out," a man's voice said, then, Rudi saw Ernst Kant coming from the kitchen.

"Kant!" Rudi said. "My God! I thought you were dead! I thought you were killed at Stalingrad!"

Rudi's old commander chuckled. "Rudi, my boy, I'm what's known as a survivor. I managed to leave Stalingrad in one of the last planes to get out of there, a little two-seater Storch. I was promoted to Lieutenant Colonel, and re-assigned to Italy. I heard you were here in Rome, so I thought I would come pay a visit to an old friend." Kant looked around the apartment and smiled. "I must say, you've done all right for yourself."

"How did you know where to come?" Rudi asked. "How did you know about my apartment and where to find me?"

"Rudi, don't be so naive, my boy," Kant said. "I merely pulled rank on an S.S. Major, whose job it is to keep tabs on everyone."

"Well, this is one time I'm thankful for the S.S.," Rudi said happily. "You've no idea how glad I am to see you, Ernst. I just knew that you, and everyone I served with, was killed or captured with von Paulus' army."

"They just about were," Kant said. Kant took the monocle out of his eye and polished it before he put it back in. "It was, as our British friends might say, one bloody mess."

"Worse than the winter before?"

Maria brought the two men a glass of wine, and they sat in the small living room while she continued to fix supper. Rudi noticed that there were already three plates on the table, and he felt grateful that Maria had accepted his friend without question, even though he was a sufficiently high-ranking German officer to really symbolize her dislike of the German military.

"I can tell you what it was like," Kant said. "You were with us the winter before. You will have a little understanding for the situation. Those who were never there will never understand. One hundred years from now they can read of our ordeal, but they will still not understand," Kant said. Kant took a sip of wine before he went on, and then in his eyes Rudi saw the pain and suffering and horror he had witnessed.

"On Christmas day," Kant said, "von Paulus gave

the men of the Sixth Army a Christmas present. He allowed us to slaughter four hundred horses for food. The night before, Christmas Eve, men crawled nearly a kilometer on their bellies through the snow, to sneak into a wheat field and cut unharvested grain with pen knives, bayonets, any tool they could find, and bring the grain back into the dugouts and redoubts. We boiled the wheat and horse-flesh to make our Christmas soup. On that same day, nearly fifteen hundred men died from frostbite, typhus, dysentery and starvation."

Maria, who had finished with the meal preparation, had come to sit on the sofa beside Rudi, and he felt her shiver under his arm as Kant spoke.

"Always there was the cold," Kant went on. "The icy wind which seemed to come straight from the North Pole itself, lashing against our skin like the cut of a million tiny razor blades. And when someone just gave up and died, the wind and the snow took them over so that less than one hour after life had left the body, a shroud of snow and ice would cover them, and only the toe of a boot, or a limb frozen to stone, would remind someone that this chunk of ice had, at one time, been a human being. Behind the ice and snow and cold wind, and beyond the last measure of food, there were the Russians, more and more of them, fat and warm and well armed." Kant laughed, a short, bitter laugh. "Hitler promoted von Paulus to the rank of Field Marshal, then informed him that no German Field Marshal in the history of warfare had ever surrendered his troops. He ordered von Paulus to continue the fight till the last round of ammunition.

"What Hitler didn't know was that the last round of ammunition had already been used. I saw men clubbing a horse to death, because they had no bullets, then they smashed open the horse's head and ate its steaming brains raw, as much for the warmth as for the food. That afternoon, von Paulus informed me that he intended to surrender before nightfall. He ordered me to take his final dispatch in the last flight out. We no longer had control of an airfield, so the pilot had to take off from one of the streets of Stalingrad. It was littered with rubble, chunks of ice, and frozen bodies, but somehow the pilot got it off the ground. I mouthed one continual prayer from the time the pilot started the engine in Stalingrad until we landed behind our own lines." Kant sighed. "To tell you the truth, Rudi, I thought I would probably be shot for desertion. After all, Hitler had ordered Russia held to the last man and the last bullet. But I think the shock of losing the entire Sixth Army was too much. I wasn't shot, I wasn't even reprimanded. Instead, I was promoted to Lieutenant Colonel, and, here I am."

Rudi reached over to take Kant's hand, and he squeezed it warmly. "I am glad you are here," he said. "I am glad to have someone from the old days, and I am glad you survived that terrible ordeal."

Kant looked at Maria. "My dear, I hope you will forgive me for such a horrible story," he said. "You have prepared such a wonderful dinner, and I have nearly spoiled it with such talk."

"Please, don't concern yourself over my sensitivities," Maria said. She looked at Rudi. "And to think that you could have been there," she said.

"Well, I am thankful that I wasn't. Now, let us eat before I begin to feel guilty for having such wonderful food."

"I say, this *is* wonderful food," Kant said, as he sat at the table and watched Maria heap the pasta on his plate. "Oh, there is another who survived and is here with me. You may want to see him too."

"Who?"

"Sergeant Heibler," Kant said.

"Heibler? Ernst, are you sure? Sergeant Heibler is here in Italy?"

"Yes. He was in Poland until this morning. I saw his orders come across my desk."

"But how on earth did Heibler get out of Russia?"

Kant laughed. "This is one time the old 19th Infantry service came to his rescue. It seems that during the optimistic days of last summer, when the High Command was absolutely certain that Moscow would be taken, they moved out all those men whom they thought did not deserve the 'honor' of being in on the kill. Sergeant Heibler, by virtue of his 19th Infantry background, was one of those transferred."

Rudi laughed. "Oh, that's marvelous," he said. "That is truly marvelous. What a wonderful case of poetic justice."

"Would you like Heibler assigned to you?"

"You could do that?"

"As easy as that," Kant said, snapping his fingers. "I'll have his orders made up tomorrow, making him your non-commissioned officer."

"Thanks," Rudi said.

"Little enough pay for a meal like this," Kant said, shoving a forkful into his mouth. "Uhmm," he said, closing his eyes and sighing. "I do believe I have died and gone to heaven."

20

IT was a lovely, soft summer day in August of 1943. It was the kind of day which, before the war, would have beckoned Frauka out for a picnic beneath the shade trees, and in the midst of the summer flowers. Frauka stood at her bedroom window and looked across the gently rolling fields which surrounded their home on the outskirts of Schweinfurt, and she stretched, lazily.

"Oh, Heinrich, isn't this a lovely day?" she asked of her husband, who was awake, but sitting up in bed behind her. He was finishing work on a plan which was supposed to decentralize the production of ball-bearings, ensuring that no more than 39% of any type bearing would be produced in any one plant. The Minister of Armaments, Albert Speer, had approved of his plan, but Hitler had balked, saying that decentralization was less efficient.

"How can any day be a lovely day when we are at war?" Heinrich replied.

"Oh, can't you forget the war for one day?"

Heinrich looked over at his wife, and he was struck with how pretty she was, and he wondered how she managed to stay so attractive, and how he could possibly ignore her to the point that this moment could come as a surprise to him.

"Sweet, I would give anything if I could forget the war for one day, or one hour, or even one minute. But how can I? Can the people of Hamburg? One hundred thousand were killed in the fire-bombings last month, and those who survived have no shelter. Can you forget the war? You talk with the fighter pilots every day who go up against these devil bombers—can you delude yourself into thinking there is no war?"

"No," Frauka said sadly. She turned back to look through the window, and the scene which but a moment before had struck her with its beauty now seemed sad, for it brought into sharp focus the contrast between peace and war. "No, I can't delude myself. The Americans bomb our cities by day, the British by night, and we've only the same handful of brave young men to send up against them again and again." Her eyes suddenly welled with tears. "Heinrich, I talk to those young men day after day, and often I have new voices to talk to, so that I can only wonder what happened to the ones I spoke with the day before. They are Rudi's age, and they are dying."

Frauka had come to sit on the bed beside Heinrich, and Heinrich put his arm around her. "I know," he said, softly. "I know."

"The war is going badly, isn't it?"

"Yes," Heinrich admitted. "We are losing men at an alarming rate in Russia, and we have been driven out of Africa. The Americans and British have taken Sicily, and it's only a matter of time until all of Italy is taken. It doesn't take a genius to see that our situation is worsening.

"I am so worried about Rudi," Frauka said.

"Rudi is a soldier," Heinrich replied. "He has faced combat before and survived. I am sure he will survive this. I'm not worried about Rudi as much as I am worried about Lisl."

"Lisl? What do you mean? She's working as a nurse, caring for infant children in the Lebensborn Home. What could be safer than that?"

"I'm not worried about her physical safety, Frauka," Heinrich said. "I'm worried about something else."

"You mean the fact that she and Paul have broken up? Don't worry about that, Heinrich, they are young. If it wasn't meant to be, then it wasn't meant to be. Better they should realize now than after they were married, don't you think so? Besides, no one ever died of a broken heart."

"I'm not worried about Lisl's broken heart, either," Heinrich said.

"Well then, what are you worried about?"

"I'm worried about Lisl's immortal soul," Heinrich said calmly.

It was afternoon before Lisl awoke. Since coming to work at the Lebensborn Home, she had moved into the Home, where she was given her own room with an outside terrace overlooking the front garden. Ostensibly, Lisl was in charge of caring for the babies which were produced by the Little Blonde Sisters; however, she herself was still available for impregnation, in the event that could be achieved. It seemed almost certain now, though, that Lisl could not become pregnant. She had certainly been exposed to enough opportunities, not only by Lange, but by as many as forty other S.S. men, none of whom had gotten her with child.

The fact that Lisl could not get pregnant did not

lessen her popularity. She was the woman most in demand by those who were selected to visit the Lebensborn Home. That was because Lisl was not only a woman of exceptional beauty, but a woman of exceptional erotic skill as well. Lisl enjoyed sex, and she made those who were with her enjoy it too, so that the supposed purpose of their cohabitation, procreation, was frequently forgotten during the pursuit of pleasure.

Pleasure had become Lisl's guideword. Nothing else had meaning to her. She had not even heard from Paul in six months, but she never thought of him anymore. She heard from her parents on a very infrequent basis, and all she knew about Rudi was that he was in Italy somewhere. She made no effort to follow the war. None of it had touched her so far, so she didn't really care what was happening. She knew that her comforts were seen to, and that she not only had the opportunity to pursue pleasure, but was encouraged to seek it.

The bright sunlight which had made the summer day so lovely to her mother now irritated Lisl, for it had moved across the afternoon sky to shine in her face. That was what awakened her, and she groaned in irritation.

"Gretchen!" she called, without getting up. "Gretchen, where are you?"

The door to Lisl's room opened, and a young, well-scrubbed, sixteen-year-old girl stepped in hesitantly. Gretchen had been hired to work in the laundry and do general housecleaning chores for the Home, but Lisl's privileged position was such that Gretchen's duties had been adjusted to the point that she was very nearly Lisl's personal maid.

"Yes, Fraulein Rodl?"

"Pull the curtains shut on that window," Lisl said. "The sun woke me up."

"I'm sorry, Fraulein Rodl, but the curtains are being laundered," Gretchen explained.

"What? You mean I have to lie in the sunlight like this?"

"I'm sorry, Fraulein," Gretchen said again. "Perhaps I can hang a bedsheet and—"

"No," Lisl said. "No, just forget it." Lisl sat up in bed and brushed her hair back from her face. She was nude, and as she raised her hand to her hair, her breast slipped out from under the sheet. There was a large purple mark on her breast, just beside her nipple, and Gretchen stared at it. Lisl saw Gretchen's eyes and she laughed. "What's the matter?" she asked. "Haven't you ever seen a hickey before?"

"A hickey?"

"That's what this is," Lisl said, putting her finger on the mark. Her fingernails were perfectly manicured and painted silver, so that the nail of her finger contrasted sharply with the purple of the mark. "My lover last night, a handsome, young S.S. lieutenant, gave it to me," Lisl said.

"How? Did he hit you there? Does it hurt?"

"How can you work in a place like this and be so naive?" Lisl asked. "No, it doesn't hurt. It felt wonderful when he did it. All he did was put my breast in his mouth and suck hard until the blood came to the surface. Here, give me your breast and I shall give one to you."

"No!" Gretchen gasped, covering her small bosom with crossed arms and retreating in fear.

Lisl laughed as Gretchen fled from the room, then she got out of bed and walked over to stand in front of the window. With the curtains gone from the window, Lisl knew that the two guards who were standing at the front gate would be able to see her if they looked around. They were common soldiers, and as such, were denied visitation rights to any of the women in the Lebensborn Home. Because Lisl knew they couldn't visit her, she also knew that the chance glimpse of her nudity would be a cruel jest. That thought made the idea delicious to her, so she tapped on the window until they both looked around.

"Hello, you poor, dumb beasts," she said softly, as she held her hands by her naked thighs in invitation. "Look, and want, but you cannot have." She licked her lips, then thrust her pelvis suggestively forward. She could almost hear them as they gasped in the agony of their frustration, and she chuckled aloud as she finally walked away from the window, denying them even that small recompense. She walked over to the bedside table then, and poured herself her morning glass of schnapps.

Frauka felt a sickening hollowness in the pit of her stomach. They were coming for Schweinfurt!

"Controller-Director, this is Valkyrie," she said, her tongue so thick with fear that she wasn't certain she could even make the words.

"Go ahead, Valkyrie."

"I have a plot on the incoming bomber stream. Their target appears to be Schweinfurt."

"Very well, I shall notify the Schweinfurt anti-aircraft batteries. You alert Wild Boar."

Wild Boar, Frauka thought. That was Max Priller. Frauka had gone so far as to find out who he was, though, other than the exchange of flirtatious remarks over the radio, she had had no contact with him. He was twenty-five, the same age as Rudi, and he had already been decorated several times. He had nearly one hundred enemy planes to his credit, and he was one of Germany's leading aces.

"This is Wild Boar," Max said, after Frauka contacted the fighter squadron on readiness call. "Valkyrie, is that you?"

"Yes," Frauka answered. "I have an action order."

Max chuckled. "Valkyrie, we can't go on meeting this way, you know. Someone is going to get suspicious."

"I, uh, have a large bomber stream, at sector G-11. Turn to course, uh, 24—wait, make that 310 true."

"Coming to course 310 true," Max replied. "Valkyrie, what's wrong with you today? You sound nervous."

"The planes," Frauka said. "They are coming here . . . to Schweinfurt, and I'm frightened."

Max chuckled softly. "Welcome to my world, love. I am always frightened. Say now their altitude."

"Eight thousand, five hundred meters," Frauka said.

"Wild Boar climbing to 9,000 meters."

"Oh, Max, stop them, please."

"Don't worry, I'll do my damndest," Max said.

Frauka projected the bomber stream and Wild Boar flights onto the large map in front of the room, then watched with the others as the bomber light source moved slowly but inexorably toward Schweinfurt.

"Herr Rodl!" Papf called down to Heinrich. Heinrich was on the floor of the two centimeter bearing assembly line, helping with the adjustment of a stator guide. Papf had come out onto the catwalk which overlooked the assembly line. "Herr Rodl, emergency! Emergency!" he called excitedly.

"Ach! What isn't an emergency?" Heinrich replied.

"Try and adjust that screw and I think it will stay in line," he said to the machine operator, just before he left.

"*Jawohl, Herr Rodl*," the operator said.

Heinrich climbed the metal stairs to the catwalk, where Papf stood, mopping his face with his handkerchief.

"They are coming," Papf said.

"They are coming? Who is coming?"

"The bombers," Papf said. "They are coming to Schweinfurt! We have just received a warning!"

"Sound the air-raid alarm quickly," Heinrich said. "Get everyone into the shelters. Get my car ready. I'm going to the gun stations."

Heinrich hurried into his office to call the anti-aircraft gun crew captain, only to learn that they had already been informed and were now bringing ammunition into position for use.

"I'll be right there," Heinrich promised the captain, and as he hung up the phone, he heard the wail of the air raid siren.

There was not a city in Germany over the population of one hundred thousand which had not yet been bombed, so the experience was not a new one to Germans. But this was the first time the bombers had ever approached Schweinfurt, so Heinrich could well understand the sense of fright which he saw on everyone's faces. Many had expressions which went beyond fright and into sheer panic. Heinrich hoped that they would be able to maintain control of themselves, for panic, he believed, would have a more harmful effect than the bombs when they fell.

"We are such a small city," Heinrich heard one of the workers saying, as they crowded toward the bomb-shelters. "Why would they want to bomb us?"

The man's question was repeated by several others, but Heinrich didn't take the time to answer any of them. He wasn't surprised that Schweinfurt was being bombed. The only surprise to him was that they had escaped this long.

Heinrich's car was waiting in the drive out in front of the building, and his driver was sitting behind the wheel, nervously tapping it with his fingers.

"To the number one gun position. Hurry," Heinrich said, slipping into the front seat beside his driver. The car was moving, even before Heinrich closed his door.

Heinrich thought of his family. Frauka was safe, he was sure of that, because she was on duty in the plotting room. The plotting room was an exceptionally well-fortified underground bunker which would survive a direct hit from one of the bombers. Lisl was in the Lebensborn Home in Guildersheim, far enough away from Schweinfurt that only a bomber badly off course would have a chance of causing her any danger. At least he didn't have the worries of his family's safety to bother him now.

The number one gun position was located at Conn Kaserne, the army barracks which was a school of Panzer training. It was here Rudi had received his training, and it was here that many of the heros of Germany's early Blitzkrieg victories had planned their operations. Here also was the airfield where Hitler had landed on the day he had come to nationalize I.G.N. Kugelwerks. A fighter wing of Messerschmitt 109's was stationed here, and even as Heinrich's car came to a stop beside the gun position, more fighters were roaring off into the sky, sucking their landing gear up under the wings, and turning northeast to join with the earlier flight led by Wild Boar.

"All the guns are manned and ready, *Herr Colonel*," the captain reported, saluting as Heinrich got out of the car.

"Good," Heinrich said. He put his hand over his eyes and stared high into the northeast.

In the distance, he could see hundreds of black dots, and the long, white scars of contrails across the sky. "Get ready, my friend. Here they come."

"Altitude, 6,000 meters!" a soldier called. He was sitting in a seat behind some kind of sighting apparatus, twisting levers and reading dials.

"Set fuses for 6,000 meters," the gun captain called, and half a dozen soldiers began adjusting the nose-caps of the shells which were stacked up, ready for use.

"Change that," the rangefinder said. "7,000 meters!"

The gun captain gave the new fuse setting, only to be changed by the rangefinder a third time.

"Wait," Heinrich interrupted. "Wait until we are sure of the altitude."

"I'm sorry, *Herr Colonel*," the rangefinder said. "I'm a bit nervous."

"We are all nervous," Heinrich said. "Don't be embarrassed by it. Just take your time and get us the most accurate finding you can."

"*Jawohl, Herr Oberst.*"

Heinrich watched as the bombers approached. Now he could hear the distant, rolling thunder, a deep resonance from heaven itself. What a magnificent sight! For a moment he was able to enjoy the pure majesty of it, putting aside the realization that there were more than three thousand American fighting men up there, all with one purpose in mind—to destroy his city.

"Altitude, 8,500 meters!" the rangefinder called out.

"Adjust the fuses," Heinrich said.

Now Heinrich could see the smaller dots flitting around the larger ones, and he knew that they were German fighter planes, nipping at the bomber squadron as a wolf pack would nip at a herd of deer. One of the formation, falling away, then disappearing in a brilliant flash.

"Attention all guns," Heinrich said. "Load, and commence firing."

Heinrich heard his order being spoken into the telephone, then almost immediately he heard the thump of the farthermost gun. Other thumps followed, moving closer and closer as the huge bomber squadron approached, until finally gun number one opened up with a stomach-shaking roar.

The sky above now was filled with metal—the sheet metal of the giant four-engined airplanes and the darting, deadly German fighters and the white-hot metal of exploding shell fragments. The sound of the engines beat down upon the ground now, and they could be heard even above the ear-splitting sounds of the rapid firing anti-aircraft guns. The fighter aircraft and the anti-aircraft guns were exacting a heavy price from the raiders, and the bombers began falling like rain. At one time Heinrich saw as many as eleven bombers spiralling down at the same time, and some of the black dots had blossomed into white puffs as scores of men were coming down in parachutes.

"Be careful of the parachutes!" Heinrich warned his gunners. "Don't hit any of them."

"Why not?" one of the soldiers asked. "They are our enemy, and they were trying to kill us."

"Because I do not approve of that," Heinrich said sharply. "Anyway, how do you know the difference between German parachutes and American parachutes?"

The bombers made a slight turn and headed for Schweinfurt, then Heinrich saw the bombs beginning to tumble out. There were thousands of bombs, and he watched in morbid fascination as they hurtled down across the five miles of vertical space that separated the city from those who would destroy it.

"Listen," someone said. "What is that strange sound?"

"It's the bombs," another said. "They whistle as they fall. I've heard them before."

The first bombs hit then, and Heinrich saw the white flash, then the smoke, followed several seconds later by the roar of the explosions. After that the bombs continued to rain down and explode in one never-ending roar for nearly fifteen minutes without pause. Finally the last bombs had fallen, and the planes turned away, heading back to the northeast in the same direction from whence they had come. Below and behind them, Schweinfurt burned.

It was dark when Frauka finally came out of the plotter's bunker, but the night sky glowed red from the fires which still burned. Hannah, at the front desk, informed Frauka that she had a message from her husband. The message was that he was not wounded, but the factory was badly damaged, and he would spend the night there to fight the fires. Heinrich would not be the only one to fight the fires on this night, Frauka thought, as she stood on the street in front of the plotter bunker, and looked out over the city. She was surprised to see that a few bombs had even fallen in this block, and though there were no fires burning here, one of the buildings was completely gutted. It was the building which had the wreath painted on the window in an understated celebration of last Christmas.

Frauka walked over to the trolley stop and stood there for a few minutes, when a military scout car pulled over and stopped.

"Why are you standing there, *gnädige frau?*" the driver asked. "Don't you realize the trolleys are not running?"

"Oh, I'm sorry," Frauka said, running her hand through her hair absently. She laughed, nervously. "I guess I'm just not thinking, I—I was in there during the bombing and—"

Suddenly the driver smiled broadly. "You are Valkyrie."

"What?"

"You are Valkyrie, I recognize your voice."

"Yes, I . . . you . . . are . . . Max?" Frauka asked quietly.

"Yes," Max said. "Get in, Valkyrie, I'll take you where you want to go."

"My name is—"

"Valkyrie," Max interrupted. "That's the way I want to know you."

Frauka got into the car, and Max drove away from the curb, steering carefully around the rubble and wreckage. Frauka looked around at the city, and the fires, and she felt a terrible, stunning numbness. "It's awful," she said quietly.

"We are lucky," Max said. "You should see Hamburg, or Nürnberg, or Berlin. Here, they wanted only the factories."

"I know," Frauka said. "My husband is Director-General of one of the factories."

"Heinrich Rodl."

"You *know* him?" Frauka asked in surprise.

"He is also Colonel of the anti-aircraft batteries," Max said. "I have met him at the air defense meetings. When I found out you were Valkyrie, I made a point to see who was lucky enough to be the husband of such a beautiful woman."

Frauka laughed. "How would you know I was beautiful if you had never seen me."

"Because your voice is beautiful," Max said. "When I am up there," he pointed toward the sky, which was now overcast, and reflecting the fires with a dull red glow, "there is only your voice connecting me to humanity and sanity. I knew you were beautiful, and now that I have seen you, I have merely confirmed it."

"You are most kind to flatter an old woman with your foolish talk," Frauka said.

"There is method to my madness," Max said. He looked at Frauka, and his eyes were deep and penetrating. "I want to make love to you."

"What?" Frauka gasped. "What are you saying?"

"I think I spoke clearly enough," Max said. "I said I want to make love to you."

"But-but you can't be serious! I'm a married woman!"

"Has there never been a married woman who made love to another man?"

"And I'm 44-years-old," Frauka added. "You are only twenty-five—the same age as my son."

Max laughed victoriously. "You know my age? Ah, wonderful, that means you were interested enough to find out. I'm not the only one with interest, eh?"

"I-I was just curious, that's all."

"That's a good sign," Max said. "Now, what do you say? Will you let me make love to you?"

"But, why would you want to? Surely there are girls more your own age?"

"I am very old," Max said. "There are no girls my age."

"Old?"

"I may die tomorrow," Max said. "One can't get any older than that. Look, Valkyrie, for men like me, all the normal rules are suspended. I haven't the time for propriety and decorum. I know only that I have become obsessed with your voice and with you. I want to make love to you more than I have ever wanted to do anything else in my life. Do you think it was an accident that I saw you at the trolley stop? No, I knew when your shift would end, and I knew that your husband would be busier on this night than any night. I commandeered this car as soon as I landed and I ran through three roadblocks to get there before you left. I was going to stand out front and ask everyone I saw where I could find Valkyrie, but I didn't have to, because you were right there waiting for me. Can't you see? It is meant to be. Now don't tease me with your age, or your son, or your husband. Tell me only what you feel deep down inside. Wouldn't you like to make love? Do this for me, Valkyrie, and when I die, I shall die a happy man."

Suddenly Frauka knew that was exactly what she wanted to do. It did not mean she loved her husband any less, it did not even mean that she felt a sense of abandonment. It just meant that she wanted to give something to this young man, to whom all Germany owed so much. It seemed inordinately fitting that she should give him a part of herself. She felt a warmth from within, an arousal which was not only sexual but spiritual.

"All right," she said. "If you want to, I'll let you make love to me."

"We'll go to my apartment," Max said. "It wasn't damaged by the bombing, and there you will be able to exercise discretion."

Frauka lay on her back, staring into the blackness above the bed. Her womb was heavy with the wetness of Max's lovemaking, and still tingling with the after-effects of pleasure. She had thought it would be, at best, a mildly satisfying experience, too undermined with guilt to be fully enjoyed. However she found that the young, virile strength of Max was enough to lift her to heights of passion she hadn't experienced in years, and for those dizzying moments of rapture she was able to suspend time, place and circumstance. Now, with her young lover sleeping beside her, and her husband working in the bombed-out rubble at his factory, time, and place, and circumstance returned . . . and she lay in the darkness and she cried.

21

Rudi stood just below the crest of the hill and looked out along the road which unwound in a series of curves before him. No more than five kilometers down that road, he knew, was the advancing American Army.

The Americans, Rudi thought. They had bombed all of Germany's cities, including Schweinfurt, and it didn't look as if they were going to stop until there were no longer two bricks standing together anywhere in Europe. They had all the artillery in the the world, and dry socks and hot coffee. They had bullets and toothpaste, gasoline and soap, tanks and ham. They had a supply system that was so untaxed that Rudi's men had found homemade cookies and record players among the American dead, and that was proof that there was even enough room to ship non-essentials into the war zone. And now they were nearly to Rome.

"Captain Rodl," a voice called from behind Rudi.

"Yes," Rudi answered. He turned and saw a soldier on the crest of the hill, standing in a way that caused him to be outlined against the sky. "Don't you know better than to stand on the top of a hill," he asked.

"I'm sorry, Captain," the soldier said, coming down from the crest. "I have a message for you."

"What is the message?"

"It is from Colonel Kant at headquarters in Rome," the soldier said. "He orders you and Sergeant Heibler to report to him immediately."

"He does, does he?"

"Yes, sir," the soldier said.

Rudi raised his binoculars and looked over to a nearby hill. "I told Mainz to bring up six tanks," he said disgustedly. "He has only four. Get a radioman for me."

"Captain?" the soldier said, surprised at Rudi's reaction. "Captain, aren't you going to report to the Colonel?"

"I'll report to the Colonel when I am ready," Rudi said.

"But, Captain—"

"I told you to get a radioman for me," Rudi said.

"*Jawohl, Hauptmann,*" the soldier said, clicking his heels together sharply.

Rudi raised his binoculars to his eyes again and went back to searching the road. Far off, he could see some movement, and soon he saw the American Army at last coming into view. They were being led by a tank, then a double column of troops which marched down each side of the road, then another tank and another double column of troops, stretching on back nearly to the horizon. There were so many of them, Rudi thought, all laughing and wise-cracking and chewing gum.

The radioman reported to Rudi a moment later, and Rudi used the radio to contact Lieutenant Mainz, and order the other tanks brought into position on the other hill. Then, when all tanks and guns were in position, he looked through the glasses again. "Sergeant Heibler," he called.

Heibler came up to him.

"Have we pre-sighted the bridge?"

"Yes, Captain. We can take it out easily."

"Wait until the first two tanks have crossed the bridge," Rudi said, "then take it out. They will be trapped on this side, and the others won't leave them. We'll have them in our killing zone for as long as possible."

"Yes, sir," Heibler said.

"Do we have a motorcycle with a side-car?"

"Yes, sir," Heibler replied.

"Have it standing by. You and I must report to Rome."

"When, sir?" Heibler asked, surprised by the order.

"Right now," Rudi said. "But I intend to wait until we have trapped the Americans in our killing zone."

"I'll get the motorcycle ready," Heibler said.

"Tell all the tanks to fire on my command," Rudi said to the radio operator, and the radio operator passed the message on.

"Just one more moment," Rudi said softly, as he watched the approaching Americans. "Are your bellies full of ham?" he asked the Americans, speaking under his breath. "Have you drunk enough coffee? Do you have to pee?"

The first tank rumbled across the bridge, followed by the infantry, then the second tank. Rudi waited until the third tank was on the bridge.

"Fire," he said.

The radioman repeated the order, and instantly the German tanks opened fire. The ground shook with the roar of twelve guns booming at the same time, and Rudi, watching through the glasses, saw the black arc of the projectiles as they slammed into the bridge. The bridge went up in a tower of smoke and fire. When the smoke cleared away, the tank which had been crossing the bridge was on its side in the gully the bridge spanned, and the infantry had dispersed to either side of the road. The two American tanks which had already crossed fired back, but they had no idea where the rounds had come from, and both American shells exploded harmlessly on a hill a full kilometer away from any of Rudi's positions.

"Fire into the killing zone," Rudi ordered, and Rudi's tanks began to fire again, dropping shells right on the American troops. Within thirty seconds there were three American tanks burning, in addition to the one which had been taken out with the opening barrage.

"Now, Sergeant Heibler, we will see what Colonel Kant has to say." Rudi turned command of the company over to Lieutenant Mainz, then settled into the sidecar as Sergeant Heibler started the motorcycle. It wouldn't be a very long ride into Rome, for Rudi's defensive position was at the very gates of the city.

Rome was in chaos. There were long streams of soldiers marching out of the city, carrying their weapons slung upside-down over their shoulders, staring dully at the back of the neck of the man in front of them as they walked along. Where were these people all going? Rudi wondered. Why weren't they out with his men, helping to defend the city?

The back packs of all the soldiers were stuffed with loot—brass candlesticks, silver cups, gold picture-frames, and similar items. One man was carrying an elaborate lacquered box, and Rudi didn't know if there was something in the box, or if merely the box itself had captured the soldier's fancy.

There were dozens of cars streaming out of the city too, many of which were civilian cars, but all of which were occupied by German officers. The officers, like the men, were carrying their share of booty away with them, and Rudi noticed that if they were no more original, they were at least greedier, being able to take greater amounts in the car than the soldiers were able to carry on their backs. It was the first time Rudi had ever seen the German Army in retreat. Even in Russia they had fought the winter, fought the Russians, suffered terribly, but stuck it out. Now they looked no different from the long lines of defeated refugees he had seen from the beginning of the war.

Heibler stopped in front of the command headquarters. Here trucks were being loaded, and Rudi saw that they were carrying out as much loot as they were military equipment.

"Careful with that painting," one major shouted to two privates who were loading a crate into one of the trucks. "That is a masterpiece and it is priceless."

"Captain, I know the colonel said he wanted to see the both of us, but I think I'd better stay with the motorcycle," Heibler said.

Rudi looked around at the tumult of the retreating headquarters. "I see what you mean," Rudi said. "If any officer tries to take it, you just promote me to one rank higher than whoever tries."

"Yes, sir," Heibler answered with a grin.

Rudi hurried up the polished marble steps of the headquarters building. It had been a museum before the German Army took it over.

"Oh, Captain, good, you have come," someone called to him. "What I want moved is in there."

The man who was speaking didn't have on his

tunic, but his trousers had wide, red stripes down each leg, and that meant he was a general.

"I'm sorry, General, but I have an urgent message for General Kesserling," Rudi answered. Rudi didn't know who the General was, but whoever he was, he knew he would be outranked by Kesserling.

"Oh, yes, well, you will find him on the second floor I believe," the General answered. "I do wish that captain from transportation would hurry. I must get out of here."

Rudi hurried on up the stairs to the second floor, which was also the floor where he would find Colonel Kant, then he pushed his way through a hall of busy, scurrying men until he found Kant's office. Kant, like the others, was preparing to leave. He looked up when Rudi called to him.

"Rudi, good, you got my message," Kant said. "Did you bring Sergeant Heibler?"

"Yes, sir, he's watching the motorcycle."

"Never mind the motorcycle, I have a car. We can give the motorcycle to someone else, or rather, trade it. Yes, that's what we shall do. We will trade it for a few extra jerry-cans of fuel."

'Trade it? Why?" Rudi asked. "Colonel, I don't follow you. What are you talking about?"

"Escape, my dear boy, escape," Kant said. "You, Sergeant Heibler, and I are getting out of this accursed place. We are withdrawing from Rome."

"That is obvious," Rudi said, holding his hand out to take in all the scurry and activity. "But I can't get out of here, I have to get back to my company."

"Why?"

"Why? Colonel, in case you don't realize it, my company is guarding the entrance to Rome. We are the only thing standing between you and the American Army."

"I know," Kant said. "How long do you think you can hold them off?"

"It's hard to say," Rudi said. "We have a good defensive position, they have only one approach. I'd say from 12 to 24 hours."

"And how long could your company hold them off if you weren't there to lead them?"

"About the same length of time, actually," Rudi said. "They are already in position. There is nothing to do now except fight."

"Then you aren't really needed there," Kant said. "In 24 hours we can be in Poland. We still control most of the road, and the road is open and clear according to our latest reports."

"But I can't do that," Rudi said. "I can't just abandon my men like that."

"Rudi, suppose you had stayed in Russia. Where would you be now?"

"In all likelihood I would be dead," Rudi said evenly.

"Precisely my point, Captain. But you aren't dead, you are alive, and you were here to put a company into a defense position which will buy enough time to allow a major portion of our army to escape intact. They can fight again, my boy, and you too. Don't you see?"

"I—I don't know," Rudi said. "I can't help but feel that this is wrong, somehow."

"It is not wrong, it is sensible," Kant said. "Besides, you no longer have any voice in the matter. I have already issued orders appointing Lieutenant Mainz as the new company commander and placing you and Sergeant Heibler on my staff, answerable to me. Now, are we going to stand here and discuss it all day, or are we going to go by and pick up Maria, and get out of here?"

At the sound of Maria's name, Rudi smiled.

"Ernst, you mean we can get Maria?"

"You don't want to leave her here for the Americans, do you?"

"No," Rudi said.

"She will go with you, won't she?"

"Of course she will."

"Then let's go get her." Ernst put on his jacket, then his pistol. He looked at the briefcase he had been packing, then he shrugged his shoulders and laughed. "You know what I was doing? I was actually packing my files, as if they were important now. Requisition orders and travel movements for an army that no longer exists. Why be burdened with the extra weight?"

Rudi followed Ernst down the stairs, passed the tunicless General who was now directing a transportation captain in the loading of furniture, and out on the street where Sergeant Heibler was explaining to a major that the motorcycle already belonged to a Colonel.

"I'd like to see that colonel, Sergeant," the major said angrily.

"I am that Colonel," Kant said at that moment. "Is there anything I can do for you?"

The major looked at Kant, then at the sergeant, and his temples worked in frustration. "No, sir," he said. "I suppose not." He turned and started to walk away.

"Major, were you wanting this motorcycle, by chance?" Kant called.

The major stopped and turned around. "What do you mean, sir?"

"You can have it you know, if we can deal."

"What sort of deal?"

"Bring fifty litres of gasoline here within five minutes, and you have yourself a motorcycle," Kant said.

The major grinned. "I'll be right back," he said.

"Where's he going to get it?" Rudi asked.

"He'll steal it, of course," Kant explained. "Better for us that he risk getting shot doing it than we, don't you think?"

"Yes, sir," Rudi agreed with a little laugh.

The major, as promised, brought the fuel a few minutes later, then Rudi, Sergeant Heibler and Colonel Kant put the jerrycans in the back of Kant's car, and, with Heibler driving, they left the scene of confusion at the headquarters building.

Rudi instructed Sergeant Heibler to go to his apartment in the Ancient City, and Heibler, who had delivered and picked up Rudi there many times over the past year, knew where to go without having to ask directions.

This part of Rome was as quiet as the other part was busy. There was nothing on the streets, no military or civilian vehicles, no horses or carts, no bicycles, not even any pedestrians. It was as if they had happened onto a ghost city, and the only sound they heard was the echo of their own engine rolling back to them from the silent walls of the empty buildings. Sergeant Heibler finally reached Rudi's apartment, and he stopped at the curb and shut off the engine. A piece of paper blew across in front of them, plastering itself against a lamp post for a moment. The poster showed a picture of a German soldier and an Italian soldier standing arm in arm. Finally, it worked its way off the post and skidded along the sidewalk until it disappeared around the corner.

"Maybe she's not home," Heibler suggested.

"Where would she be?" Rudi asked.

"I don't know," Sergeant Heibler said, "but I don't like the looks of it. Why don't you wait here, Captain, and let me go up and see."

"I'll go," Rudi said.

"If you don't mind, I'll go with you," Heibler said.

"That's a good idea," Kant said. "The two of you go on up. I'll stay with the car."

Rudi and Sergeant Heibler got out of the car and started toward the narrow stairway between the empty tobacco store and the deserted straw basket shop. A cat suddenly jumped out from behind a trashcan, screeching loudly and knocking over a pile of wine bottles.

"What the—" Rudi shouted, and he and Sergeant Heibler both trained their weapons toward the sound before they realized what it was.

"It's just a cat," Heibler said with a little laugh.

"Look at that," Rudi said, pointing to the wall of the tobacco store.

Written on the wall, in blood-red paint, were the words: "Death to all Germans, Free Italy!"

"I don't like the looks of this," Sergeant Heibler said. He pulled back the bolt on his machine pistol, chambering a round. "I'm going up first."

"Be careful when you pass the open doorways," Rudi warned.

Slowly, Sergeant Heibler began climbing the stairs, moving the barrel of his gun back and forth in front of him as he went up. Rudi was behind him, tensed and ready for action. When they reached the door to

Rudi's apartment, Sergeant Heibler stopped and looked
back toward Rudi. "Shall I try the door?" he asked.

"Yes," Rudi said. "Open it."

Sergeant Heibler tried the door, found it unlocked,
then pushed it open. He stepped inside, then, quickly
came back outside, looking ashen-faced.

"Captain, don't go in," he said in a pained voice.

"What? What do you mean don't go in? Sergeant
Heibler, what is it? What's wrong?"

"Let's go," Sergeant Heibler said, putting his hand
on Rudi's shoulder and trying to push him back down
the stairs.

"Sergeant, get out of my way!" Rudi said, and, impatiently, he pushed by him, then ran up the last three
steps to the door. He stepped inside, took one look,
then turned and threw up.

Maria was hanging by her feet from the ceiling light
fixture. She was naked and her body was badly muti-
lated. A sign was pinned to one of her breasts with a
dagger.

**DEATH TO ALL GERMAN WHORES.
FREE ITALY.**

22

"I'll tell you what I think," *Obersturm-bannführer* Dietzl said to *Sturmbannführer* Lange. "I think those bureaucratic bastards in Berlin just don't understand the problem here. I can kill ten thousand stinking Jews a day, but I can't get rid of them. The furnaces? Don't make me laugh. If you try to burn one hundred thousand bodies in ten days, you'll have a fat deposit build-up on the inside of the chimneys which could explode like gunpowder."

Lange felt a little queasy, and he put his hand to his forehead.

"Feeling bad? Here, have a drink," Dietzl said, and he poured a glass of schnapps for his visitor.

"Thanks," Lange said, taking a swallow, then wiping the back of his hand across his mouth. "I'm sorry," he said. "I don't want you to misunderstand. I whole-heartedly believe in the final solution to our—"

"Final solution my ass," Dietzl interrupted. "That's another piece of bureaucratic bullshit that I don't approve of. Why don't they come out and call it by its right name? I'm proud that I have been selected to kill Jews. I overheard Eichmann tell someone that he could jump into his grave happily, knowing that he had killed over a million Jews. Well, I'm telling you I can match Eichmann Jew for Jew."

"Yes," Lange said. "I'm sure. You, uh, do understand the purpose of my visit here, do you not?"

"You want to see the Jew Paul Maass," Dietzl said.

"Yes, if I may," Lange said. "He is still alive?"

"My orders were to keep him alive," Dietzl said. "I follow orders, no matter how personally distasteful they may be. What was he, some kind of an actor or something?"

"He was an orchestra director," Lange said. "And a very good one, too. The Führer once publicly proclaimed him to be the best in Germany."

Dietzl laughed. "That must have come as a shock to a few people. I mean, the Führer complimenting a Jew."

"No one knew that he was Jewish then," Lange said. "In fact, he is only one-half Jew."

"Half piss and half beer is still piss," Dietzl interrupted.

"Of course," Lange agreed. "And that is why he is here. However, there are extenuating circumstances which make it important that Maass be kept alive."

"And you want to see him, just to make sure he is alive, is that it? You can't trust my report?"

"Please, *Obersturmbannführer*, it does not indicate a lack of trust, merely the thoroughness of procedure which my superiors require of me."

"I know," Dietzl agreed. "Bureaucracy, I understand completely." Dietzl pushed a button on his desk and a sergeant stepped into the room. "Bring the stinking Jew Maass to me," he ordered.

"*Jawohl*," the sergeant answered with a click of his heels.

"Tell me," Dietzl said, after the sergeant left. "How does it go at the trial of the traitors who attempted to murder Hitler?"

"The trial is a lesson to anyone who would be foolish enough to ever try such a thing again," Lange said. "Judge Freisler is conducting it." Lange laughed. "He had the belts taken from the defendants, and in the case of Field Marshal von Witzleben, his pants were so large that the old man had to hold them up with his hands. Right there in court, Judge Freisler shouted at him, 'You dirty old man, why do you play with yourself?' "

Dietzl laughed heartily at the idea of a Field Marshal so humbled. "It is about time the arrogant Army bastards learn who is in control of things around here. Who all was involved, do you know?"

"There have been nearly seven thousand arrested," Lange explained. "I can tell you who has been condemned so far. Garl Goerdeler, has already been executed, so has Colonel General Ludwig Beck, and Colonel von Stauffenberg. Stauffenberg, of course, is the traitor who placed the bomb. General Friedrich Oldbricht, and Major General Helmuth Stieff, and Admiral Canaris have also been executed. General Delligiebel and General Oster have both been sentenced to die."

"It is too good for them," Dietzl said. "They should be given to me, and I would give them the same treatment I give the Jews. A 'bath and disinfectant,' " he said, laughing, referring to the gas chambers which were designed to look like showers.

"It is my belief that many other high-ranking Army officers will suffer the same fate before too long," Lange confided. "I know that the Führer wishes to promote the S.S. Officers to positions of greater importance in the military. This is especially true now that the Americans and British have made a successful landing in France."

"If Hitler would let the S.S. take over the war effort now, we would throw the scum back into the sea within a week," Dietzl bragged.

"We would never have let them off the beach in the first place," Lange added.

Paul Maass was trying to make a lamp work. It was not something the guards told him to do, for if they had told him to do it, he wouldn't have. Paul learned soon after his arrest that, for some reason, he had been singled out to be kept alive. Twice he had been broken out of the group which he later learned was going to the gas chamber. There had been no particular reason for his being selected for the gas chamber, he was just in the wrong place at the wrong time. But there was also no reason for his being saved, and in a way that was even more perplexing. At least those who were being executed were there by the chance of random selection. He had been singled out to be saved. But why?

At first Paul was bothered by it, because he felt that the others may think he conspired in some way to save his own life. Then he realized that the "others" generally weren't around long enough to formulate such opinions. The average life expectancy of those who came into camp was no more than ten days. Paul had been here for ten months, having been arrested on October 15, 1943. He remembered the date well, because it was the day after the largest Schweinfurt air raid, and he was arrested as he dug through the rubble of the destroyed concert hall.

Once Paul realized that the Nazis were sparing him

for some reason, he began to play a macabre game with them. The rules of the game were simple. The Nazis had been ordered not to kill him, so he was determined to make them violate those orders. He worked only when he chose to, and only on those things he chose to work on.

Though he had been ordered to descend into the death pits to handle the corpses of the thousands who were killed, he steadfastly refused, and he told his guards that the only way he would go into a pit of corpses was if he were one of them. The S.S. guards had not encountered that before, and, as they had strict orders not to kill Paul, they didn't know what to do. So, they did nothing.

"Jew Maass," a guard called to him from the door.

"What is it, swine?" Paul answered defiantly.

"You have been ordered to report to the commandant."

Paul considered for a moment whether he would obey the order. If he just sat here, would the guard shoot him? Paul thought about pushing it, to see if the guard would shoot him, but he decided against it, choosing instead to go with him to see what the commandant wanted. It was more a matter of curiosity, than an act of preservation.

Paul walked through the campground toward the commandant's building. It was hot and sticky and the furnaces were going, and from the chimneys smoke boiled up with the sweet, cloying smell of human fat being burned. When Paul first arrived, the smell had made him sick. Now he seldom noticed it.

"In there," the guard said, pointing to the door.

"I know where it is, you ignorant bastard," Paul said.

The guard glared at Paul, but his orders had been very specific. Paul would not be killed. To the limited mental power of the guards, that also translated into his not being harmed in any way, though in fact there was no such order in effect.

"Jew Maass," Dietzl said. "Someone is here to see you."

Paul looked over toward the visitor, and felt a knot of anger inside. "Lange," he said quietly.

"Ah, I see you remember me," Lange said. "And do you remember our little tests?"

"I remember," Paul said. He smiled dryly. "I believe you certified me as 'non-Jew,' didn't you?"

"Yes," Lange said. "Although I later reexamined the results and found that I had misread some of the results. My tests now confirm that you are, indeed, a Jew."

"I am glad you were able to find your error," Paul said sarcastically. "Why am I being kept alive?"

"Ah, why indeed?" Lange said. "Perhaps it is because we can't kill the Jewish part of you without killing the rest of you."

"That hasn't stopped you with killing others who are only partially Jewish," Paul said.

"Well, perhaps it is because you have a friend in a high place."

"Are you talking about Hitler? Tell that swine I would rather be friends with Satan."

"You would do wise to watch what you say about the Führer," Dietzl ordered.

"Why?" Paul challenged. "Are you going to put me in a concentration camp?" He laughed bitterly. "Or perhaps you will kill me. You ignorant bastard, I want to be killed, don't you understand that?"

Dietzl sighed. "As you can see, *Sturmbannführer*, we are carrying out the orders not to kill this man, but he is making things very difficult for us. He is, singlehandedly, having a totally disruptive effect on the morale of my men."

"I shall get a further disposition on him as soon as I can," Lange said. "When I do, I shall let you know if it is all right to kill him."

Dietzl smiled. "When that moment comes, I shall kill you myself, Jew Maass."

"Do it now, swine."

"By the way, Maass, isn't it a shame about Lisl?" Lange asked.

"What?" Paul asked, and the steel curtain he had put on his eyes suddenly faltered. Lange laughed, for here was the chink in Paul's armor he had been looking for. "What do you mean?"

"You remember Lisl, surely," Lange said. "She is the sow you once rutted with. She became a soldiers' whore. I soon tired of her, so she shared her charms with others. Hundreds of others," he laughed. "I'm afraid she wasn't very particular. But then, she never was, was she?"

"For me, Lisl no longer exists," Paul said, trying to recover his composure.

"Ah, poor Lisl," Lange said. "She was turned out of the Lebensborn Home long ago . . . her mother and father have disowned her, and for you she no longer exists. She has left Schweinfurt. I'm afraid I don't know where she is now, or even if the poor wretch is still alive. I did think you might be interested."

"I am not interested," Paul said.

"I have some fascinating film," Lange went on. "Perhaps you are in need of some entertainment for your men," he suggested to Dietzl. "This woman, Lisl, is really quite a beautiful woman, and an interesting case study. You see, her former association with the Jew Maass corrupted her, and altered her personality

so that she became a creature with no more morals
than a men's room cockroach. As a result, this beautiful young woman became a totally amoral creature,
as I mentioned earlier. We took film of her rather in-
ventive sexual exploits with men and women. I doubt
that there is anything she didn't try at least once, and
she never seemed to find the presence of a camera
inhibiting."

"These are motion pictures?" Dietzl asked, and the
expression in his voice showed that he was already
looking forward to it.

"Yes. I'm sorry to say, however, that there is no
sound. And that is too bad, for the sounds she makes
while rutting about are the really most interesting—"

Paul suddenly turned and left the room.

"Jew Maass, where are you going?" Dietzl called,
laughing. "Don't you want to hear about this?"

"So," Lange said, after Paul left. "He is not a man
of iron."

"Have you ever met Hitler?" Colonel Kant asked
Rudi.

"No. My father and my sister have met him, but I
never have."

"Well, I won't say you are in for a treat," Kant said.
"But I will say you are in for an experience."

Colonel Kant and Rudi were riding in a car with
Major General Dietrich von Cholitz. Sergeant Heibler
was driving, and they were headed to Wolf's Lair,
Hitler's headquarters in East Prussia. This was also
the place where he had been the victim of an assassination attempt one month earlier. They had been summoned there so that Hitler could give Cholitz personal
orders on the defense of Paris.

After leaving Italy, Colonel Kant managed to get

himself assigned as an aide to General Cholitz, and in that position, he pulled strings to have Rudi and Sergeant Heibler assigned to him as well. It was a good, safe billet, and Kant, who privately confessed to Rudi that the war was lost, felt no compunction about finding the safest assignment possible to ride out the rest of the war.

General Cholitz had the reputation of being a destroyer of cities. In 1940, he had ordered the destruction of Rotterdam, leaving almost eighty thousand wounded or homeless. During the siege of Sebastopol, he took the city, only after totally destroying it. General Cholitz was also in command of the German rear during the final retreat from Russia, and he left behind a scorched earth which added to his infamy. And now he was in command of Paris.

"I must confess to you, Ernst," General Cholitz said, opening his tunic and scratching his rather large stomach. "If I am forced to destroy Paris, I fear I will go down in history as one of the most destructive men of all mankind. It has always been my lot to defend the rear of the German Army. And when this happens, I am ordered to destroy each city as I leave it. I fear this is what I will be ordered to do now."

"And will you, *Herr General?*" Kant asked.

"I am a soldier, Colonel Kant," Cholitz answered. "I must do what I am ordered to do."

A soldier stepped out with his hand up to stop the car as Sergeant Heibler arrived in front of the bunker. The soldier saluted the officers who returned their salute.

"You will all have to be searched," the soldier said.

"Searched?" Cholitz replied. "Searched for what reason?"

"I'm sorry, General, but it is the Führer's orders.

Anyone who comes to see him must be strip-searched."

"Strip-searched? This is outrageous!" Cholitz replied. "I will not be subjected to such indignities."

"You have no choice, Cholitz," Field Marshal Keitl said, stepping out of the building to greet the three men. "That is, not if you wish to continue being a general. Come, I will go in with you, it won't be such an ordeal."

Grumbling, Cholitz, Kant, and Rudi, went into a room to remove their clothes. Sergeant Heibler, who wouldn't actually see Hitler, wasn't subjected to the same requirement, so he was allowed to remain with the car undisturbed.

There were three S.S. guards in the room, and as Rudi and his two senior officers began undressing, the guards took their clothes from them, one piece at a time, searching each piece carefully. Finally the three men stood naked before the amused eyes of Field Marshal Keitl.

"Well, Dietrich, it is obvious to me that when you are around your two aides, you should remain in uniform. Naked, they are clearly more impressive than you," he chuckled.

"Are you *quite* finished now?" Cholitz asked the guards.

"*Jawohl, mein General,*" the sergeant who was in charge of the guards answered.

Cholitz got his uniform back and began redressing.

"You have to understand that the Führer is still badly shaken over the incident last month," Keitl explained. "Now he sees traitors behind every bush, and an assassin in every crowd."

"I am constantly amazed at the number of officers who were involved," Cholitz said. "I had no idea it was so widespread."

"I'm sure there will be more uncovered as we go along," Keitl said. "Now, if you are dressed, we will see the Führer."

Rudi followed the others along a gravel path, under a spread of trees, to a small, stone building. It had the look of a cool, quiet park, and Rudi could almost imagine hearing the laughter of children as if a family were enjoying a picnic nearby.

"It's a lovely setting," Kant said, looking around.

"Yes," Keitl said, non-committally. "Ah, there is the Führer now."

Hitler was dressed in his brown uniform, wearing the billed cap which he always wore. His right ear was stuffed with cotton, and he was standing quietly with his arms folded in front of him, his left hand grasping his right wrist. The fingers of his right hand dangled loosely, showing the injury he had suffered.

"General Cholitz," Hitler said, as Cholitz and the others saluted. "I trust you will forgive me if I do not return your salute."

"Of course, my Führer," Cholitz said. "All Germany was horrified to hear of the tragic events of last month, and heartened that you are recovering so quickly."

"What happened here has given me absolute assurance of the fact that my destiny will be played out," Hitler said. "Providence has spared me for great deeds."

"I agree, my Führer," Cholitz said.

"Come," Hitler ordered. "I will show you the operations room where it happened."

"I'm sure it has been cleaned up by now, Führer, and—"

"It has *not* been cleaned up!" Hitler suddenly shouted, and he brought his left fist up and slammed it down as if slamming it against an imaginary podium.

"It will stay just as it is, so that the world will be able to view for all eternity that a monstrous crime was attempted here. Can you imagine? Someone actually trying to kill me, at the hour when Germany needs me more than ever before? It was the vilest treason in history. I will show no mercy to anyone involved, not anyone, do you understand?"

"That is as it should be, my Führer," Cholitz said, a little surprised and somewhat shaken by Hitler's sudden and unexpected outburst.

"I will kill every worm who was involved, and their wives and their children and their children's children!"

By the time Hitler finished his tirade, they had arrived at the operations building, and Hitler stood in the doorway and pointed to the destruction, almost, it seemed to Rudi, with a perverse sense of pride.

"I was there," he said, pointing to a place on the far side of the mangled room. "The traitor put the bomb under the table, right in front of me. One of the others, one of the innocent victims, moved the bomb, thinking it was only a briefcase because it was in his way and he could not get to the map. That was a fortuitous move, for the heavy table-leg absorbed the blast and saved my life. Nevertheless, I was still thrown from there to here by the effect of the explosion." Hitler pointed out where he wound up after the explosion was over.

"My Führer, the briefing map is in place," Keitl said, interrupting Hitler's musing.

"What? Oh, yes, yes, the briefing. Come, General, we have much to discuss," Hitler said.

Hitler and the entourage left the shattered operations room and walked over to another room which was serving as the new operations center. There, on a huge table, was a map of Europe, with the situation outlined in color codes. Rudi looked at it, then gasped. The American Third Army, under General Patton, had thrust out in a bold pincers movement, all the way to Le Mans. The German Armies, the Fifth and the Seventh, were in danger of being cut off, as was Paris itself.

"Well, Captain, I see you can read a map," Hitler said.

"Yes, sir," Rudi answered quietly.

"As you can see, my Generals, those who weren't traitors," he added with a snarl, "have nearly lost in two months all that I won during the entire war. I am surrounded by incompetency. But that's all being taken care of." Hitler leaned onto the table, and brought his face right up to Cholitz's face. Rudi could see now that Hitler was bathed in perspiration, and saliva was literally running out of his mouth. He began trembling, and as he trembled, the table shook in his grasp.

"Since July 20, 1944, *Herr General*, scores of generals, literally scores, have danced from the end of a rope because they attempted to prevent me, Adolf Hitler, from fulfilling my destiny! I . . . will . . . have . . . no . . . more . . . treason!" Hitler took a long, audible gasp after the sentence. "I . . . will . . . have . . . no . . . more failures!" Another audible gasp. "I . . . will . . . have . . . no . . . more . . . excuses! Do not defy me, General, do you hear me?" Hitler began pounding on the table, crying out with each blow of his fist. "Do . . . you . . . hear . . . me?"

"Yes, my Führer!" Cholitz answered, clearly frightened by Hitler's rage.

Hitler suddenly swept a pile of loose papers off the table, then, with a cry, he dropped to his knees and leaned forward to grab the edge of the rug. To Rudi's shock and amazement, Hitler put the carpet in his mouth and began chewing, making growling, animal-like sounds as he did so. Saliva rolled down his chin, and his eyes were wild with the frenzy of something inhuman. Rudi looked at the others, and Cholitz and Kant were as shocked as he was. Only Keitl appeared to be unmoved, and the Field Marshal stood quietly in the background, examining his nails as if nothing extraordinary was happening.

"Uhnnn, uhnnn, uhnn," Hitler growled. "You . . . you . . . do understand me?" Hitler finally managed to gasp.

"Yes, my Führer!" Cholitz answered again.

Hitler got up and wiped his sleeve across his mouth, then took a few breaths, and somehow managed to compose himself. "Now," he said. "This is what I want done with Paris. It must be totally destroyed. When my Army leaves, nothing must be left standing—not one public building, not one church, not one artistic monument."

"But the opera house, my Führer, you love that building so, that—"

"It, too," Hitler said. "I want everything destroyed. Then, I want you to destroy the water supply. I am told that pestilence can gain a rapid foothold in a city without safe water."

"That is true," Cholitz said.

"Good, good," Hitler said. "Destroy the water."

Cholitz stood there for a long moment, but Hitler said nothing else. Hitler began looking at the map, as if studying something, then, after a moment, he looked up at the general and his aides.

"Are you still here?" he asked.

"Yes, my Führer."

"*Go*," Hitler said, dismissing them with a wave of his left hand. "Go, and carry out my orders."

Cholitz clicked his heels and saluted, as did Rudi and Kant, then the three of them left the bunker and walked quietly back to the car. No one said a word as they got in, and Heibler knew to drive away only because Cholitz signaled him with a wave of his hand.

They left Wolf's Lair and drove in absolute silence for nearly ten minutes before Cholitz spoke.

"He is a man gone mad," Cholitz finally said. Cholitz pinched the bridge of his nose between his thumb and forefinger. "I have dedicated my life and my honor to an insane fool."

"General, you won't destroy Paris, will you?" Kant asked. "You don't really intend to carry out those orders?"

"No," Cholitz said. "God help me, I have no intention of carrying them out." He sighed. "I want the three of you out of Paris. I may not be able to save it, but whatever happens now I want it known by someone that I had no intention of destroying Paris."

"General, we can't leave you alone to face the Americans, the Free French, and possible reprisals by Hitler," Kant said.

"Colonel, you once told me you are a survivor," Cholitz said. "You survived the fall of Stalingrad, you survived the fall of Rome, and now I intend to see that you survive the fall of Paris. Do not argue with me. You are leaving Paris at once. Do you understand?"

"Yes, *Herr General*," Kant said.

Rudi wondered if it really would enhance his chance of survival to leave Paris. Might it not be better to fall with the city, and leave the war now? But he said nothing.

23

THE Ardennes was covered with a mantle of snow, and in an American rest encampment, brightly colored Christmas ornaments hung from every available pillar and post. Incongruously, within the gaily decorated camp, there lay half a dozen burned out half-tracks and jeeps. Supplies were scattered in disarray on the snow, and the soldiers who were picking through them were not American, but German, members of the 5th Combat S.S. Panzer Battalion.

The German soldiers were there because three days earlier, on December 16, 1944, Hitler had ordered a massive counter-offensive against the Americans who were advancing toward the German West Wall. Four German armies, consisting of two hundred fifty thousand men, had been hurled into the attack against eighty-three thousand American troops, deployed thinly across an 85-mile Ardennes front.

The Americans had been totally unprepared for the onslaught and the Germans poured through with stunning success, recapturing in hours ground it had taken the Allies weeks to take. Tons of equipment were abandoned by the Americans as they retreated from the German advance. Thus it was that Rudi, who reluctantly found himself acting as the executive officer in a *waffen* or combat S.S. unit, was one of the soldiers milling around the American rest camp.

Rudi drained some gasoline from an overturned American jeep, then put it into the little American stove. He worked with it for a few minutes, then lit it, and was rewarded wih a steady blue flame. He held his hands out over the stove, grateful for the warmth.

S.S. Major Sachs trudged through the snow toward Rudi and put his hands out over the stove as well.

"The Americans can come up with some wonderful inventions," Rudi said. "See how small and simple this stove is. If we had possessed twenty-five thousand of these in Russia, we would have won the battle there."

"If the Waffen S.S. had been in Russia, we would have won," Major Sachs said. He sniffed loudly, and wiped his running nose with the sleeve of his tunic. "Just as we are winning here."

"The attack is but three days old," Rudi said. "I would suggest, Major, that it is too early to judge whether we have won or not."

"Victory is just around the corner, Rodl," Major Sachs said. "I know this. Why, it's just like the days of the Blitzkrieg!"

"Were you a part of the Blitzkrieg, Major?" Rudi asked.

"Well, no, not exactly," Major Sachs hedged. "I had important duties in Germany at that time."

"I'm sure," Rudi said rather derisively. "If you had been a part of the blitz, you would realize that we carried our own equipment and did not have to rely upon captured goods to supply our army. We are living on borrowed time now, Major."

"Bah, you are just like everyone else in the army," Major Sachs scoffed. "You have no faith in the Führer, or his plans. Well, the Führer has had enough, and that is why he has given spearhead command to S.S. General Dietrich. In just three days we have put right all the wrong done by the army."

"How privileged we of the army are to be in the company of the brilliant Waffen S.S.," Rudi said sarcastically.

"There will be a reckoning," Major Sachs said, pointing an accusing finger at Rudi. "Do not think, Captain, that people like you will escape re-examination for political reliability. Those who are found wanting will be dealt with most harshly. And don't think your Iron Cross First Class is going to save you," he added, pointing to the medal Rudi wore.

"I'm sure it's worthless," Rudi replied.

"Captain, would you like some of the American field rations for your lunch?" Sergeant Heibler called to Rudi. When Rudi had drawn the assignment, he had asked for and received permission to take Heibler with him.

"The Americans always have bellies full of ham," Rudi said. "Is there any ham?"

"How do the Americans say ham?"

"It is spelled h-a-m," Rudi said.

"There is something called ham and beans," Sergeant Heibler said, pronouncing the word with a long *a*, so that it came out *bains*.

"*Bohne*," Rudi said. "Yes, that would be good. Perhaps we could heat it over this stove."

Sergeant Heibler brought the can over to the stove. "I'll be," he said. "Look at this, at how ingenious it is." He demonstrated a small, finger-held can opener. He opened the can, then held it over the stove.

Rudi chuckled. "We must thank the next American prisoner we see, not only for leaving us these fine tins of food, but also for providing us with the means to open them."

"I'm afraid that will be impossible," Major Sachs sneered.

"Impossible? What do you mean?"

"We will see no American prisoners, because there are no American prisoners."

"But surely there are," Rudi said. "No one, not even the Americans, could so effectively withdraw their army that no prisoners are taken."

"Not even the Americans," Major Sachs repeated in a sarcastic, sing-song voice. "Captain, you seem to be obsessed with the greatness of the Americans."

"I fought against them in Italy," Rudi said. "I know their capabilities."

"Well, what do you think of their capabilities now?" Major Sachs sad. "We have thoroughly routed them and killed thousands. That includes anyone who tries to surrender—so that is why you will see no prisoners."

"What?"

"We are taking no prisoners," Major Sachs explained patiently. "We have orders to shoot anyone who tries to surrender. Colonel Peiper has already executed several hundred Americans."

"Major, are you telling me that we are murdering prisoners of war?" Rudi asked in shock.

"Murder, Captain? We are at war. Killing during time of war is not murder."

"By all the rules of civilization it is, if you are killing prisoners," Rud said. "I will not be a party to such a crime."

"Tell me, Captain, what do the rules of war say about the bombing of German cities?" Major Sachs wanted to know. "Do you have any idea how many German women and children have been killed by the barbarism of your civilized Americans?"

"I'm going to see Colonel Kant," Rudi said.

The ham and beans Sergeant Heibler had been heating were just completed, and Heibler started to give the can to Rudi.

"Your American *schinken und bohne*," Major Sachs said. "Aren't you going to stay and eat it?"

"You eat it," Rudi said.

"Thank you, I will," Major Sachs said. He took the warm can from Sergeant Heibler and took a big bite. "Uhm, delicious."

"I'll drive you, Captain," Sergeant Heibler offered, picking up his automatic rifle and slinging it over his shoulder.

"You're right about one thing," Major Sachs said, taking another big bite. "The Americans do have good food."

"I just hope they didn't leave behind several cases of poisoned food," Rudi said as he climbed into the little scout car.

"Poison?" Major Sachs said, coughing and choking on the food in his mouth.

Rudi laughed as he and Sergeant Heibler drove away.

"I'm afraid that what Sachs told you is true," Kant said, answering Rudi's question about the American prisoners of war.

"Ernst, can't you see what this does?" Rudi asked. "Not only does it mean that our men can expect the same treatment, it will also stiffen the American's resolve. If there has been any weakness in the American soldier, it has been that he doesn't fully understand why he is fighting on foreign soil in some foreign war. But this . . . this will give them steel in their backs."

"I agree with you, Rudi. In fact, I couldn't agree with you more. But there is nothing I can do about it. I didn't originate the orders, and I can't suspend them."

"I won't follow such orders," Rudi said.

Kant shook his head. "You have no choice. Major Sachs will report you and you'll be shot for disobeying an order."

"I don't care," Rudi said. "I will not murder American prisoners, or any other prisoners."

Kant sighed. "Rudi, we are survivors, you and I. We've come this far, don't do something foolish now. After all, what difference does it make if you kill an American before he is captured, or after. You have certainly killed your share in battle."

"In battle, yes," Rudi said. "But I won't do murder."

Kant removed his monocule and polished it vigorously. "Very well, I'll tell you what you do. There is a deposit of American fuel at Baugnez. I am going to give you command of the 19th Panzer Battalion. Your assignment will be to take the fuel supplies at Baugnez."

"The 19th Panzer Battalion? I've never heard of it," Rudi said.

Kant smiled. "There is no such unit. There won't be a unit until you make it so. I'll assign you a few men, and maybe you'll even get a tank or two after you get the fuel. You may never get operational, Rudi, but at least you will have an independent command, free of S.S."

"I'll do it," Rudi said.

Kant took a piece of paper and scribbled on it. "Here

is authorization for you to draw twenty-five men from the replacement depot," Kant said. "Baugnez is that way." He pointed to the west.

"Look at them," Sergeant Heibler said to Rudi, as he and Rudi walked down the road at the head of the men. They were split into two columns, one column on either side of the road, and most were carrying their weapons upside down, as if not expecting any action. "Absolute raw recruits," Sergeant Heibler spat. "Old men and young boys."

"At that, I'd rather have them than be assigned to the S.S.," Rudi said.

"Captain, look!" Sergeant Heibler suddenly called, pointing down the road in front of him. Rudi looked up to see some American soldiers diving into a ditch on the side of the road.

"Quick!" Rudi ordered his men. "Into the ditch!"

The soldiers with Rudi ran and dived into the ditch, and Rudi breathed a sigh of relief that no one shot themselves in their inexperience.

"How many did you see?" Rudi asked.

"I don't know," Sergeant Heibler said. "I just saw two or three, but there may have been several more."

"Surely not," Rudi said. "I thought we controlled this sector." Rudi rubbed his chin, and raised up to look across the road. "Well, we can't stay here all day. We've got to get across the road. I'll take a group, you cover me."

"Right," Sergeant Heibler said, crawling up to the edge of the ditch.

Rudi looked back down the ditch toward the men who were now in his command. "You," he said to the first soldier. "Begin the count."

"*Ein.*"

"Zwei."

"Drei."

The count continued until number 24.

"Odd numbers stay with Sergeant Heibler. Even, come with me," Rudi shouted, and he climbed out of the ditch, onto the road. Rudi fired in the direction of the American soldiers, and ran, crouched low, across the road for the ditch on the other side. But the men with him, exposed to enemy fire for the first time, stopped and tried to return the fire from the middle of the road. The fire from the Americans was deadly accurate, and many of the German soldiers were cut down.

"Get out of the road!" Rudi shouted, and finally, the ones who were not hit finished the dash across the road. Six lay on the road.

"Sergeant!"

"Yes, Captain."

"Tell those idiots with you to keep moving when you come across."

"Yes, Captain," Sergeant Heibler answered.

Sergeant Heibler and the rest of the men started across the road then, and again, the Americans, who had an excellent defensive position and a good field of fire, poured withering fire into the German ranks. Four of Sergeant Heibler's men went down, and one very old man froze in fear, stopping right in the middle of the road to stare, woodenly, at the men who had already been hit.

Sergeant Heibler had nearly made it across when he saw the old man stop, and he turned and went back for him, grabbing him and pulling him by the arm. The Americans fired again, and Sergeant Heibler went down.

"Heibler!" Rudi called. "Heibler!"

The old man Heibler tried to help walked slowly across the road, amazingly unhit.

"Captain, what are we going to do?" one of the men called.

"We'll all be killed," another shouted.

"Give me that radio," Rudi ordered to a crouching radio man. The radio man handed it to Rudi, and Rudi called the Panzer unit they had just passed on the road, and asked for a tank to be sent up. "Now, give me that scarf," Rudi said, pointing to a white scarf around one of the men's neck.

"Captain, are we going to surrender?"

"No," Rudi said. "I'm going to ask the Americans for permission to get our wounded off the road."

Rudi tied the white scarf to the end of a rifle, then waved it back and forth above the edge of the ditch.

"What is it?" one of the Americans called. "What do you want?"

"We want to get our wounded," Rudi replied. "Will you allow us to do this?"

There was a moment of hesitation, then the Americans called back. "Go ahead, pick them up."

Rudi lay the rifle down, then signaled to four others to lay down their arms. They climbed out of the ditch and walked to the middle of the road pulling the wounded and the dead into the ditch. Rudi dropped to one knee and looked into Heibler's face. The sergeant's eyes were open, but unseeing, and his mouth was open. A dark, sticky stream of blood ran down the side of his head from a bullet wound in the temple.

"Good-bye, old friend," Rudi said quietly. He stood up, and looked toward the ditch where the Americans were. One of the Americans was standing up, watching them. "We have a tank coming," Rudi said to him. "If you surrender now, you'll save yourself."

"Just get your wounded," the American called back. "Then do your damndest, because we'll be waiting for you."

Rudi stood in the middle of the road until all the wounded and dead had been dragged across the road to the safety of the ditch on the German side. Finally all movement stopped.

"The truce is over, Americans," Rudi called.

"Then take that, kraut!" one of the other Americans replied, and he stood up and fired an entire clip. The Germans returned the fire, but Rudi kept them in the ditch to wait for the tank.

The tank came about five minutes later, clanking and rattling in the supreme confidence of its invulnerability. It was a Royal Tiger tank, 34 feet long and 12 feet wide, weighing 68 tons, with steel armor seven inches thick. The .88 millimeter cannon tube was 17 feet long, and it traversed around toward the Americans, flashed once, and the roar of its firing was so loud that it split the pants legs of some of the soldiers, and left the ears of all ringing.

Rudi watched the round explode in the ditch, and it seemed inconceivable that anyone could survive such a blast. He waited for one full minute, looking to see if there were any sign of life.

"Captain," the tank commander called, sticking his head up from the turret. "We've got orders to pull out of this sector."

"Pull out?"

"We're turning our attack. Everyone has to be back. You'd better go kill any survivors."

"Very well," Rudi said. He looked at the men he had

left. "Put the wounded and the dead on the tank," he said. "Then follow it back to headquarters. I'll be along."

"*Jawohl,*" a corporal, the senior of his remaining men said. They began loading their casualties as Rudi ordered.

Rudi pulled his pistol and walked over to look down into the ditch. Amazingly, there were only four soldiers there. Four Americans had held off over twenty Germans.

One of the soldiers groaned and moved. Rudi saw that there was a bar on his collar—the rank of lieutenant in the American army. The lieutenant reached toward the man beside him. The man beside him wore stripes on his arm, the rank of sergeant.

"Mel, my God," the American lieutenant said.

So, Rudi thought. The American officer lost his sergeant, as I lost mine. Had he been with him as long as Rudi had been with Heibler? Did he owe his life to him?

"Your friend?" Rudi asked, and the American officer jerked around in surprise to see Rudi squatting at the top of the ditch. Rudi had his pistol pointed at the American Lieutenant.

"Yes," the American answered. "He is my friend."

"I'm sorry," Rudi said. "Are you the officer?"

"Yes."

"It was you who let me retrieve my men?"

"It was all of us," the American officer said.

"I lost many men here, too," Rudi said. "Your men put up a good fight."

"Thanks," the American said.

"The fighting has gone too long now. I think it is time for the war to end. We are beaten."

"Yeah? You'd have a hell of a time proving it by me right now," the American said.

Rudi stood up. "Lie down," he said, pointing his pistol toward the American officer.

"What? What are you going to do?" the American asked fearfully.

"Lie down," Rudi said again. "I have been ordered to take no prisoners, to kill all who surrender. I don't wish to kill you. I will shoot into the ground beside you. Pretend that you are dead. Do not move until the sound of the motors has gone, then you will be safe. Your army will move into here soon."

Rudi watched the American roll over onto his stomach, and he aimed his pistol into the dirt beside the American's head. He fired three shots into the ground.

"Good luck, my friend," Rudi said quietly, as he turned and walked away.

24

LISL pulled the coat around her more snugly as she walked along the nearly deserted street. It was a cold, clear night and high overhead the full moon hung like a great, silver lantern, shedding its soft light on the city below. The light from the moon was the only light, for the city was observing blackout conditions, though that seemed to most residents to be an unnecessary precaution. Though the other cities of Germany lay in bombed-out ruin, it was now February of 1945, in the sixth year of the war, and Dresden was as yet unbombed.

There were many reasons given for the fact that Dresden had not been bombed. Some said it was because the British and the Americans intended to make Dresden the capital of the newly occupied Germany after the war was over. No one doubted now, that the war would be over soon, or that Germany had lost. Others spread the story that Churchill had relatives who lived in Dresden; the allies would not bomb the city for fear of harming them. Most believed however, that Dresden was spared because it was a center of culture, art and history, and had no military targets of significance. Whatever the reason, Dresden had been spared and because of that, it was now a city of well over one million people, its population swelled by refugees seeking to escape the terrible rain of destruction which tumbled from the German skies over the other cities of the beleaguered nation.

Lisl was one of those refugees. She had fled Schweinfurt after the last bombing. She had walked through the streets of the town in which she was born and raised, but could not even tell where she was, because block after block of buildings had been reduced to charred piles of broken brick and mortar. She did find where the concert hall had been, and she stood in the wreckage and wept bitter tears when Lange told her that Paul Maass had been killed in the bombing. Lange had laughed about it, saying that the Americans killed the Jew for him, and now he didn't have a hold on her anymore.

"But of course, you and I both know that the safety of Maass was but a sham anyway, wasn't it? You have stayed because you loved it. I could have killed the Jewish pig long ago, and you would have stayed."

"No," Lisl cried hotly. "No, that's not true!" And yet, even as she denied his allegation, she knew that it was true, and she hated herself for it, and wished that she had been killed in the bombing along with Paul.

Lisl left the Lebensborn Home with the mocking laughter of Lange ringing in her ears. She was filled with remorse and shame, so much shame that she couldn't even face her parents, so she fled Schweinfurt and wound up in Dresden, where she would be away from the bombing and the war. In Dresden she found work in a bakery.

The bakery was owned by a husband and wife, both in their fifties. The man had a wooden leg from the first war, and because of that was spared the last, universal conscription which extended the age limit to sixty for all men. And yet, even with the wooden leg and the advanced years, the baker was still a man, a commodity increasingly more rare in Germany now, and his wife guarded him jealously, and was most antagonistic toward Lisl because she perceived Lisl's beauty to be a threat.

Lisl accepted the woman's jealous attacks stoically. How could she tell the woman that she had spent the last three years as a whore, and as a result didn't care if she ever saw a man again? That which had once brought her so much pleasure now filled her with shame and self-loathing. She wore the shabbiest clothes, and did nothing to her hair, choosing to look as unattractive as possible.

Lisl liked the work in the bakery. It was hard, back-breaking work, and it began at midnight, so the first loaves would be ready by the break of day. But at least Lisl didn't go hungry, and the heat of the ovens also kept her from being cold. She also liked the fact that she was able to enjoy long hours of absolute silence, during which time she could be totally alone with her thoughts. At those quiet times, she begged forgiveness from God for all her sins.

Lisl heard the gong of the town hall clock, indicating the hour of midnight. How wonderful it was even to hear a clock strike in these days. In those other cities which had the ornate clocks for which Germany was famous, the clocks had long ago been taken apart and encased in concrete and steel bunkers to protect them from bomb damage. Dresden was so secure in the knowledge that it would never be bombed, that the clock had remained, and it was a visible and audible link with a more peaceful past.

Lisl heard another sound, shortly after the clock stilled. It was a sound she had heard before, and it sent a cold chill down her spine. It was the distant thunder of heavy bomber engines.

Fearfully, Lisl looked up into the night sky. There were no crisscrossing searchlight beams, and no bursting anti-aircraft shells, so perhaps there was nothing to fear. Perhaps the planes were bound for Berlin, 162 kilometers to the north. Yes, that was it, she decided. They were going to Berlin. Lisl saw the airplanes then, or, more accurately, their shadows, when hundreds of dark objects moved across the shining face of the moon. They looked like bats from a cave, and the illusion was frightening.

Then Lisl heard something which caused her heart to stop. It was the whistle of thousands of bombs, plummeting toward the city from the bombers, high overhead.

"No," she screamed. "No, there has been a mistake! This is Dresden! This is Dresden!"

The bombers flew serenely over the city, unopposed by fighter aircraft, unopposed by anti-aircraft artillery, not even pinpointed by searchlights. For the bombers it was as routine as delivering the mail. But for the one million residents below, it was the opening of the gates of hell.

When the first bombs began bursting in the center of the city, about three thousand meters from Lisl's location, she dived to the sidewalk along the wall of the building, and put her arms over her head. She heard the steady thump of explosions as the bombs fell, then, after several minutes of constant explosions, she heard the roar and lick of flames.

When finally the bomb bursts stopped, Lisl stood up and brushed herself off. She looked down the street toward the bakery, and saw a wall of fire. The bakery was on the other side of the fire, so there was no way she could get there. Dazed and not knowing quite what to do, she sat down on the steps in front of the building beside which she had taken shelter and watched almost disinterestedly as people began running in the street, screaming in panic. She saw one figure running from the wall of fire, then collapse on the street, and only then did Lisl realize that the person was burning.

A fire truck passed by in front of her, its siren sounding, its firefighters hanging onto the side. What a puny, insignificant sight it made, she thought, one fire truck, and six men, against a blazing city.

The explosions started again, and at first she thought it was explosions set off by the fires, then she realized that it was a second wave of bombers, dropping bombs onto a city whose fires lighted their way. These explosions weren't as loud as the first, and when she saw a bomb cluster land on the roof of a building across the street from where she was sitting, she knew why. They weren't high explosive bombs, they were incendiary bombs, setting fires wherever they fell. The new fires spread rapidly, and soon joined with the older fires, which were now consuming entire city blocks. Now, all the fires had merged into a howling firestorm. As the firestorm superheated the air around the flames, the air rose, creating a suction which drew air into the inferno, feeding it with fresh oxygen, making it even hotter and sucking in even more air.

At first Lisl was only aware of the heat which warmed what had been a cold winter's night. But the heat increased, becoming uncomfortable, and finally, nearly unbearable, and she had to twist around on the steps, and turn her back to the approaching wall of flame to shield herself from its scorching effect. It was several minutes before Lisl actually realized the true danger of her situation, and when she did realize it, it was too late, There was only one true bomb shelter in Dresden, and it was reserved for the use of the *gauleiter*. The other million people had to find shelter where they could, and they began crowding into doorways, or pushing down into basements in a vain effort to escape the blistering heat which now extended over the entire city.

To the crackle of flames and muffled explosions, was added the whistling rush of wind which was now blowing in hurricane fury. But even the banshee wail of the wind could not shut out the sounds of a dying city—the screams of terror, cries of pain, and, here and there, a last, blasphemous oath of anger.

Finally there was a crash, then a roar unlike any sound Lisl had ever heard. She looked toward the noise and saw a giant wave of fire, shooting between the canyons of the buildings, filling the street from wall to wall, and turning the street into a blast furnace, consuming everything in its path. The fire moved like something alive, as if it were some monster escaped from the gates of hell, and Lisl, knowing there was no escape, got up from the steps and walked out into the center of the street to wait for it. She opened her arms to welcome it, as she would welcome a lover. As the first tongues of flame touched her, she suddenly realized that this was Ash Wednesday. All who are truly repentant of their sins should wear ashes on this day. The irony of it struck her, and she laughed.

The sign out front said, "Twenty-Fifth Panzer Corps Headquarters," and uniformed guards stood by the entry to the bunker, snapping salutes as sharply as if they were on parade in Berlin. Rudi returned their salutes as he stepped through the door, and walked past the operations room just inside. A large wall map showed all the American, British, French, and other Allied positions, accurately locating them well inside of Germany, thrusting toward Berlin. The map also showed German Army positions opposing the advancing allies, with the Twenty-Fifth Panzer Corps, outlined in red.

The map was accurate with regard to the American positions, but it was inaccurate with regard to the 25th Panzer Corps' positions. The 25th had no positions, because there was no 25th. It was a paper army, dreamed up by the generals to help create the grand delusion they were now weaving for Adolf Hitler.

With the Allied armies advancing from the west, and the Russian army advancing from the east, Germany was like a pecan in a nutcracker, slowly, but steadily being crushed. Kant, like Rudi, had seen the writing on the wall from the moment the Ardennes offensive had failed and the army had been forced to retreat back across the river. Had Hitler not launched his offensive but kept his army intact to fight a defensive battle, the total collapse might have been delayed by as much as a year to eighteen months, perhaps long enough to effect a surrender which would ensure Germany's survival. Now, it was Easter Sunday of 1945, and total collapse was only weeks away.

Kant, unlike Rudi, was able to do something to effect his own survival, and when he learned that a paper army was being created, he had himself assigned to the command staff. Once Kant was assigned, he drafted orders shifting Rudi over to the 25th, thus taking both of them out of combat units, and putting them in the position of being mere window dressing.

There was a time when Rudi might have protested that move, but no more. He was thankful to Kant for arranging it so that both of them would survive.

Rudi studied the battle maps every day, and monitored the progress of the advancing army. The thin line of gray-clad soldiers defending Germany today bore little resemblance to the iron legions which had captured most of Europe in the early days. That army was gone, and most of the men of that army were dead. Seven million Germans had died, and the graves of fine fighting men like Kaspar and Heibler, and Mainz, were spread from the Steppes of Russia to the deserts of North Africa, and from Sicily to Normandy Beach. Those few men who had seen the early battles, and were still here, were, like Kant and Rudi, survivors. And like Kant and Rudi, their sole objective now was to stay alive until the final shot was fired.

"Ah, Rudi, I was about to send for you," Kant said, as he saw Rudi looking at the map.

"What's up?" Rudi asked.

"I just saw a message in some S.S. radio traffic which might interest you. Paul Maass is alive."

"Paul Maass is alive?" Rudi said. "I think there must be some sort of a mistake. Paul was killed in one of the bombing attacks on Schweinfurt."

"No, he wasn't," Kant said. "It turns out that was merely a ruse to cover his disappearance. The S.S. arrested him on the morning after the raid."

"But, I don't understand," Rudi said. "Why would the S.S. arrest him?"

"It's all very strange and convoluted," Kant said. "But then what about Herr Himmler's perverse empire isn't? Anyway, it seems that Paul is a Jew. Or at least, one-half Jew. Did you know that?"

"I knew he had a half brother who was Jewish, but—"

"Not a half brother," Kant said. "They had the same father, though the father died before Paul was born, and his mother remarried. Thus the confusion and the different name. Anyway, the S.S. had a problem. Paul Maass had been publicly praised by Hitler as a musical genius. Now, Hitler couldn't very well say such nice things about a Jew, could he? So, it seems that the S.S. had to grit their teeth and bear up to the prospect of a Jew going free. But Paul was more than just a Jew, it turns out he was doing occasional work for the underground. The Gestapo discovered it, and he was arrested. But, though he was arrested, no one would take the authority to order his execution, until they knew exactly where Hitler stood on the matter."

"And where does Hitler stand?" Rudi asked.

Kant laughed. "Well, now no one knows because no one had the courage to tell Hitler a Jew was still alive and being held. They would have to tell Hitler that he had been wrong when he proclaimed Paul Maass a genius. Therefore, they have kept him in custody since they arrested him back in October of 1943. He is in Stachen, and the commandant wants to know what disposition is to be made of him."

"Stachen? That's very near here, isn't it?"

"About 30 kilometers," Kant said.

Rudi took his hat off and rubbed his hand through his hair. He looked around to make certain that no one was close enough to overhear him, then he spoke. "Ernst, let's go get him."

"What? Are you crazy? What do you mean?"

"We can do it," Rudi said. "I know we can. We could just go over there and take him—at gunpoint if need be."

"Listen, if he has survived this long, he'll survive till the end of the war," Kant said. "Why risk our lives now when it may not even be necessary?"

"But what if he doesn't survive until the end of the war?" Rudi asked. "What if the camp officials decide that it would be best if no one survives?"

"Oh, I'm sure that decision has already been made," Kant said. "But there is no way the S.S. can kill that many prisoners, and dispose of them that quickly. No, I think Paul's chances are pretty good."

"Ernst, we have to do this," Rudi finally said. "Don't you understand?"

"No," Ernst said.

"We have stood by, you and I, while this has gone on."

"We had nothing to do with it," Ernst said. "And there was nothing we could do about it."

"How do we know?" Rudi said. "We never tried. God help Germany, Ernst, but no one ever tried. And if we let this war end without taking one small step, somewhere, our souls will be damned for all eternity."

"You are really serious about this, aren't you?" Ernst said.

"Yes."

Ernst scratched his chin. "Well, we can't go in and take him out at the point of a gun, but—"

"You have an idea?"

Ernst smiled. "Suppose a couple of high-ranking S.S. officers went to Stachen to see the commandant, and requested Paul Maass be turned over to them. Do you suppose the commandant would comply?"

"You mean us?" Rudi replied. "We'd have to pass ourselves off as S.S. Generals. Do you think we could get away with it?"

"We wouldn't have to be Generals," Ernst said. "The

commandant of Stachen is an *Obersturmbannführer*, the same as a lieutenant colonel. We will go in the uniform of *Oberführer*. That's a special S.S. position that doesn't exist in the army, but it ranks between Colonel and General. It's the perfect rank, don't you see? It's high enough to pull rank on the Commandant, yet as it is not a General's rank, it won't be too conspicuous."

Rudi smiled broadly. "You had this in mind all along, didn't you?"

"I don't know why," Ernst replied. "I have prided myself on being a survivor. This is about the dumbest damn thing I have ever done."

"I don't know," *Obersturmbannführer* Dietzl replied, looking at the orders the two men in the S.S. *Oberführer*'s uniforms had just given him. "I was told that I would be responsible only to *Sturmbannführer* Lange with regard to the prisoner, Maass."

"What?" Kant exploded. "You would be responsible only to a man of inferior rank to you? It's bad enough, Dietzl, that you would question the authority of the rank of *Oberführer*, but now you tell me you are answerable to a mere Major—and you a Lieutenant Colonel! My God, no wonder the Führer is having trouble with his leaders, if they are anything like you they are all dunderheads."

Kant's explosive outburst had the effect of wilting the camp Commandant, and he shrunk back in fear. Kant followed up while he had the Commandant reeling. "Get Maass in here, at once," he demanded. "Unless you have already had him killed. If that is the case, Dietzl, I'll have you shot by your own guards!"

"No, no, Maass is not dead," Dietzl said. "He is not dead!"

"Then get him in here at once!"

Dietzl started to pick up the telephone on his desk, but Kant grabbed the receiver and slammed it down. "I told *you* to do it, Dietzl, not have it done."

"But, surely you don't expect me, the camp Commandant, to go down into the barracks and—"

"That is *exactly* what I expect you to do," Kant said. "Maybe next time you will think twice before you question a superior officer."

"Yes, *Herr Oberführer*," Dietzl said, "I'll get Maass." Dietzl hurried from the room, and Ernst and Rudi watched him go, then Rudi chuckled.

"Do you think . . ." Rudi started, but Kant, quickly, put his finger to his lips, and looked toward another door. He pointed quietly, and Rudi walked across the room softly, then jerked the door open. There, standing on the other side, was an emaciated scarecrow of a man, with a head which was little more than a skull, covered by gray, featureless skin. He was holding a mop and pail, and he was wearing the gray and white striped uniform of an inmate.

"My God!" Rudi said, shocked by the man's appearance.

"What are you doing there?" Kant asked, gruffly.

The man said nothing, but held up his pail and mop.

"Get out," Kant ordered. "Get out of this room, out of this building. I don't want to see your stinking face again."

Expressionless, the man turned and left the room. Kant watched him in silence until he had gone through the front door, and closed it behind him.

"Why were you so harsh?" Rudi asked. "Didn't you see him? I swear, I don't know how he has stayed alive this long."

"I had to be harsh," Kant explained. "If he is working in here, he might be spying and reporting back to the Commandant. We can't take any chances."

"Yes," Rudi said. "Yes, I see what you mean." Rudi walked over and looked through the window, out onto the camp. The prison yard was now full of inmates, all carbon copies of the man he had just seen. Oddly, the impact of so many seemed so great that he couldn't assimilate it, and this sight didn't affect him as much as the unexpected confrontation with the lone prisoner had a moment ago.

It was all Rudi could do to keep from shouting out loud, when Dietzl brought Paul into the office. Paul Maass looked no different from the man with the mop and pail; in fact, he could have *been* the man with the mop and pail, so much alike did they look. And yet, despite the total emaciation, there was something about him Rudi was able to recognize. This was Paul Maass.

"This is the stinking Jewish Pig, Paul Maass," Dietzl said. "And this is the film." He handed a gray film container to Rudi.

"Film?" Rudi asked. "What film?"

"The film which is to be shown to him three times a day."

"I'm not aware of any film requirement," Ernst said. "What is it?"

Dietzl grinned broadly. "I thought everyone in the S.S. over the rank of major had seen this film. You know the one, it's the film of Lisl Rodl having sex with five men and a woman." He laughed. "The sow was this Jewish Pig's fiancée."

"Oh, *that* film!" Kant said, laughing. "Yes I've seen it many times. I just didn't make the connection with Maass, that's all. You know the film, don't you?" he said to Rudi. "The first time we saw it, we had to go out and get a couple of whores."

"Yes," Rudi said, forcing himself to laugh. "Yes, I know the film."

"Well, gentlemen, if you ask me, I'm just as glad to get rid of Maass anyway," Dietzl said. "Frankly, I have no stomach for a Jew that I can't kill. And I'm beginning to have trouble finding people who will show this film. You can only take so much of it, you know, and then it'll drive you crazy. I don't know how Maass has been able to stand it. I must admit, it is a delightful bit of torture. Here," he said, handing a clipboard over to them. "You must sign for him. I may outrank Lange, but he has connections, very high connections, and I don't mind telling you, he frightens me."

Rudi signed the paper on the clipboard, then Kant signaled to Rudi and Paul that they must go. Silently, the three men climbed into the open scout car, and drove away from the death camp. Not until they were safely away did Rudi turn in his seat and look at Paul, who had been staring straight ahead with a fixed gaze.

"Paul," Rudi said softly. "Paul, have you still your wits about you?"

Paul looked over at Rudi, but said nothing.

"Do you know who I am, Paul? Do you know where you are, and what's happening to you?"

Paul raised his bony hand and put it on Rudi's and tried to squeeze, though there was no more strength in it than there would have been in the frail hand of a ninety-year-old woman. He said something, but the words were so quiet that Paul couldn't hear.

"What's that?" Paul asked. "What did you say?"

"I asked you where your sister was," Paul said. "Where is Lisl?"

Rudi looked down at Paul's hand, and he covered it with his other. "She's dead," he said. "She was killed in the bombing raid on Dresden."

Paul was quiet for a long moment. "I loved her," he finally said.

"You don't have to say that," Rudi said. "I . . . I know what Lisl became. I know what she did to you, to my parents, to everyone. You don't have to tell me you loved her."

"I loved her," Paul said again. "The S.S.? They thought showing me the film was torturing me. The ignorant bastards, they didn't understand that seeing Lisl every day was the only thing that kept me going. Don't you know, Paul? Doesn't anyone know? Lisl became what she became in order to save me. Lange bragged about that."

"Lange," Rudi said. "I should have killed him long ago."

"No," Paul replied. "Lange belongs to me."

"Paul, do you really think you will ever find him?" Ernst asked. "When this war is over, he'll go into hiding and no one will ever see him again."

"I will," Paul said resolutely. "I'll hunt the son of a bitch down if it takes me forty years to do it."

25

ADOLF Hitler and his wife of a few hours, Eva Braun, committed suicide in the Führer Bunker, April 30, 1945. Dr. Goebbels and his wife Magda then killed their six children and took their own lives, joining their Führer in this last, dramatic act of the *Gotterdammerung*. The government was turned over to Admiral Karl Doenitz, who immediately set about trying to negotiate Germany's surrender.

Rudi and Ernst Kant didn't wait for all that. They negotiated their own truce on the Easter Sunday they rescued Paul Maass from the concentration camp at Stachen. Rudi came home to Schweinfurt, to nurse Paul back to health, and to sit out the remainder of the war. Kant refused Rudi's invitation to join him in Schweinfurt, saying that he preferred to leave Germany altogether if possible, and then surrender himself to the English or the Americans at some point after the war was over. Kant feared that the Russians would be given most if not all of Germany, as repayment for their terrible loses, and he had no wish to wind up in Russian hands.

Ernst Kant had a grandiose scheme for escape. He

arranged with the pilot of the four-engine flying boat, to take him to one of the secluded bays in Greenland, where, stocked with books, food, and drink, Kant would await the final results in Europe. The flight to Greenland would be routine—the pilot had made it many, many times during the war in the quest of long-range weather forecasting. In fact, the German pilot and the pilot of the English weather plane had often crossed each other's paths during their reconnaissance flights, and though it couldn't be said they were friends, they always gave each other a wide berth, and neither had cause to fear the other.

Ernst Kant, the survivor who had figured all the odds, did not figure this one, however. He did not figure the odds of an American P-51 fighter pilot becoming an ace before the war's end. With Hitler dead, and the war collapsing, there were practically no German airplanes aloft, and an American pilot with but four kills to his credit had very little opportunity to notch the fifth, and thus become an ace. On the morning the four-engine flying boat took off with Ernst Kant, his books and food aboard, an American fighter pilot with four swastikas painted beneath the canopy of his plane spotted the huge Dorneir. He did a wingover, then lined up on the German airplane with his guns blazing. The flying boat was full of gasoline for the long trip and it exploded in a giant fireball. The P-51 did a series of victory rolls as it sped across the bay, leaving the burning residue of its victim scattered on the water.

Rudi didn't learn of Kant's death until he had already been arrested and interned by the Allies. There, one of the other prisoners had heard of it, and it was he, who conveyed the news to Rudi.

Rudi had not been too disturbed when the American Military Police showed up at his father's home to arrest him. After all, he had been an officer from the beginning of the war, and there was a mania of arrests, so he felt that, as one of the officers in the early days, he might be found guilty of contributing to the German war effort. But when he saw the charge sheet listing the offense for which he was to be tried, he was shocked.   ,

> *Whereas Rudolph Rodl, serving as an* Oberführer *in the S.S., at 1400 hours on the 19th day of December, 1944, did, in the city of Warsaw, Poland, murder Father Stefan Stakowiach, it is hereby ordered that* Oberführer *Rudolph Rodl be charged with the crime of murder.*

Rudi attempted to explain that he was not an *Oberführer* in the S.S., but a captain in the Army. The military police laughed, and told Rudi that *Reichsführer* Himmler had been arrested, passing himself off as an Army private. Besides, they had irrefutable evidence that Rudi *was* an S.S. *Oberführer*. They had an eyewitness to the murder, and they had Rudi's signature on a document, in which he signed as an *Oberführer*.

The document was the release document which Rudi signed to get the camp commandant of Stachen to turn Paul over to him. The eyewitness was the man with the mop and the pail Rudi had seen in the commandant's office. He signed a sworn statement that he had also been present in Warsaw, when the murder was committed, and he had seen Rudi do it. He wasn't sure until he saw Rudi again, when Rudi came to the camp at Stachen.

Paul tried to testify on Rudi's behalf, but Paul had been in Stachen on the nineteenth of December, not in Warsaw, so his testimony was disallowed. Rudi tried to tell the American authorities that he was in Belgium on the nineteenth, as part of the Ardennes offensive, but he had no way to prove it, for the survivor Kant, in an effort to obliterate the trail by which the Army would be able to trace them down when they deserted, had destroyed all records of his and Rudi's service. Now Kant was dead, Heibler was dead, even the S.S. Major Sachs had been killed. The ghost battalion which Rudi commanded had never existed on paper, and Rudi had no way of proving his statement. It was his word against the word of the prisoner who had identified him.

Rudi was incarcerated in a detention camp in Schweinfurt, until such time as he could be moved to Nurnberg. For that, Rudi was grateful, for he could at least stand out in the prison compound and see the familiar fields and trees of his youth.

The prison was at Conn Kaserne, and the Kaserne was now occupied by American soldiers. They had moved into the barracks and taken over the officers' club and all the other facilities. Two big buildings near the prison area were being used to store the bodies of American airmen who had been shot down during the Schweinfurt raids.

Rudi had talked with his father about the Schweinfurt raids, and nothing seemed more indicative of the terrible waste of the war than those raids. The Americans had tried to bomb by day, so they could prove their concept of precision bombing. They weren't really that precise, because the bombs fell not only on the factory complexes, but throughout the city as well, and about seventy percent of Schweinfurt was destroyed. The small city of Schweinfurt had the dubious distinction of being as gutted as her more populous sister cities. The Americans paid an exceptionally heavy price for the raids, though. Well over a thousand airmen had died in the raids, and their flag-draped coffins now sat in row after row in the huge warehouse next to the prison compound. But, for all the destruction, the German war industry never suffered for lack of ball bearings. Heinrich Rodl had merely moved equipment underground, and had diversified ball bearing production to the point that within a few days after the last raid, production was back to the wartime peak.

Rudi was fascinated by this close-up glimpse of Americans. Though the enlisted men did salute their officers, they did it with a type of nonchalance which bordered on insolence, and Rudi wondered why the officers would accept it. Then he noticed that, even among the officers, there was a degree of laxity which seemed counter to all sound military dicta. He also noticed that everyone seemed to have one of the little open cars called Jeeps, and sometimes there would be an absolute traffic jam, complete with honking horns and swearing drivers. Had Rudi's situation not been so desperate, he would have enjoyed this opportunity of observing the Americans so closely.

There were other prisoners in the camp, some of whom Rudi felt were as innocent as he was. But many had been members of the S.S. death squads, and they bragged openly of it. Rudi avoided them as much as he could. He didn't avoid them to make a show of separating himself from them; he avoided them because he couldn't stand them.

Rudi was assigned a lawyer, and though the lawyer had been unable to find any substantiation that Rudi was in Belgium in 1944, he thought that letters Rudi had written and newspaper accounts of his heroism, would at least establish his claim as being in the Army. "But that still won't clear you for the crime with which you are charged," he cautioned. "For that, we have to put you somewhere other than Warsaw on the nineteenth of December."

"I'm going to plead guilty," Rudi finally said.

"You mean you *were* there?"

"No," Rudi replied. "I was in the Ardennes. But I am going to plead guilty, as all Germans should plead guilty. We condoned and supported the action of Hitler and the Nazis, and therefore we are equally as guilty as those who operated the death chambers."

"You cannot be tried for collective guilt," his lawyer said. "You can only be tried for a specific crime."

"I fail to see the distinction. If I am going to be found guilty for a crime I didn't commit, then I shall at least take the satisfaction of knowing that it is just punishment for the crime for which we all must bear guilt."

Rudi's declaration soon spread to the other prisoners in the compound, and they began to avoid him, lest his philosophy contaminate them. Then one afternoon, less than a week before Rudi was to be transferred to Nurnberg, he saw an American officer standing on the other side of the fence, looking in. There had been many curious Americans before, and the prisoners, not wishing to provide a show, normally turned their backs on them. Rudi started to turn his back when something about the American caught his attention.

The American turned and started to walk back to his jeep.

"American lieutenant!" Rudi called, starting toward the fence.

The American continued to walk, ignoring Rudi's call.

"American lieutenant, please, I must speak with you."

The American stopped, but he didn't look around.

"I have nothing to talk to you about, you Nazi bastard," he said.

"Please, Lieutenant, you recognized my flag of truce once before. Won't you do so now?" Rudi asked.

The American turned around, and Rudi could see the look of shock registering on his face. Rudi was all the way to the fence now. "Please," Rudi said again. "I must talk to you."

The American returned to the fence. "Are you?" he started, then he looked at Rudi more closely, and the recognition appeared in his eyes. "You are the German officer at the ditch," he said. "You are the one who fired into the ground beside me."

"Yes," Rudi said. He smiled. "I see you took my advice and lay quietly until your own men came."

"Yes," the American said. "Yes, I did. They came within a few hours."

"Ah, how different our fortunes became after that," Rudi said. "I was a Panzer officer without tanks, a commander without men, a warrior without hope. I reached my own truce on Easter Sunday, 1945. For me, the war ended on that day, for on that day I returned home to Schweinfurt."

"Why are you in here?" the American asked.

Rudi smiled. "My American friend, that is where you can help me," he said.

"Wait a minute," the American interrupted. "Listen, I'm grateful to you, whatever your name is."

"*Hauptman* Rudi Rodl," Rudi said, clicking his heels together automatically.

"Yes, well, Captain Rodl, I'm grateful to you for saving my life on that day. But I don't think I can do anything for you here, this all—"

"Do you remember the date?" Rudi asked.

"I beg your pardon?"

"Do you remember the date I saved your life?"

"Yes," the American said. "I remember it well, because that was also the date you killed my friend, Mel."

Rudi remembered the scene in the ditch, with the American officer lamenting his friend and Rudi remembered his own friend, Sergeant Heibler.

"It was an act of war, Lieutenant," Rudi said quietly. "You killed many of my friends on that day as well. Do you remember the date?"

"Yes," the American snapped, "I remember the date. What is so damned important about the date?"

"I am only charged with one crime," Rudi said. "I have been identified as the German officer who executed a Polish Catholic priest in Warsaw. The day the priest was killed was 19 December, 1944."

"Nineteen December?"

"Yes."

"You couldn't have been in Warsaw," the American officer said. "You were in the Ardennes. Can't you prove you were there?"

"How?" Rudi asked. "I was attached to a rover unit. We were supposed to capture our supplies from the Americans, our fuel, even our food. We were independent of any major command, so I cannot verify my whereabouts by official orders."

"But surely one of your men—"

"Dead," Rudi said. "Every man you saw with me on that day is dead. I am the last survivor of an army that never even existed as far as anyone is concerned. Lieutenant . . . what is your name?"

"Anderson," the American said. "Jim Anderson."

"Lieutenant Anderson, you are the only person alive who can put me there on that day. Will you do it?"

The American looked at Rudi for a long, quiet time, and Rudi could almost see in his eyes the memory of that cold day near Baugnez. They had shared that day, from opposite sides to be sure, but they had been united by fear, misery, and sorrow.

"Yes," Lieutenant Anderson said. "I'll do it."

Lieutenant Anderson turned to leave, then he realized he had spoken in German, so he said it again in English. "Thank you."

Lieutenant Anderson turned to leave, then he stopped and looked back toward Rudi.

"Good luck, my friend," the American said.

Rudi smiled at him. That was the same thing he had said to the American that day at the ditch.

Rudi watched the American officer go back into the headquarters building to make the report which would free him, and he thought of the American's words as he left. *Good luck, my friend.*

"I have used all my luck," Rudi said quietly. "And I have survived."

Frauka had a special homecoming party for Rudi after he was released. Paul was at the party, too, and of course so was Heinrich. It was a quiet party with little food, because there wasn't much. It was quiet also because the ghosts of those who weren't present dominated the scene.

Lisl wasn't there, but her beauty and the infectious

enthusiasm of her laugh was, and there was scarcely a person who didn't close their eyes at one time or another to call her picture to mind. Kurt Papf, Heinrich's production foreman, wasn't there; he had been killed in the last Schweinfurt raid. *Gauleiter* Anton Dietering, the official who had loaned Paul the car, wasn't there either. He was dead by his own hand, committing suicide shortly after he heard of Hitler's death. Baumann, Paul's concert master, was dead. Max Priller, the young Luftwaffe pilot whose code name was Wild Boar, and with whom Frauka had made love one afternoon, was also dead. Of course, it would not have been proper for Frauka to invite him anyway. But his spirit was there with her, as surely as the spirits of Kaspar, and Heibler and Mainz, and Kant were there with Rudi.

And there was one other person whose spirit was there. Manfried Lange had not been seen or heard from since the last week of the war. Some thought he was dead, others insisted he had made good his escape.

"I don't believe he is dead," Rudi said, when his name came up. "But he should be."

"I don't believe he is dead, either," Paul said. "But he will be. I intend to find him and see to it that he gets his just reward."

"Oh, Paul, there are already people doing that sort of thing," Frauka said. "Can't you leave it up to them and get back to your own life? You've your music career to consider."

"My music career?" Paul asked, laughing bitterly. "What about the music careers and the writing careers, and the teaching careers, and the business careers of the millions who were murdered? No, Frau

Rodl, I'm sorry, but no. I have only one career now, and that is in hunting down Manfried Lange."

"But how will you support yourself?" Frauka asked.

"He need not worry about that," Heinrich said. "As long as I have the money to support any of us, I will support Paul in his endeavor."

"And I, as well," Rudi said. "Paul, we have much to make up for. We may never find atonement in this generation, but there are many of us who are going to give it one big try."

Paul held his glass up toward the others, and his eyes, like the eyes of everyone else in the room, were covered with a sheen of tears.

"My friends, for the first time in a long time, I am proud to say I am a German."

THE END

Author Robert Vaughan talks about
himself and wars he has known

I was born November 22, 1937 in Morley, Missouri, a tiny settlement on the Missouri side of the Mississippi River, just across from the location of the fictional town of Mount Eagle, Illinois (the hometown of the Holt family in *The Brave and The Lonely*).

I grew up in Sikeston, Missouri, a somewhat larger community, and, as a boy during the war, I watched the trains pass through loaded with soldiers, trucks, guns and tanks. I also remember the scrapmetal drives, the newspaper collections, ration points and air raid blackout drills.

When my father was drafted we followed him to army bases in Arkansas, Alabama and Oklahoma, before he went overseas. Thus, I was exposed to army camp life, particularly the housing shortage, to say nothing of the money shortage of an enlisted man's family.

I joined the army in the middle of the 1950s, entering army aviation, where I became a Warrant Officer, flying helicopters. I served, or traveled in, 30 countries, including Germany, France, England and Japan. Because of my interest in history, I studied the war in those countries, including visits to the libraries and archives, and had lengthy conversations with the people.

When the war heated up in Vietnam, I went over for my first tour in the early part of 1966. I flew helicopter recovery missions during this period, and over the next 18 months I saw a great deal of combat.

The most hazardous operation I participated in was one called *Junction City*, a major search and destroy operation. Near an area called "The Iron Triangle" I was part of a 13-ship element. Eight of those ships were shot down, and, as recovery officer, I had to recover each of them. It was for this mission that I was awarded the Distinguished Flying Cross. During my tours in Vietnam, I also received the Purple Heart, the Bronze Star, the Air Medal with several oak-leaf clusters, the Meritorious Service Medal, the Army Commendation Medal, the Vietnamese Cross of Gallantry, and several, lesser awards. I served eighteen months during my first tour and eighteen months on a later tour, for a total of three years in Vietnam.

My early writing reflected my military background. My first novel was a story of the U.S. Army along the DMZ in Korea. I have also done three books about Vietnam: *Brandywine's War, The Valkyrie Mandate*, and, under a pseudonym, *Junglefire*. Over 9,000,000 copies of my books are in print, most of them under various pen names.

I played football in my younger days, and I love all sports. I am now quite active as a football and track and field coach in Sikeston, Missouri, where I live with my wife, Ruth Ellen, and young sons, Joe and Tom.